The Organ Grinders

Also by the author

PEST CONTROL

the

ORGAN GRINDERS

Bill Fitzhugh

AVON BOOKS ◈ NEW YORK

AVON BOOKS, INC.
1350 Avenue of the Americas
New York, New York 10019

Copyright © 1998 by Reduviidae, Inc.
Interior design by Kellan Peck
Visit our website at **http://www.AvonBooks.com**
ISBN: 0-380-97651-X

Library of Congress Cataloging in Publication Data:
Fitzhugh, Bill.
    The organ grinders / Bill Fitzhugh.—1st ed.
        p.   cm.
    I. Title.
PS3556.I8552074   1998   98-4492
813'.54—dc21   CIP

First Avon Books Printing: September 1998

FIRST EDITION

QPM   10   9   8   7   6   5   4   3   2   1

For Mary B. Farrington,
my godmother, who fought so.
And to Lawrence for fighting alongside.

And finally for Kendall,
my personal life support system.

preface

The Organ Grinders is based on research currently underway at biotechnology companies and universities around the world. With one exception, all of the medical and agricultural biotechnology referred to in this book is real. The one exception being a certain type of transplant, which, I believe, even a casual reader will be able to identify as suspect. From what I could gather, the surgery is, at least, feasible—at worst, it is not so far fetched as to be dismissed out of hand. As far as I know, this operation has never been attempted; however, I can't say for certain because not a single one of the specialists I contacted regarding the matter would return my call.

And although I obtained excellent information from many experts in other fields, the odds are good that I still got something wrong somewhere in here. These errors are mine and I will not share them.

As for the statistics in the book, I cannot vouch for their accuracy. But the numbers regarding the supply and demand for human organs come primarily from the United Network for Organ Sharing and other reputable organizations. The statistics about the world's human population, as well as the facts about solid waste disposal, vivisection, air and water pollution, male hormone therapy, the financial costs of organ transplantation, and industrial espionage in the biotechnology industry, also come from what would have to be considered reliable sources.

I did take one liberty in my portrayal of the transplant co-ordinator's profession. However they may be paid, rest assured that they do not work on commission.

Finally, the ideas contained in this book do not intentionally represent the beliefs of anyone who consulted on this work, nor of the organizations for which any of those people work. This is a work of fiction based on factual science.

The Organ Grinders

San Mateo County, California, March 1975

Paul had big butterflies in his stomach. He was nervous because he was on his way to meet with Mr. Jerry Landis. *The* Mr. Jerry Landis, one of the most important men in the country, according to every business magazine Paul had read. And since other important men had a hard time getting an appointment with Mr. Landis, everybody was impressed that Paul had been granted an audience with him—especially since Paul was just fifteen years old.

He was sitting in the back of the bus looking at the blood on his finger. Paul chewed his nails whenever he was anxious, and this time he had torn one below the cuticle, drawing a crimson reminder of his apprehension. Paul took a deep breath and tried to relax, but he would need more than air to settle his nerves today. He was delivering an important document to Mr. Landis and he prayed it would make a difference. Paul just wanted to make the world a better place.

The reason Paul had been invited to meet with Mr. Landis in the first place was a civics class project designed to demonstrate the power and importance of a participatory democracy. The project involved writing a letter to someone in a position to influence government or corporate policy. Some of Paul's classmates wrote to city council members; others wrote to senators or representatives. But Paul wrote to Mr. Landis because of something he had read about in the newspaper, something called the Landaq Sierra Nevada Development Project.

According to the newspaper, Landaq had recently purchased a vast tract of land in the foothills of the Sierra Nevadas, a pristine wilderness area where Paul had attended summer camp as a child. Paul still felt the wondrous charge of emotion he'd experienced when he first saw that land. The stunning granite peaks painted with corn lilies and Indian rhubarb were still vivid in his eyes. He had waded in the clear creeks lined with grass hummocks, bushy splashes of green and bright yellow. He could still smell the sugar and ponderosa pines that dusted the cool lakes with patterns of pollen while mergansers paddled noiselessly about. The dogwoods that bloomed fragrant next to maple and cottonwood alive with noisy squirrels and Stellar's jays had somehow gotten into his blood. And the giant sequoia—awesome, ancient, and primeval—had moved his young soul. This land so inspired awe that it must have been created, as John Muir wrote, by tender snowflakes noiselessly falling through unnumbered centuries. It was the world the way it should be, Paul thought.

But Jerry Landis thought it could be improved. Or, as Landaq's press release said, "developed." The newspaper article quoted Jerry Landis: "Landaq merely intends to capitalize on some of the area's natural resources." And Paul knew that meant the land would be destroyed. Paul had read that Jerry Landis supported politicians who helped open national forests to logging, who moved aggressively to scale back clean water programs, and who referred to the Environmental Protection Agency as "the Gestapo of government." Whenever Jerry Landis "developed" a wilderness area, he strip-mined mountainsides, or clear-cut old growth forests, or drilled and spilled crude oil, or dumped toxic wastes, or all of the above.

And his shareholders didn't care one whit. Just so Jerry Landis increased dividends.

But Paul wasn't interested in that sort of return. Paul wanted this small part of the world—his Eden—to remain as it was. He didn't want to see it destroyed. So he wrote to Mr. Landis and asked him to reconsider. Paul said he would write a plan suggesting alternative uses for the land. A few weeks later Paul received an invitation to meet with Mr. Landis to discuss his ideas. Paul threw himself into the project. He stopped playing with his friends after school. Instead he stayed at the library until it closed. He stopped watching television, except for *Chico and the Man* and *Hawaii Five-O*. He spent ungodly hours researching and learning and writing about his subject. He started using terms like "aquifer water volume" and "forest biomass density." And after two months of grueling work, Paul had completed his proposal.

And now he found himself sitting in the back of a city bus going from Atherton to Menlo Park. The bus driver had forced Paul to pay full fare because he looked older than fifteen. Paul was big for his age. His classmates teased him, not terribly, but enough that it hurt. Something about Paul's looks—half adult, half kid—kept him from being in any of the cliques. He was big and awkward, no longer a cute boy but not yet the handsome young man he would become.

Sitting several rows ahead of Paul were a woman and her son. The woman looked tired, sad, and troubled. The boy was about Paul's age, and there was something terribly wrong with him. His eyes were strange, and Paul wondered what he saw through them. The boy made loud noises instead of words and periodically he screamed and hit himself. When his mother tried to restrain him, the boy would hit her too. The woman looked embarrassed and frightened every time this happened, and Paul felt sorry for both of them. Paul knew the last stop for this bus was the state hospital at Woodside. He imagined this overwhelmed and battered woman was taking her son there. She couldn't deal with it anymore.

Everyone else on the bus tried to ignore them, but Paul couldn't, it bothered him too much. It was so unfair, he thought, that someone could be that way through no fault of his own and that nothing could be done to help. Paul became angry when he heard people shrug this sort of thing off with "it's not a perfect world" platitudes. Paul knew it wasn't a perfect world just as sure as he knew it didn't have to be nearly as imperfect as it was. One of Paul's teachers told him he was just too sensitive. Paul could never figure out how that was possible. It seemed to him that no one else was sensitive enough.

Paul got off at the next stop, leaving behind the mother and her autistic child. He hoped the hospital could give both of them what they needed. It was hot for March, and the sun was beating on the people by the side of the road who were waiting for the bus. Paul started the half-mile walk to Mr. Landis's office. And he worried every step of the way. After a while Paul had to stop and take off his suit coat. It was too hot. He was wearing his suit because he had been taught that children should show respect for their elders. Paul was very good in that regard. He believed what his teachers told him. He did as he was told. Grown-ups liked him.

As he marched up the sidewalk Paul held his proposal carefully so as not to crease the pages. He wanted to make a good impression. He knew how important first impressions were. That was one of the things his father had impressed upon him.

"I just hope you don't get me canned," Paul's dad had said with a smile. He had said this months ago after Paul had announced at dinner that he was writing to ask Jerry Landis not to go ahead with the Landaq Sierra Nevada project. It turned out that Paul's dad worked for Jerry Landis, if only indirectly. He was a bio-organic chemist doing contract work for the research-and-development arm of an agricultural biotechnology subsidiary controlled by one of Mr. Landis's many corporations. Up until that moment, it had never occurred to Paul that his actions might have negative consequences for his father.

"I won't send the letter if it's going to get you in trouble," Paul said.

Paul's dad smiled again. "Don't worry about me," he said. "If you believe in what you're saying, send the letter. I'm behind you a hundred percent."

"What if you get fired?" Paul asked.

His dad paused to give the question some thought. "Well, then you'll either have to support the family or I guess we could sell you into slavery. The choice will be yours." He winked at Paul.

Paul's mother shook her head. "Frederick," she said, "I wish you wouldn't say things like that." She only called him Frederick when she was trying to sound serious.

"Why?" Paul's dad asked. "You don't think he'd fetch much on the slave market?" He reached over and felt the muscles of Paul's arm. "He's got some pretty good meat on those arms. He's probably good for a few thousand bucks."

Paul loved it when his dad kidded around like this. He thought his dad was pretty funny. "If it'll help," Paul said, "I could start lifting weights."

"Don't encourage your father," Paul's mother said. "You just go ahead and send the letter. If your dad gets fired, we'll look into selling *him*."

Paul and his dad broke up at that one. Mom didn't make many jokes, but when she did you had to laugh. After dinner that night Paul's dad sat down with Paul and together they went over the letter to Mr. Landis. It was a good letter, well written and polite. And the next day Paul mailed it. And now, several months later, Paul was walking up a sidewalk toward a new ten-story building, a grid of black steel interspersed with mirrors reflecting the hot sun and the blue sky. The gleaming silver sign on the roof said LANDAQ INCORPORATED. Paul's anxiety doubled as he thought about meeting with Mr. Landis somewhere in that forbidding building. He tore another nail to the quick and headed for the door.

Paul was so nervous he was afraid he would throw up. He bit the inside of his cheek, hoping to distract his stomach. He stopped at the door, slipped his coat on over his sweat-soaked shirt, then went inside where the air was chilled and corporate. He signed in with Security, then rode the elevator to the top floor under the disdainful eyes of several adults. He entered the reception area of Landaq Incorporated at 2:50 P.M. He told the receptionist he had a three o'clock appointment. Paul was embarrassed when he saw her looking at his nubby fingernails—or was it his sweaty shirt? She told him to sit down and wait. He took a seat near the door to Mr. Landis's office. As he waited, Paul read and reread his proposal and worried about what he would say to Mr. Landis when they finally met. The clock suddenly chimed three, and Paul's young stomach tightened as if to eject something. He'd never been this nervous in his life. His hands were cold and clammy. He stood in anticipation of being shown into Mr. Landis's office. But the receptionist never looked his way. Instead, a humorless businessman brushed into the reception area and announced his presence. "Go right in," the mean-looking receptionist said. "He's expecting you."

Paul didn't know what to do or say. He was standing there with a stupid I-was-supposed-to-have-the-three-o'clock-appointment look on his face. He thought about asking if there had been a mistake, but he didn't want to show any disrespect. So he just sat back down and looked at his plan. It was twenty pages long. Just looking at the cover made him proud: "Alternatives for Landaq's Sierra Nevada Development." Paul was certain this was the sort of official-sounding title that got results. He read the plan for the hundreth time, and when he looked up at the clock he saw it was 3:45.

Paul glanced at the scowling receptionist and decided not to ask what had happened to his three o'clock appointment. Paul knew children weren't nearly as important as adults, so he'd just sit there and wait until they called him. He fidgeted in his seat and kept thumbing through his proposal. Every now and then he wiped his hands on his pants so the pages wouldn't get wet. The longer he waited, the more nervous he got, and as the afternoon dwindled, the ticking clock only made matters worse. Paul was beginning to worry that Mr. Landis was too busy to see him and his report. Several more people had come and gone from Mr. Landis's office, and no one had ever bothered to tell Paul why there was a delay. Paul felt stupid and insignificant. It was 4:30.

When the clock finally chimed five Paul wondered if he should just apologize and leave. But he thought that might be disrespectful so he sat there feeling stupid, not knowing what to do. And then, suddenly, the door to Jerry Landis's office opened and the man himself stepped out. He was tall and decisive looking with thin lips and angular facial features. He was wearing an expensive suit that was a 100 percent wool way of saying "I have enormous amounts of power and money; what do you have?" Paul knew what he had was worn out and didn't fit. It was almost the same color as Mr. Landis's, but the effect was completely different.

Like all young boys wearing suits, Paul looked and felt like an impostor, an attempted adult. Contrary to what his mother had said, Paul's ill-fitting suit gave him no credibility. Paul was ashamed that he had worn such a crappy suit, but it was his only one. He stood and hoped Mr. Landis wouldn't notice.

"You must be Paul," Jerry Landis said with a big, warm smile. "I hope you can forgive me for making you wait so long. I promise to make it up to you. Please, come in." Jerry Landis turned to the receptionist. "Ask John to come on up."

Mr. Landis put his arm around Paul and led him into the office. "You, sir, are a better man than I. I have no excuse for my rudeness. I fell behind my own schedule and, well, I do apologize. Sincerely." Mr. Landis was shaking his head as if ashamed of himself.

"It's okay," Paul said. He couldn't think of anything else to say. He was too stunned. Paul couldn't believe that he'd been so worried and nervous all this time. Mr. Landis was a great guy! "I really haven't been waiting that long," Paul said with a shrug.

Mr. Landis smiled. "Now, don't let me off the hook that easily, Paul. That'll just make me feel worse than I already do." Jerry Landis suddenly thrust his hands out, palms up. "Mea culpa!" he said dramatically. Paul had no idea what that meant, but he could tell by the way Mr. Landis said it and by the sparkle in his eyes that it was funny, so he laughed. "Can I get you something? A soda? Anything?"

"No thank you, sir. I'm fine," Paul said.

Mr. Landis gestured at a chair. "Please, sit." Jerry Landis propped himself on the corner of the desk facing Paul. He glanced at the document in Paul's hand. "Is that your proposal? I can't *wait* to read it." Jerry Landis made Paul feel like the most important person in the world. "Can I see it? It certainly looks thorough."

"Yes, sir, it is." Paul handed it to Mr. Landis and began reciting some of the facts and figures. "According to the Nature Conservation Group—"

Just then a man with a fancy camera entered the office. "John! Come in," Mr. Landis said to the photographer. "John, this is Paul." Paul stood to shake hands. "Paul is *very concerned* about the Sierra Nevada project. In fact, he's even written a lengthy proposal addressing his concerns about it. Isn't that right, Paul?"

Paul was embarrassed by all the attention. "Well, it's not that big a deal. It's just—"

Mr. Landis waved Paul off. "Don't sell yourself short. I bet there are some *great* ideas in here," he said. Jerry Landis held Paul's proposal up in the air. "This is the future, Paul. *You* are the future. It's people like you who usher in change. Us old guys get stuck with one way of thinking. We need bright young people like you to get us out of those ruts." He turned to John. "Am I right or what?"

"You're always right, Mr. Landis," John said with a smile.

Mr. Landis winked at Paul. "He's a bootlicker. Probably wants a raise, don't you think?"

Paul smiled and nodded. He was part of the inner circle now, sharing jokes with his friend Jerry. He couldn't wait to show off his charts and graphs. Mr. Landis guided Paul over to a wall of books. "Paul, if you don't mind, John here is going to take some photos of our meeting. I want to get a story in the paper about you and the proposal you've written."

Paul could hardly believe it. His picture in the paper! With Mr. Jerry Landis. His mom was going to be so proud. "Wow," Paul said. "I don't mind at all."

Mr. Landis positioned himself facing Paul. "John, let's do this with Paul handing me the proposal," Mr. Landis said. John measured the light and moved Paul a little to the left. Paul held his proposal out and Mr. Landis reached for it. "Big smile, now." *FLASH!*

"Mr. Landis," Paul said, "will someone need to interview me?"

"I wouldn't be surprised," Mr. Landis said. "John, let's get one of us shaking hands *and* exchanging the proposal. If that's all right with Paul."

"Sure," Paul said. "That's a great idea." Paul puffed his chest out proudly and smiled.

FLASH! "That's terrific," Jerry Landis said. "Now let's do the same shot from the other side." Paul smiled as the photographer moved him into position. He felt like one of those important people at an international summit meeting. He couldn't wait for the interview. The photographer jockeyed around to the other side and *FLASH!* A perfect photo to accompany the story of how Landaq CEO Jerry Landis took time out of his schedule to meet with a local youth concerned about the environment. It was all part of the "At Landaq, we care" PR campaign.

"You know, Mr. Landis, my dad works for one of your companies," Paul said proudly. "He's a bio-organic chemist and he's working on some kind of enzyme that penetrates the cell walls in rice, I think."

"No kidding? That's terrific," Mr. Landis said. "John, make sure we get an extra set of these photos for Paul's dad." John nodded to his boss before disappearing behind the camera again. *FLASH!* John took one last photo. "Paul," Jerry Landis said as he took the proposal from Paul's hand. "I have a flight in about an hour and, if you don't mind, I'd like to take this and read it on my way to Zurich."

"Really?" Paul said. "That's great."

Mr. Landis handed the proposal to John and then put his arm around Paul. They headed for the door. Paul suddenly knew how it felt to have influence with powerful people. It was, even in this short time, intoxicating. "Again, please accept my sincere apology for the wait, Paul. I will read this and get back to you within the week."

"That would be fantastic," Paul said enthusiastically. They were at the door now, and Jerry Landis launched Paul like a ship toward the elevator.

"Have a good trip!" Paul said as he sailed away, giddy about the meeting and participatory democracy. He couldn't wait to tell his mom and his civics class. Paul was halfway across the reception area when he realized he had not thanked Mr. Landis. It would be unforgivable if he left without expressing his gratitude for the courtesy this man had shown him, a mere boy. He turned back and saw that the door was still open. And he saw John looking at the proposal, laughing. John handed it to Mr. Landis, who laughed even more. Paul felt a sickening sensation. He felt like a fool. Then he saw Jerry Landis drop his proposal into the wastebasket. And with that simple act, Jerry Landis taught Paul a painful lesson. But as much as it hurt, it wasn't the worst thing Jerry Landis would ever do to him.

Palo Alto, California, March 1998

In a perfect world it would have been a perfect day for speeding up the 101 toward San Francisco. However, this was by no stretch of the imagination a perfect world, and thus northbound traffic was snailing along at the speed of drying paint.

Paul—big, fit, and handsome at thirty-eight—was driving. Sitting next to him was Georgette, the love of his life. They were on their way to visit Paul's father, something Paul tried to do regularly. Inching their way north in what was jokingly referred to as the fast lane, Paul and Georgette had already counted six moving violations by other motorists—and they hadn't been on the road for five minutes yet. "Look at that nitwit," Georgette said, pointing at a pale blue Ford Taurus. "Merging left with his right signal flashing. I guess the state just hands out a license to anyone who can find their way to the DMV with twelve bucks."

"I still like your idea of using paint guns to tag cars when drivers screw up. *Bam!*" Paul said, hammering his big fist on the steering wheel. "A big yellow splotch on the trunk marks the driver as a fugitive scum turn signal violator."

"Exactly," Georgette said, taking Paul's bait. "And the

next time the idiot stopped, decent citizens could pull him from his car and shoot him right there on the sidewalk."

"Seems a bit extreme," Paul said.

"Beat him senseless, then."

"For a turn signal violation?"

"Okay, ridicule him until he apologizes."

"I notice you keep saying 'him,' " Paul said.

"Hey, I needed a pronoun," Georgette replied.

Paul smiled. "And of course there wouldn't be any disputes over who did what wrong."

"It's not a perfect world," Georgette said. She turned in her seat to face him. "Seriously, if you could, would you?"

Paul considered that. "Nah, I prefer working within the current system."

"In other words," Georgette said, "even though it drives you nuts, you're willing to waste your entire life waiting for the Department of Blessed Motor Vehicles to enact a more rigorous driver's test to get these chuckleheads off the road instead of taking some action on your own."

"I'm funny that way," Paul said.

Georgette leaned over and kissed Paul on the cheek. "And that, my dear, is what makes my love for you such a fucking mystery." Which was true. Georgette had always been an activist in the literal sense of the word. She'd been suspected of sabotaging bulldozers and she'd been questioned about cutting tuna nets in the past. And since Georgette's old boyfriends tended to be the tree-spiking types, it surprised everyone—Georgette included—that she had settled down with Paul, whose approach to solving the world's problems was a bit more passive, even when dealing with Jerry Landis, his long-time nemesis. But that philosophical conflict aside, Georgette loved Paul completely and thus was willing to go with him to things like Save the Rain Forest rallies— which is exactly where they had just been.

❖   ❖   ❖

While the northbound lanes of the 101 were clogged like a bad artery, the southbound lanes were wide open, and at the moment—roughly ten miles north of Paul and Georgette—there were exactly eighteen cars taking full advantage of that fact. Screaming south at ninety-five miles an hour was a stolen Saturn SC2. At the wheel of the Saturn was one William Kemmler, idiot extraordinaire. Following the Saturn were seventeen black-and-white California Highway Patrol cruisers whose light bars were attempting to convey a certain urgency. The squadron of colorful cars made for a high-speed parade of red and blue lights. Though Mr. Kemmler had never been one for parades, he nonetheless continued leading this one to the south, at increasingly higher speeds, straight toward Paul and Georgette.

Going to the Save the Rain Forest rally had been Paul's idea. And while Georgette agreed with the philosophy and goals of the pro–rain forest people, she didn't think their methods were very effective—as evidenced by the fact that there were far fewer acres of rain forest now than before the protesting started.

Georgette referred to Save the Rain Forest as "one of Paul's pet causes." The phrase annoyed Paul because it trivialized the importance of the movement. Georgette hoped the annoyance would turn Paul's tepid verbal protests into something more heated and substantial, though she was never specific about the alternatives. Paul's concern about the environment began when, as a child, he saw the ancient sequoias. It was cemented the day Jerry Landis threw his proposal into the trash. And it was maintained by a big electronic sign that Paul had seen years ago outside the Hard Rock Cafe in Los Angeles. The words above the sign read:

ACRES OF RAIN FOREST REMAINING: 1,963,063,000

The number was constantly diminishing. It was a ticking clock and Earth was the bomb. Every now and then

Paul thought about the sign—it was his own personal reminder of humankind's lunacy. The words might as well have read:

ACRES OF GOOD SENSE MANKIND HAS LEFT

Forests were being clear-cut, burned, and bulldozed, resulting in the biggest loss of plant and animal species in history. Paul knew it was being done in the name of "development" and because of increasing demand for the packaging of consumer goods of dubious value.

Though Georgette derided Paul's methods of protest, she never accused him of apathy. In Paul's mind he was doing all he could to solve the world's problems while still playing by the rules. He organized meetings and protests, and, of course, he voted. The fact that he was betrayed by most of those he helped elect didn't dissuade him. He believed the system eventually would work. He *had* to believe that since the truth of the matter was Paul was a coward. At least he felt like he was. In the darkest corner of his soul where those nasty, personality-defining truths festered and mocked the self that he presented to the world, Paul feared that he lacked true conviction and the courage thereof. He secretly admired the work of the so-called eco-terrorists and he wished he could do what they did. But he couldn't. And this gnawed at Paul. It was a sign of weakness. He still felt like the little coward who let Landaq destroy a part of the Sierra Nevadas.

So he overcompensated. Paul began fighting every fight he could find until he became completely paralyzed by the sheer number of problems he felt he had to solve. Industrial pollution, overflowing landfills, diminishing wildlife habitats, starving children, nuclear waste dumps, and on and on. There was so much information—and whose statistics should you believe? Paul raced from one cause to the next, spreading himself so thin and accomplishing so little that he eventually realized he had to change his approach. Paul's solution was to focus his energies on one thing. But instead of choosing to pursue a single cause, Paul decided to pursue a single man. And the choice was obvious. It would be Jerry Landis—not only for what he had done to the Sierra Nevadas but, more significantly, for what he had done to Paul and his father. And though Paul did devote most of his energy to defeating Landis, he still went to the odd Save the Rain Forest rally.

Paul's environmental bent led him to buy a fuel-efficient car with a low emission rating. Typical of such cars, Paul's was roughly the size of a small washing machine. Unfortunately, Paul had grown from a big awkward kid into a six-foot-four-inch model of a man. He was thick as an inside linebacker, which was the position he ended up playing when he was at Cal. He was All-America handsome, his perfect black hair and winning smile the stuff of sorority dreams.

Georgette, who had attended Stanford on a basketball scholarship, was a striking six feet tall and beautifully proportioned. After college she went from beautiful child athlete to postmodern punk. She had short brown hair that she frequently moussed into a flat, spiky ponytail. A sparkling diamond stud pierced her right nostril. Even those normally put off by such jewelry found her irresistible.

Cramped inside their tiny car, Paul and Georgette continued north, doing their part for the ozone layer. Georgette glanced at the speedometer. They were going thirty in a sixty-five zone. "Let me ask you," she said. "What does it mean when the state sets more vigorous testing procedures for an embalmer's license than a driver's license? I mean, thousands of people die each year because of bad drivers, but how many people do embalmers kill? What does that mean?"

"I believe that's one of the signs of the apocalypse, honey," Paul said.

"What it means is there are too many unqualified drivers on the road. And that keeps insurance rates up, slows traffic down, increases pollution, and keeps mass transit from working."

"So, we should put all our energy into solving that problem instead of saving the rain forests?" Paul asked.

"See, that's what pisses me off," Georgette said. "You have to focus all your energies on one problem at a time, and even then you get nothing accomplished."

"You mean we're just wasting our time?" Paul asked.

"Utterly," Georgette said.

Paul loved Georgette more than all the rain forests in the world, but it broke his heart that she'd become so cynical. When they met, Georgette had been an ardent activist, but lately she seemed to be giving up. She still went to the protests, but her heart seemed elsewhere. Paul curled his lip out to pout. Though Georgette was kidding, Paul wanted her to know he didn't like hearing that he was wasting his time trying to save the rain forests. Paul's pout—a sort of sad puppy look—was more than Georgette could stand, so she leaned over and kissed him again. "But that's no reason to give up," she said.

"What I find curious," Paul said, "is how you know about embalmers' testing procedures."

Georgette wiggled her sleek eyebrows devilishly. "You'd be surprised at the things I know," she said.

Paul and Georgette would both have been surprised to know that half a mile ahead of them the world's fastest parade was hurtling their way at ninety-five miles an hour. However, to absolutely no one's surprise, Mr. Kemmler refused to pull over. He was in a hurry to get anywhere but where he had been. At the moment, Mr. Kemmler was supposed to be in his cell at San Quentin awaiting execution, but, impatient with the state's slow-motion death machine, he had slipped out through the prison sewage system, stolen the warden's sporty new coupe, and headed south without so much as putting on his seat belt.

Ten years earlier, Mr. Kemmler, who had a long history of overreacting to minor annoyances, made the mistake of videotaping himself as he used a fireman's ax to chop the head off a young trick-or-treater one grim Halloween night. In his defense, Kemmler explained that he was tired of people ringing his doorbell over and over and over and not only that but he thought the young boy was actually Freddy Krueger Jr. Although one juror initially felt the defense made a lot of sense and thus held out for the first two days of deliberation, Mr. Kemmler eventually was found guilty and sentenced to a life of pointless legal appeals (though at the time the jury was under the impression it had sentenced him to die).

Georgette was the first to notice all the colorful lights on the CHP cars. Just as she pointed them out, Mr. Kemmler, who hadn't been behind the wheel of a car in a decade, overcorrected badly in response to a Plymouth Duster making a sudden and unannounced lane change ahead of him. Kemmler began to lose control and, as usual in situations like that, panic set in. And the only thing worse than a bad driver on the run from the cops is a *panicked* bad driver on the run. Kemmler's sphincter puckered tighter than a knot as his car began to spin.

It appeared the parade was going to have a big finish.

Paul and Georgette watched the whole thing wide-eyed in what seemed like slow motion: The Saturn went sideways, caught some air, and flipped. It started rolling, over and over, hurtling across the median directly toward them and their efficient, but air bag–less, little car. Georgette screamed as Paul jammed on the brakes. The tiny tires smoked and skidded to no avail. The stolen car was headed directly at them and there wasn't a damn thing Paul could do to stop it.

Sitting in his Menlo Park office on the eve of his forty-seventh birthday, Jerry Landis was hard in the grip of the fear of death, and for good reason. The biotechnology company he had founded seventeen years earlier, the cryptically named Xenotech, Incorporated, had failed to find a cure for his disease, despite the millions of dollars

Jerry Landis had poured into it. Expecting the Grim Reaper to knock on his door at any minute, Jerry Landis was reflecting on his extraordinary life. A life which, according to the specialists, was going to end very soon.

It was at times like this that the rhythmic *whir-pffft whir-pffft whir-pffft* faded almost to nothingness . . . *whir-pffft whir-pffft whir-pffft* . . . but it never went away completely.

The disease had made its mark. It had bent the spine, forcing Landis into a painful hunch. His skin had the texture of thick wax paper. His eyesight and hearing were fading as fast as his memories. And no matter how many times he showered each day, he had an unusual essence about him. One had to get close to smell it, but it was there. It was almost as if he were rotting.

Twenty-seven years earlier Jerry Landis had burst onto Wall Street at the tender age of twenty, a brash whiz kid picking big-time winners. *Barrons* and the *Wall Street Journal* quickly deemed him a seer, a visionary, "the Prophet of Profit," and he quickly amassed a net worth of more than $350 million by looking into the future and telling others what he saw—and, more often than not, being right.

The whole thing started with rape. Landis was researching an agribusiness company based in Saskatoon when he came across a magazine article about a scientist experimenting with rape, an old world annual plant (*Brassica napus*) of the mustard family and cousin of the turnip. For years rape was grown primarily as ground cover and as a forage crop for livestock. But this scientist had discovered that the seeds of the plant yielded an interesting oil he called canola. According to the article, the scientist wasn't sure if the oil had any practical uses, but he thought it was worth looking into.

It was while reading that article that Jerry Landis had the first of his many epiphanies. Jerry Landis went to visit this scientist, and what he heard convinced Mr. Landis to invest heavily in the scientist's company and in rape futures.

On Wall Street they say "Timing is everything."

At roughly the same time that the American public discovered the dangers of saturated fat in their diets, the scientist discovered that canola oil was lower in saturated fat than most other oils. Since people preferred not to die of saturated-fat-induced heart attacks, the rape crop, which heretofore had been worth only a few million dollars a year as cattle feed, was about to begin generating in the neighborhood of two billion dollars annually. And with researchers looking at ways to turn canola into an industrial oil as well as a vehicle fuel, that number might easily double.

Thus was Jerry Landis a seer. A visionary who suddenly had more money than most people knew what to do with. But Jerry Landis was not most people: Like Jules Verne, turning nineteenth-century fascination with science and invention into mass-market literature, Jerry Landis suddenly knew that the future of investing was in agricultural biotechnology. Over the next ten years, in addition to his own money, Jerry Landis raised hundreds of millions of dollars for start-up agricultural biotechnology companies in the United States, Germany, and Canada. Ag-biotechs, as they were called, were new and scary to most investors at that time. But Jerry Landis saw the commercial potential invisible to others, and he had the ability to convey that vision.

The products of ag-biotech companies had what Jerry Landis considered an obvious payoff. People would always have to eat, so any company that created (and patented) a more efficient way to produce food—or created new types of food or safer food products, like canola oil—would be a regular dividend machine. And he figured this was especially true in a world whose population seemed to be growing endlessly.

One of the companies in which Jerry Landis invested developed microorganisms—specifically, a genetically altered fungus called *Penicillium bilaii*—which helped plants take in phosphate, a critical plant nutrient. The company also refined the use of rhizobium, a naturally occurring bacterium which helped legume crops absorb more nitrogen. All of this helped farmers double their crop yields per acre, and farmers all over the world are willing to pay good money for products like that. Another of Landis's ag-biotechs perfected the genetic manipulation of tomatoes and strawberries so they would withstand harsh weather and become more pest resistant. It didn't matter that the resulting fruits were chewier and less flavorful than pink cotton balls—the point was these babies could be grown and sold year-round, and consumers, always willing to lower their standards, were buying them as fast as the trucks got them to market.

After years in New York, Jerry Landis and his wife moved to Menlo Park, California, the West Coast home of venture capital. There he roamed the landscape of investment possibilities, picking both winners and losers in industries ranging from aerospace and fiber optics to lumber and strip mining. And soon his fortune was estimated at five hundred million dollars.

But all that was before the damned diagnosis. *Whir-pffft whir-pffft whir-pffft.*

Since then a lot of things had happened. First, he bought a struggling medical biotechnology company and redirected its research efforts. Second, his wife left him. And third, he had gotten a lot older than the intervening seventeen years would account for. And now, as he approached his forty-seventh, and possibly his final, year— Jerry Landis was reviewing the facts of his life.

It was not an ordinary life by any standard. It had been punctuated by revelations about the future. He had taken these visions and applied them to the stock market, and the results could best be described as miracles. Miracles performed in the laboratories Jerry Landis had created with his own money. It was creation in the purest sense of the word, something springing from nothingness.

Jerry Landis had done wondrous things.

As these thoughts of miracles and wonder danced on his cortex, something happened to Mr. Landis, something he couldn't stop. As if he were a puppet controlled by a higher power, the long-forgotten words of Thomas Car-lyle suddenly issued from Landis's mouth: "The hero can be poet, prophet, king, priest or what you will, according to the kind of world he finds himself born into." He repeated the words slowly: "the kind of world he finds himself born into." Jerry Landis considered this for a moment, unsure of the meaning. But he was sure of something else. He was certain that he had been chosen.

And suddenly he felt the warm hand of Almighty God upon him. A brilliant golden light illuminated the room and the truth was revealed to him.

He had never thought of it this way, but now, with the golden light showering down upon him, it seemed so obvious. In his brief lifetime, Jerry Landis had been visited with revelations and he had performed miracles. He had also been visited by a plague of sorts and was facing an untimely death like many saints and martyrs. Men like that didn't come along every day, he reasoned, so it seemed to Jerry Landis that this could mean only one thing: He would be a vessel, a medium, an agent, an instrument—something. But what?

A instant later Mr. Landis thought he heard a voice. It said, "I have chosen thee in the furnace of affliction." He recognized the words of Isaiah, but who had said them? And why? The golden light was comforting, and it made Landis receptive to the voices. Matthew spoke next: "For many are called, but few are chosen."

"Yes," Jerry Landis said. "Few are chosen." Chosen for what? he wondered.

"Ye have not chosen me," John said, "but I have chosen you."

And suddenly Mr. Landis was clear as the sky. He had been chosen to see the future. He was a prophet. Either that or the second son of God, and prophet seemed to him more likely.

The golden light grew brighter and he gazed around his office. He saw angels in the architecture, spinning in infinity, and in this state of grace he rose from his chair and crossed to the wall of books that dominated the room. A wide variety of texts filled the shelves. But only one of them mattered right now: the King James Version of the Bible, the sacred scriptures of Christianity. Jerry Landis pulled the book down and it fell open to the Book of Genesis. His eyes landed where he imagined God wanted them to: "Be fruitful, and multiply, and replenish the earth, and subdue it."

To some the message would have been unclear, but not to Jerry Landis. He understood what the Lord wanted, even expected, of him. God wanted Jerry Landis to replenish the earth in his own likeness. But in order to do that he would have to find a way to cheat the certain death he had been promised by the specialists.

It was a test.

Ultimately, this passage of Holy Scripture was telling Jerry Landis that God wanted him to live. Jerry Landis wanted that also, but the specialists had told him that wasn't going to happen. Jerry Landis suddenly saw the irony. Without even knowing it was God's will, he had started many years ago the process of keeping himself alive. But the thing he had begun as a way of circumventing the ravages of a rare disease (and which, coincidentally, also stood to make him one of the wealthiest men on earth) he now saw as a mission. A mission from God, no less.

He could think of two ways to succeed at the task God had set for him. The first was already well under way at Xenotech, Incorporated, a company he had founded years ago. The second way was to have children—sons, specifically—who would bear his name. If he had enough sons, then no matter what happened at Xenotech, Incorporated, Jerry Landis's name would live on just as God wanted.

"And God said, Let us make man in our own image, after our likeness; and let them have dominion over all the earth and over every creeping thing that creepeth upon the earth."

Yes. That is what Jerry Landis would do. But how? He had only four children, and only two of them boys, and only one of them heterosexual, and *he* was impotent.

Thus, as things were, when Jerry Landis and his two sons died, there would be no one to carry on the name. And clearly this was not what God wanted. Worse, Jerry Landis's wife had left him five years ago. She had tired of never seeing her husband. He was always at work, completely obsessed with the company he had founded. The thing that bothered her most was that she didn't know why he suddenly had become so obsessed with his work. Even when they lived in New York and Jerry was ruling Wall Street they spent much of their time together.

For reasons that were unclear even to himself, Jerry Landis never explained it to her. He never told her about the diagnosis, so she was in the dark and confused and feeling unloved, so she left with a hundred million dollars and returned to New York.

And now Jerry Landis needed someone—a woman, obviously—to help him execute God's plan. But with his time running out, one woman probably wouldn't suffice. This was God's way of telling Jerry Landis that he needed *many* women. Hey! Hallelujah! The golden light was almost blinding now. Jerry Landis had been visited by God the Father and told to find and impregnate as many women as he could.

Thy will be done, he thought.

But what if the disease had left him shooting blanks? How would he get around that?

It was another test.

Jerry Landis went to the window and looked out on the fine buildings dotting Menlo Park. Some of the buildings brimmed with ideas that mankind had never imagined. Other buildings offered the path to the capital necessary to bring those innovative ideas to fruition. After a moment's reflection, Jerry Landis realized the answer to his quandary was right outside his office. He lived in the Santa Clara Valley, also known as Silicon Valley, home of advanced computer science and biotechnology. It was indeed the Valley of Miracles. If there was any place on God's green earth where Jerry Landis could get a third testicle attached to his reproductive system, this was it. And if anyone had the contacts to find out who dealt with such matters, it was Jerry Landis.

Whir-pffft whir-pffft *whir-pffft whir-pffft* . . .

The slums stretched for miles. Dead and dying bodies littered the squalid, putrid alleyways connecting the wretched mud huts and lean-tos. Few cities in the modern world could rival Calcutta for overcrowding, unemployment, poverty, and sheer human desperation.

And, as any good businessman knows, where there's desperation there's money to be made. Good money.

For the lucky ones in this part of the world, home was four sheets of rotting plywood topped with rusting peels of metal. Starvation had made them too weak and too slow to catch the diseased rats which came and went as they pleased, gnawing at the emaciated children on the floor more often than being eaten themselves.

But the new day had brought hope to some. There was a man—a doctor—who had come to help those most in need, and word had just reached Indira. She was small and gnarled, the result of childhood malnourishment and rickets. Her gaunt face, with bulging eyes and slack jaw, gave the impression of a howling skull. She gathered what little strength she had left and made her way to the makeshift office where the good doctor was seeing the downtrodden. The room was small and windowless. Thick, humid air slowed the ceiling fan to a worthless spin. Flying insects jockeyed for position to get at the moist human flesh below. It was spring in Calcutta.

Indira was desperate and afraid. But her fear eased when she saw this great man. He looked exactly as she expected a distinguished American doctor to look. His round belly filled with good food, his scalp bare from contemplation, a look of jowly wisdom. Indira explained to the interpreter that she had a dozen sick and starving children at home and that her husband had died recently. She needed money for food and medical care or, if by some miracle she came into enough of it, she could use it as a dowry with which to attract a new spouse, and then she could be blessed with even more children.

Through the interpreter, the man calling himself Dr. Gibbs explained to the impoverished woman that he could help. "Tell her I understand," he said, his tone sincere. He smiled warmly at Indira as he spoke. "Tell her I have children of my own and I can't stand the thought of hers going hungry."

The interpreter conveyed this to Indira, and she began to cry in the presence of this saint who had come offering salvation. Through her sobs she managed a few words. "She says she'll do anything," the interpreter said.

"Good. Then tell her I'll give her sixty-five bucks for one of her kidneys, but it has to be this afternoon." Dr. Gibbs was in India searching for one of the little bean-shaped organs because the nephrons of a particularly wealthy client in Hong Kong had ceased collecting the waste products from his blood and he was thus on the verge of death or a lifetime of dialysis. The client was eager to part with $20,000 (U.S.) if doing so would get him off the damn machine. And if money guaranteed anything these days, it guaranteed that the wealthy need not suffer dialysis.

The reason Dr. Gibbs was in India instead of, say, Indiana, was that India was one of the few countries in the world where the human organ trade was still legal. The United States outlawed trade in human body parts with the National Organ Transplant Act of 1984, possibly in reaction to imprisoned felons who were trying to sell their organs in order to raise money to fund their pointless appeals. In the United Kingdom, the British Parliament passed the Human Organ Transplants Act of 1989, which made illegal the sale of human organs from both live and dead donors. But India, making a bid to be the ultimate free-market economy, kept the organ trade legal—so legal, in fact, that it was a thirty-million-dollar-a-year business. In this part of the world, it wasn't at all unusual for people to have kidneys and other organs removed in the same way people have their wallets snatched on the streets of New York.

China was considered an up-and-coming second in the human organ business. Never one to miss an opportunity for committing human rights violations, Chinese authorities were said to harvest and broker the organs of the prisoners they executed. And, if you believed what some people said, one enterprising Chinese hospital announced a transplant package deal including airfare, the organ of your choice, and the necessary surgery, all for the can't-beat-it price of $18,000!

Recent medical advances had made these dangerous times.

His business card said simply "Dr. L. Gibbs" and he tended to overemphasize the "Dr." when he introduced himself. He was a bit defensive, what with his degree coming not from Harvard or Yale as his parents had wished, but rather from the Port-au-Prince School of Medicine (known as Voodoo U to the American students attending). It was the medical school equivalent of Betty Jo's Pet Grooming Academy.

His suspect credentials notwithstanding, the good doctor was making a decent living—but not so decent that he was going to be able to retire early. And at age fifty, retirement was something he was thinking seriously about. On top of that, the work was not particularly rewarding from a self-actualization point of view, and he had to travel a good percentage of the time and always to the filthy, overpopulated cities of the third world where he could ply his trade legally.

Now and again (usually during happy hour), Dr. Gibbs would entertain the thought of trying to go "black market" back home in the States—he knew there were plenty of poor and desperate people there. But he feared that the moment he had a good two feet of small bowel in his greedy little hands the door would come crashing down and the cops would storm in and take him away. Either that or he'd find himself on the business end of a *60 Minutes* interview. Trouble like that Dr. Gibbs didn't need, so he always shelved the idea when he sobered up. Besides, he got lots of frequent flier miles traveling the way he did.

Dr. Gibbs didn't actually install the kidneys he procured—that wasn't the sort of thing one learned in Haitian medical schools—but he did know how to remove them. And the patients usually survived his surgery. He had done it a hundred times before, but lately he found himself growing tired of the grind.

Indira listened intently as the interpreter conveyed the doctor's generous offer. At first there was some confusion in the translation, or at least Indira thought there was. She asked for clarification. When she found she had heard right the first time, her expression was one of astonishment; she looked as if someone had just reached in from behind and yanked her kidney out bare-handed.

Dr. Gibbs looked at his watch, growing impatient. He had to get downtown to a warehouse to look over a shipment of eyeballs before they went bad. They'd been in storage for just over three weeks, so they were nearing spoilage. Eyes were a great export item in this part of the world. As someone once said, they're hardy as olives, but worth lots more by the pound. They went for the unbeatable price of $90 a pop in this wretched corner of the world as compared to as much as $4,000 per in the United States. Best of all, the transplantable part, the cornea, was bloodless and thus would not be rejected by the recipient. On top of that the cornea was the only body part you could legally sell in the United States after 1984.

Dr. Gibbs swatted at a fly buzzing around his large, oily ears that protruded from the sides of his head like small satellite dishes. You never knew what sort of disease a mosquito or a fly might be carrying around here so the effort required to shoo them away was generally worth it. The insect landed on his sweaty, wrinkled white shirt and he slapped it. Blood and God-knows-what-else stained the moist all-cotton oxford. Dr. Gibbs wiped his hand on his pants and shifted his overweight frame in

the creaky wooden chair before pulling a tissue from his
pocket and dabbing at the perspiration beading on his
balding head. "Well, does she want the fucking money
or not?" Dr. Gibbs asked. "I've got an appointment
downtown, and I want to pick up some curry before
I go."

The woman shook her head and spoke to the
interpreter.

"She thinks you're lowballing her," the interpreter
said. "Says her cousin got eighty for his kidney."

"Sweet Jesus! Eighty bucks!" Dr. Gibbs looked over
the results of the blood tests. The match was nearly perfect. "All right, but she'll have to sign a nondisclosure
agreement. I don't want word getting around that I'm
paying that much. It'd put me out of business."

As the stolen Saturn hurtled toward Paul and Georgette in a violent roll, both of its air bags deployed and
the protective steel cage did its best to protect the feloni-
ous Mr. Kemmler. It was over in a matter of seconds,
too fast for Paul and Georgette to do anything but start
a prayer—and up until that point, neither had really been
the praying type. Given more time, Georgette might have
prayed that she and Paul not be horribly disfigured so
their friends and family could enjoy a nice open-casket
wake.

Paul would have prayed for a victory over Jerry Landis.
Just one victory and he'd be all right to die. As it was,
Paul's win-loss record in terms of causes was unimpressive: Rain forests were still falling, landfills were overflowing, and the percentage of children living in poverty
was on the increase. Most of his elected officials had
been indicted and far too many had been convicted of
charges ranging from sexual harassment to misappropria-
tion of public funds and worse. Yet Paul's idealism was
still intact. He didn't expect a perfect world, but he did
want to bring about at least one improvement to the
world before he died. But right now it looked like Paul
was going to check out batting zero.

That is, until the Saturn ground to a halt, upside-down, its crumpled bumper nosing the Greenpeace sticker on Paul's tiny car.

Traffic ground to a halt and irritated motorists leaned on their horns—horns Mr. Kemmler would never hear. It was dumb luck the convicted murderer didn't kill anyone with his stunt driving, especially Paul and Georgette. Kemmler himself might have walked away from the crash but for the fact that he wasn't wearing his seat belt. Ironically, as the Saturn had rolled sideways across the median, the owner's manual had been thrown from the glove compartment and, like a scolding mother, was open to the reminder that air bags are only a supplementary restraint system.

The adrenaline rush that comes with the fear that your life is about to end in a grisly manner is sometimes enough to trigger cardiac arrest, but Paul's and Georgette's athletic hearts were robust from their years of physical training. Still jittery, however, they got out of their car and stood by the roadside surveying the scene. After a minute Paul turned to Georgette. "What color paintball you think this deserves?" he asked.

"I think this scumbag ought to be dragged out of his car and shot with a real gun," Georgette said, her diamond stud sparkling in the sun.

"That might be redundant at this point," Paul responded.

"I don't care," Georgette said. "It's the symbolism that counts." Adrenaline still coursed through her veins.

Kemmler, in fact, wasn't dead, at least not officially. But until the jaws of life got him out of the crumpled coupe, no one would be able to measure what was still alive about him.

Georgette turned to Paul. "What were you thinking?"

"What? Just now?"

"Yes, just now when you thought you were going to die. Did anything cross your mind, like maybe how much you love me and how you could never live without me so maybe you were hoping that if I died, you'd die too? Something along those lines maybe?"

"I hate to say it," Paul said, "but I thought about Jerry Landis."

"What?" she blurted. "You're about to die, sitting six inches from your better half, or your consort, or life partner, or whatever I am . . ."

"My reason for living," Paul said.

"Thank you. So your reason for living is about to kick the bucket and you think of Jerry Fucking Landis? How do you think that makes me feel?"

"It wasn't a conscious thought process," Paul said. "I'm sure I would have thought of you next."

"Small comfort." Georgette punched Paul's shoulder. "I can't believe I'm playing second fiddle to that son of a bitch."

"I just sent him another letter," Paul said.

In fact, since the day Jerry Landis threw Paul's proposal in the trash, Paul had written him many letters, none of which had had any impact whatsoever on the course of human events. Landaq, Incorporated, went ahead with its "development" plans. It clear-cut the sequoias and, since it had recently discovered a way to extract the trace amount of gold that was in the granite, it strip-mined the land as well.

Unable to bring himself to sabotage the bulldozers or spike the trees, Paul felt like a perfect coward as he stood by and watched as his Eden was raped. The upside, as he saw it, was that he had not broken any laws. He hadn't stooped to that.

The igneous rock yielded only enough gold to break even on production costs, but there was a nice tax break on equipment depreciation so, on balance, it looked profitable for Landaq.

Lacking the courage to do anything else, Paul swore a young man's vow to use "the system" to prevent such things from ever happening again. He joined Greenpeace and sent twenty dollars to the Sierra Club. He also participated in some protests, and he even painted some of the signs they used. It felt good to be a part of the solution.

After gouging the land, Landaq increased its profits by dumping toxic waste from one of its chemical manufacturing subsidiaries into the gaping holes left behind.

When Paul heard about that, he swore once again to make Jerry Landis's life as difficult as he possibly could. And to that end he worked feverishly to crush his foe, writing letters to senators, lobbyists, and the Department of the Interior. And as if that weren't enough, Paul volunteered to go door-to-door to collect petition signatures for the National Resources Defense Council.

Landaq completed the Sierra Nevada Development Project three months ahead of schedule. It put in a few splintery picnic tables, and with help from a sympathetic congressman, sold the land to the federal government for use as a public camping site. And finally it made the whole transaction part of the "At Landaq, we care" PR campaign.

And when it was all over, Paul was outraged. However, as often happens, his rage softened with time. Plus, at that age, girls became a major distraction.

During the second year of his crusade, Paul's failure to have even the slightest impact on the fortunes of Jerry Landis began to diminish his determination somewhat. And, of course, getting his driver's license didn't help matters any. It's hard to be a dedicated eco-warrior after you've installed a good eight-track player in your Ford Galaxy. Paul tried not to let all this distract him from his cause but it wasn't easy. He still wrote letters whenever he could, and he started using some pretty damn strong language too.

By the time he was eighteen and old enough to vote, Paul was ready to surrender to the folly of his oath. But then something happened that renewed Paul's rage and his vow. The event was devastating and unalterable and Paul used it as fuel.

During the years that followed, Jerry Landis would grow to hate Paul for his persistence. He was "that annoying letter-writing son of a bitch" who wouldn't go away. Politicians could be bought and policy makers influenced, but not Paul. He was a pit bull pain in the ass, always telling the press about the evils of Landis's deals. Paul's campaign of letter writing and protesting actually started to cause problems for Landis—extra scrutiny on environmental impact studies, delays on acquisition of tracts of National Park land, stuff like that. But the problems were relatively minor and always solved by crossing another palm. Still, they were problems, and like Chinese water torture, after twenty-three years it was enough to make a man crazy.

"Let me give you some advice," Georgette said. "Next time I ask what you're thinking about after we've shared a life-threatening experience, just say you were thinking about me. It's a safe bet that'll be the right answer."

Paul smiled. "I swear on a stack."

"And I'm sorry I hit you."

"Me too," Paul said, rubbing his shoulder.

Georgette was a serious athlete who packed a serious punch. She had started for three years as power forward for Stanford's women's basketball team. She still lifted weights and played ball every Wednesday night with pals from the old team. It wasn't unusual for a player to come away from those games with a puffy mouse under the eye, the result of going in for a rebound against Georgette. On court she was known for her peripheral vision—eyes in the back of her head, they said, green and clear as centuries, sexy and sly and framed by dark, sleek eyebrows that tapered to sharp points. Her silky hair was brown and cut short, easily stuffed inside a baseball cap or moussed punkishly into that spiky little ponytail. "I'm going to see if that piece of shit in the Saturn is still alive," Georgette said, demonstrating how she had earned her share of technical fouls.

A highway patrolman approached Paul. "Can I get your name, sir?"

"Paul Symon," he said.

The patrolman looked over Paul's six-foot-four frame. "I thought Garfunkel was the tall one," he said.

"The last name's spelled different," Paul said. "It's S-Y-M-O-N."

The patrolman erased the *I* and corrected Paul's last name. As he did his paperwork, Georgette returned from talking to the paramedics. "The guy's unconscious. They're taking him to South Bay Memorial, said it doesn't look good."

"That's what happens when you flip your car without your belt on," the patrolman said.

"Paul," Georgette said, "are we done here? If we're still going to the cemetery before I play ball tonight, we've gotta go."

The paramedics loaded the comatose Mr. Kemmler into the ambulance and sped away as the flatbed tow truck left with what remained of the disabled Saturn. The little coupe still had a few parts that could be salvaged, and for that matter, so did Mr. Kemmler—assuming he had signed his donor card.

3

The cemetery was surrounded by a crumbling brick wall. As Paul and Georgette passed through the rusting wrought iron gates at the entrance, Paul noticed the graffiti spray-painted below the bronze Belmont Memorial Cemetery sign. It read A GATED COMMUNITY.

Something about the cemetery silenced Paul. Whatever it was also seemed to have silenced the rest of nature. It was odd. There were no birds chirping, no chattering squirrels, and no buzzing insects. Georgette honored the quiet as Paul led the way through the field of crosses, obelisks, and other monuments.

Despite daily maintenance, the cemetery itself appeared ready for burial. The marble grave markers were corroded and pitted and cracked. The shrubbery along the walls was stunted and gnarled. Even the plastic flowers left behind on some of the plots looked sickly and spent. The grass was thin and composed of more brown than green. The company managing the cemetery tried putting down some extra fertilizer once but to no avail.

The cemetery was situated a couple of miles west of the massive West Bay Industrial Manufacturing Park, which was located along a terminally fouled inlet at the south end of San Francisco Bay. Notwithstanding the

Clean Air Act of 1967 (and the obviously impotent amendments of 1970, 1977, and 1990), the towering smokestacks of the profitable industries in this manufacturing park spewed nitrogen oxides, nonmethane hydrocarbons, sulfur dioxides, and peroxyacetyl nitrate twenty-four hours a day. The westbound clouds passing overhead absorbed these gases before drifting across Highway 101 and Interstate 280, from which they gathered the emissions of roughly 520,000 cars and trucks each day. Then, saturated with these noxious elements, the clouds continued drifting west until they backed up against the Santa Cruz Mountains. Once stalled, the clouds drizzled acid rain into the Upper Crystal Springs Reservoir, a state fish and game refuge, and the cemetery.

When they arrived at Paul's father's plot, Georgette gently leaned the bouquet of flowers against the damaged headstone. The inscription was simple: FREDERICK SYMON—LOVING FATHER AND HUSBAND. The dates on the marker showed that it had been twenty years since they buried Mr. Symon. Paul and his mother had chosen this plot because it was in the shade of a tree whose canopy had still been green when they buried Paul's dad. Paul remembered thinking that his dad would enjoy looking up at the lush, leafy branches for the rest of time. Sadly, after so many years of acid deposition, the tree had the look of a large scarecrow with a skin disease. Paul silently apologized for the landscaping as he stood over his father's plot.

Fred Symon had worked for himself. He was a bio-organic chemist working as an independent contractor. He called his company Symorganics. In early 1978 he landed a contract with an agricultural biotechnology company called Cel-Tech Labs. Cel-Tech was a subsidiary of Landaq, Incorporated. Jerry Landis had built Cel-Tech after making his fortune with canola oil.

Fred's contract with Cel-Tech called for him to help create a viral clone, attaching genetic material via a novel (and proprietary) bio-organic enzyme-delivery system. Among other biologics, Fred worked with the cancer gene responsible for the unregulated cell growth for which cancer is famous. The end product was designed to be sprayed on rice paddies. A series of enzymes on the surface of the virus would allow it to penetrate the plant's cell walls and deliver the genetic growth factor material to the rice's genetic makeup. The result, at least in theory, was larger grains and an increased crop yield.

Fred Symon loved his work. In 1978 this was cutting-edge science. It was exciting and potentially hazardous, which was part of the fun. And, being an independent contractor, Fred was, in every sense of the word, his own boss. He got to call his own shots as long as he delivered the goods. He loved his independence.

There were several phases in the cloning process, some of them sensitive and dangerous, during which—if one were exposed to it—the virus was capable of infecting human cells, causing massive cell growth until the "shut-down" gene took over and stopped it. That's why Fred and his fellow scientists did their work in biological safety cabinets, or "hoods": biohazard cabinetry work spaces that met a series of NIH and CDC standards designed to make it safe to manipulate infectious microbiological agents. The primary safety feature of the hoods was the negative air pressure created by a fan that sucked air from the lab into an elaborate filtering and exhaust system.

Because several competing biotech companies were working on variations of the same viral-enzyme process, Jerry Landis had ordered double shifts around the clock. He knew the kind of payoff that awaited the winner, and he didn't want someone else beating him to market.

The only problem was that when Jerry Landis built the lab he saved some money by cutting a few corners—nothing you could see, of course, just stuff like a 40 percent reduction in the size of electrical conduits and the concomitant use of smaller-gauge wire. Little things like that, at the end of the day, added up to real money. But when it came to the biological safety cabinets, Jerry Landis didn't skimp. There was no point: He knew he'd never get a qualified scientist to work in a conspicuously unsafe workplace. So Cel-Tech Labs had hoods that met all government requirements—even though, as a private lab, it wasn't burdened by such regulations.

When the lab was finished, building inspectors checked all of the electrically driven safety devices against building and safety codes. They found that each one passed. However, they never tested all systems simultaneously. A couple of years later, with a double shift working on the viral rice project, the electrical system was, for the first time, maxed out. Thanks to the conduit shortcut there was severe overheating in the overhead wiring of Fred Symon's biological safety cabinet. This led to an electrical fire which cut off power to the exhaust fans, resulting in a positive air pressure in the BSC. Finally a sensor picked up the smoke, tripping the fire alarm. As Fred looked around to see why the alarm was sounding, the intense heat in the crawl space melted a part of the hood, which then fell onto the Erlenmeyer flasks containing the cancer gene component and the viral enzymes, thus releasing airborne viral material. At the sound of shattering glass, Fred and the other researchers left the lab immediately. However, unaware that his fan had stopped, Fred inadvertently breathed in a gulp of the infected air before escaping.

Fred, and everyone else in the lab, went through the normal decontamination procedures that day, and they underwent a basic physical exam. Everyone vetted clean, and within a couple of weeks they had resumed work in a new lab.

Meanwhile, the cause of the fire was investigated. Cel-Tech's insurance company discovered the problem and refused to pay for damages, saying the wiring shortcut had voided the policy. Cel-Tech paid a small building code violation fine and got on with business.

A few months later, during the summer between Paul's senior year in high school and his freshman year at Cal, Paul and his father were in the backyard tossing a football. Fred took tremendous pride in the fact that Paul was going to play Pac-10 football and get such a highly regarded education. He couldn't wait to see his son on the field at Memorial Stadium. He was living for the day. "Okay," Fred said. "Put some mustard on this one." He clapped his hands and called for the ball.

Paul pretended to take the snap from center. He faded back behind an imaginary offensive line. "Stabler sets up in the pocket," he said, doing his own play-by-play.

His father cut across the middle of the yard, waving a hand wildly, pretending that he had found a hole in the zone coverage. "I'm open! I'm open!"

Suppressing his urge to laugh at his dad's antics, Paul resumed the call. "He sees Casper moving awkwardly across the middle and he delivers the ball." Paul zipped a sharp pass to his dad, who caught the ball, jogged a few yards, and crossed a fictional goal line. Once in the end zone, he spiked the ball and did a silly victory dance. Paul thrust his hands in the air. "Touchdown! Raiders!" He burst out laughing as his dad strutted about the yard celebrating his victory.

Fred laughed too for a second before his face suddenly twisted into a mask of pain and fear. Paul watched in confusion and horror as his father reached for his chest and fell forward onto his face without a sound. Paul screamed for his mother as he raced to where his father lay. He was dead before Paul reached him. Paul rolled his dad onto his back and tried to revive him but it was too late. Fred would never see Paul on the field at Memorial Stadium.

It looked like a garden-variety heart attack, but they did an autopsy anyway. The coroner found that Fred's lungs were choked with a massive cancerous growth. Microscopic examination of lung tissue also revealed contamination by an unusual virus. The coroner said Fred had died of a heart attack, resulting from complications caused by the mysterious cancer in the lung.

There was nothing mysterious about the cancer to Paul and his mother. They knew where it had come from and, thanks to the results of the fire investigation, they believed Jerry Landis was ultimately responsible for Fred's death. So they contacted an attorney and told her what had happened. They wanted to know if Cel-Tech's president, Jerry Landis, could be held criminally liable for Fred's death. Paul and his mother felt someone had to be held responsible. The attorney contacted the appropriate authorities on behalf of the widow Symon. After reviewing the facts, the district attorney's office concluded that Fred Symon was an independent contractor. He had signed a contract with Cel-Tech wherein he specifically assumed risks never assumed by employees. The contract included a rider that Fred had signed. The rider stated that he had inspected the Cel-Tech facility and its safety mechanisms and found they met or exceeded government standards. Of course, Fred had never crawled around looking to see if the building's wiring was done to code, but his signature said otherwise. According to the district attorney's office, the wording in the contract and the rider was clear, unequivocal, and conspicuous. The contract was found to be enforceable and, thus, Cel-Tech was not criminally liable for Fred's death. There would be no charges filed.

So a civil suit ensued. At trial it was determined that the growth-factor cancer gene had infected Fred Symon's lung cells, causing them to multiply at unnatural rates. As the cancer spread, fluids eventually became a prominent component of the lung surface, rendering the lungs ineffective in oxygen transport, especially during periods of physical activity. The diminished oxygen supply placed an extraordinary burden on Fred's heart, resulting in a heart attack and death.

Paul attended every deposition, every pretrial hearing, and every day of the trial. He didn't understand most of what was going on but he was there. He was in a state of shock about his father's death, and he couldn't shake the image of his father's face when his heart quit. That look of terror and loss would never fade. Paul couldn't believe his dad was gone. He couldn't believe his mother

was alone now. He couldn't believe his path had crossed
Jerry Landis's again, not like this.

The key to the case was in proving by a preponderance
of the evidence precisely when and how Fred Symon
was exposed to the virus. Defense attorneys for Cel-Tech
argued that it was entirely possible Fred Symon had been
careless in his handling of the materials at some point
prior to the fire, in effect infecting himself.

Every scientist Fred Symon had worked with over the
past six years testified that Fred was without peer in
the care and caution with which he handled any sort of
biohazardous material. To their knowledge, he had never
made a mistake in that regard. On cross-examination,
however, the scientists were forced to admit that even
someone who was very cautious *could* make a mistake.
The possibility existed.

Cel-Tech paid handsomely for unimpeachable expert
witnesses from Yale and Harvard to testify that it was
impossible to prove one way or the other precisely when
and how Fred Symon was exposed to the virus. Cel-
Tech's expert arson investigators testified that no one
could say whether the fan in Fred Symon's BSC had
stopped working before or after the Erlenmeyer flask
broke. Based on this and other testimony, the judge instructed the jury they had no recourse but to find in
favor of Cel-Tech.

Paul's mother knew before the judge spoke that they
had lost. Her husband was dead and no one would be
held responsible. She put her arms around Paul and held
him tight. It was just the two of them now. Paul looked
around the courtroom and saw that Jerry Landis wasn't
even there. He had sent his attorneys to get the good
news and bring it back to him. When the verdict was
announced, Paul cried for his dad. Jerry Fucking Landis
had killed his father and walked away, living proof that
Ambrose Bierce was right when he said that corporations
were ingenious devices for obtaining individual profit
without incurring individual responsibility.

Someone suggested appealing the verdict in the civil

suit but the Symons didn't have enough money for that sort of litigation and they couldn't find an attorney to take the case on contingency; every capable lawyer in the Bay Area knew it was a loser. Many of those lawyers believed that the fact that the Symons were probably correct in assuming Jerry Landis was ultimately responsible for the death and yet had escaped damages was proof positive that a properly set up corporation (or limited partnership or limited liability company) was indeed a beautiful thing. At a meeting of the San Mateo County Bar Association a week after the trial, two prosperous attorneys were talking. One commented that, legalities notwithstanding, he was shocked—*shocked!*—that decent, righteous people could get so screwed by the American justice system. When the second attorney finally stopped laughing, the two of them agreed to skip the presentation on legal ethics and go have a drink.

For the Symons, it was over. Paul's mother would have to get by on a meager savings account, the life insurance, and Social Security payments. And she would be all alone.

Paul had to get packed. The quarter was about to begin. He had already missed several weeks of summer practice. Football season was about to start. The day before he was to move into the dorm, a letter came. It was from their insurance company. The letter said that as a result of Cel-Tech's expert witnesses' pointing out the possibility that Fred had mishandled the viral material and infected himself, the company refused to pay on Fred's life insurance policy. They were very sorry.

It was getting late and it was time to leave the cemetery. Paul turned to Georgette. "You know, Landis never even apologized to my mom. Didn't even send a sympathy card." He looked up to the gathering acid rain clouds.

Georgette wiped a tear from Paul's cheek. "C'mon, sweetheart," she said. "Let's go."

Hidden deep in the piney woods of south-central Mississippi, on the fringes of the DeSoto National Forest, was a ten-thousand-acre property encircled by two fifteen-feet-high, electrified fences. A ten-yard-wide no-man's-land separated the two fences, and the overall impression was that of a medium-to-high-security prison.

Some of the curious residents of Deckern County, Mississippi, where this property lay, speculated that it was a compound for one of those fringe groups like the Freemen in Montana or the Republic of Texas wackos. Others said they had heard rumors about weird experiments of some sort but were unclear on the details. Still others said they had heard unnatural animal-like noises coming from beyond the tree line inside the fenced area. They described it as a screeching, barking sound that no native animal made.

All of the employees who worked there also lived on the grounds in a stylish dormlike building. They had come from out of town, somewhere in California, as rumor had it. They were periodically replaced, the grapevine said, always by more Californians.

The mysterious place had been there for going on twenty years, and the land records at the Chancery Clerk's office indicated the property was owned not by an individual but by a company called Xenotech, which had been incorporated in San Jose, California. The records showed that a Mr. Jerry Landis was the chief executive officer and president of the corporation.

Out in these piney woods, Xenotech, Incorporated was doing business as the Biomedical Research Center of the South. Most of the property was given over to the woods but there was a paved airstrip and several buildings, including the dorm. Near one end of the airstrip was a large hangar for servicing the corporate jets that periodically came and went. Next to the airstrip was a twelve-acre clearing where the physical plant was located. It consisted of two large laboratories, the dormitory, a cafeteria, and the security department. And it was in this last building where two men were having drinks.

The larger of the two was William Robert "Billy Bob" Needmore. He was the new head of security and former sheriff of Deckern County and was the first local to set foot on the ten thousand acres in nearly two decades. The former head of security had died under mysterious circumstances, if you can call being chewed up in an old cotton gin mysterious in this part of the country. And although it appeared he might have died as the result of a large knife wound to the chest prior to having his fiber separated from his seeds, the local coroner, who helped extract the body from the machine, said such speculation was "damn fool nonsense" and he would testify to that in open court. He then got into his brand-new Dodge Ram pickup truck, which many people believed to be far beyond his means, and went back to his office.

"Make me a nuther one of them Klanberry cocktails while you're up," Billy Bob said with a laugh. "Then I'll tell you the rest."

Billy Bob's cousin, H. Merle Grimes, was already drunk, but he figured another couple of ounces of vodka and cranberry juice would make his girlfriend look better, so he was going to make a couple more and then listen to this crazy story Billy Bob had been threatening to tell for the last couple of hours.

As Merle mixed the drinks he glanced over at Billy Bob, who was trying to thread a needle. "Owwshit!" he said when he stuck the needle into the soft pad of his index finger.

"I better give you a little extra to kill the pain," Merle said. He poured Billy Bob two extra fingers of the vodka.

"Good idea," Billy Bob replied.

Things had changed somewhat in Mississippi in these slightly more modern times. And they had changed so gradually that neither Billy Bob nor Merle could remember when they had stopped drinking beer and started with the fruit drinks, but neither of them would argue with the merits of vodka. They also couldn't remember when the local women had started becoming doctors and lawyers and politicians and had stopped doing the sewing, which is what Billy Bob was attempting to do at the moment.

"C'mon, Billy Bob, just tell me," Merle said as he set the drinks on the table.

"Just hold yer water, son. Soon as I get the button sewed back on this here shirt, I will," Billy Bob said. "But I sware yer not gonna believe me."

"All right," Merle said, hoping to prompt the rest of the story out of his cousin, "so this cumpny from California buys the property, puts up 'at big fence and brangs in some buy-ologists and rocket scientists, and—"

"I never said nothin' 'bout no damn rocket scientists," Billy Bob said.

"Well, whatever. All I'm sayin' is it don't make no damn sense to me why they'd brang a buncha eggheads out here to work on a secret project, that's all."

"It's the damnedest thing too, Merle. It's all about genetics. Gene splicin' and hybridizin' lack they does with corn and soybeans and dairy cows, only these fellas is doin' it with damn monkeys!"

"Get out!" Merle said, spilling some cranberry juice onto his shirt.

"And I'm tellin' you the truth, these is some damn big monkeys. Ain't never seen nothin' lack 'em and I even been up to 'at zoo in Jackson where they keep a whole mess of 'em. All different kinds of monkeys up air, but not a one like they got here, nosir."

"Izzzzaaright?" Merle said.

"Goddamn right. I got to talkin' with one of the fellas what's doing the work and he sorta 'splained how they been doin' this here gene splicing, trying to make 'em even bigger."

"Bigger'n they already is?"

"Yessir, 'at's what he told me."

"Dee tell you why?" Merle asked.

"Said he didn't have no idea. Said he was gettin' paid good money just to do the work and not to ask any questions," Billy Bob said.

"Doan sound natch'rll, if you ask me."

"Sure don't," Billy Bob agreed. "I ain't even s'posed

to have nobody out here on the property, 'at's how top secret it's posed to be."

"Shoot, like I care," Merle said. "I wanna see these damn things."

"Can't see most of 'em. Most of 'em's out in the woods." Billy Bob looked around furtively and gestured with his head. "But they's got one of 'em over to the lab building they's fixin' to ship outta here back to California. They ship one of 'em out 'bout once a month."

"Well, she-it, cuz," Merle said. "What're we waitin' on?"

Billy Bob looked around nervously. "Well, first off, you gotta *sware* you ain't never gonna tell nobody about none of this," Billy Bob said. "I want yer oath."

"You know I ain't like 'at," Merle said. " 'Sides, who'd I tell anyway?"

"Sware! I ain't lettin' you see nothin' less you sware not to tell nobody."

"All right, I sware I ain't never gonna tell nobody nothin'."

" 'At's good," Billy Bob said. "You ain't gonna be sorry, neither."

Merle jumped up and mixed two more drinks and then they walked over to the lab building. Before going in, Billy Bob insisted on blindfolding Merle in a cheap attempt to heighten the drama of the moment. Drunk, Merle agreed and offered his own, rather crusty, handkerchief.

As Billy Bob led his titillated cousin into the room, Merle's olfactory senses responded to a strange and overpowering smell. "Whew! 'At is one stanky monkey," he said.

Turning the dimmer, Billy Bob eased the lights up to full brightness. He turned Merle to face him in the proper direction, then quickly yanked off the blindfold.

When Merle's eyes finally focused, he gasped and dropped his glass. "God damn!"

"Goddamn is right," Billy Bob said. "What're you doin' droppin' your glass in here? Mop 'at shit up!"

But Merle was too stunned by what he saw to worry about cleaning up his mess. On the far side of the room was a massive steel cage and inside the cage was a huge, primitive-looking beast. It was like nothing Merle had ever seen in all his life. Of course since Merle had never been out of Deckern County that didn't mean much. But this was like nothing he had even seen on television, which expanded Merle's frame of reference quite a bit. He especially liked National Geographic Specials.

This one was a male. *Papio ursinus*, commonly known as the chacma baboon, *normally* the largest species of the steppe baboons—but this wasn't at all normal. In fact, though neither Billy Bob nor Merle would ever know it, this baboon was larger than *Dinopithecus*, the Ice Age baboon that was the size of a full-grown male silverback gorilla, nearly six feet tall when standing on its hind legs, weighing almost five hundred pounds—and all muscle.

The baboon regarded the two men with suspicion.

"I told you it was a big motherfucker," Billy Bob said. "That nose kinda makes him look lack a big dog, don't it?"

Merle nodded slowly, staring at the animal's long, bulky muzzle that looked like it was made from oily black rubber. Tremendous canines extended from the elongated jawline. Merle had never imagined teeth like these—long, slightly curved, and with ventral edges keened by grinding against lower teeth every time the mouth opened and closed. He figured those giant fangs could bite through his truck's tailgate—and he was right.

The chacma of southern Africa is also known as the dog-faced baboon. Its fur is a smooth silvery-brown with an unusual green tint along the back. The adult male chacma usually grows to about ninety pounds and is, even at that size, a formidable fighter using his disproportionally strong limbs, thick sturdy legs, and awesome jaws. Multiplied by a size factor of five, this specially bred baboon was capable of frightening displays of strength and violence.

Billy Bob and Merle stared in silence at the giant primate, awed, the only noise that of the baboon's rhythmic breathing as it stared back at them. In the hush, the power of nature inspired a sense of wonder in both of the species as they looked into one another's eyes.

Suddenly, and for no good reason other than the vodka, Billy Bob yelled, "Boo!"

Merle nearly wet himself and the baboon went ape, screeching and slapping the floor of the cage. The huge baboon snatched the large automobile tire that was in the cage and, in a terrifying demonstration of its power, ripped it in half as if it were so much cardboard.

"Shut up yer yellin'!" Merle said, his eyes wide in wonder. "Are you out of your rabbit-assed mind? You see how strong 'at thang is? Damn! You doan wanna get somethin' 'at big pissed off."

"Too late," Billy Bob said, finishing off his drink.

The baboon turned and farted in their general direction. It was a long, primitive fart that sounded like a ragged fire hose spewing chili. It was the ugliest, rudest, most ill-behaved thing either of them had ever seen: the baboon's ischial callosities were vividly colored, like a giant pulsating red-and-purple flower.

"So whaddya thank about *that*, cuz?" Billy Bob asked.

Merle inched slightly closer to the cage for a better look. "I tell you what I thank," he said. "I thank I'd lack to know what the hell they's gonna do with it."

Arty was dizzy as usual when he left the Central Coast Blood Products building in downtown San Jose. It was a dizziness he had come to enjoy—a Just Say No high. And the best thing was he got paid for it. Contrary to what he had said in his pre-pint interview, Arty had given blood earlier that day up in Redwood City. Sure, it was against the rules, but the rules didn't take into account that Arty was just trying to make a living without actually holding down what most people think of as a job. Arty was way too smart for regular employment. He had tried retail sales and knew instantly he was destined for something else. He had decided long ago there was no reason to waste a single day (much less your entire life) selling things you didn't believe in to people you didn't care about. Arty had things figured, and nine-to-five with two weeks paid vacation and a crappy HMO was nowhere in the equation. He considered himself a medical researcher, at least that's what he told people who asked about his employment status. Arty just wanted to live comfortably and, depending on your definition of the word, he was doing just that.

He lived in a rented mobile home in Sunnyvale, California, not far from the Great America Theme Park. It was only a single-wide, but that suited Arty fine since he was on the smallish side anyway, about five-four with curly blond hair and an impish grin. Arty didn't require much room, or much of anything else for that matter, just a comfortable chair and a color TV and he was set. Arty ventured out only to sell his renewable natural resources (blood and sperm), to participate in medical experiments, and to do his volunteer work at the orphanage. Arty wanted to give back a little to the community that had given him so much and to that end he worked ten hours a week at the Cupertino Children's Home doing whatever needed to be done.

His choice of charities was an easy one. Arty himself had been orphaned. The only thing Arty knew about his parents was that his father was a fisherman, his mom a fisherman's friend. Arty was only a year old when his father abandoned them. His mother decided she really didn't want the seven children either, so she left one day and never came back. The social workers distributed the children to various foster homes and orphanages. To this day Arty didn't even know he had any siblings. He was raised by the people at the Children's Home—the old one near Monte Vista, not the new one in Cupertino—and to Arty they were his family. The Home was where Arty's heart resided and it's where he always spent Christmas.

Early in life Arty discovered something remarkable

about his body. He was eleven years old when a searing abdominal pain located roughly between his right hipbone and his navel caught his attention. Before he knew it, Arty was at the county hospital staring dumbstruck at his appendix suspended in formaldehyde. Like other young boys fascinated by the creepy world of insects, Arty was completely captivated by the idea that you could have parts removed from your body and stuck in a jar for entertainment and display purposes. While most patients would have been laid up for the better part of a week after having the worthless little wormlike organ removed, the doctors let Arty return to the orphanage the next day, saying they had never seen anyone heal so quickly after emergency surgery. Arty was a fast healer and it was just a matter of time before he figured out how to use that to his advantage.

For now Arty figured that by selling his bodily fluids for a living he would never have to deal with overbearing, ignorant supervisors or back-stabbing co-workers who were trying to make it up the corporate ladder at anyone's expense. He had it all figured.

As his two-pint dizziness passed, Arty made his way to the bus stop and, taking advantage of his sickly pallor, quickly panhandled enough change to catch an express up to Palo Alto. Arty didn't drive. The way he saw it, there were too many idiots on the road who didn't have a clue as to what they were doing. Arty liked mass transit. The drivers were professionals and the vehicles were bigger than just about everything else on the road. And he liked making new friends—striking up conversations with his fellow passengers, whom he saw as orphans of the road.

The bus hissed to a stop and Arty climbed aboard. He sat down next to a retired nun who said her name was Sister Meg. "I used to teach geometry and typing." She held up her hands and showed Arty how her little fingers were bowed inward. "I used to tell my students if I can type, anyone can." She smiled kindly—something she rarely ever did in typing or geometry class. "Where are you off to?" Sister Meg asked.

"I'm on my way to a medical experiment at one of the local biotechnology companies," he said. "Well, actually it's just an interview," Arty said. "Always interview first, that's my policy. Make sure their design is all right." Arty swooned slightly from blood loss, and his lack of color made the sister nervous.

"What sort of experiment?" Sister Meg asked as she inched away.

"Something to do with short-term nerve damage," Arty said proudly. "I don't have all the details, but the way I understand it is they'll be severing some major nerves in my arms and legs to see how they recover with the help of a new grafting procedure."

Sister Meg grimaced. "Won't that hurt?"

"Maybe at first," Arty admitted stoically, "but they're paying pretty good, so what do I have to lose, right? I hardly ever need all of them at the same time, right?" He elbowed the nun and winked. Arty explained that in the past year he had consumed radioactive liquids for a gastrointestinal system analysis, had bronchitis artificially induced by exposure to massive quantities of sulfur dioxide, and had electrodes clipped to his gums for a highly rewarding pain threshold experiment.

"You know, a group of us older nuns get together every couple of weeks and compare our ailments," Sister Meg said. "We talk about what's giving out and what's still working. We call those our organ recitals." She smiled.

Arty laughed. "You look like you're in pretty good shape, Sister."

"I suppose I'm blessed," she said.

"Me too," Arty replied. "I'm a fast healer. And I'm nobody's fool either." Arty explained that with some of the money he had earned from his research activities he had purchased an accident and dismemberment policy which covered the loss of limbs and sight. The payoff was fantastic by Arty's standards: $1,000 for loss of a single arm or leg; $2,200 if he lost any two at the same time. And if he were lucky enough to have an eye gouged from its socket, they paid the princely sum of $3,500. "Of course I'm not planning on losing anything, but you never know," he said. "This ain't a perfect world, after all." Being an orphan, Arty knew whereof he spoke.

The bus pulled to the curb and Sister Meg said good-bye as she transferred to the bus heading for the convent. Arty continued north to Palo Alto, planning the rest of his day. After his interview with the nerve graft researchers, Arty would go to the Cryogenic Life Clinic and Sperm Bank in San Mateo for his favorite, and most satisfying, part of the day. He began singing, "Hi ho, hi ho, it's off to work I go . . ."

The emergency room doctors ordered X rays and CAT scans. As a matter of routine, they sutured Kemmler's lacerations and set his broken bones, but their hearts weren't really in it as they suspected he wasn't long for this world. The results of the scans confirmed their suspicions and the admitting doctor won the twenty-dollar ER pool for closest diagnosis without technical assistance: Mr. Kemmler was the proud owner of a severely damaged cerebral cortex and as such he was going to be doing a good Sunny von Bulow imitation for a while— his only possible use in the upcoming hospital talent and sketch show would be in a nonspeaking role.

Kemmler was in a deep coma—a persistent vegetative state, as they like to say—probably irreversible, though it's surprising what people in comas have done. For example, in March of 1991, a man from High Point, North Carolina, emerged from an eight-year coma and fingered the two people who had beaten him senseless with a log eight years earlier. Go figure.

"Is he dead?" a pretty nurse named Helen asked the intern, who was looking at Mr. Kemmler's nearly fixed and dilated pupils.

"Depends on how you define *dead*," the intern said. "There's whole-brain dead, where both the cerebral cortex and the brain stem irreversibly cease to function. And then there's higher-brain death, where only the cerebral cortex is terminally damaged and the brain stem is largely intact." The intern was trotting out all he knew about the subject. He wanted a date with Nurse Helen and hoped this display of knowledge would impress her enough that she'd agree to go out with him, or would at least agree to a quickie in one of the unoccupied trauma slots. "The whole-brain standard was endorsed in '83 by the President's Commission for the Study of Ethical Problems in Medicine and has since become law in more than thirty states. Only a few states have adopted the broader higher-brain criterion. You know, they say the left side of the brain dominates the right. I could tell you more about it over dinner. What do you say?"

"I'd say my boyfriend's about twice your size," Helen said. "And president of his NRA chapter."

Not wanting to spend any unnecessary time in the ER, especially not as a customer, the intern abandoned his quest for the shapely nurse and sent Kemmler off to ICU, where he lay hooked up to an impressive system of tubes, wires, and monitors, which were in turn connected to a central nurses' station on the floor.

Meanwhile, in a demonstration of efficiency rarely seen in the administrative department of any hospital, a Mr. Lance Abbott was already on the phone with the warden at San Quentin trying to find out about next of kin and organ donor status vis-à-vis Mr. Kemmler. Mr. Abbott wasn't actually an employee of the hospital. He was a consultant known as a transplant coordinator whose small office just happened to be on the same floor as the intensive care unit. Lance Abbott worked for a company called SCOPE, Santa Clara Organ Procurement Enterprises, and he shared his office with the ICU because that's where most of SCOPE's products originated, warm and fresh from the oven, so to speak.

It was Mr. Abbott's ghoulish job to approach the grieving relatives of the recently dead and the currently dying to ask permission to harvest their loved ones like a patch of ripe tomatoes. Of course he never used words like *harvest* for obvious reasons—as a "family approach specialist" Lance Abbott was trained to be somewhat more sensitive than that. Part of his training involved recognizing when to approach the family for the goods. As they like to say in the organ procurement business, "Timing is everything." That's why Lance Abbott let the relatives go through what was referred to as a "decoupling" period, the time necessary for the family to come to terms with the inevitability of the situation. Only after the finality of it all had been absorbed was the time right to move in and ask about the availability of, say, the liver.

Lance was six feet tall with an olive complexion coming from an Italian branch somewhere in his family tree. He had a permanent five o'clock shadow and he dreamed that he looked like Al Pacino. Lance Abbott was proof that dreams don't always come true. Though not classically trained for the job (most transplant coordinators were RNs), Lance was nonetheless well prepared for the task. In fact, he had one of the highest commission rates of all the transplant coordinators on the West Coast.

Lance had come west after graduating from Illinois State University with a degree in theater. He had studied under both Jean Bruce Scott and Randy Reinholz at ISU's vaunted theater department. Lance moved to Los Angeles but after two years had only one paying gig, in an episode of *Renegade*, portraying a bystander who got to yell, "Hey!" before being shot by the bad guy (and presumably being shipped off to *ER* or *Chicago Hope*, where his organs were harvested). Souring on the film and TV business, Lance drifted north to the Bay Area in search of work and found it with SCOPE. He continued doing some dinner theater on weekends, keeping his chops up, but Monday through Friday he was perched, vulture-like, in his office at the hospital. From ISU to ICU, go team go!

Whenever it became apparent that a patient was about to go the way of all flesh, Lance assumed his character: bereaved, slightly confused by the mysteries of life and death, yet holding out a candle of hope to the surviving relatives. He would gently usher them into a quiet room decorated in warm, giving colors. He went to great lengths to put the people at ease, speaking very softly, never sitting directly across from them, never touching, and with his eyes trained on his shoes. His movements slowed, his arms remained down, his palms open, head tilted slightly to the side. Sometimes he actually had a hat, which he kept in hand, tugging at its brim as he made what appeared to be the most difficult request of his life.

His performances were legendary. Although SCOPE provided scripts for its family approach specialists, Lance preferred writing his own, and he frequently improvised, as actors are wont to do, depending on the audience. For example, fifteen minutes after meeting the born-again parents of an adolescent who had just been killed in a drive-by shooting, Lance had them on their knees singing like the Dixie Hummingbirds, praising the Lord, and begging for the harvest to begin—they actually used the *H* word, thinking it sounded biblical. Another time Lance got a hard-line Christian Scientist to agree to give up the usable solid organs of his rapidly departing wife. But in his most famous performance, he not only obtained written permission for all the organs of a man killed in an automobile accident, but the man's wife actually offered one of her own kidneys right there on the spot.

Needless to say, Mr. Abbott saw a handsome bonus check that week.

And why not? Organ procurement was not a matter of charity, it was big business. Every time a donor set sail across the River Styx without a full set of goods, he or she set in motion anywhere from $500,000 to $1 million in medical procedures. Big business indeed. In a world where the science to transplant human organs had been perfected, the only practical problem in this potential multibillion-dollar industry was rejection and the severe shortage of organs.

The warden at San Quentin told Lance he'd have to call him back. It was past five, so Lance decided to call it quits for the day. He locked his office and headed down the hall, passing Mr. Kemmler's room, where the heart monitor and respirator hummed the rhythm of the saints and the life-support system played the intensive care lullaby for Mr. Kemmler's persistent vegetative state. Inside, the shapely Nurse Helen was at Mr. Kemmler's bedside, marveling that the hospital was taking such extraordinary steps to keep the man alive so that the state could execute him as soon as he was released. Just for fun she pinched his nose closed. A moment later, the door eased open. A doctor, wearing green scrubs and a surgical mask, entered the room.

Startled, Nurse Helen quickly let go of Kemmler's nose and pretended to check his breathing. "Hi, Doc, nothing new here," Nurse Helen said. "No need for the mask either, this guy's not contagious."

Ignoring the nurse, as MDs often did, the doctor studied Kemmler's chart before crossing to the life-support system. There she examined the line connections and the respirator settings. "Do me a favor," the doctor said. "Go tell whoever's at the central station not to worry if it looks like Mr. Kemmler here flat lines in the next few minutes. I've got to make some adjustments on this."

"Right away, Doctor," Nurse Helen said as she left the room.

A moment later, as casually as unplugging a vacuum cleaner, the doctor pulled the plug on the respirator that was giving Kemmler the appearance of life. Surprisingly, Mr. Kemmler unplugged continued breathing. Oops, this was not what the doctor ordered. A sudden panic threatened to overwhelm the MD's murderous calm. Visions of Karen Anne Quinlan danced limply in the physician's head. Should she smother him? Oh Lord, what would Dr. Kervorkian do?

Suddenly there was a hiccup in the breathing pattern and a moment later the struggle for oxygen began—a few minutes without the precious gaseous element and

what little activity there was in Mr. Kemmler's underde-
veloped brain would cease irrevocably, his life slip-sliding
away. The doctor calmed and watched curiously as the
patient's stressed respiratory system fought for air. Then,
when the breathing stopped altogether and the *beep-
beep-beep* of the heart monitor yielded to the steady tone
of death, the doctor pulled a gleaming ice pick from
under her gown. She placed the tip of the ice pick against
a carefully chosen area of Mr. Kemmler's chest and
pressed down hard, puncturing the superior vena cava.
Next she poked a hole in the descending aorta and then
the pulmonary artery and the left ventricle. Then she
got busy.

Georgette was in a mood. She seemed distracted. Paul knew something was on her mind, but he couldn't get her to admit it, much less say what it was. He knew badgering would only make matters worse, so for now Paul was just going to keep his mouth shut. Georgette would talk when she was ready. She always did. And as long as he had time to think about other stuff, Paul could always mentally draft his next letter to Jerry Landis.

They walked in silence down a long, dingy hallway under the watch of the still, oil-painted eyes of Pythagoras, Sir Thomas More, Tolstoy, and George Bernard Shaw. Finally, Georgette spoke. "I'm as antihandgun as anybody," she fumed, "but if I'd had one, I swear . . ."

"I don't doubt you for a second, sweetheart," Paul said. "And if it makes you feel any better, I wouldn't testify against you."

On the drive over to the meeting hall, Georgette and Paul were trapped behind two cars driving parallel with one another, ten miles under the speed limit, for seven frustrating miles. Georgette tried tailgating, honking, flashing lights, and all the traditional hand gestures but neither driver would yield. In fact, neither of them was paying any attention to her or any other car on the road.

And it wasn't the estimated four minutes she lost that bothered Georgette, it was the principle. "It's either arrogance or ignorance and neither one is a good excuse," she said. "It's like no one else matters to these idiots. The rest of us will just have to do as they please."

Since the driving infraction had occurred only recently, Paul knew it wasn't the issue that had been gnawing at Georgette all day. It was something else, something personal. At the end of the hall Georgette stopped and glanced up at the paintings. "I see they conveniently left a couple of adherents off the wall."

Paul was examining Mahatma Gandhi. "Really? Who?" he asked.

"Adolf Hitler, for one," Georgette said. "And I think Mussolini, though I don't think he was a full-timer."

At a friend's urging, Georgette and Paul were on their way to a meeting of the Vegetarians Association of Central California. Though Paul and Georgette occasionally enjoyed a nice pork loin chop with a savory mustard cream sauce, they knew fruits and vegetables were healthier than tons of meat. Another reason Paul wanted to attend the meeting was that sign:

ACRES OF RAIN FOREST REMAINING: 1,145,829,000

Paul knew one of the reasons the rain forests were disappearing was so cattle barons could make more pasture for grazing cattle to satisfy the ever-increasing demand for meat. Paul knew it took X acres of land to feed a cow which, when butchered, would feed only Y number of people, and that the same acreage planted with grain could feed Y^2 people, or something like that. Paul also knew that Jerry Landis had significant financial interests in foreign cattle ranches that were involved in this sort of "development" of the rain forests, so he hoped to get some new ammo with which to shoot at his longtime foe. But mainly they were hoping to pick up a few good recipes and maybe some coupons.

The Vegetarians Association of Central California was

no middle-of-the-road outfit. They had pulled their little vegetable cart far to the right (or left, depending on your point of view), and they would not suffer the fish or chicken eaters who called themselves vegetarians.

"Hitler was a vegetarian?" Paul said.

"Yeah," Georgette said, "but I read that he fell off the wagon and ate pig knuckles occasionally. Other than that he was inordinately fond of asparagus tips, cauliflower, and killing Jews." She smiled, opened the door, and made a sweeping, doormanlike gesture. "Shall we?"

They entered the auditorium, where the meeting had already started. A frail blonde was leaning against the podium leading the crowd in some sort of prayer. The herd of plant eaters spoke weakly, but in unison, "No longer now, he slays the lamb, who looks him in the face, and horribly devours its mangled flesh." This pledge of vegetarian allegiance came from Shelley's epic poem "Queen Mab," not, as many of those in the crowd believed, from his *Vindication of Natural Diet*, an obscure pamphlet he published in 1813.

Paul and Georgette took seats in the back of the room and listened—Paul intently, Georgette amused. Georgette didn't care much for the vegetarians she had met; they tended to give the otherwise commendable lifestyle a bad name with their holier-than-thou snootiness. Vegetarianism seemed to be a magnet for the intellectually flighty, their logic undermined perhaps by too much fiber. On the one hand they argued against killing other living things for food, yet it was somehow all right to kill plants. And, as measured by the number of dead insects in the grills of their cars, in the course of an average day, vegetarians killed as many insects as did their carniverous counterparts: Was it all right to kill insects because they weren't as cute as lambs? Or because you couldn't make eye contact with them the way you could with a cow?

And Georgette loved the famous animal rights philosopher who proclaimed that the line between the animals which had inalienable rights and those which didn't was to be drawn between the crustaceans and the mollusks.

Such arbitrary, hypocritical notions grated on Georgette's nerves. But at the moment, Georgette was less focused on the vegetable issue than on what she had to tell Paul. And she *did* have to tell him. But when and how? Maybe on the way home, stuck in traffic behind some more idiots.

"I'm glad to see so many of my fellow antipreophogists here tonight," the woman said. "Now before we get on with new business, let me just say something that bears repeating, and that is that the eaters of dead flesh depend on others to do their slaughterhouse dirty work and on euphemisms so they won't be reminded what they're really eating is not just flesh but all the violent energy also necessary to kill animals in the first place!"

As the crowd applauded listlessly, Georgette leaned over to Paul. "Was that a complete sentence there, or did I miss something?"

Before Paul could answer, the woman continued. "The Buddha practiced vegetarianism and preached the doctrine of Ahimsa, a philosophy of harmlessness to all living things." Except fruits and vegetables, Georgette thought to herself. Maybe *now* was as good a time as any to talk to Paul. Certainly the speaker wasn't saying anything new or intriguing. But Georgette couldn't just blurt it out; she needed an introductory remark of some sort.

The speaker was blathering something about the osmosislike transference of evil and violence via the rump roast when a dull-eyed young man in the front row stood up and pointed an accusing finger at the woman onstage. "I saw you at Denny's yesterday eating an omelette!"

The audience let go with a feeble murmur. Georgette nudged Paul, "This should be good."

"Well, yes, that's true," the woman said from behind the podium. "They have an economical breakfast special. But I substituted pancakes for the sausage. What's your point?"

"The point is you can't be a vegan *and* eat eggs!" the man said.

"I never claimed to be a *pure* vegan," she said with a hint of shame. "I'm ovum-tolerant."

"Ovum tolerant?" The man pulled an egg from his coat

pocket and held it aloft. "This is where life begins and you dare eat it? You're a murderer! You're no better than a butcher!" He threw the egg as hard as he could at the woman but it fell short and hit the front of the podium.

Another woman in the audience stood up. "He's right! You're eating the unborn!"

Georgette couldn't stop herself. "Chickens aren't born, Einstein, they're hatched," she yelled.

"Fine!" the woman said with equal fervor, "she's eating the unhatched!"

"Hey," someone too weak to stand said. "I saw you drinking from a carton of milk outside. That sort of thing doesn't fly in here."

The diplomat next to the milk drinker shot back, "For your information, she's a lactose-lenient vegetarian. It's a perfectly legitimate and acknowledged form of—"

"What a crock!" This came from a rope-thin young man who was trying to stand up to make his point more forcefully, but he didn't seem to have the strength. "Am I the only true vegan in this room? Somebody help me stand up, so I can . . . oh, never mind, I'm too tired." He took his seat to catch his breath.

What happened next was historical in the annals of vegetarianism. After a few more sharp words, Paul and Georgette witnessed the official split between the lacto-ovo-tolerant and the pure vegan factions of the Vegetarians Association of Central California. The lacto-ovians took the left side of the room and the pure vegans the right. Georgette and Paul remained nonaligned in the back of the room (though Georgette did put five bucks on the lacto-ovians to win). Accusations and insults traversed the center aisle like Civil War cannon volleys. The stronger members of each faction moved toward one another and, inevitably, a fistfight broke out. But without any real protein behind the punches, little was accomplished and soon the combatants lost their strength.

However, when one of the vegans was poked in the eye with a stalk of celery, the anti-pro-ovum-protester began heaving eggs across the auditorium and a second charge began. Paul tried to play peacemaker, but no one would listen—even Georgette told him to shut up and sit down as he was interfering with their bet. Emotions ran strong; these issues had been buried under a layer of couscousian congeniality for too long. Tolerance gave way to violence despite the fact that most of these people hadn't eaten so much as a short rib in over a decade.

Georgette found it all amusing and nonthreatening because, with the exception of Paul, she was the biggest, strongest, and healthiest person in the room. And if one of these herbivores threatened her with so much as a snap bean, she'd gladly demonstrate how she'd managed to get more rebounds than any other woman in the history of Stanford basketball. And if that didn't impress anyone, she'd show how she'd fouled out of more games than any man or woman in the history of the Pac-10 Conference.

As she watched the warring factions, Georgette thought again about how to tell Paul what was on her mind. She wanted to ease into it, not just blurt it out. Suddenly a voice of reason came over the loudspeaker system. A man with sunken eyes was at the microphone. "What about the plant kingdom, man?" he said. "Have you never heard the scream of a squash ripped from its vine?" It was the emaciated leader of a pro-plant group who had infiltrated the meeting. "Plants feel pain, man!" The Vegan Guard slouched onto the stage to subdue the intruder. As they struggled to drag him away, the man yelled, "Flowers weren't born in vases, man!"

Screw it, Georgette thought, I may as well just say it and get it over with. "There's something I have to tell you," she said to Paul.

"Let me guess, you want to up the bet to ten bucks?"

"Well, sure," she said. "But there's something else." She paused before saying it. "I'm pregnant."

All the madness and the noise and the fighting suddenly faded to nothing in Paul's mind. He was going to be a father. He had created a life. It was wonderful. It was amazing. Hell, it was God-like. He had always wanted children—well, a son anyway—and now it was happening inside the woman sitting next to him. Paul stood up and pulled Georgette to her feet and he hugged her. "I love you so much!" he said.

"I love you too," she wheezed. "But sometimes you squeeze me too hard."

"Sorry." Paul relaxed. "I'm just so excited!"

"Yeah, me too," Georgette said without the proper enthusiasm.

"So why's my ambivalence detector suddenly pegging?" Paul asked.

Georgette sighed. "There are things I want to do that I can't do if I'm pregnant. I won't be able to play ball for months. And anyway, what kind of world is this to bring a child into?"

Paul smiled and hugged her again. He whispered in her ear, "We'll just have to make it better before he gets here."

"I notice you said 'he.' "

"Hey, I needed a pronoun," the proud father said.

Georgette scanned the room. "Looks like the lacto-ovians are winning."

"All right, I owe you five bucks."

"Ten; we raised the bet."

"Ten it is . . . Mom," Paul said.

Georgette smiled. "You can buy me lunch, Pops," she said. "I'm hungry."

"Great," Paul said. "What do you feel like?"

"I'm thinking double bacon cheeseburger."

Lance Abbott rushed down the hall toward Mr. Kemmler's room as soon as he heard. Outside the door he stopped and gathered himself and said a silent little prayer, much as he used to do before going on stage at Illinois State. Then, using another of his thespian techniques, he yanked out a few nose hairs so he'd be teary-eyed for his audience. Even though he was expecting to find only hospital personnel inside, Lance entered the room quietly, almost religiously, not wanting the employees to think of him as too much of a buzzard.

As expected, there was an orderly in the room. But

Lance was surprised to see an older man in a dark suit looming at Mr. Kemmler's bedside looking more confused than bereaved. The man was old enough to be Kemmler's father, or uncle perhaps. The man looked over at Lance without speaking. Inadvertently making eye contact, Lance quickly lowered his gaze, folded his hands, and eased into the creases and the shadows near the wall in an attempt to be as nonthreatening as humanly possible. This can't be, Lance thought as a rattling, deep emotion tingled his brain. San Quentin said no next of kin. Shit, okay, no problem, just do your thing. Estimated decoupling time . . . Lance looked at his watch and waited. What seemed like an eternity passed as Lance struggled not to look at what the man in the dark suit was doing at the bedside. Maybe it was some sort of last rites ceremony. Lance decided it was better if he just kept looking at his shoes for a while. But he couldn't wait forever; there were organs in need of harvest.

When the man finished whatever it was he was doing, Lance gently seized the moment. He broke the ice, speaking softly to the floor. "At times like this, and I know how difficult this is, but at times like this, the hospital likes to offer the family the opportunity to bring life to others."

The man in the suit chuckled and looked under the bedsheet.

Lance had seen a lot of different reactions from grieving relatives asked to hand over the kidneys, but chuckling was a new one. The situation had to be reassessed. He looked at the chart—it was William Kemmler all right. But something else was wrong. Where was the familiar beeping noise that usually served as the sound track for these tense little scenes? Lance saw the heart monitor was turned off, as was the respirator. "What happened?" Lance asked.

"That's what I'd like to know," the man said. "I'm a detective with Santa Clara PD."

Who would believe it? Lance thought. The dead felon's next of kin was a cop. "Are you his, uh . . ." Lance left the blank open for the cop to fill in with "father" or "uncle" or whatever, but the detective was too busy poking around at the late Mr. Kemmler to play fill-in-the-blank with Lance, so the silence hung in the air for a while. Finally Lance tried again. "I don't understand, are you related to Mr. Kemmler?"

"We're all in the family of man," the detective said flatly. This time the orderly chuckled.

Lance wasn't sure how to interpret that one, so he simply introduced himself. "Well, uh, I'm Lance Abbott with SCOPE, and time is of the essence."

"Not for this guy," the orderly said. The detective smirked as his head bobbed up and down.

Lance couldn't take it any longer. He didn't know what the hell was going on, but there was a full set of perfectly good organs lying in the bed in front of him and that meant a bonus check if he could just get the ribs spread. "Detective," Lance said, "exactly what relation are you to Mr. Kemmler, if I might ask."

"No relation," he said. "Why? You think there's some resemblance?"

The orderly suppressed a laugh.

"Well, if you're not related," Lance said, "what the hell are you doing here?"

"I'm in Homicide."

That seemed to limit the options, Lance thought. But ever the optimist, he gave it one last shot. "And you think Mr. Kemmler killed someone?"

The detective turned to the orderly while throwing a thumb in Lance's direction. "I take it this is the organ grinder you were talking about?" The orderly nodded. "Look, I hate to be the one to tell you, Dr. Frankenstein, but I'm not here investigating any of the heretofore unsolved murders Mr. Kemmler may have committed, I'm here to investigate the murder *of* Mr. Kemmler."

"But he was in a car wreck," Lance said.

"That was yesterday," the cop said. "Today he was murdered."

Like thin wisps of smoke, Lance saw his bonus check floating away on the wind. "When?" Lance asked desperately. "I mean, how long ago? How long's he been dead?

We can still use some of the organs if he hasn't been dead too long." Lance was now at the side of the bed opposite the detective, feeling Mr. Kemmler's cold, stiff arm. He began rubbing it as if to revive him. The orderly and the detective exchanged queer glances that didn't speak well of the transplant coordinator.

"Sorry, pal," the detective said. "But unless you need a colander, Mr. Kemmler here's not going to do you much good." Lance's blank stare asked his next question as well as any words could have. "Somebody came in here with an ice pick a couple of hours ago and poked holes in every organ in his body, including the eyes," the detective said.

"Goddammit!" Lance blurted. "Shit. I thought I had a full set. A full set!" Lance slumped into a chair and continued cursing. He had a hard time decoupling from his bonus.

"Hey, Detective," the orderly said. He seemed to be pointing at Mr. Kemmler's ear. "There's something under his head, a piece of paper or something."

The detective grabbed Mr. Kemmler by the hair and struggled against the stiffening neck to lift the head from the pillow. Using a pair of hemostats he found on the bedside table, the detective gently slipped the piece of paper out and studied it for a moment as the orderly read over his shoulder. "What's it mean?" the orderly asked.

"It means I'll have to keep driving the same piece-of-shit car I've had for the past seven years," Lance said as he walked over to see what they were looking at. "That's what it means."

The detective had a different interpretation. "Well, first off, given Mr. Kemmler's history, I suspect this note's from a radical pro-death-penalty group. They take their executions very seriously and they don't like it when the state screws up and paroles these people."

The orderly was nonplussed. "They paroled a guy who chopped a kid's head off?"

"No, but they let him escape," the cop said. "Not much difference to these anti-murderer nuts." Before he slipped the note into a plastic evidence bag the detective looked at it once again. "Gonna have to get this translated." He held the note up to the light. "You know, a company here in Silicon Valley created the world's most sophisticated police database network. It lets all the police departments in the Bay Area talk to one another. If I need a sheet that's in San Jose, *boom*, got it. Need a fingerprint from Oakland, *boom*, got it. Need something translated, I send it to the language experts in San Francisco, and *boom*, I got it." The detective paused a moment as Lance looked over his shoulder at the note. "Well, anyway, that's how they say it works. Supposed to be pretty amazing." The detective sealed the note in the evidence bag.

The note said simply, "!Terra tuebor!"

Dr. Gibbs was queasy despite his good fortune. Instead of just one kidney, he had two plus a heart. He could have had a full set of organs, but his little Igloo would hold only the three. They were packed for the trip back to Hong Kong, cooling in the slushy sterile saline ice solution. The kidneys had a shelf life of seventy-two hours, the heart only six, so if Dr. Gibbs was going to make a sale there, he had to hurry. He had already called his Hong Kong contacts to let them know a good pump was available on a first come, first served basis. Some bacon-eating big shot who had been at death's door would probably be prepped for the transplant by the time Dr. Gibbs arrived. And that's the best time to negotiate the price.

Dr. Gibbs's queasiness came after Indira croaked while under his knife. This had happened before to Dr. Gibbs but it still bothered him. It wasn't that he had become attached to the woman but there was still enough humanity left in the man that he felt a little compunction when he killed someone. Fortunately, Indira had signed all the requisite documents and Dr. Gibbs's local assistant was dealing with the authorities on his behalf just as he had in the past.

Dr. Gibbs was in a taxi heading downtown on the way to a warehouse in one of the many industrial areas along the filthy Hooghly River. The smell in the taxi wasn't nearly as bad as the scent outside thanks to the turmeric, cardamom, fenugreek, and the fifteen other spices that made up the large sack of curry the doctor had picked up at the market in the city. The taxi pulled up to the loading docks of Warehouse 47, where Mr. Albert Cavanagh was eagerly awaiting Dr. Gibbs's arrival. Mr. Cavanagh's family had been in Calcutta since Albert's great-great-grandfather retook the city after the nawab of Bengal seized it in 1756 and sent thousands to their deaths in the cramped and stifling little room known as the black hole. Since then, the Cavanaghs had thrived as major players in a black market that handled everything from opium to human eyeballs. "Ahh, my friend, the good doctor," Mr. Cavanagh said. He was English by ancestry, but after a lifetime in Calcutta his accent was thicker than the Bhagwan Sri Rajneesh. "Come, come. I have a most wonderful package of goods for you, and I know you are in such a hurry."

Dr. Gibbs carried the Igloo with him.

"I am telling you," Mr. Cavanagh said, "I have had a great many other offers for these ocular delights, but my word to you is good, so I have saved them for you. Come, let us go inside and effect our transaction so that others might see."

"Cut the crap, Albert," Gibbs said. "The only thing you're interested in seeing is a profit."

Mr. Cavanagh smiled. "Yes, you are quite right, my friend, quite right. Come, come."

As they entered the vast warehouse, Dr. Gibbs did something he had never done before. He began reflecting on his thirty-five years in sales. Thirty-five years of listening to suppliers tell wholesale lies about how they had done him this favor or that favor in transparent attempts to get a higher price for whatever crap they were selling. And thirty-five years of turning around and telling the same lies at retail prices. Ever since he earned his third-rate medical degree and let his parents down, Dr. Gibbs had been on the road selling. He'd sold everything from iron lungs to vivisection contraptions and for years had survived on a smile and a good shoe shine, always a half step ahead of the bank while complaining about how refrigerators and washing machines were designed to fall apart the moment you got them paid off. The good doctor was simply trying to stay current on his insurance payments and maybe get a little bit ahead, get a little security in case the bottom dropped out on him. But lately the grind had started to wear on him. It wasn't that ethical problems related to buying healthy organs from desperate people bothered him. It was the traveling: rushing needlessly through crowded airports to catch flights that would spend an hour on the tarmac before taking off, all the bad airline food, sleepless nights in cheap hotels, bribing officials, yanking organs from hapless peasants to sell to some arrogant, wealthy asshole who didn't appreciate the shit he had gone through to get the pancreas, or whatever.

For years Dr. Gibbs had measured himself against the standard of being well liked by his customers and suppliers. But now he thought maybe it was time for a new standard. He needed to examine the quality-of-life issue—the quality of his own life. He wanted to take a vacation, go somewhere with nice restaurants and great hotels. Maybe he'd go to New York and see some shows, maybe catch some of the plays of Arthur Miller if they were still being performed.

"My friend," Mr. Cavanagh said, "please be cautious with your step. There was a most unfortunate accident here last week with my nephew. He was not properly checked out on the new forklift, so the floor here is in need of a cleaning." Cavanagh had refined the art of understatement. The floor was wet and slick with God-knows-what. Here and there were inch-deep puddles of something with the viscosity of egg whites or jellyfish. "Here we go, my friend." Mr. Cavanagh stopped at a large Styrofoam container sitting atop a wooden pallet. "You know, the human eye is very much like a camera with its iris and variable focusing abilities."

Except a crate of Instamatics doesn't start to stink after

three and a half weeks in a filthy warehouse, Dr. Gibbs thought. He didn't want to say it aloud because he wasn't sure if the stench was wafting in from the river, coming from a shipment of rotting fish, or was, in fact, seeping from the container of eyeballs. "C'mon, Albert, nothing personal, but let's have a look at these starry orbs you're peddling," he said. "I got a flight to catch."

Mr. Cavanagh shrugged and opened the container. The two merchants nearly threw up when they got a whiff of what was inside: four dozen blind, putrefying eyes staring up at them through the fetid air. The sclera had broken down in decay and vitreous humor oozed into the bottom of the container; a furry blue-black mold thrived on the perimeter of several of the eyes, lending the appearance of raised eyebrows and creating a scent that made spoiled Roquefort seem like honeysuckle.

Like the nawab of Bengal, whom his grandfather had defeated four generations ago, Mr. Cavanagh was not one to surrender, even in the face of obvious defeat. He thought for a moment before speaking. "You know, my friend, I am telling you, if we just rinse these off a little . . ."

Dr. Gibbs picked up his Igloo and headed for the door.

"Perhaps I could interest your clients in some sunglasses?" Mr. Cavanagh said.

Dr. Gibbs waved him off and began walking faster. He wanted out of the gamy warehouse before he lost his lunch. He wanted to get to Hong Kong, makes his sales, and get back to California, where he could do some more reflecting on his current and future situations, maybe take a look at the job market, see if he could get off the road.

"Come, come, my friend. I believe I have a shipment of Ray•Bans that might be of interest to you," Mr. Cavanagh offered.

Dr. Gibbs turned suddenly to say something, and as he turned he hit one of the puddles of slippery goo and flipped ass over teakettle. His little Igloo soared across the warehouse carrying several lives with it, Dr. Gibbs's included. When it crashed onto the concrete, the top popped open, spilling the heart and the two bean-shaped organs onto the filthy floor. Desperate and confused, his nerves jangled and his future unsure, Dr. Gibbs rushed over and fell to his knees. He began desperately scooping the organs back into the container with as much of the saline ice solution as he could collect. He picked large bits of grit and grime from the sinus of one kidney. On the other, what appeared to be a dead fly was trapped in a thin envelope of Gerota's fascia that remained on the kidney's exterior. As Dr. Gibbs worked urgently to extract the demised insect, he had what is commonly referred to as an out-of-body experience. He floated out of himself and from above he looked down on a most pathetic scene: A generally decent man on his hands and knees in a grungy warehouse in Calcutta trying to herd a few human organs into a small beer cooler—a smug black-marketeer standing nearby shaking his head in contempt.

How had it come to this? Had he done something terribly wrong in a previous life? Was this kismet's idea of a joke? He was just trying to make a living, for God's sake. He never put a gun to anyone's head demanding their organs; they did it of their own free will. Doesn't that count for anything? Sure, he paid bottom dollar, but that's a basic tenet of business: buy low, sell dear. He was doing the same thing a zillion other people were doing every day.

Down below, on the warehouse floor, the real Dr. Gibbs struggled mightily to maintain his composure. He plucked the fly from the hilum, tossed the contaminated kidneys into the cooler, and snapped it shut. He stood and brushed the dreck from his pants and he made a vow: When he got back to California he'd take some time off to do a little research, see if he couldn't find a better way to make a living with the skills he had polished over the years. He prayed that his future lay somewhere other than on the floor of this filthy warehouse.

o   o   o

"Promise me you won't hurt anybody," Paul said.

Georgette leaned out the driver-side window. "I never hurt anyone who doesn't deserve it," she said, causing Paul's eyebrows to arch. "Okay," she conceded, "rarely."

"I've seen you play, sweetheart," Paul said.

"Well, then you know. If I get the rebound and some-body gets hit by an elbow, it's because they're just too damn close." Georgette closed her eyes and tapped her lips with an index finger. "Now, kiss me, I gotta go." Paul bent down and kissed her good-bye, and off she drove to her weekly game of hoops. She was almost out of the parking lot when something occurred to her. "Oh, shit!" Georgette slammed on the brakes and screeched the little car into reverse. She raced backwards through the grocery store parking lot to where Paul was standing. Seeing this, Paul looked down at his pile of stuff and saw Georgette's gym bag. He picked it up and walked it over to the car. "Jesus!" she screeched. "I can't believe I drove off without my bag. What were you doing with it?" She sounded agitated as she got out of the car.

Paul was surprised at her tone. He shrugged. "I wasn't doing anything with it. I just grabbed it by accident when I was unloading my stuff."

Georgette took the bag and tossed it into the back seat. Then she stopped and put a hand over her eyes for a moment before speaking. "I'm sorry, honey. I didn't mean to snap at you." She kissed Paul's cheek. "Do I seem more irritable to you lately? I kind of feel like I have been."

"You seem fine to me," Paul said. Then he smiled and opened the car door for Georgette. "But I feel sorry for whoever has to guard you tonight."

Georgette stuck her tongue out at Paul before putting the car in gear. She glanced in the mirror and saw Paul setting up his card table just as he'd done a thousand times before. As she turned out of the parking lot and lost sight of her hopeful crusader, she wondered if he would ever really get Jerry Landis while playing by the rules. She wondered if anyone could.

Paul set up his table by one of the two doors leading into the Safeway supermarket. The boxes and bags piled around the table contained clipboards, flyers, pamphlets, pens, books, liquid-filled test tubes, blown-up photographs, and paperweights to keep everything from blowing away in the breeze. Paul was here to gather signatures for a petition he intended to send to the Environmental Protection Agency. He was greatly concerned about a certain limited-liability company that planned to leave ten million tons of uranium mill waste sitting on the banks of the Colorado River near Moab, Utah. It was a 130-acre slag heap of uranium tailings and heavy metals that was leaking contaminants into the water supply for tens of millions of people in Utah, Nevada, southern California, and Arizona. The company was called Landaq Minerals, LLC. Mr. Jerry Landis was the chairman of the board.

Ten years ago when medical authorities first noticed clusters of malformed babies living downstream of Moab, a flack for Landaq Minerals actually had the nerve to issue a press release noting that the parents of all these children were the right age to have been hippies. He further suggested that the deformities were probably due to the LSD and the other recreational chemicals undoubtedly taken by the parents of these children. An opinion poll taken shortly after national news organizations picked up the press release showed that 83 percent of the general public felt that parents whose children were deformed due to recreational drug use got what they deserved.

For the past eight months, the chairman of the U.S. Nuclear Regulatory Commission had been talking with a straight face about simply putting a clay-and-rock cap over the radioactive slag heap despite the fact that it was situated on a floodplain over a fault zone. Jerry Landis was all for moving the radioactive mound, provided the government paid the bill. Various environmental groups as well as the National Park Service and the Department of the Interior had been fighting Landaq Minerals in the courts for years, but as one of Landaq's representatives pointed out with a smile, "in a democracy like ours, these things take time."

Paul had written to his senators and his congressmen about the matter. In reply he had received form letters thanking "Dear constituent" for "sharing your thoughts and concerns." Vague promises were made about having staff members "look into this very important matter." At the end of the letters was a form which allowed the constituent to contribute money to the next election campaign.

The democracy route having failed, Paul had conceived of his petition. It was aimed at forcing Landaq to move the slag heap and do an EPA-approved cleanup at its own expense. It also called for a substantial fine against Landaq Minerals for damage done to the environment. Paul wanted to include a provision that would have provided jail time for Jerry Landis but he knew the EPA wasn't in a position to mete out punishment, so he scrapped the idea.

Paul unfurled a large cardboard sign and taped it to the front of his card table. It said:

LANDAQ MINERAL$ HURT$ EVERYONE!

Paul slowly unpacked the bags and boxes, setting the table for that night's petition drive. He was tired, anyone could see that. He had put in another ten-hour workday as an underpaid fund-raiser for United Citizens, a nonprofit, nonpartisan lobbying organization designed to promote honest and accountable government, support Green Party candidates, and fight corporate welfare. Paul had made some unsuccessful door-to-door cold calls in the morning and had spent the afternoon being abused and rejected over the phone. Now he had to summon the energy necessary to convince individual citizens of the importance of signing his anti-Landaq petition.

This was Paul's life. He did this sort of thing every time he had the chance. If it wasn't a petition drive, he was leading protests outside Landaq's main offices. And if he wasn't leading a protest, he was organizing a letter-writing campaign. He was relentless. And when anyone pointed out the futility of his efforts, Paul nodded and said, "It certainly tests my patience." But he never stopped thinking about his dad. How he had collapsed and died without having a chance to say good-bye. The expression of stark terror when he knew his life was suddenly over. What had gone through his mind in that moment? The paramedics told Paul there was nothing he could have done to save him. The only thing he could do for his dad now was to not let bygones be bygones. Jerry Landis kept Paul going whenever his patience was tested.

Georgette frequently helped, but never on Wednesday nights. Her ball games were important to her and Paul insisted she go. After all, this was his fight. Georgette could pick her own at the gym.

Paul never sat; he didn't even bring a chair. He stood near the table so he could be more mobile, so he could approach anyone who showed the slightest bit of interest in his cause. Few did. The store did a brisk evening business, mostly because families in his neighborhood couldn't survive on a single income so shopping had to be done at night. The downside was that most people just didn't want to be bothered by that point in their day. They wanted to get home so they could spend a few minutes with their spouses and children before surrendering to exhaustion. Paul understood that. He knew that he had to convince these people that his cause was legitimate and important. The hard part was in conveying this in the ten or fifteen seconds between the time they came into the range of Paul's voice and when they disappeared into the store.

He had to grab them with one-liners but he also had

to avoid sounding like a crackpot. Say something like "Landaq is killing us with radiation!" and most people look at you as if you were one of those half-baked Area 51 fruitcakes. Open with a statement about the dangers of high concentrations of selenium and the half-life of radium and you might as well be speaking Martian. He once tried "Are you concerned about the quality of the water you drink?" but most people simply said "Yes, that's why I buy bottled."

After all this time, Paul knew all the dodges. He could tell from twenty yards out how any given shopper would deal with him. A third of the people who parked in the near half of the parking lot went out of their way to use the far door just to avoid him. Of those who walked past Paul, half of them lied about their resident status, saying they weren't registered to vote in California. Others simply stared straight ahead to avoid eye contact. Many feigned deafness. Every now and then someone would respond to Paul's pitch with a madman's stare—never saying a word but figuring that Paul wouldn't bother them if they looked crazy or potentially violent. Mostly, Paul was ignored, slapped in the face with apathy. Yet he persevered.

After a few minutes, a man came around the corner of the building. He was big as a bear and he had a yellowish gray beard that looked like a large shrub with a nose sticking out of it. He was broad-faced and florid and he wore a tattered and filthy topcoat. The resulting look was decidedly biblical. The man never said a word to Paul. He just rooted through the overflowing trash can on the other side of the door, looking for food like everyone else.

Paul's first potential signature arrived in a Lincoln Town Car moments later. The driver pulled into the handicap parking spot just across from where Paul was. This was encouraging because in Paul's experience the physically challenged tended to be more understanding about causes than others. But it was an able-bodied man wearing a suit who got out of the car and headed for the store. He casually flicked his half-burned cigarette onto the ground as if that were the right thing to do. Jesus, that chapped Paul's ass. There was a large, sand-filled ashtray conveniently situated at the entrance to the store but this prick couldn't be bothered to use it. He was just like all the assholes who tossed burning butts out of their car windows when they had perfectly good ashtrays in their cars. One of these days Paul was going to say something to one of these people but right now he had signatures to collect. He offered one of his flyers and asked the man if he was registered to vote in California.

The man never broke stride. He turned his head toward Paul and exhaled indignantly before disappearing into the store. "Thank you for your time," Paul said.

It looked like it was going to be one of those nights. Paul turned back to the parking lot to spot his next potential signature. What he saw was the biblical man stooping to pick up the creep's burning cigarette in a malignant variation on the recycling theme. The man noticed Paul looking at him.

"What?" he asked, his eyes darting about nervously.

Paul smiled. "You registered to vote in California?"

"Yeah," the big man said proudly. "As a matter of fact I am. 'Course I voted to get the homeless off the streets and you see how much good that did." The big man lumbered over, snatched a pen, and signed the petition. "So how come you're not out really doing something about this?" he asked Paul.

"What do you think this is?" Paul pointed at the petition.

"Uh huh." The big man picked up one of the flyers and perused it. "And they said *I* was delusional." He started to walk away, then he stopped and turned back to Paul. "You might want to rethink your strategy." He took a long drag on the cigarette before continuing around the corner of the building whence he had appeared.

For the next two and a half hours Paul stood outside the grocery store trying to talk to the people who came and went. He tried being funny: "Hey, how many radioactive elements does it take to screw in a lightbulb?" But no one laughed. He tried being serious: "Utah's Division of Radiation Control says the contaminant concentrations in the river are at deadly levels." But no one cried. People said "Sorry, I'm in a hurry." And "Good luck." And "Nuclear power is the future, dickhead." And on and on. By ten-thirty he had gathered a total of only six signatures. He knew the EPA wouldn't respond to a petition signed by fewer than a thousand concerned citizens. At this rate, the slag heap would be about as dangerous as mother's milk by the time he got enough signatures. Either that or another ice age would have come and made it a moot point.

Paul let out a long sigh and admitted to himself that tonight wasn't his night. Maybe it was time to pack his bags and cut his losses. Georgette would be coming to pick him up, and he wanted to be ready when she arrived. But when he saw a woman coming his way Paul decided to wait. The woman paused to look at one of the flyers on the table. Paul opened with "Landaq Minerals is poisoning the Colorado River with—"

"Yeah, yeah, yeah," the woman said as she glanced at the photos of the slag heap.

Okay, Paul thought, she didn't exactly sound like an ally but at least she was still reading the material. "I'm sending this petition to the EPA," Paul offered. "Care to sign it?"

"So, what, you're a nuclear engineer?" she asked.

"No," Paul said, "just a concerned citizen."

"Right," she said. "And why should I think you have the slightest clue what you're talking about, huh? You know all there is to know about this stuff?"

"No," Paul admitted, "not everything, but—"

"But bullshit," the woman said. "Then you don't know what you're talking about. You're just repeating what someone else said."

"Well, yeah," Paul admitted. "Utah's Division of Radiation Control."

"In other words," she said, "you're not fully informed about it, right? You have no way to evaluate what they've said. Let me ask, you think making decisions without being fully informed is a good idea?"

"No, that's why I've got all this other information," Paul said.

The woman gestured at the literature Paul had spread across the table. "This is your idea of fully informed? This is bullshit. You'd need a Ph.D. in chemistry before you came close to knowing the truth about whatever dangers your slag heap might pose, and you know what, I don't have the time to get a Ph.D., so I'm never going to know the full truth about it, just like I'm never going to know all about the ozone layer or acid rain or radon or any of that kind of shit, and you know why, because I've got a life to live, I've got to go shopping and I've got to cook meals and I've got a job that takes up fifty-five hours a week and I spend another fifteen hours a week stuck in my fucking car driving to and from that job and to and from day care and the grocery store and the post office, where I have to stand in line for half an hour getting nothing done, then my doctor tells me I need to exercise six hours a week and my dentist says I need to floss two times a day and my family therapist says I need to spend at least one hour of quality time every day with my kids and my marriage counselor says I should spend another hour with my husband and my analyst says I need to take an hour a day for myself." She stopped and took a big breath before continuing. "So tell me, Mr. Sign-my-petition-to-save-mother-earth, when do I have time to get fully informed about all this shit or should I just sign anything anyone shoves under my fucking nose?"

Paul stared at the woman for a moment, amazed and disappointed. It was the same thing night after night. It was exhausting. How was he supposed to get through to people? Why should he even bother? "Maybe you're right," Paul said. "Maybe we should just throw up our hands and surrender. Maybe Landaq and Exxon and

Union Carbide really are looking out for our best interests." Paul grabbed one of the large test tubes from the rack on the table. It was filled with a greenish yellow liquid. "Maybe selenium is actually good for you." He pulled the cork from the top and handed the test tube to the woman. "Go ahead, drink it," Paul said. "I'm just some half-informed crackpot, right? Knock yourself out. Probably make your hair shinier and more manageable." While the woman stared at the test tube, Paul began packing his stuff angrily. "What are you waiting for?" Paul barked. "Drink up!" The woman stared, slack-jawed, at the glowing green liquid. Suddenly Paul grabbed it from her. "What's the matter?" he said. "I'm just a lunatic, right? Here, how's this?" Paul abruptly gulped the contents of the test tube. "I've got plenty more where that came from," he said as he grabbed another test tube, popped the cork, and gulped the green goo.

"What are you doing?" the woman shrieked, and grabbed Paul's arms to stop him.

"I'm assuming you're right," he said.

"Well, stop it!" she shouted. "I don't know any more than you do. Just tell me where to sign. Jesus!"

Paul started to look surprisingly satisfied for a guy who had just gulped two test tubes of selenium. He handed her the clipboard and a pen. "I appreciate this," he said. Then he burped. "Excuse me." The woman signed the petition, then backed slowly into the store, never blinking. Her jaw twitched once though, like a lizard's. "Don't worry about me," Paul said, "I'll be fine." He broke out in a big smile and got back to work, no longer thinking about packing it in. Whenever Paul got a new signature, his vigor was renewed. All the rejection that came before was forgotten and he started fresh. *Now* he was getting somewhere.

Georgette arrived a few minutes later. She stopped in a far corner of the parking lot and watched Paul for a few minutes. He was so dedicated, so passionate about his beliefs. That was just one of the reasons she loved him so. Georgette could tell by his body language that things were going well, and she didn't want to interrupt that feeling; it came so infrequently for him. She was happy just to watch him doing what he wanted to do— what he had to do. He was going to be such a great father.

About twenty minutes later it looked like no one else was coming in for late-night shopping, so Paul began to pack his wares. Georgette pulled the car up to the curb as Paul folded up his LANDAQ MINERAL$ HURT$ EVERY-ONE sign.

"How'd it go tonight, hon?" she asked.

"Slow," Paul said, "but I got a few. How was basketball?"

"Not bad," she said. "My jump hook was on and . . ." Georgette noticed the empty test tubes. "Oh my," she said, picking one of them up.

"Yeah," Paul said sheepishly. "I had to."

Georgette shook her head, then picked up the entire rack of test tubes. "What is this stuff, Squirt?"

"Mountain Dew," Paul said.

5

Seventeen years ago, just after his thirtieth birthday, Jerry Landis and those around him began to notice something strange: Jerry Landis suddenly started to gray, and not just a little at his temples, but everywhere and completely. At first they thought it was the result of his eighteen-hour days and international travel schedule, but when his bones began to brittle and liver spots took dominion over his rapidly wrinkling skin, he decided to see a doctor.

His primary care physician, as the doctor was called, did several tests but the results didn't explain anything. The primary care physician's specialist friends ran dozens of other tests before discovering the problem. "Mr. Landis, I'm afraid you've got what's known as Werner's syndrome," the specialist said gravely. "Very, very rare. Only three people in a million have it, mostly Japanese, so the odds against your having it are tremendous."

Like someone struck by lightning, Jerry Landis took little comfort in knowing that he had beaten the odds. "Is there a cure?" he asked.

The specialist shook his head. "But we do know what happens." Werner's syndrome, the specialist explained, caused premature aging. Those affected by it appeared completely normal through their teenage years, but in their twenties they began aging rapidly. It wasn't as severe as Hutchinson-Gilford syndrome—the victims of which typically died before the age of thirty—but all the problems associated with the aged—osteoporosis, diabetes, arteriosclerosis, cataracts, cancer—nonetheless started showing up decades ahead of schedule and the patient invariably died before the age of fifty. "We suspect it has something to do with a defect in a protein called a helicase. Helicases sort of undo DNA so strands can be repaired or replicated, but if defective they might allow biochemical mutations during cell replication."

"Fifty?" Jerry Landis said. "I'm going to die before I'm fifty?"

"Well, there's no guarantee," the specialist said. "I mean, a few researchers are trying to isolate the gene, and you never know when they'll find a cure, but . . . uh, well, yeah, you probably won't have to worry about the solvency of the Social Security system." The specialist thought some levity might help lighten the situation.

"But I'm thirty," Jerry said. "Didn't you say it starts while you're in your twenties?"

"Yes, well, sometimes it starts late," the specialist improvised.

"So that means I've got 'til I'm sixty?"

"No, that's the bad news. But the good news is *Murder She Wrote* and *Matlock* reruns will soon be very entertaining for you." The specialist laughed. "Just kidding. The real good news is people with Werner's have a remarkably low incidence of high blood pressure and Alzheimer's disease," the specialist said. "And I'm telling you, there's nothing worse than neuritic plaques and neurofibrillary tangles. Still, if you haven't got your will together . . ."

Jerry Landis didn't hear the rest of what the specialist said. He was thirty years old and the veritable king of Wall Street. He had the Midas touch. With three phone calls he could make miracles happen, at least financial miracles. But now, according to the specialist, his time was coming to an end. Or not, if Jerry Landis had anything to do with it.

Jerry Landis loved his life and he damn sure wasn't going to have it taken from him, not without a fight anyway. No, he'd put his mind to it and hope for another revelation. A miracle, a medical miracle this time. The way he saw it, anyone who could beat the odds and get Werner's goddamn syndrome in the first place could probably get lucky and find a cure. His first step was to buck the conventional wisdom of portfolio diversification and concentrate his position in the arena where he'd had his original success: biotechnology. But this time, instead of ag-biotech, he would focus on med-biotech. He returned to the library, figuring if research could lead him to the promised land once, it could do it again. He spent the next few weeks poring over hundreds of issues of *Science*, *Nature*, and *Chemical & Engineering News*. Here and there were intriguing bits of information which by themselves didn't solve his problem, but together— together he sensed they might add up to something.

It was while reading an obscure article in an obscure medical journal that Landis had his new revelation. The headline was ORGAN SHORTAGE PROMPTS QUESTIONS. But for Jerry Landis, it prompted only answers, answers he knew were years away, but they were out there and now was the time to start looking. By the time he finished the article, all the intriguing information he had gathered over the past weeks suddenly fell into place and, puzzled together, they appeared to add up to big money and— more importantly to Jerry Landis—to life itself.

Soon he was in his opulent conference room, standing before a group of sophisticated investors, a loose affiliation of millionaires and billionaires. Here he more or less repeated the performance he had first given a few years earlier on the virtues of ag-biotech and the seed of the rape plant. "Gentlemen," he said to the gathered capitalists, "I have seen the future, and the space between its nostrils is narrow." The investors nodded knowingly as if Jerry Landis had just said "The annualized yield on two-year treasury notes will be roughly five point seven-six percent." But that's not at all what he had said, and furthermore he continued by saying of the future that its small eyes were deeply set under a prominent brow, its ass pink and puffy. At this, the room of monied men looked skeptically at one another, unsure what to think. They wanted to think big return on investment, but the image of the future with such an ass had thrown them.

"Baboons, gentlemen! Yellow, olive, chacma!" Jerry Landis said, referring to the different species. "Trust me when I tell you there are staggering sums of money to be made in baboon futures." These men wanted badly to trust Jerry Landis. Their portfolios were in need of something new and vigorous with long-term growth potential, but . . . baboons?

When he first hit Wall Street, Jerry Landis made what appeared to be some odd and risky investments but, the gathered investors had to admit, they had all paid off. So now if Jerry Landis was selling baboon futures, well, goddammit, they would seriously have to consider buying some.

Arty had no problem finding a lawyer to take his case. After he lost the use of his right arm and left leg in the nerve graft experiment, the president of the heavily insured biotech company was eager to settle out of court so as not to see the value of the company's stock, not to mention his own fortune, swoon to anemic levels. Although not exactly delighted about his situation, Arty had no problem finding the silver lining in it: He was getting a hundred thousand dollars, a tricked-out wheelchair, and a handicap parking placard. Of course, since Arty didn't drive, he planned to sell the placard for some extra cash. And all of that was before he cashed in his own accident and dismemberment policy. When all was said and done, Arty would certainly be able to buy something nice at Christmas for the kids at the Cupertino Children's Home.

Arty's attorney had been more than fair with regard

to her fee. Initially set to receive 33 percent of the settle-
ment, she later agreed to take only half of that—her
thinking being that anyone crazy enough to make a living
the way Arty did was crazy enough to do damn near
anything and she didn't want to be on the receiving end
of that sort of madness. So, sitting next to his fair and
slightly frightened attorney, Arty signed the nondisclosure agreement, took the check, and guided his shiny
new wheelchair out to the bus stop where he'd catch an
express back to the trailer park. And that's where he
encountered his first example of handicap discrimination.
His own trailer, lacking wheelchair accessibility, betrayed
him, leaving him stranded outside the front door. Doggonit, Arty thought, he could have snapped the fingers
on his one functional hand and the biotech's insurance
company would have paid for a nifty little ramp and
wider doorways throughout the trailer. Heck, if he got
his attorney to sit up and bark loud enough he could still
probably get them to do it, but right now he just needed
to get inside the trailer so he could pee.

Arty wheeled his swift new machine over to the trailer
next door. He knew Bonedigger was home because he
saw the Harley parked out front and he could smell
something rancid wafting out the kitchen window. Arty
was headed for the doorbell, but since he wasn't yet in
complete command of his motorized chair he crashed
into the chopped-out bike, knocking it to the ground.
This worked better than the doorbell, which Arty never
would have reached anyway.

The hulking owner of the hog exploded out the door
with three feet of heavy chain dangling from his leather-
gloved hand. He was a hairy, tattooed bastard with a Fu
Manchu that spread out at the jawline like two giant
pork chops. The man was huge and dangerous looking,
glowering from underneath a simian brow—though his
menace was undermined somewhat by the tiny black egg-
shell motorcycle helmet he wore. It was one of those
useless helmets bikers wore to comply with the state's
helmet law, the thinking being that by wearing a helmet

which met only the minimum requirements they were thumbing their noses at an overly intrusive government. The Darwinian nature of such thinking escaped these people and the fact that the helmet looked like a lacquered yarmulke and, in a typical motorcycle accident, would be about as protective as a thick coat of hair spray apparently didn't matter. The biker was about to do something violent when he saw it was his little neighbor, Arty, attempting to right the bike with one arm.

"The hell happened to you?" Bonedigger asked.

"Hey, Bones," Arty said. "Sorry I knocked your bike over; the steering on this chair's a lot more sensitive than I thought."

Bonedigger shook his head and righted his motorcycle, checking for damage. "No harm done, at least not to my bike." He scratched an armpit and looked at Arty, whose right arm was hanging uselessly to the side like a dangling conversation. "But I gotta be honest, little man, *you've* looked better."

"I'll tell you all about it if you'll help me into my trailer," Arty said. "I gotta pee real bad." A few minutes later, a glow of relief on his face, Arty told Bonedigger all about how the nerve graft experiment had gone south on him and how willing the biotech company was to settle. Bones had never seen a check with that many zeros on it, at least not a legitimate one. "And that's not the best part," Arty said. He pointed at the small table near his hulking friend. "Do me a favor, look in that drawer for a big legal-sized envelope."

Bones pawed through the drawer and pulled out the envelope. He handed it to Arty, who used his good hand and his teeth to pull out the insurance policy. He began flipping through, looking for the relevant clause. "You're gonna love this," Arty said. He was reading fast, skipping lightly over the boilerplate, until he crashed, eyes-first, into the relevant clause. "Doggonit!" he said.

"Smatter?" Bones asked.

"Well," Arty said, "if I'm reading this right, it says here

that I can't collect just because I've lost *use* of my arm and leg."

"Bummer."

"Bummer is right," Arty said. "I thought I had an extra twenty-two hundred bucks coming in. I was going to invest it in one of these biotech companies around here. I read in the paper where one of them was selling shares for about ten dollars one week, then the next week, after this drug they made got FDA approval, their stock went to sixty bucks!"

Bones was impressed. "No shit? I didn't know you followed the stock market."

"You kidding? Independent contractor like me, without security? I gotta be careful with my money. Stick it in savings and cost of living'll eat it alive. You gotta invest. Mutual funds are a good way to go." Arty wasn't the most sophisticated investor in the South Bay area, but he watched *Wall Street Week* now and then and had learned enough to beat inflation.

Bones stood up. "Listen, Arty, I gotta go. I'm cooking up some meth and if I don't get back to it, the trailer's gonna blow up and then you'll be able to cash in that policy, if you're still alive." He laughed and hit Arty on his good shoulder, leaving him at a slight tilt.

The little wheels in Arty's head started to turn. "Hey," Arty said. "You just gave me a great idea. Go turn off your burner and do me a favor, come back over when you're done. I'm gonna need your help." Bonedigger shrugged, said he didn't have anything else to do, and left.

When he returned a few minutes later, Arty was just hanging up the phone, visibly excited. "This is such a great idea, Bones, I swear, sometimes I scare myself. I just got off with a guy at the hardware store said they got everything we need. So here's the plan . . ."

As Arty outlined his plan, Bones fidgeted and became increasingly nervous, and not just because of the half-cooked speed he had just snorted. Arty's plan went beyond anything Bones or any of his biker buddies had ever dreamt up, much less done—and the crowd Bones ran with wasn't exactly squeamish. Still, being a good neighbor, Bones was willing to help. "Guess I'll have to get the truck," Bones said. "Can't tote all that shit back here on my bike."

"That's great," Arty said. "I really appreciate your help. And I'll pay for the gas."

At first the truck refused to start. Bonedigger growled as he squeezed his 280 pounds underneath the dashboard to get to the fuse panel. It looked like the head of Medusa with different colored wires curling out in an impossible jumble and all held together by duct tape. A screwdriver was jammed into the box, apparently to make an otherwise hopeless connection. Bones twisted together a couple of the snaking wires and reached up to turn the key. There was a small spray of sparks as the truck came to life. Bones tossed Arty into the cab of the old pickup and gassed it onto the road. First they went to the bank so Arty could deposit his check and get the cash he needed for the hardware store. Arty waited in the cab while Bones got the stuff on the list. When they returned to the trailer park, Bones, grinding his teeth from the effects of the speed, carried everything inside, including Arty. "Now what?" Bones asked.

"Let's nail a few of these two-by-fours together first," Arty said.

Bones, who had worked construction for a few years, hammered expertly while Arty, a natural righty, flailed ineffectively with his left hand, failing to hit the nail on the head even once. "That ought to do it," Arty said after he hit his numb right hand for the third time.

"Tell me again how we're gonna do this," Bones said.

Arty smiled and tapped his temple with his index finger. "See, I need to build a ramp and some wider doorways because of the wheelchair, right? So we're doing some construction, right? And the next thing I know, ooops, I cut my arm and leg off with that circular saw and bingo! An easy twenty-two hundred bucks."

"Ohhhh." Bones finally understood. "Great idea. How much do I get for helping?"

"What do you think's fair? A hundred?"

"A hundred'd be great," Bones said as he examined the gleaming new saw. "But the rip fence on this thing's gonna make it tough. Oh, hang on, it's adjustable." Bones spun the wing nut that controlled the width setting on the rip fence, then he slid it completely off. He set the lower guard retracting lever on maximum and screwed the blade-tilting lock down as hard as he could with the blade set straight.

"There we go," Arty said. "Now we're getting somewhere." Arty took the phone and dialed 911. He was on hold for a couple of minutes. "This is going to be great," he said.

Finally a voice came on-line. "Emergency operator."

"Hi, yeah, listen," Arty said. "There's been a construction accident over at Los Trancos Trailer Park, space twenty-two. Send an ambulance, okay?" Arty hung up the phone and snickered giddily.

"Did they buy it?" Bones asked.

"I guess. I mean I don't see why they wouldn't," Arty said. He thought for a moment. "Listen, let's have a beer first. I want that ambulance pretty close by the time we're done."

"Good idea," Bones said. He grabbed a couple of big malt liquors from the fridge.

Arty held out his can for a toast. "Skoal!"

They clinked cans. "To your health," Bones said before inhaling the entire sixteen ounces.

Arty slurped his down quickly and set his can on the table. "Don't forget," he said. "It's the *left* arm and the *right* leg."

"I know," Bones said. "You already told me."

Arty suddenly wondered if Bones knew left from right, but he didn't want to ask for fear of insulting him. As crazy as Arty was, he knew insulting a cranked-up biker with a circular saw wasn't the smartest thing one could do. Arty suddenly yelled, "What's that on your right hand?"

Bones looked at the correct hand. "Oh, that was my lizard tattoo. It reminded me too much of my ex-girlfriend Elizabeth. I been tryin' to peel it off ever since she dumped me. I'd rather not talk about it."

"Sorry, man." Arty sounded relieved. He let Bones pick at the scab for a moment before speaking again. "I'm telling you," Arty said proudly, "I don't know where I get these great ideas of mine. I just don't know."

"Yeah, me neither," Bones said as he picked up the saw. *RAAAANNNNHHHHH!!!!!* Bones squeezed the trigger switch and the blade's sharp, jagged teeth ran in vicious circles. Bones looked at Arty. "You ready?"

Georgette was conflicted about a host of issues. First she had to decide whether she wanted Oreos or Chips Ahoy. Nearing the midpoint of her first trimester, Georgette was eating prodigious amounts of baked goods. She and Paul were at the Safeway, shopping to the Muzak version of "Bridge Over Troubled Water." Georgette solved the first problem by getting both Oreos and Chips Ahoy. But that wasn't the only thing Georgette was conflicted about. "I don't think I want bridesmaids and groomsmen and all that traditional stuff," she said.

"That's fine, G," Paul said, using her basketball nickname. "I can go either way. Whatever you want. I just want you to be happy."

Somewhere on aisle two, near the capers and pickles, Georgette had announced out of the blue that she felt it was time they got married. Paul nearly dropped his gherkins. In the five years they had lived together Paul had asked Georgette to marry him several times but she had always dismissed the idea as being too bourgeois.

Paul could see she was conflicted—wanting, on the one hand, to do the traditional thing and get married now that she was pregnant, and, at the same time, objecting to the idea of a traditional ceremony. "Okay," Paul said, "here's an idea. What if we do it in the redwoods instead of a church? Remember Mike and Sally's wedding out near Point Reyes? Like that."

"That's perfect," Georgette said, obviously pleased with the idea. "We can get one of those whole-wheat ministers and write our own vows." While they shopped, Paul and Georgette planned the entire wedding, including musical selections—G would march down the aisle to "I Do It for Your Love" as performed by two close friends who had formed a surprisingly smart bagpipe/zither combo. Paul and Georgette also sketched an outline of their vows on the back of the grocery list. They had a lengthy debate on aisle six, near the boxed table wines, on whether or not to invite Paul's cousin Richard, who had a history of lewd behavior at family functions. Paul was against the idea, but Georgette thought it might cause more problems if they didn't invite him. As they neared the end of aisle nine, around the frozen yogurt, Paul asked the key question. "How soon do you want to do this?"

"Soon," Georgette said as she loaded a quart of premium coffee-flavored ice cream into the cart. "I don't want to be showing in my wedding pictures." Thus began the date debate.

Paul smiled. He couldn't remember Georgette's ever being vain. "Okay, we'll do it soon," he said with a small laugh. "I'll call Mike and Sally and get the number for that place in the redwoods." Paul knew that planning a wedding was a time-consuming nightmare and that it would necessarily cut into his assault against the evildoings of Jerry Landis, but, he figured, you only get married once and Jerry Landis would still be there after they said "I do."

At the checkout stand Paul pulled out his canvas bags. He was still smiling, happy about getting married and having a child with the woman he loved so. It felt like his heart was singing its favorite song and hitting all the notes just right. But his good mood vanished when the bag boy asked a question with shocking ecological implications: "Paper or plastic?" he said for the millionth time that day. He was talking to the older woman in front of Paul and Georgette.

"Do me a favor," the woman said. "Give me double paper in double plastic. And put my meat and frozen foods in those little plastic bags, and do the same for the soap and the detergent."

Like they're all not packaged enough already, Georgette thought.

Paul imagined the old woman lived only three blocks from the store. He suspected she would go straight home, unpack her groceries, and throw the bags straight into the trash. Maybe she just wasn't aware of the problems she was causing. Paul wanted to say something. He hoped he could screw up the courage to do that much. But before Paul could do or say anything, the sign flashed in his mind:

ACRES OF RAIN FOREST REMAINING: 1,000,974,000

Paul knew that Americans threw out over 180 *million* tons of garbage each year. Did this woman have any idea how much space a ton of garbage takes up, let alone 180 *million* tons? Georgette noticed the veins standing out at Paul's temple and on his neck. "You're going to stroke out if you don't calm down," she said. "Besides, there's nothing we can do about it. She's old, ignorant, and she doesn't care." The woman heard the comment but wasn't sure it was aimed at her.

Paul turned to the old woman. "Ma'am, did you know that each year Americans throw away enough steel, plastic, and aluminum to produce two million cars, enough wood to build a million homes, and a half million house trailers worth of aluminum?"

The woman flashed some yellow teeth at Paul. "Isn't that interesting?" she said. The old woman kept her eyes on the checker, making sure she wasn't being overcharged for her individually plastic-wrapped portions of synthetic cheese substance.

Paul felt good about himself for speaking up. Maybe it wasn't as bold a move as spiking a tree, but it was a start. "Don't you see?" Paul pleaded, "we *have* to stop throwing out so much garbage, and one of the best places to start is by not using all these paper and plastic bags."

Paul hoisted his own cloth bags as evidence of the better alternative.

"Your total comes to thirty-eight sixty-six," the checker said. The old woman reached into her purse and pulled out her checkbook.

Georgette stared in disbelief. She couldn't believe the old woman had waited until *now* to start writing her check. They'd be here forever. Some people were so rude. Georgette wanted to get home to start on a second draft of the wedding vows.

Paul didn't know if he was getting through to the woman, but he wasn't about to stop. "Ma'am, it's really important. I tell you what, how about if I buy you a few cloth bags? We'll save a small forest somewhere."

The woman handed over the check, then put her checkbook back into her purse and snapped it shut, never looking at Paul.

"Did you know people are actually talking about using the Grand Canyon as a landfill?" Paul asked.

The old woman put her purse into the child seat of the grocery cart, then turned to Paul. "Young man, you should mind your own business," she sniffed. "I will not be around by the time things are that bad." She smiled her old lady smile. "So I really don't care about any of that."

The words echoed in Paul's head. *I. Don't. Care.* The woman assumed a superior countenance as she watched the bag boy wrap a two-pound wad of fatty ground beef inside two plastic bags before putting it in the doubled-up paper-inside-plastic sacks.

Paul chewed on his lower lip, wondering what it took to get through to people. After a moment, Paul shouted, "Well maybe it's time you *started* to care you self-absorbed, blue-haired jackass!" He slammed his hand down on the checkout stand.

Everyone froze. The last person to scream like that inside the store had been wielding a shotgun. Georgette looked up, startled yet keenly interested in where this was heading. In the silence, the old woman slowly turned around to look at her accuser.

"What about your children or your grandchildren?!" Paul yelled across the store. *"They'll* be around! Don't you care about the world they'll be living in?!"

"That will be their problem," the old woman said. "So . . . so . . ." she seemed to be searching for words with extra impact, words she didn't get to use much at her bridge games. "So just go screw yourself you web-footed tree hugger!"

Paul looked like he might simply explode. *"Their* problem?! That's your justification? It'll be *their* problem?!" Paul stared at the woman for a moment before continuing. "Has your narrowed little mind just withered up inside your tiny fucking head?!" Paul gestured with both arms. "Look around, people," he said. "Do the goddamn math! How many trees were felled because you won't do something as simple as use canvas bags? There are forty thousand goddamn grocery stores in this country and this is going on twenty-four hours a day! Can't you see how that adds up? We're going to bury ourselves alive!"

"What goes on in the rest of the country doesn't concern me," the mother of six at checkout stand five said. "I've got my own problems." She had two grocery carts filled with over-packaged frozen dinners, plastic shrink-wrapped sixty-four-packs of individual-serving cereal boxes, and thirty pre-made high-fat lunch kits bundled in hard molded plastic, sealed in cellophane, and boxed in cardboard. "Besides, recycling's a pain in the ass," she said.

"Hey! Wake up," Paul said, "the health of this planet isn't a matter of your personal convenience!"

A young man passing by mumbled, "Ecofreaks."

And so it went. Everyone in the store had turned on Paul and Georgette. The old woman tottered out of the store feeling victorious. Paul finally surrendered to the idiocy, refusing to respond to a perverse accusation involving snail darters and Paul's sexual inclinations.

Georgette turned to the guy at the cash register. "What do we owe you?"

"Eighteen forty-three," he said. Georgette handed over a twenty.

Paul was dispirited. He felt like he was on the banks of a wide river. On the other side, millions of people were threatened with a horrible death unless they got across the water. Paul was trying to explain to them where the crossing was. But his voice wasn't loud enough or his directions were unclear or the people on the other side just didn't care what happened to them. Suddenly, a voice reached Paul. He turned and looked in the direction of the voice and realized he was still in the grocery store.

The bagboy looked at Paul with dull eyes and blinked once before speaking again. "Paper or plastic?"

Late one cloudy Wednesday night, Mr. Shart Lemsling was walking to his car in the parking lot of Western Environmental Industries. His car was parked in the space reserved for "CEO/Owner." As he keyed the car door, he suddenly felt a sharp pain in his lower back as if someone were holding an ice pick to his spine. Mr. Lemsling glanced quickly at the car window and caught a reflection of the person standing behind him. Taller than himself, broader shoulders, but the face was obscured by a mask crudely fashioned from a large plastic milk carton. The guttural voice, altered as it was by the ill-fitting mask, said, "Do not turn around, just give me the keys."

Not wanting to confirm whether or not the pain he felt was, indeed, being inflicted by an ice pick, Mr. Lemsling did exactly as he was told and soon found himself being chauffeured out of the parking lot, blindfolded and tucked comfortably in the spacious trunk of his Mercedes. The kidnapper drove for half an hour on surface streets. After that Lemsling figured he could be as far south as Cupertino, as far north as San Carlos, or somewhere in the Los Trancos Woods.

The car turned onto a dirt road and continued for another five minutes before stopping. Based on the quiet, Lemsling was fairly certain he was no longer in the city. As he listened to his kidnapper outside doing something, Lemsling began to notice an unpleasant smell which quickly turned to rank stench. He had to struggle to keep from vomiting.

The masked abductor opened the trunk and ordered Lemsling out. Blindfolded, Lemsling had no idea if his kidnapper was armed with only the ice pick or if he was about to be shot where he stood. The only thing he was certain of was that it smelled god-awful wherever it was he had been taken. "What's going on?" Lemsling asked. "What are you doing?"

"You've been kidnaped, you idiot. What did you think, I was going to open the trunk and all your friends from the County Solid Waste Subcommittee were going to jump out from behind the furniture and yell 'Surprise!'?"

Mr. Lemsling got a queasy feeling in the pit of his stomach. Someone apparently had taken exception to some recent events that had transpired behind doors that were supposed to have been, as they say, closed. It turned out that Mr. Lemsling's Western Environmental Industries was a deceptively named company that controlled the extremely lucrative landfill business in the South Bay Area. Thanks to some creative (if not publicly disclosed) financial arrangements, several previously uncommitted members of the County Solid Waste Subcommittee had recently voted to award Western Environmental Industries not only a new six-year contract but also a waiver which allowed it to begin dumping solid waste in a sensitive wetland area known to be the last remaining regional habitat for several endangered species of waterfowl.

Someone had also made arrangements for a hefty pile of environmental impact study paperwork to be filed and "okayed" by several unsuspecting members of the environmental impact subcommittee. By the time the matter could be straightened out in the courts, Mr. Lemsling—

along with the next two generations of Lemslings—would be long gone.

The masked abductor grabbed Lemsling by the arm and led him forcefully over the uneven terrain before kicking him hard in the back of the legs. Lemsling crumpled to his knees and felt moisture seeping through his expensive trousers. That close to the ground the stench grew decidedly worse. "This is about the wetlands, isn't it? You're worried about those goddamn hooded mergansers," Lemsling said. "Listen, we can work something out."

"Mergansers? You think I'm worried about some stupid fucking waterfowl? Sorry, pal, my attention's focused a little higher up the food chain. Now, dig!" the kidnapper said.

"With my hands?" Lemsling asked.

"That or your mouth, asshole, the choice is yours."

Lemsling reached down and started to dig, very slowly, with understandable trepidation—understandable because Lemsling now knew exactly where he was. He was somewhere in one of his six landfills, each of which was roughly the size of Rhode Island. And if Lemsling knew anything, he knew there were all kinds of things buried in landfills into which you didn't want to be sticking your hands.

"Faster. I don't have all night," the kidnapper said while kicking Lemsling in the ribs.

Lemsling thrust his hands into the wet garbage and immediately felt something sharp and ragged cut deep under one of his manicured fingernails. Shit, he knew it, probably the rusted top of a moldy dog food can. The stench was getting worse. Lemsling had smelled a lot of garbage in his day, but this was unnaturally sickening. "What the hell is that smell?" he asked.

"Looks like disposable diapers to me," the kidnapper said. "Seem to be an inordinate number of them in this particular part of the dump."

The smell of festering baby shit filled his nostrils, testing Lemsling's gag reflex. "Goddamn environmentalists," he muttered.

The masked abductor laughed. "Yeah, those evil bastards, encouraging personal responsibility and ecological sensitivity. Who the hell do they think they are? Do both of us a favor, pinhead," the kidnapper said, "shut up and dig."

In the next twenty minutes Lemsling dug himself quite a hole. And his abductor was right, this part of the landfill did seem to be diaper-heavy—and if you think a freshly removed baby diaper stinks, you should sample one that's been under the sun for a few days. The smell was so awful Lemsling finally surrendered to the urge to vomit. His fingers were throbbing from some nasty, soon to be infected, cuts. His pants were soaked from the moist garbage he knelt in. And as bad as the vomit dribbling down his chin smelled, it was still unable to overpower the diapers. The president and CEO of Western Environmental Industries was reduced to whimpering. "I think I'm going to throw up again," Lemsling said.

"Knock yourself out," the kidnapper said. "You know, it's amazing how many of these diapers are out here. But then again, maybe not. I mean, a baby must go through, what, eight or ten diapers a day for, what, about two years? Let's see, that's about eight thousand diapers per baby and they must take twenty or thirty years to decompose. And when you think of the ninety-five million babies born every year, damn, that's a lot of disposable diapers."

"So why are you doing this to me? I mean, why not someone from the diaper company?"

"It's a metaphor, dipshit. And you get to play mankind." The kidnapper told Lemsling to stop digging. He was standing in the deep hole when the masked abductor began kicking used diapers in all around him. When they reached ground level, the kidnapper tamped them down so tightly around Lemsling that he couldn't move anything but his mouth.

"You're not going to leave me here like this, are you?" Lemsling asked pathetically.

"Of course not," the kidnapper said before stuffing a particularly foul diaper into Mr. Lemsling's mouth. "I wouldn't want you out here yelling all night. You might disturb the mergansers."

Desperate to get off the road and make the most of his pre-retirement years, Dr. Gibbs returned to his home in Sunnyvale to try to find an answer to the question: Is there a place in the Santa Clara Valley for a guy with a suspect medical degree and extensive experience in the human organ market? Since he didn't have any friends who could answer the question and since the want ads proved useless, the public library seemed as good a place to start as any. As he walked past the long window leading to the library's entrance, Dr. Gibbs paused to study his reflection. What he saw was unsettling. He looked like the unholy offspring of Friar Tuck and Mama Cass. A sagging tire looped his midriff and a mangy ring of thin dark hair circled his large round head. Making matters worse, Dr. Gibbs had made the mistake of letting the hair in the back of his head grow long and then, compounding that mistake, he had tortured the stuff into a thing he called a ponytail. He thought it made him look like some Hollywood producer and he was right.

He hadn't always looked like this, he thought. How had he come to look so . . . pathetic? Why was he soft in the middle when the rest of his life was so hard? What he needed was an exercise program and a shot at redemption, which is exactly what he hoped would result from his research. Since Dr. Gibbs hadn't been in a library since his second year of medical school, he was surprised to find the dreaded Dewey decimal system no longer operating out of the ancient wooden index-card filing cabinets that he grew up fearing. Instead, it had been rendered even more inaccessible by being squirreled away on a hard drive.

Since there was no one at the underfunded library's

reference desk, Dr. Gibbs soon found himself lost in front of a computer screen hitting the Esc key over and over until he got to a help screen that was of no help whatsoever. An hour later, he still hadn't figured out how the damn thing worked, so he paid a bright-eyed eleven-year-old five bucks to be his computer consultant. He told the kid he wanted to find some newspaper or magazine articles on any of the local industries which might potentially employ a man with the skills and experience he possessed.

"Sure, no sweat," the kid said. She was helpful in two ways. First, despite the fact that it was one of the biggest employers in the region, she didn't waste Dr. Gibbs's time by suggesting the computer industry as a possible employer. Secondly, she mentioned the industry which employed both of her parents.

"What do they do?" Dr. Gibbs asked.

"They work for Genetek Enterprises," the girl said. "You know, gene splicing and DNA and chromosomes and stuff."

A dim glimmer of recognition lit inside Dr. Gibbs's head. He was vaguely aware that biotechnology was a big industry in the South Bay Area. "Aren't there a lot of biotech companies around here?" Dr. Gibbs asked.

"Like tons of 'em," she said. "They have this, like, big softball tournament every summer and there's like a whole bunch of teams that play. My parents' team has this *stupid* song they sing all the time at the games." The girl suddenly started singing, "Mama don't take my chromosomes. Leave your strand so far from home; Mama don't take my chromosomes awwaae-yeah." She paused a moment before saying, "They think it's real funny, but I don't get it."

Dr. Gibbs didn't get it either. But he suddenly realized that the biotechnology industry might be his next employer. He was, after all, in the medical profession, more or less. He got the kid to search the database and kick out articles on local biotech firms. The first article was about the company where the girl's parents worked. They were doing R&D on gene therapy for non-Hodgkins lymphoma. The next article was about a start-up developing a technology to accelerate the discovery of proteins and peptides and a treatment for septic shock. The third article was about a company whose researchers had isolated a bone protein called RZ-77. The company licensed this bone protein to a major pharmaceutical company to develop as a treatment for osteoporosis and other bone disorders.

Dr. Gibbs was beginning to think negative thoughts. Bone proteins. Big deal. How much can an isolated bone protein be worth? Who the hell even knows what a bone protein is? They probably have to sell a truckload of it to make a buck. He was ready to give up on the biotech idea altogether when he started reading the fourth article, an intriguing little piece revealing the potential value of some of the biotech products.

It seemed that on a picture perfect morning in October of 1994, the FBI arrested a UniMed biochemist named Alexander Williamson when he handed over a brown attaché case to one Alexis Rurik in the parking lot of a Sack n' Save. Inside the case was a genetically engineered cell line apparently capable of producing the human hormone erythropoietin, an antianemia drug with worldwide annual sales of more than $1 billion. The FBI said Williamson, a former employee of Integrated Genetics, had taken the cells from his former employer a year earlier. Rurik had bragged of connections with some former KGB officials who were now working in the private sector and were willing to buy the cells for $300,000—ostensibly so a Russian firm could manufacture the erythropoietin and sell it on the black market. Unfortunately, Rurik's KGB contact turned out to be an FBI agent.

A billion dollars annually? Dr. Gibbs was impressed. It seemed biotech might be quite profitable, depending, of course, on what it cost to genetically engineer a cell line capable of producing erythropoietin. Dr. Gibbs read several more articles that the kid had retrieved for him and each one reinforced his belief that before he gave up on biotech as a potential employer, he needed to talk with someone in the business. He just hoped he could find the right name.

"Here's what you really need," the girl said upon returning from some nether region of the library. She dropped a large book onto the table. It was a directory of every biotech firm in the United States, listed alphabetically, with details on the nature of their research, a list of corporate officers, with locations, phone numbers, fax numbers, and E-mail addresses.

It was everything Dr. Gibbs was looking for. Suddenly euphoric, he gave the girl another five bucks and started reading from the front. Affymetrix, Biopharm, Chromatech, Darwin Molecular. There were nearly 1,600 companies listed, but, through the Ds at least, none of them seemed to offer any obvious employment opportunities for someone with Dr. Gibbs's skills. These companies were creating drugs for nerve and brain diseases, developing intrastromal corneal rings, and marketing oligonucleotide-based leukemia drugs. These, it turned out, were not areas of study offered at the Port-au-Prince School of Medicine while Dr. Gibbs attended.

He turned to the back of the directory and his eyes fell immediately upon the listing for Xenotech, Incorporated. The entry indicated Xenotech was doing research primarily in the area of immunosuppressive drug strategies employing mycophenolate, FK506, methotrexate, azothioprine, and cyclosporine A. Finally! Something Dr. Gibbs actually knew about. Well, "knew about" was overstating it. He *recognized* the word *cyclosporine*. He didn't know it occurred naturally in a certain Norwegian fungus called *Tolypocladium inflatum*, nor was he aware that its medical effects were first observed in 1972 by a Swiss biochemist. What he did know was that cyclosporine was approved for clinical use in the United States in 1983 and before that in countries with less rigorous medical testing procedures. He knew that because once it became available in most of the world, it had helped triple his organ procurement business.

Prior to cyclosporine, most organ transplants failed—not because of any difficulty in connecting the organs to recipients, but because the recipients' immune systems naturally rejected foreign tissues. Cyclosporine suppressed the body's immune system—specifically, it blocked T cell activity, which would otherwise attack the foreign tissue. But as good as cyclosporine was, Dr. Gibbs knew it wasn't perfect and that explained why this Xenotech, Incorporated was working on other antirejection drugs. And as long as it was working in the field of organ transplantation, perhaps it could find a place for Dr. Gibbs. He felt his background in organ procurement would somehow mesh with this company on the cusp of new anti-organ-rejection drugs resulting in—what was the word they used now? Synergy? Yes, he hoped there would be some of that. Dr. Gibbs copied the pertinent information and stuffed it into his pocket. He would go to Xenotech, Incorporated, which was just a few miles up the road. He would take an updated résumé and see if he could get a meeting with the company's president, one Jerry Landis.

1963  Dr. Thomas E. Starzl and Dr. Francis D. Moore, working separately, lay the groundwork for human liver transplants. Dr. Starzl performs the first human-to-human liver transplant on March 1, 1963, at the University of Colorado, Denver.

6

When Georgette asked Paul to join her at the rally he was thrilled; it meant she still cared enough about important causes to attend a demonstration. Paul was so excited, in fact, that he never asked G what the rally was about. So he was caught somewhat off guard when the main speaker, a woman, stepped up to the microphone and said: "Recently, a doctor attending a psychoanalysts' conference in Buenos Aires got into a taxi and asked to be taken to his hotel. Instead, he was taken to a clinic where his kidnappers removed one of his kidneys. He was then taken back to the convention center and dumped on the sidewalk, alive, but roughly a pound lighter." A murmur trembled through the crowd.

"Wow," Paul said. "That's horrible."

"It's not a perfect world," Georgette said with a shrug. They were in Lytton Plaza among a group of about seventy people who had gathered in front of a small stage. Standing at the podium was an attractive woman in her early thirties. She had a crinkly smile, a head of somewhat unruly blond hair, and several degrees in biological

sciences. Overhead was a banner: BAY AREA BACKERS OF
ONGOING NATURAL SELECTION (BABOONS).

This outing, on a sunny Saturday afternoon, had three
components. The first was the rally. Second, Paul and
Georgette would go to the grand opening of the new
McBaby World, where they hoped to find on sale all the
infant stuff they'd be needing in four or five months.
Third, they hoped to agree upon the actual wedding date.

"In Guatemala," the BABOON woman continued, "infants are routinely stolen from their cribs and strollers
and their organs are sold on the black market." Paul
shook his head as he thought of his own impending child.
"The only reason things like this happen," the Darwinist
said sternly, "is that medical science has made it profitable. And as repellent as we might find this hideous market for human organs, it's not the worst problem such
advances have created. The real problem is that these
advances undermine the process of natural selection. And
the undermining of natural selection will eventually undermine the human species."

Paul weighed the woman's comments before joining
in the enthusiastic applause which was started by the
BABOON ringers spread throughout the audience. "The
biotechnology and biopharmaceutical industries are going
to kill us by keeping us alive," the woman said. "Biogen,
Ciba-Geigy, Creative Biomolecules, Scriptgen, Xenotech—these and hundreds of others are genetically engineering our demise and something must be done about
it!"

The name Xenotech didn't mean anything to Paul
since Jerry Landis had dozens of corporations and holding companies and Paul certainly didn't know the names
of all of them. While the BABOON woman chattered
on, Paul's concentration wandered, and he soon found
himself distracted by the people standing next to him, a
young boy holding his father's hand. Paul began to
daydream.

It was a sunny day; not a cloud was in the sky. Paul
and his own beautiful young son were on the banks of a

cool river, the greens of summer serving as a backdrop for a game of catch. Paul smiled as he lobbed a softball to his joyful little boy, who giggled when the ball rolled between his legs. Paul made a face of comic surprise and pointed behind the boy. "Get the ball, Sonny!" The boy turned and, with his little legs churning as fast as they could, raced after the runaway sphere.

Lolling in the warm sunlight on a blue-and-white checkered blanket, Georgette watched happily as she ate a crisp red apple. "He's fast," she said to Paul. "Gets that from me."

Paul nodded. "The coordination too," he said as Sonny did a face-plant into the soft grass. "You okay?" he asked.

After a moment with his nose deep in the zoysia, the boy stood and showed the world his hands. "I'm otay," he said proudly before bounding off after the fugitive orb. His bones were still soft, his spirit resilient. Then, with the ball in his tiny, excited hands, Sonny ran back to his father and said, "Any wildlife biologist will tell you that a herd must be thinned in order to maintain a healthy gene pool and balance with the ecosystem within which it exists."

Paul returned from his bucolic fantasy and he tried, mostly in vain, to follow what the BABOON woman was talking about. "We cannot allow the fetus worshipers to terrorize us or to keep us from our mission," she said. "Those who would argue that a zygote is a human would say an acorn is an oak tree and that a blastocyst deserves due process and they are meddling with the primal force of natural selection!" she bellowed.

Paul felt he must have missed something important in the middle of her speech because he certainly wasn't following her point. But looking at Georgette, he could tell she was enthralled. "We must stand firm against the cornucopian myth! The earth does not *have* infinite resources! We must stop undermining natural selection or else face extinction! We must stop the pharmaceutical giants from curing all diseases and promoting ever longer life spans," the BABOON woman said, "or we will have no life spans at all." She continued by arguing that the ultimate goal of the giant pharmaeceutical companies was to do nothing less than create an everlasting consumer. She asserted that if nothing was done to stop them, humankind would come face-to-face with the irony that natural selection created a brain smart enough to make us live forever and that, in turn, would be the cause of ruin for the planet which was the source of natural selection in the first place.

The BABOON woman then talked about the fairly recent cultural phenomenon of irrational sentimentality toward fetal life. Her point, which seemed harsh to some, was that only in the past few hundred years or so had humans come to romanticize children and pregnancy. Prior to that, she said, childbirth itself proffered no degree of sanctity to the newborn. Actual admission to a community or society came only after the community's needs were considered. Now, she argued, the good of the whole was scuttled in favor of the individual's desires. Romanticism defeated pragmatism in the age of the individual.

The woman leaned close to the microphone and delivered her message. "Individual human beings must start making the choice—worldwide—to stop reproducing at the rate the species has been for its entire history or something much less pleasant is going to do it for us."

Another one of the BABOON people began circulating printed information which included the names and addresses of various biotech companies in and around the Bay Area. As the flyers were distributed, the BABOON woman began to wrap up her presentation. She spoke eloquently about solutions, about energy usage and environmental stress and the earth's optimal sustainable population (suggesting that two billion was the right number). She reminded everyone that the United States was the world's third largest nation and had the world's highest per capita resource consumption rate. She urged the audience to join the fight, but Paul feared this was more than he was capable of fighting against. He decided he would sign their petition but otherwise he would maintain his course against Jerry Landis and whatever he was currently up to. And maybe, if he had the time, he would write some letters to his elected representatives. That way, by the time his boy grew up, maybe the world would be the fine, sunny place Paul daydreamed about.

Dr. Gibbs was exhausted and jittery. For the past eight hours he had been in his crummy office updating his résumé and working on his letter to Jerry Landis—the man Dr. Gibbs hoped would be his salvation. He was halfway through his second pot of coffee and in the throes of his third draft, which had him "interested in a lateral move to an exciting new field," when the phone rang.

"This is Dr. Gibbs," he said, emphasizing "Dr."

"Dr. Gibbs, it's Lance Abbott with SCOPE," the voice said with a certain expectation. There was a long pause as Dr. Gibbs searched his mental Rolodex. "We met at the American Society of Transplant Surgeons conference last year," Lance said. "In Vegas. The MGM?"

"SCOPE?" Dr. Gibbs said, tugging on his emaciated ponytail. "Doesn't ring a bell."

"Santa Clara Organ Procurement Enterprises," Lance said. "We exchanged business cards at the reception after the presentation on liver transplants."

"I'm sorry," Dr. Gibbs said. "I don't remember."

"Sure you do," Lance said. "I told that paté joke you thought was so funny."

"Ohhhhh, yeah, I remember now," Gibbs said, figuring it was easier to lie than to have this man retell the joke. "What can I do for you?"

"Well, first of all, this is not a SCOPE matter. Now and then I do some freelance OP work for, well, let's say for some private parties. In any event, I have a client who is interested in getting off dialysis and uh, how do I say this? He can afford to be in a hurry about it. So I was wondering if we could make arrangements for a trip

to India. I believe that's where you said you did most of
your kidney business."

"That's right," Dr. Gibbs said. "But I'm afraid you've
caught me as I'm trying to ease out of that line of work."

"Oh." Lance assumed this meant Dr. Gibbs wanted to
know exactly how much of a hurry this client of his could
afford. "My client is the president of a major software
company based here in the South Bay. I'm sure he can
meet your fee."

"I don't doubt that," Dr. Gibbs said. He knew how
much money some of those software people had made.
"But right now I'm talking to a local biotech outfit about
a position and I can't afford the time to go to India. I'm
sorry, I'd like to help, but . . ."

"Well, what about a local procurement?" Lance asked.
"My client is able to pay."

"I'm afraid that's illegal, Mr. Abbott. I'm sure you
know that."

"Sure," Lance said, "but I remember you saying something at the conference about how you might be willing
to turn a blind eye, especially if a life was at stake . . ."

Dr. Gibbs was beginning to get impatient. He really
wanted to get his résumé shaped up and in the mail,
plus all the coffee he had consumed was beginning to
test the limits of his tiny bladder. "Look, if he just needs
a kidney, his life's not at stake," Dr. Gibbs said.

"I know that, but I just assumed you meant it was a
matter of money, and my client . . ."

"I know. Your client can afford to pay," Dr. Gibbs
said, crossing his legs.

"Well, his exact words were, and I quote, 'Mr. Abbott,
I'd toss a blind baby into a sausage maker to get off this
goddamn dialysis machine,' end quote. He's willing to
pay quite well."

Dr. Gibbs considered that imagery for a moment before speaking. "Here's the bottom line, Mr. Abbott. I
can't help you. I'm sorry. But if I should hear of anything,
I'll call."

Lance Abbott paused as he considered another counter

to the doctor's objection, but then reluctantly surrendered. He gave Dr. Gibbs his phone number and thanked him for his time. The moment he hung up, Dr. Gibbs had a thick, uneasy feeling in his stomach. A bird in hand came to mind. The impatient president of a successful software company would probably be willing to part with $75,000 for a functional kidney. Xenotech, Incorporated (playing the role of the two birds in the bush here) would still be around by the time he got back. Couldn't he postpone his career change for a few weeks? As Dr. Gibbs mulled that question, his olfactory memory offered up a mental sniff at the container of gamy eyeballs in the warehouse in Calcutta. His career decision thus made easy, Gibbs headed for the door. He had to get to the men's room fast. Unfortunately, when he opened the door to the hall, he was greeted by a head of curly blond hair sitting atop a small, one-armed, one-legged guy perched in a state-of-the-art wheelchair.

"Whoa! You must be psychic," Arty said. "I didn't even knock." It had been two weeks since Bonedigger helped Arty defraud the insurance company, and as expected, Arty had healed up faster than anyone in the history of amputation. His accidental death and dismemberment policy had just paid off and now, with his money safely in the bank, Arty was getting back to work. "You must be the doc. My name's Arty." He held his left hand out to shake. "A mutual friend gave me your name and address."

Dr. Gibbs already didn't like where this was going. "A mutual friend?" he said.

"Yeah, Scott Matthews over at Amputech. Said you might be interested in some of my . . . products. Mind if I come in?" Arty didn't wait for an answer. He nudged the wheelchair's joystick and plowed forward so quickly that Dr. Gibbs couldn't get out of the way. When Arty hit one of the doctor's clunky wing tips, the chair flipped onto its side. "Whoa!" Arty spilled onto the floor. "Man! This thing is quick, isn't it?" Arty wiggled around on the floor like a walking catfish as he tried, unsuccessfully, to right the wheelchair and crawl back into it. Finally he looked up to Dr. Gibbs. "Could you give me a hand?"

Dr. Gibbs wanted to go to the bathroom more than anything, certainly more than he wanted to pick up this wiggling amputee, but something in him made him stoop down, pick Arty up, and put him back in the chair's lamb's-wool seat. Despite the fact that Arty was surprisingly light, down to about seventy pounds without the extra arm and leg, the strain put tremendous pressure on Dr. Gibbs's overfilled bladder. "You're a salesman?" Dr. Gibbs asked. He felt some professional courtesy was in order for a fellow pitchman, or maybe it was sympathy.

"Exactly," Arty said with a smile. "And I just found out I've got some new products in my warehouse that I was previously unaware of."

Dr. Gibbs didn't try to decipher the meaning of Arty's statement. He was eyeing the door and trying to find a way to excuse himself without seeming rude.

"You seem a little distracted, Doc. Have I caught you at a bad time?"

"Uh no, sorry, go ahead." Dr. Gibbs remembered his days going door-to-door and the constant emotional defeat one faced in that job. And he tried to imagine how tough it must be if you're handicapped. He decided he'd try to hold it long enough to hear what the man had to say.

"Well," Arty said, "like I was saying, I was talking to Scotty, showing off the new chair here and catching up, right? So I'm telling him about how things are going, what's my latest experiment, what's the going price for a shot of spermatozoa and—"

"Excuse me?" Dr. Gibbs hoped he hadn't just heard what he thought he heard.

"Sperm, the male germ cell."

"I know what it is," the doctor said.

"Yeah, well, I make pretty good money selling mine," Arty said, leaning forward slightly in the chair. "I don't mind telling you I got some big coconuts down here that make plenty of the milk, if you follow me."

Dr. Gibbs's expression said he felt like he was tailgating.

Arty smiled again; he loved the look on peoples' faces when they realized what he did for a living. "Let me cut to the chase, Doc. I was talking to Scott and your name came up."

"In what context?" Gibbs asked, hoping the answer didn't involve sperm-bearing fluids.

"In the context of you get organs for people who need them," Arty said.

The unexpected direction of the conversation briefly distracted Dr. Gibbs from his need to pee. "Well, I'm actually getting out of that line of work. It involves too much travel."

"Yeah, Scott said you do most of your work in India and the Philippines. I imagine that gets old after a while." Just then, Arty inadvertently hit the joystick on his chair and it spun around in a tight circle, nearly throwing him onto the floor again. "Whoa!" He was facing the wrong direction now, so he jockeyed the joystick until he faced Dr. Gibbs again. "Look, here's the deal. Scotty told me something that nearly knocked me out of my chair. He said there was a nice market for human organs, especially kidneys, and you were the guy who knew what was what."

"Well, I know what I know," Dr. Gibbs said cryptically. He was trying to figure out the story behind this one-armed, one-legged man in the swift wheelchair. He said he was a salesman, but what could he be selling? His inquiries seemed to be more along the lines of someone wanting to buy. He imagined Arty had been in a hideous industrial accident and, in addition to the limbs, he had lost his kidneys and, while on a break between dialysis treatments, he was here shopping for a new one. "Well, it's true there's a market," Dr. Gibbs said, "but it's illegal in this country to buy and sell human organs. I'm sure Scott told you that."

"Sure he did, but we're consenting adults, if you get my drift." Arty winked.

"So, are you wanting to *buy* a kidney?" Dr. Gibbs asked.

"No, no, no. The way I understand it, I got too many as is," Arty said. "I'm here to sell."

"Oh." That explained the "new products in the warehouse" comment. The uneasy feeling in Dr. Gibbs's stomach suddenly thickened. Not five minutes ago, Lance Abbott had called offering a large sum of money for a kidney, and now one had rolled into Dr. Gibbs's office with a For Sale sign on it. It was starting to look like Dr. Gibbs still had that bird in hand after all. But taking advantage of the situation would require him to break the law, something he had avoided for many years. "Excuse me," Dr. Gibbs said. The pressure in his bladder suddenly reached a threshold which he could not endure. "I'll be right back." He moved quickly to the door.

"Forgive me if I don't stand." Arty chuckled as Dr. Gibbs shuffled out of the room.

Dr. Gibbs raced down the hall to the bathroom. There, leaning with one hand against the wall, he considered the implications of brokering a deal with this man's kidney: If he could make a deal without having to go all the way to India, he could still pursue the Xenotech matter. And he could always use the money; there was never any question about that. It wouldn't take much time, just a couple of phone calls. And it seemed unlikely this was a sting operation since those are almost always directed toward someone who has been committing a particular crime on an ongoing basis. On top of that he felt certain a jury—if it came down to that—would buy the "I was just trying to help" defense. This seemed to be a perfect opportunity to make some easy money. It felt good. It felt right. Or perhaps he was confusing the merit of this idea with the satisfaction he was getting via urination. He'd never know for sure.

Dr. Gibbs returned to the office only to find Arty wiggling around on the floor again, this time trapped under the chair. "Oh hi, Doc. Sorry, I was practicing wheelies and I flipped over. I have *got* to get control of this thing!"

Having relieved the awful pressure in his bladder, Dr. Gibbs was feeling saintly, so he once again put Arty back in his chair.

"So what do you say, Doc? Do us both a favor, lighten my load. . . ."

Dr. Gibbs rubbed at his tired eyes. "Let me make some phone calls."

Arty smiled and slapped his hand on the armrest. "Now we're talking!"

"I am Grand Dragon of the Realm," Merle said ominously. "Who are you?"

"I am Grand Titan of the Dominion, and these are my six furies," the man said as he waved the salted rim of his glass at the two other men gathered at the table.

"They ain't but three of us altogether, you dumb shit," Merle said with a cracked smile.

They all laughed raucously at the higher mathematics of the joke. It was late and Merle Grimes and two of his cousins were drinking margaritas in the Jeff Davis Room of the local Holiday Inn. They were pretending to be members of the local klavern of the Klan and, as such, were retelling their favorite O. J. Simpson jokes from days gone by. "So O. J.'s boy asked O. J. if he could borrow the Bronco to go on a date." Merle paused to take a sip from his icy green drink before delivering the punch line. "And O. J. says, 'I don't know, I'll have to ax yo mama!' "

The table exploded into gales of politically incorrect laughter. They were pretending to be Klan members mainly because of the margaritas. None of them was a deep-in-his-heart racist. They completely lacked the level of hateful commitment that organizations like the Islamic Jihad managed. There wasn't a man at the table willing to strap a bomb to himself and go, for example, to a Jackson State/Grambling game just to make a point. Ultimately, these were underemployed, undereducated, good ole boys who longed for the good ole days when just being white trash guaranteed you a decent job.

When the laughter subsided, Brutha, as Merle's second cousin was known, leaned across the table toward Merle. "Now gone and tell us about this here safari you wanna take us on," Brutha said.

Merle didn't want to get his cousin Billy Bob in any kind of trouble, but he sensed a damn good opportunity here to make some easy money. Besides, what could go wrong? "Arright," Merle said, "but you gotta sware you ain't never gonna tell nobody, 'specially Billy Bob, 'cause he'd get in trouble or he'd get all mad at me."

Brutha's first cousin (Merle's second) Jimmy was getting visibly excited about the prospects. Jimmy loved huntin' more than just about anything, certainly more than things like going to school. His IQ tested somewhere in the low eighties, but then that IQ test was culturally biased toward people with some degree of measurable intelligence. "What sorta game you talkin' 'bout, Merle, lack deer and such?" Jimmy asked.

"Hell pecker no!" Merle replied defiantly. "I ain't talkin' 'bout no damn deer. Shoot. I'm talkin' 'bout some damn exotic game, not some old coon 'r possum. This is a for-real wild animal. You put this thang's head on yer wall and strangers'll accord you some respect, I gare-un-tee." Merle proceeded to tell Brutha and Jimmy all about the huge and powerful beast Billy Bob had shown him that night in the laboratory on the grounds of the Biomedical Research Center of the South. He finished by telling them how the great ape had ripped the car tire in half.

"Hot butt nuggets!" Brutha said as he looked, wide-eyed, at Jimmy. "I'd sure lack to get a shot at one of them puppies."

"Billy Bob says they's more of 'em out in those woods." Merle lowered his voice. "And for twenty frogskins apiece, I'll git you in there for a little target practice."

"What about them 'lectric fences?" Jimmy asked, squinting.

"You let me worry about that," Merle said. And faster than Merle could say "George Wallace is a traitor" his cousins slapped their money onto the table and they began to plan their hunt. They drank margaritas until the bar closed and then spent the next several hours collecting all their hunting gear and loading it into Merle's truck. Then they drove slowly through the piney woods toward the giant fenced compound.

Merle's plan for getting over the fence involved a rickety contraption made from a couple of aluminum ladders held together by hinges and thrown over some scaffolding perched on top of the cab of his truck. The design was based on something Merle had seen on a CNN report about Mexican drug smugglers. The smugglers welded a collapsible ramp on top of a large truck and pulled it up to the fence on the U.S.-Mexican border. The ramp unfolded over the top of the fence and other, smaller trucks carrying drugs and illegals drove over the ramp and into the desert of southwest Arizona.

In the half-light before sunrise, Merle, Jimmy, and Brutha managed to get the aluminum ladder contraption over the electrified fences without electrocuting themselves. They took this as a good sign for the coming hunt. Once into the compound, Merle pulled on a rope which lifted the ladder off the ground so that none of the baboons could escape if they came across it. He tied the rope to a tree and they headed into the woods. Merle explained to his two cousins that baboons were ground-dwelling herbivores who slept mostly in the afternoon, so dawn was the best time to hunt them since the big monkeys would be grazing and fairly easy to find. Of course Merle had made all of that up since it justified being where they were at the moment. As they made their way through the dense woods and the occasional grassy clearing, they saw evidence of a flourishing ecosystem. The flora was thick from the abundant rainfall and the long, warm summers. They were surrounded by longleaf, shortleaf, loblolly, and slash pines. And of course the southern longleaf yellow, the heaviest and strongest of the pines, and the favorite of the region's timber growers. They also saw deer, racoons, and squirrels, but no baboons.

Finally, after about an hour, Brutha spoke up. "Dang, Merle, I want my money back. They ain't no damn exotic monkeys nowhere 'round here. You crazy."

Just then, Merle saw something in a patch of tall grass ahead of them. "Oh yeah?" Merle whispered as he crouched. "Then what the hale you thank 'at is up air ahead?"

Brutha and Jimmy crouched down next to their cousin. "I'll be damned," Jimmy said. "You 'spect 'at's one of 'em?"

"No," Merle said, "it's one of the Oak Ridge Boys, you dumsumbitch."

They readied their weapons. Merle and Brutha had twelve-gauge shotguns and Jimmy had a 30-30. "C'mon, let's get us a closer look at that there," Jimmy said.

The three of them crept closer and closer until Brutha suddenly started laughing. "Shit. 'At's yer big, wild exotic monkey? Shoot, you don't need much more'n a twenty-two to keel that little thang." A month-old baboon had slipped away from its mother and was playing on the ground when the great white hunters found it.

"It's kinda cute," Jimmy said.

"Cute my ass," Brutha replied. "I'll show you cute." He reared back and kicked the little baboon, which let out a surprisingly loud yelp.

Wildlife biologists who have studied baboons tell us that they have a close-knit social structure; their family ties are very strong. They live in troops of up to two hundred members—consisting of juveniles, females with their young, subadults, and less-dominant males. These members are controlled by the large, dominant males, who act as peacekeepers within the troop and as defenders from outside attackers.

Observing a baboon defending its troop against an aggressive Cape hunting dog, a zoologist reported that a dominant male baboon took the fifty-pound dog by one of its hind legs and swung it around over its head like a rope before smashing it to the ground. The mangy black-skinned dog which had strayed from its hunting pack regrouped and attacked again. This time the baboon seized it with powerful hands and sunk his huge canines into the dog's neck. It then pushed it away with its powerful arms and legs until it tore out the dog's throat. On another occasion the zoologist saw a fight between a single dominant male baboon and a leopard that attacked a weak juvenile baboon which had lagged behind the roving troop. It was a terrible struggle, with the baboon briefly overcoming the big cat's hundred-pound weight and strength advantage before the fight was finished. When it was over, the baboon was sitting erect against a tree with a fatal neck injury. Ten yards away, the dead leopard lay in a pool of its own blood and intestines.

"I'm tellin' ya, they get a lot bigger'n this," Merle said. "This ain't nuthin' but a pup."

"Well shoot," Jimmy said, "let's go find us some of the big uns."

Brutha picked the scared little baboon up by the scruff of its neck and held the barrel of his shotgun to its face. "Bet this'd make a mess outta this little monkey's head."

That's when Merle thought he noticed movement in the trees surrounding the clearing, as if something had climbed down the trunks of all the trees. While Merle had guessed correctly that baboons were diurnal, that was the only thing he was right about. He was wrong to say they were strictly vegetarians and he certainly didn't know that they slept in trees. The little baboon yelped again when Brutha jabbed the rifle into its soft stomach. "Sure is a noisy little shit," Jimmy said.

The next thing the cousins heard was a screeching, barking sound. It was unlike any noise made by any animals native to the region, and it seemed to be coming from all around them. The men looked at one another, hoping for a cue that would tell them whether they should be terrified or just a little spooked. "Get down!" Merle said.

Brutha and Jimmy squatted fast. All around them, in

an ever-tightening noose, the tall weeds rustled. "Shoot, what're we squattin' in here lack a buncha girls for?" Brutha said. "I ain't scared of a bunch of little monkeys." His bold posturing notwithstanding, Brutha started crawling through the weeds, away from the baby baboon. Merle and Jimmy crawled off in different directions. The barking noises were getting closer and resonating so deeply that even someone as pig-ignorant as Brutha knew it was time to take the safety off the shotgun. But stooped over in the weeds like an old scrubwoman, he found the long, heavy weapon unwieldy and awkward to handle. Before he was able to flip a simple switch, one of the dominant male baboons broke through the weeds and came to a dead stop face-to-face with Brutha.

Baboons are quadrupeds, with compact bodies and robust limbs. And this particular male was best described as huge—four hundred and eighty pounds of muscle and instinct, balanced and threatening. It was three times the size of Brutha, who, until now, had never in his life been paralyzed by fright. His shotgun might as well have been a broomstick. Using his keen olfactory senses, the baboon sniffed the still air until he caught scent of the baby baboon on the frightened hunter. The huge animal suddenly started to slap the ground, pant-grunting a terrible threat. He tilted his head backward and, opening his jaws, displayed his five-inch-long canines.

Merle somehow slipped past the circle of encroaching baboons and was at the tree line waiting for his cousins when he heard Brutha make a horrible sound. It wasn't a scream or a yell; in fact, Merle would never be able to describe accurately the noise Brutha made the moment he died. But after hearing the hideous sound of death—and it was unmistakably that—Merle started running through the woods toward the truck. He never heard Jimmy make any noise, never heard Jimmy's gun fire, never saw him again.

Merle glanced back and saw a large male baboon chasing him. Merle pumped his shotgun on the run. He hoped to God he could get over that fence without confronting the baboon. Behind him the barks and screeches faded into background noise as he fled. Ahead he saw the rope tied to the tree suspending the hinged ladder contraption—his only way out of the compound. He fired the shotgun, hoping to hit the rope and drop the ladder to the ground, but apparently Merle had used up his quota of luck for the day by getting safely over the fence in the first place. He pumped the shotgun again and pulled a hunting knife from his belt. Huffing, sweating, and sick from the margaritas, Merle dropped his shotgun and was cutting desperately at the thick rope when the baboon pounced. It grabbed Merle by his leg and with both hands began swinging him around over his head. Then it let go. Leading with his face, Merle hit a loblolly pine about six feet off the ground. Three of his teeth broke off in the soft, sappy wood. Then he landed in a bed of pine needles. Under normal circumstances Merle would have been out cold, but adrenaline kept him going. Wild-eyed and bleeding profusely, Merle realized he still had the knife in hand.

The baboon was jumping up and down excitedly as if guarding the rope and daring Merle to "bring it on." Merle accepted the challenge and attacked like a rabid Cape hunting dog with a knife. The pain of the knife wound sent the baboon reeling, but not before knocking a few more teeth loose from Merle's bloody, mutilated mouth. With the baboon bleeding and temporarily out of the way, Merle cut the rope. The ladder flopped to the ground and Merle scampered over the fence like a spider monkey, leaving a trail of blood that would have embarrassed O. J. himself. He fired up the truck and threw it into reverse without lifting the aluminum ladder contraption.

The baboon jumped for the last rung and grabbed it just as the retreating truck brought the ladder into contact with the electrified fence. There was an explosion of sparks and the smell of burning baboon flesh filled the air. The primate screeched and dropped from the ladder. Inside the truck, Merle's hair stood on end until the ladder cleared the fence. He spun the truck around and drove like a bootlegger through the woods to a dirt road that led back into town.

The local authorities found Merle sitting in the cab of the truck in the parking lot of the Holiday Inn later that morning. He was weak from blood loss and barking like a baboon.

Much to Dr. Gibbs's relief, the kidney deal with Arty and the software mogul went off without a hitch. The doctor who performed the surgery commented to Dr. Gibbs that the donor, in addition to being quite a character, had needed absolutely no post-operative care. "Healed faster than anything I've ever seen," he said.

In the meanwhile, Dr. Gibbs had sent his letter and résumé to Jerry Landis and had promptly received an invitation for an interview. Dr. Gibbs arrived at the sleek, modern building in Menlo Park that housed Xenotech, Incorporated and took the elevator to the top floor. He was nervous as this was his first job interview in thirty years. The secretary showed Dr. Gibbs into the office and said Mr. Landis would be right with him. He was looking at the wall of the books when Mr. Landis and his *whir-pffft whir-pffft whir-pffft* entered the room.

Dr. Gibbs was surprised to see a large, withered old man with yellowing white hair. He looked as if he had once been six-four but had recently shrunk to five-ten. He appeared to be near eighty despite the fact that on the phone he sounded much younger. Dr. Gibbs was also surprised by the unusual mechanical noise issuing from somewhere within the man. "Mr. Landis?" Dr. Gibbs hadn't intended it to sound like a question.

"Ahhh, Dr. Gibbs," he said. "Don't let my appearance throw you. I'm not the old man I appear to be. Well, actually—it's a long story. Have you ever heard of Werner's syndrome?" Jerry Landis explained his genetic abnormality. When he finished the story about the specialists, premature aging, and his imminent death, Dr. Gibbs didn't know what to say. There was something otherworldly about Jerry Landis; he was old, he was young, he was peculiar, and there was something strange about his eyes. Dr. Gibbs tried not to stare.

Jerry Landis walked arthritically to his desk, gestured for Dr. Gibbs to sit, then eased himself into his own chair. On the desk, plastic models of human organs served as paperweights and, apparently, as decoration. "So, Dr. Gibbs, tell me what you know about what we do here at Xenotech," Jerry Landis said, peering over a plastic pancreas.

"Well, I know you're doing research with immunosuppressive drugs like cyclosporine, but beyond that, to be honest, I don't really know. I had hoped you'd be doing organ transplant research since organ procurement is my background."

"So it is," Jerry Landis said. "And that's exactly why I responded to your letter." He leaned forward onto his elbows. "I have the feeling you are just the man I've been looking for."

Dr. Gibbs couldn't hide his smile. This was music to his ears. A job at a big outfit like this could mean security, and security would mean no more dealing for the duodenums of the downtrodden, no more begging for bowels, no more crawling around on gooey warehouse floors. But the music in Dr. Gibbs's ears stopped abruptly when Jerry Landis fixed his milky eyes on his guest and asked an embarrassing question: "Doctor, do you know what xenografting is?"

Dr. Gibbs looked down at his shoes, fearing that his ignorance about xenografting would seriously diminish his employment chances with a company called Xenotech, since it seemed highly probable that the two things were connected. "I'm afraid not," Dr. Gibbs said, a hint of shame in his voice. "Technically, I've never practiced medicine. My parents wanted—"

Jerry Landis waved his hand like a magic wand to make the doctor's shame disappear. "It doesn't matter," he said. "I was just curious. Most people don't know what it is, or at least they've never heard the term. Sometimes its called xenotransplantation."

Through his business dealings, Dr. Gibbs knew of several other kinds of transplants, or grafts, but not xenografts. He knew an autograft was when you transplanted tissue, like skin, from one place on your own body to another. An isograft was where an identical twin gave up an organ to his or her genetically identical sibling. Autografts and isografts were very successful because the tissue matches were essentially perfect. The more problematic type of transplant, the kind people usually thought of when they heard about organ transplants, was the allograft, where one person gets an organ from another, unrelated, person. The main problem encountered with allografts was rejection—the T cell attack on foreign tissue. But with cyclosporine, FK506, mycophenolate, and other immune system suppression drugs—the sorts of drugs Xenotech was researching—allografts were now routine.

With all this in mind, Dr. Gibbs conjured a statement he hoped would give him some credibility. "You know, in my business, I dealt almost exclusively with allografts."

"And allografts are fine, as far as they go," Jerry Landis said. "But as an organ procurement man, I'm sure you know all about the supply-and-demand problem." *Whir-pffft whir-pffft whir-pffft.*

Dr. Gibbs nodded knowingly. "I know there's more demand than supply," he said. "Especially in the States, where sales are illegal. That's why I spent so much time overseas. I mean, if you can't make a profit on having your organs removed, where's the incentive?"

"Exactly," Jerry Landis said. "As a man who knows the business side of the organ trade, you're aware that it's all about numbers, isn't it, Doctor?"

"You can't argue with numbers." Gibbs had no idea what numbers he was referring to.

Jerry Landis knew the numbers and he loved reciting them, just as he did when speaking to a room full of investors. Each year, he explained, in the United States alone, nearly 43,000 patients with bad hearts were denied potentially lifesaving transplants because of the organ shortage. At any given time 35,000 people, just in the United States, were waiting for a functional kidney. And it wasn't just first-time patients lined up out the door— since most transplanted organs required replacement within ten years, there were plenty coming back for seconds.

Whir-pffft whir-pffft whir-pffft. For the life of him, Dr. Gibbs couldn't figure out what was making that noise. It sounded like a small washing machine inside Jerry Landis's stomach. Landis picked up the plastic heart from the desktop and absentmindedly disassembled it as he spoke. "The human body is like an automobile engine," he said. "It has so many parts that can break down, leaving you stranded by the side of the road of life." Dr. Gibbs listened as Jerry Landis stretched his analogy thin. He talked fuel pump (heart), air filter (lungs), and oil filter (kidneys). He said these and other parts could cease to function, leaving you to call the medical equivalent of the auto club, which in this case was the American Society of Transplant Surgeons. Dr. Gibbs knew Jerry Landis was making a point, though he wasn't sure what it was, so he opted for a fairly safe comment. "That's a wonderful analogy."

"Yes, and I'm sure I was making a point with it too," Mr. Landis said. He put the plastic heart back on its stand. "My mind sometimes wanders these days," he said, trying to remember where he was. "Oh yes, the supply-and-demand problem. I must confess, I get confused talking about xenografting. My motives are mixed now, compared to when I first entered the biotech business." *Whir-pffft whir-pffft whir-pffft.*

"How so?" Dr. Gibbs asked, not that he was interested, but rather because he knew people responded positively to questions about themselves.

Jerry Landis stood and walked slowly across the room as he spoke. "When I started, I was just a businessman," Jerry Landis said. "Profits were my only goal. Then I was diagnosed with Werner's syndrome and self-preservation became my primary motivation." Jerry Landis laughed. "But the money still talks to me, if you know what I'm saying."

"Its voice does carry," Dr. Gibbs agreed.

Jerry Landis crossed to a large globe and spun it on its axis. "Think about it, Doctor. Seventy thousand patients on the official organ transplant list in a country of only two hundred and sixty million people. Multiply that out in a world of five and a half *billion* people and that works out to one million, four hundred thousand potential transplants—Per. Fiscal. Year," Jerry Landis said. Dr. Gibbs was shocked. If he had known these numbers while he was in business, he'd have been charging much, much more for his services. "But," Jerry Landis continued, "there are only enough organs to do about twenty thousand transplants a year. And what does that leave you?"

"A lot of eager patients," Dr. Gibbs said.

"A lot of *clients*. Most of whom will die without your product." *Whir-pffft whir-pffft whir-pffft.*

"It's a tragedy. I've been saying that for years," Dr. Gibbs said for the first time in his life.

"Those numbers showed me the future," Jerry Landis said. "And as it always does, the future offers tremendous opportunity."

"No question about that," Dr. Gibbs said enthusiastically. He just hoped that opportunity would have something to do with him. And soon.

"Xenografting, Dr. Gibbs, is the process of transplanting organs from one species of animal into another, in this instance, from baboons to humans."

Dr. Gibbs was pleased to know he wasn't as far out of the loop as he originally feared. "Oh, like Baby Fae and the baboon heart," he said.

"Exactly," Jerry Landis said. "But Baby Fae only lived two or three weeks with that heart and that's not much of a solution. But we're working on that and all the other problems inherent with xenografting; that's what Xenotech is all about." Jerry Landis moved stiffly from the spinning globe to the bookshelf. Dr. Gibbs was fascinated by all of this but he couldn't imagine what sort of job Jerry Landis might offer him since he didn't know the first thing about immunosuppressive drug research. But his afternoon was already shot, so he decided to stick around and see where the meeting went. Jerry Landis pulled an economics book from the shelf and flipped through it as he spoke. "Given the free market's ability to create solutions to supply-and-demand problems, you have to see opportunity at times like this," Jerry Landis said. "And not just a *financial* opportunity, though it certainly is that."

Dr. Gibbs was beginning to wonder whether Landis really had a job for him or if he was just some wealthy lunatic with a biotech company who needed someone to listen to him rant. Jerry Landis pulled another book down from the shelf and opened it. It was the King James Bible. "Tell me, Doctor, are you a religious man?" *Whir-pffft whir-pffft whir-pffft.*

Oh shit, Dr. Gibbs thought, this smelled like a trick question. He'd have to think fast if he hoped to land a job here. Okay, let's see, the man asking the question was suffering from a rare and life-threatening disease and he was opening a Bible. It seemed rather obvious. "Why yes, I am," Dr. Gibbs said.

"That's good," Jerry Landis said. He then read from the Book of Genesis. " 'And the Lord God caused a deep sleep to fall upon Adam, and he slept: and He took one of his ribs, and closed up the flesh instead thereof; and with the rib, which the Lord God had taken from man, made he a woman.' " He closed the Bible. "Do you realize what that means, Doctor?"

Not wanting to alienate his potential employer by misinterpreting this particular passage, Dr. Gibbs shook his head no.

"It means the first transplant was performed by God and all we're doing is carrying on his will." *Whir-pffft whir-pffft whir-pffft.* Dr. Gibbs knew he didn't have the medical or the theological expertise to argue the point.

Besides, like many people who interpreted scriptures, Jerry Landis had a look about him that invited only agreement—sort of a Jim Jones, David Koresh look. It was in the eyes.

"I could see that," Dr. Gibbs said.

Jerry Landis gently closed the Bible and slipped it back onto the shelf. He then took Dr. Gibbs by the arm and led him to a sofa, where they sat facing one another. Jerry Landis put his frail hands on Dr. Gibbs's shoulders and looked into his eyes. The act itself was mesmerizing. Mr. Landis spoke calmly, hypnotically, with the rhythmic *whir-pffft whir-pffft whir-pffft* purring softly in the background. "In the five years after the introduction of cyclosporine, doctors in the United States performed ninety-three thousand organ transplants. Let's say each one generated payments of one hundred thousand dollars, which is low, but it makes the math easier. That's nine billion, three hundred million dollars in five years, in the United States alone. And that's with a short supply of organs."

Something stirred deep inside of Dr. Gibbs. He was utterly captivated, not only by Jerry Landis's magnetic eyes and the mysterious noise but by the numbers swirling thick and curious in a world of advanced medical procedures and immunosuppressive drug therapies. Jerry Landis smiled, knowing he had touched Dr. Gibbs's soul. "Now imagine filling *every* request for organs worldwide. That's one hundred thousand times one million, four hundred thousand. That's one hundred and forty *billion* dollars a *year*, Dr. Gibbs. So you see I have two motivators here. If I succeed, I not only live but I live like few others in history."

Dr. Gibbs was putty. He could only listen to what this supernal man said.

Jerry Landis shook him slightly. "Have you ever experienced a period of grace, Doctor?"

Dr. Gibbs thought of that moment in the warehouse in Calcutta when he had his out-of-body experience, but decided not to go into that. "No, I haven't."

Landis told Dr. Gibbs about the night the golden light filled the very room they were in. When he was finished with his fantastic tale of divine intervention, Dr. Gibbs was lost. Only an hour ago, Jerry Landis had said Dr. Gibbs was just the man he was looking for, which was great. Then he had explained the potential value of xeno-grafting, which was astounding. Finally he had made a stunningly original interpretation of Genesis which ulti-mately suggested that God wanted Jerry Landis to repro-duce immediately and prodigiously. "Can you help me, Dr. Gibbs?"

Dr. Gibbs had never experienced anything like what happened next. It was a soothing sensation, as if he had been dipped in warm water. It was comforting and pow-erful. He felt he was in the presence of a great and troubled man who could, indeed, see the future. Jerry Landis was not like anyone Dr. Gibbs had ever met. He was a most peculiar man. He was a dying prophet and Dr. Gibbs would do anything he could to help him. "I don't understand what you want from me," Dr. Gibbs said weakly. "Is there some sort of a job you want me to do?"

Jerry Landis smiled. "Yes. I have a very important job for you, Doctor. For if I am to fulfill God's will, I will need another testicle," Mr. Landis said. *Whir-pffft whir-pffft whir-pffft.*

Despite his trancelike state, Dr. Gibbs was taken aback. "Come again?" he said.

Jerry Landis winked at him. "I need another grape in my gunnysack."

"Sorry?" Dr. Gibbs said.

"Doctor, I'm forty-seven calendar years old, but that's nearly ninety in Werner's syndrome years. I've had the tests done and my sperm count isn't what it used to be."

"But . . ."

"No buts, Dr. Gibbs. It's very simple. You're in organ procurement, right? I need another ball to play the game. Get me one and install it and you will have a staff posi-tion here."

Had he heard that right? Was this man for real? A staff position? "And all you need me to do is procure a testicle?" Dr. Gibbs asked.

"And attach it," Landis reminded him. "I'm thinking of a salary in the hundred-thousand-dollar range, plus benefits *and* stock options."

Although he dare not say it, Dr. Gibbs couldn't imagine that such surgery would work. First, he had never heard of a testicle transplant. Second, would there be room in the scrotum or would they have to add on to the existing one? Third, whose DNA would surf those milky white waves if all three testes fired simultaneously? But for a staff position, it would be worth a try.

Jerry Landis stood to show his guest to the door. "Doctor, I have seen too many miracles in my day to think this isn't possible. And I know *you* are the man to pull this off." He put his hands on Dr. Gibbs's shoulders again and looked into his eyes. "I want that gonad."

And as Dr. Gibbs made his way toward the elevator he wondered where in the world he was going to get one.

"Pardon me while I hurl," Georgette said sourly. And with that she disappeared into the bathroom. Paul felt the violent, heaving contractions every time she threw up but, other than sympathize, there was nothing he could do. Morning sickness simply had to run its course.

They had been wrestling with a calendar in an attempt to choose their wedding date when the bride-to-be felt the urge to pray to the porcelain god. Paul tried to distract Georgette by reading from the flyer he got at the BABOON rally. "Listen to this. It says overpopulation is the most serious problem facing humanity as it's the root cause of deforestation, waste disposal problems, children living in poverty . . ." Georgette struggled with a dry heave. "You okay?" Paul rubbed her back gently.

"Yes, the wretching guttural noises mean I feel great."

"Just checking," Paul said before he continued reading. " 'With each medical advance that the biotech industry foists onto a desperate and gullible public, the gene pool is weakened and the population increased by virtue of interference with the natural death rate.' " Georgette stood and went to wash her face. Paul handed her a washcloth and continued reading. " 'We, the Bay Area

Backers of Ongoing Natural Selection, believe that the evidence supports the assumption that natural selection is an operant process which, by selecting against certain deleterious genetic traits, culls living forms not fitted to our environment. So, for example, the death of a person by cystic fibrosis (though a personal tragedy) is, in fact, a benefit to the species (assuming the death occurs before the person passes on the gene). It benefits the species because cystic fibrosis is deleterious and is therefore best expunged from the gene pool instead of being passed on to succeeding generations. But the biotech industry is on the verge of finding a way to keep cystic fibrosis carriers alive, therefore allowing the gene to be passed on to the next generation. This is doubly problematic because not only are carriers of deleterious genes allowed to live (and therefore consume limited resources) but they then reproduce, not only passing on the deleterious genes, but also creating other carriers who then strain the earth's carrying capacity by their consumption.

'In a world of unlimited resources this would not be a problem, however we do not live in such a world.

'By preventing the process from selecting out the carriers of deleterious genes, the biotechnology industry has become a key contributor to both a weakened gene pool and to overpopulation that will doom humankind to a slow demise featuring grotesque battles over dwindling resources.' "

Paul put the BABOON flyer down. "I don't buy the argument," he said. "Except for the part about overpopulation being the big problem. I mean, the logical extension of the argument would prevent you from using antibiotics and aspirin."

Georgette dried her face and turned to Paul. "I don't know," she said suspiciously. "Maybe they're on to something. I mean, think about it. The entire scenario is made possible only because two longtime adversaries have inadvertently ended up in cahoots."

Paul encouraged her. "You think it's a conspiracy?"

"No question," she said. "It's only because the Church,

with a capital *C*, successfully sells the mystical notion that humans are somehow sacred, like cows in India, and are thus worth keeping alive at any cost. Science, with a capital *S*, steps obligingly to the plate and, doing its newest voodoo, keeps the tithing penitents alive." She arched her eyebrows conclusively.

Paul pointed at Georgette as if she had proved the Kennedy assassination conspiracy theory. He went to the phone in the next room and picked it up.

"What are you doing?" Georgette asked.

"Calling Oliver Stone."

Georgette smiled, kissed Paul, and grabbed the car keys. "I gotta go, smart guy. Tell Oliver we want complete creative control."

"Give the doctor my best," Paul said. Georgette headed off for her monthly prenatal checkup and Paul returned to the flyer, which cataloged vital information on some of the local biotech companies involved in the vicious cycle dooming humankind to its slow demise. These outfits dealt in derivative blood products, tissue engineering, peptide technology, baculovirus protein expression services, and a host of other novel products and procedures. And among the companies was a name with which Paul was all too familiar: Mr. Jerry Landis, President, Xenotech, Incorporated. Surprise, surprise, Paul thought. The synopsis said Xenotech was a leader in immunosuppressive drug research in the xenografting arena. However, unlike all the other companies in this arena, Xenotech was attempting to solve the transgenic *baboon* organ rejection problem instead of the transgenic *pig* organ rejection problem.

Intrigued, Paul went to his computer and got on-line. Keyword: Xenograft. A list of helpful and informative cyber-addresses came onscreen, and soon Paul was visiting various home pages—http://www.os.dhhs.gov (U.S. Department of Health and Human Services); http://www.nih.gov (National Institutes of Health); listserv@wuvmd.wustl.edu (organ transplant forum); and http://www.primate.wisc.edu (primatology site). Paul was fascinated by what he learned—and he knew Mr. Landis would be shocked at some of the information too. An hour later Paul had all he needed, so he set about to bring about change the way he always did:

> Mr. Landis:
>
>> Here we go again.
>> Recently I attended a rally presented by the Bay Area Backers of Ongoing Natural Selection and it was there that the name of one of your companies, Xenotech, Incorporated, came up. After a little research it occurred to me that the federal government . . .

Paul wrote that while the BABOON theory was, admittedly, a bit far-fetched, it did lead to some other concerns. Concerns that might be of interest to the bureaucrats within the NIH, FDA, and the CDC. Finally Paul suggested that he and Jerry Landis should meet and discuss the issues to see if there wasn't something they could do to solve some of these problems, specifically the problems that Xenotech's research might lead to. When he finished, Paul was confident that Jerry Landis would invite him in for a meeting, their first since 1975. Only this time, Paul would have the upper hand.

Sitting in the small waiting room, there was no way for Georgette to escape the conversation between the two bulbous women who looked to be in their third trimesters. "It's such a wondrous thing," one of them said in a dreamy, fatuous voice. "We're actually creating *life*." The woman placed her hands on her belly like Jesus laying his hands on Lazarus.

"I know," her friend said. "It's"—she gazed heavenward, searching for the perfect word—"just a miracle." The women leaned together and hugged.

"Oh, Christ," Georgette muttered just loud enough for the women to hear and know the comment was directed at them. Insipid nitwits. Georgette looked straight at them. "There's nothing miraculous about it. It's cells dividing. Every dumb animal on the planet is capable of doing it." The women were horrified that one of their own would blaspheme their glorious state. One of them wound up to take issue with the impious thoughts. However, when Georgette stood to move away, revealing her rebounding stature, the woman thought better of the notion and settled on a stare of superiority.

Georgette wasn't keen on women who tried to turn the mere act of breeding into some sort of passion play starring themselves and their zygotes. For reasons she still didn't understand, Georgette was also annoyed whenever she overheard the pregnant discussing their gestation as if it hadn't been done ten or twenty billion times before. You'd think they'd found a cure for cancer when all they'd done was gotten knocked up. Georgette wondered why she lacked this sappy fascination with her own pregnancy. Every pregnant woman she had ever known had come down with the same maudlin symptoms—every woman but herself. Maybe she was suffering from a hormone shortage. The problem is all inside your head, she said to herself. But deep down inside she worried that something was really wrong with her.

A nurse appeared from behind a door and read from a file. "Georgette Hobson?"

Later, after the requisite palpating and fluid sampling, Dr. Nemeth scribbled a note on the file, then looked over her glasses. "Physically everything's fine, Georgette. So tell me why you're so anxious."

"There's nothing to tell." Georgette wasn't a very good liar, but she was tenacious and Dr. Nemeth knew it. She and Georgette had played ball together for two years, so the doctor knew there wasn't any point in trying to force the truth out of her friend the power forward.

"Suit yourself," Dr. Nemeth said. "I'll see you next month." She draped her stethoscope around her neck and moved to the door. "Call ahead if you decide to do the amnio."

"Thanks," Georgette said. "I will." As the door was closing Georgette thought of one final question. "Hey, Doc! How much longer can I play ball?"

Her old friend smiled. "Assuming you keep your elbows out like you used to, you ought to be able to get a rebound and make an outlet pass just as you go into labor."

"Thanks," Georgette said. "Oh yeah, Paul says hi."

Driving home, traffic was a nightmare. Surface streets were gridlocked so Georgette hopped onto the freeway, which was worse. She was trapped behind a diesel Mercedes, a four-wheeled Auschwitz threatening to asphyxiate her. God knows what the fumes were doing to the embryo within, she thought. Two wild-eyed homeless men, sensing a rare employment opportunity, burst from the scrubby bushes on the roadside where they lived. They ran into traffic spitting on windshields, making thin mud from the soot and dirt and ink as they smeared ragged pages of newspaper across the glass. They held out grubby hands and cursed those who refused to pay. A baby boy began to cry in the car next to Georgette's. The child's father turned and smacked the boy in the head for making too much noise. Behind, a car filled with teenagers turned up their booming stereo loud enough to pancake the Nimitz Freeway. Perhaps it was the vibration from the throbbing mega-bass rattling her brain stem or maybe it was the diesel fumes, but Georgette began to see what appeared to be the future.

It was a dystopian panorama, one that Georgette had seen many times before. The landscape was barren, the burned-out remains of automobiles perched like dead animals on tree stumps as garbage blew by in the hot, dry wind. The sun was a dim bulb in a yellow-brown sky. The ground was rock, the topsoil long gone. There was nothing green. But there were people everywhere, millions of them, ragged, hungry, desperate, pregnant. A young girl in worn clothes squatted by a fetid pool of water and dipped her hand in to get a drink. Suddenly her mother stopped her. "Don't drink that," Georgette said. "It's contaminated." She pulled her daughter to her side. "We'll look somewhere else."

"I'm hungry," the girl said.

"Everybody's hungry, sweetheart. Maybe your dad will find something for us."

They walked on through the grim landscape in silence for a while before Georgette spoke. "It wasn't always like this, you know."

The girl looked at her mother. "What happened?"

"Nobody did anything, I guess. At least nobody did enough."

The little girl took her mother's hand. "So why did you have me?"

Suddenly a horn honked and traffic finally began inching forward. Georgette, still in a diesel-fume-induced haze, drove ahead vacantly. She got off at the next exit and drove aimlessly for half an hour as she considered her malignant fantasy. Finally, as if someone else had taken the wheel, her car turned into a driveway leading to a complex of medical offices. There was a young girl in the parking lot, preaching to a crowd, singing sacred songs and reading from the Bible.

Georgette got out of her car, and as she approached the abortion clinic, a fervent man in his thirties with a frighteningly conventional haircut grabbed her by the arm. "Don't do it!" he screamed at Georgette. "Save the ba—" was the last thing the man said that day. Georgette was in no mood to have her rights impinged upon, so wielding a solid right elbow, she put the presumptuous son of a bitch on his back and went inside.

"Dammit, get out of the way! I'm on a fucking mission of mercy!" It was near the end of a long Thursday and Lance Abbott was in a hurry to get across San Francisco Bay. He wanted to beat his competitors to the scene of an accident. However, Lance's fellow motorists didn't share his sense of urgency about crossing the bridge so he was reduced to pleading with them. "Move, you goddamn idiot!"

The go-getter that he was, Lance kept a police scanner in his car for just this sort of situation. He had been driving south out of Oakland, where he had attended a seminar on new organ procurement protocols, when the police scanner squawked the news. Lance didn't get all the details but from what he could put together it seemed that an eight-fingered performance artist who scoured Bay Area Rapid Transit tunnels for the dead bodies of small mammals (which he mounted on remote-controlled mechanical devices used in his performance pieces) had discovered the body of a somewhat larger mammal known as Mr. Randall Hirschoren. The police had called for an ambulance to meet them at the scene, so Lance suspected the man was still alive. The question was, how long would he remain that way?

Lance was tuned to all-news radio waiting for a traffic report, which was due in five minutes. In the meanwhile the news reader was updating a story that lately had captured the imagination of South Bay radio listeners. "Los Altos police say they have turned up a curious new clue in the investigation of the mid-week kidnapping of landfill mogul Shart Lemsling, who was abducted in the parking lot of Western Environmental Industries Wednesday night. Jennifer Mullen, spokesperson for the company, said they had received a note but would not comment on the nature of that note other than to say it wasn't of the ransom variety. Los Altos police detective Geoff Young, who is heading the investigation, said only that the note indicated Mr. Lemsling was alive and waiting to be found."

The next voice was that of Detective Young: "Extortion does not appear to be the motive. At this point, considering Mr. Lemsling's business, we believe a radical pro-environmental group is responsible. We're looking into the possibility that the kidnappers may be an offshoot of Earthfirst! due to the use of exclamation marks in the group's name." Detective Young went on to say that the name of this heretofore unknown pro-earth extremist organization appeared to be written in Latin. He pronounced the name "terra two-bor." "My guess," the detective said, "is that the 'terra' is Latin for 'terrorism' and terrorism is nothing more than error-ism without the T, if you follow what I'm saying." Detective Young said that his department and the other police departments in Silicon Valley were part of the world's most sophisticated police computer network and that soon after he scanned the terrorist note into the optical character recognition program and E-mailed it to their language experts they'd know more about the actual translation. And after that, they'd surely catch whoever had committed this senseless crime.

Lance recognized the words "terra tuebor," but he couldn't remember where he'd heard or seen them. Perhaps it would come to him later. Meanwhile, since Lance knew that kidnap victims usually turned up dead or dying, he made a mental note that after checking on the man in the BART tunnel he would go straight to Western Environmental Industries to express SCOPE's sympathies and to see if anyone knew whether Mr. Lemsling had signed an organ donor card. But first he needed a traffic report to tell him whether he should go ahead to the San Mateo Bridge or double back and take the Bay Bridge to get over to Daly City.

"The traffic report is next," the announcer said, "but first, good news about your health! In a study published today in the New England Journal of Medicine, researchers at Boston General hospital say that green tea may help prevent all forms of cancer. The study—"

"Nobody cares about greenfuckingtea!" Lance screamed at the radio. "Give me the goddamn traffic report!"

It turned out that traffic sucked in every direction. Lance calmed slightly when he realized that nobody else could get there any faster than he could.

When Lance Abbott arrived at the scene of the accident, Mr. Randall Hirschoren was being removed from the tunnel. Actually, only the top third of Mr. Hirschoren was being brought out. The bottom two thirds had already been extracted and laid on a sheet of heavy plastic by the side of the tracks.

After snapping on their rubber gloves, Bay Area Rapid Transit investigators and a detective from the San Bruno police department put the two parts together like an idiot's jigsaw puzzle and looked to see if they could determine the cause of death. Lance peered over the detective's shoulder. "Anything salvageable?" he asked.

The detective poked at something in Mr. Hirschoren's body cavity that might or might not have resembled a human organ. "Lemme guess," the detective said, "you're with one of those organ procurement outfits?"

"Yeah, Santa Clara Organ Procurement," Lance said. "How'd you know?"

"Ever since cyclosporine, I've seen more body parts people than reporters at accident scenes." The detective looked at the victim's mangled giblets. "The fact that Mr. Hirschoren here has been split in two by the steel wheels of a BART train makes me doubt you're going to find anything for resale here," he said. He tossed a sliver of something at Lance.

Lance dodged it, then bent down to look. "The hell is that?" he asked.

"I'm guessing liver," the detective said. "Let me ask you." The detective stood and pulled off his rubber gloves. "Why would a lawyer be lying on the tracks in a BART tunnel?"

"How do you know he's a lawyer?"

"We called his employer," the detective said. "Daly City Chemicals, they make industrial solvents. This guy's in-house counsel, just got a nice bonus and a new parking spot. Misses work for the first time in ten years and he shows up like this."

"A chemical company, huh?" Lance rubbed his chin, intrigued by something. "You know, I just heard a news story about some landfill guy who got kidnapped. The cops in Los Altos think some crazy pro-environmental nutcase did it."

The detective perked up at the news. "No kidding?

I'll check it out on our new interdepartmental computer system, supposed to be pretty amazing. Thanks for the tip."

"No problem," Lance said. Since there was nothing for him here, Lance returned to his car. Maybe Mr. Lemsling had turned up semi-alive in the last fifteen minutes. And if not, Lance now had something else he wanted to look into.

The detective was intrigued about what Lance Abbot had said about the possibility of a connection between the man in the BART tunnel and the kidnapping up in Los Altos, or Los Gatos, or wherever. If a group of environmentalist radicals or even a single extremist was on some sort of homicidal rampage, then there might be more related cases strewn about the Bay Area, and cracking such a case would almost certainly mean a promotion.

When he got back to the station, the detective went to the computer and got busy. He logged on with his "DKTRCY" password and began trying to navigate around the brilliantly designed program linking all the databases of all the police departments in the Bay Area. Every now and then the detective was forced to refer to the instruction manual, but it appeared that the author of the manual spoke English only as a third language, which confused matters worse than they already were. Finally, after two frustrating hours of inputting the information he believed the program was asking for, the detective took a deep breath and hit ENTER.

There was a pause before the computer began to make the comforting sound it does when the disk motor activates and the actuator arm swings the read/write head over the spinning hard drive. Then an important message popped on-screen: SHARED CODE ERROR. CANNOT INITIALIZE. ABORT, RETRY, IGNORE? The detective considered the message, then hit R for retry. Again the disk motor spun the hard drive and again the message: SHARED CODE ERROR. CANNOT INITIALIZE. ABORT, RETRY, IGNORE?

After several of the detective's colleagues restrained him from tossing the CPU out the window, they suggested he call the free customer support line that the software manufacturer offered to customers. He did so.

"Thank you for calling CrimePerfect Programming. If you have the three-point-two or the three-point-three version of CrimePerfect, press one. If you are calling about errors in specifying default percentages, press two. If you are calling about errors in sorting secondary files, press three . . ." The detective listened patiently as the list of potential errors paraded by. Eventually, one spoke to him. "If you are calling about initialization or shared code errors, press star forty-nine." He did so. "Welcome to CrimePerfect Programming's Free Customer Support Line. Please have your credit card number ready for the next available operator." The detective was on hold for seventeen minutes listening to a classic rock station that the software company's marketing department had selected as having the most appeal for the demographic who used their product in this market in the past three months. He was halfway through a syrupy version of "Keep the Customer Satisfied" when the next available operator came on the line and explained that before he answered any questions, he'd need the detective's credit card number.

"But it's a *free* customer support line!" the detective argued. "Why do you need my credit card number if the support is free?"

"Here's how it works, sir," the next available customer support person said. "You give me your credit card number, then I check to see that it's valid. Once I have confirmed the card is valid, I charge fifty dollars to the account. Then I transfer you to someone in customer support. You will explain your problem to customer support and they will tell you how to solve the problem and whether the problem is our fault or yours. If we determine that the error is our fault, we will then issue a credit to your account. If the problem is your fault, you will see the fifty-dollar charge on your next statement.

Do you understand?" The customer support person sounded like he had just Mirandized the detective.

Feeling he was close to solving the computer problem, the detective gave his credit card number, assuming (incorrectly) that the department would reimburse him. After the credit card was found to be valid, the detective was put on hold for another twelve minutes of classic rock. Then the next available voice came on the line. "Customer support, this is Ryan."

The detective explained the problem to Ryan and Ryan had the detective go to DOS and dink with some codes. When that failed to solve anything they went to the file manager. When that failed, they went to the program manager. When that failed, they went to a diagnostics program. When that failed (and another thirty minutes had elapsed) Ryan said the problem was the detective's fault and he would be charged fifty dollars. Then Ryan hung up.

This time the detective considered using his gun, but thinking better of it (and not wanting to do all the paperwork that comes with discharging his service revolver in the building) he hit A for abort and called it a day.

Dr. Putnam watched impassively as the beveled needle pierced the papery skin of Jerry Landis's abdomen. Liquid crimson swirled into the whitish fluid as Landis's palsied, liver-spotted hand doubled its feeble grip on the syringe and forced the plastic plunger downward. The black rubber bulb herded the insulin into his subcutaneous tissue. From there, the protein of twenty-one amino acids would find its way into Landis's deteriorating circulatory system. Diabetes was the latest manifestation of the accelerated aging process eating away at Jerry Landis, his pancreas the most recent organ to betray him. The rhythmic *whir-pffft whir-pffft whir-pffft* was evidence of an earlier betrayal.

"Technically, the entire pancreas hasn't gone bad, sir," Dr. Putnam said. "It's just a small group of cells within the pancreas called islets of Langerhans. They secrete the hormones that regulate your blood sugar levels." He picked up the plastic pancreas that was on Landis's desk and pointed at the offending islets. "See, these are—"

"Shut up and give me the report." Jerry Landis tossed the syringe into a trash can and tucked in his shirt. He was in a mood.

Dr. Putnam was a certified cardiac surgeon and Xenotech's top researcher, and he was here to bring Jerry Landis up-to-date on the two areas of research on which the company was focused: (1) solving the cross-species organ rejection problem, and (2) curing Werner's syndrome. Of the two, Landis would have preferred the cure, but if that wasn't going to happen he at least wanted to be able to replace his organs as they failed.

"Well, sir," Dr. Putnam stalled as he searched for a good spin to put on the bad news. "Last week's trial was a success in the sense that we eliminated the latest antirejection drug."

"Among other things," Jerry Landis said. *Whir-pffft whir-pffft whir-pffft.*

Dr. Putnam looked at the floor, caught. "Yes, sir, uh, there was nothing we could do."

"Don't sweat it," Jerry Landis said. "It's the price that must be paid for progress."

"Yes, sir, it is," Putnam agreed.

"You just better hope we make some goddamn progress before you're the one paying the price," Landis said with more than a hint of threat. He looked at the interior of the model pancreas. "I assume another trial is imminent?"

"Yes, sir, we have several scheduled over the next few weeks. I honestly believe we're very close now. In the past month we've completely overhauled the daclizumab monoclonal antibody protocols. And we're getting tremendous results with both the CTLA4-IG and the 5C8 protein studies."

"What about the bone marrow stem cell project?" Jerry Landis asked.

"It's progressed much faster than any of us imagined."

Jerry Landis threw the plastic pancreas at Dr. Putnam. "For the amount of money I'm pumping into this I'm expecting better imaginations! Now, goddammit, what about the helicase research?" *Whir-pffft whir-pffft whir-pffft.* Jerry Landis's face began to blanch.

"Well, we've narrowed the location of the gene to a stretch of chromosome three. But it contains about a million individual bases," Dr. Putnam said, referring to the chemical information which was telling Jerry Landis's body to age at twice the normal rate. Suddenly, Jerry Landis looked severely distressed—and not because of the magnitude of the chromosome three problem. He pitched forward violently onto his desk, scattering the plastic organs onto the carpet. The force of hitting the desk pushed some air up through his windpipe, "Oooophf." Desperately, he extended his right arm toward one of the desk drawers, but he couldn't reach it. *Whir-pffft whir-pfff whir-pffft* . . . Something was going wrong, Dr. Putnam thought, but what the hell was it? A stroke? My God, that would be horrible; he'd be unemployed. He leaned down to listen as his boss struggled to say something. It sounded like "Elvis."

"Elvis, sir? What about him?" Perhaps something had prompted Mr. Landis to do an Elvis impersonation—and it wasn't a bad one if he was going for Elvis on the bathroom floor.

Whir-pffft whir-pffft whir-pffft whir-pffft . . . It was slowing dangerously.

Landis gathered his last bit of strength and said it again, this time more clearly. "L-VAD."

"Ohhh!" Dr. Putnam said. "It must be your batteries."

A few years ago, Mr. Landis had been betrayed by his heart, and it wasn't love gone bad, it was simply that his pump was giving up. It turned out the solution was not a heart transplant but rather a left ventricular assist device, an L-VAD, a low-tech-looking device about the size of a hamburger that was implanted in his abdomen and connected by a spray hose to his left ventricle. The noisy little pneumatic device weighed about a pound and a half and was attached to an external battery belt which Landis wore like a fanny pack. The only problem with batteries is they don't last forever.

Whir-pffft whir-pffft whir-pffft whir-pffft . . .

Dr. Putnam hurried to the desk drawer and found a second battery pack. He plugged the electrical jack into the charged pack and Jerry Landis jerked back to life. *Whir-pffft whir-pffft whir-pffft!* He turned blue and looked as if he had been struck by lightning. Dr. Putnam slapped his boss hard on the back, causing him suddenly to suck in enough air to deflate a blimp. "Sweet Jesus!" Jerry Landis gasped. "It took you long enough!" Landis adjusted the electrical flow down a few amps to the regular setting. *Whir-pffft whir-pffft whir-pffft.*

"Sorry, sir, I thought you said 'Elvis.' " He got on his knees and began gathering the plastic organs.

"Goddamn idiot! What does it look like, I'm going to Graceland?"

"No, sir, I . . ."

"Can't you see I'm dying? Get your ass back to the lab and find me a cure!"

"Yes sir." Dr. Putnam tossed the spleen onto the desk and scurried away.

Jerry Landis sat back in his chair ready to kill, but damn sure not ready to die.

Paul was part of a network of activists who kept in touch via E-mail and electronic bulletin boards. They used Internet resources to gather information and to post their protests and invite one another to help out at demonstrations. Over the past several weeks, Paul had spent all of his spare time getting the word out on a protest he planned on staging. He told his fellow activists that he would write and distribute the press release and make the signs if they would just show up to march and yell slogans for a few hours. Paul had stayed up until three in the morning painting and stapling the placards for the protest—and it showed. Dark circles underscored Paul's tired eyes, and he stifled a yawn as he unloaded the last of the signs he had made.

"You okay?" Georgette asked.

"Yeah, just a little tired."

It was dawn and Paul was there with the signs, several boxes of doughnuts, and a thermos full of coffee. He hoped some of the morning news shows would send camera crews out to film the demonstration and maybe do an interview, thus exposing the bad guys.

The protest was aimed at Cel-Tech Foods, Inc., a wholly-owned subsidiary of Cel-Tech Labs, where Fred Symon had worked twenty years earlier. Cel-Tech Foods had become the nation's largest producer/processor of genetically engineered fruits and vegetables. It was also a fast-rising power in the world of agribusiness influence. However, since there's no point in staging a protest if no one sees it, this one wasn't being held at Cel-Tech's facilities in rural Stanislaus County, near Modesto. Instead, it was being staged in Menlo Park in front of the offices of Cel-Tech's parent company, Landaq, Incorporated.

Through his network of activist contacts, Paul had learned about some sealed grand jury testimony regarding Mr. Gilbert Healms, the current secretary of agriculture, and his ties to Cel-Tech Foods. It seemed that Cel-Tech had given Secretary Healms some gifts, trips, and favors totaling $350,000 in exchange for some preferential and highly profitable treatment by the USDA, the government entity charged with overseeing food product companies. Cel-Tech had also funneled $40,000 in soft money to the failed congressional campaign of Secretary Healms's brother, Ross Healms. This was Jerry Landis's idea of participatory democracy, and Paul felt it was his obligation to expose such behavior.

After a doughnut and a cup of coffee, Paul picked up a sign and started marching. Georgette, eating for two now, had a second and then a third doughnut before joining the picket line. A steady stream of traffic passed by but no one seemed to care. Even when Paul waved his Honk for Corporate Honesty & Governmental Integrity sign, no one did. No one stopped to offer support. They were too lazy or just plain apathetic or they had other things to do. It was discouraging but Paul tried to not let it show. He figured other protesters would show up at any minute. Georgette hoped, for Paul's sake, that somebody would. This was what Paul lived for, and she knew how a bad turnout like this chipped away at Paul's spirit. Paul never complained about his lack of support. But he would sometimes offer unsolicited explanations and excuses for why no one had shown up. "You know," he said to Georgette after an hour, "I think the problem is that PETA is having a big antifur rally at Fisherman's Wharf today. I should have scheduled this better."

"Don't worry about it," Georgette said. "We're doing fine on our own."

Paul looked toward the mirrored windows of the Landaq building and wondered if Landis was standing there, with Paul's latest letter in his hand, watching. Every time he staged one of these demonstrations, Paul hoped he would have a chance to confront Jerry Landis. But he never showed up. No one ever showed up. Paul joked that he had them on the run but he knew the truth was that he just didn't have anyone's attention.

They marched alone for another hour before another activist finally showed up. He looked like a lost Dead-head, right down to the tie-dye T-shirt and the dilated pupils. *"Que pasa?"* he said. "Oh, wow, like doughnuts!" He ate several before joining the protest. He said his name was Tom and his conversations were short and wild. "Man, like I remember Three Mile Island like it was yesterday. I was there, man. I was backstage with the Stones. Whoa, wait a minute, dude, I'm thinking of Altamont."

It went like that for about an hour before Georgette asked Tom if he was willing to try a new type of transcendental meditation protest. All he had to do was walk with his sign while silently chanting "Om." It worked fine except that Tom soon fell into a trance and dropped his sign.

Eventually a television news crew showed up but decided not to do a segment since two and a half people protesting without the help of some graphic visual aid didn't make very good TV news. "I need some good pictures," the producer said. On top of that, since Paul didn't have any solid evidence about the sealed grand jury proceedings the producer decided to go look for a house fire or something more "visually newsworthy."

After the television crew left, Tom snapped out of his trance and said he had to go. Bob Weir was doing a concert in Golden Gate Park and Tom had the acid concession.

It was early afternoon and obvious that no one else was going to show up. Paul convinced Georgette to take it easy and sit in the shade. She was pregnant and he didn't want anything to go wrong with that. For the next hour she watched her Don Quixote, all alone, tilting at the windmill. She shouted encouragement and told jokes in the hope of maintaining his sense of commitment. She knew how important this was for him and she didn't want him to lose that.

But by mid-afternoon Paul decided it was time to call it a day. Georgette looked like she needed something to eat. Besides, Paul was exhausted and, though he'd never admit it, he was beginning to feel like a fool marching around out there with his sign all alone.

January 23, 1964  Dr. James D. Hardy transplants a chimpanzee's heart into a human. The patient lives for approximately ninety minutes.

8

Dr. Gibbs had put it off as long as he could. Although collecting testicles was not exactly what he'd had in mind when he decided to make a career change, he knew that if he wanted to get off the road and get that hundred-thousand-dollar job with Xenotech he'd have to make the call sooner or later, so he picked up the phone and dialed.

The answer came on the second ring. "Arty here."

"Yes, Arty, hello, this is Dr. Gibbs." He sounded chipper and professional. His years in sales had resulted in a polished insincerity that few detected. "How's that kidney?"

"It's working overtime, Doc. Thanks for asking," Arty said. "How're you doing?"

"Good, thanks. Listen, I was wondering if you might be interested in . . . well, in another transaction?"

Arty didn't hesitate. "Long as you don't want my other kidney, I'm game." Arty laughed at his clever renal humor.

"No," Dr. Gibbs said, forcing a chuckle of his own. "No, as a matter of fact, it's something you still have two of. Could you come to my office so we can discuss it?"

"Sure thing, when's a good time?"

"The sooner the better," Dr. Gibbs said. He wanted to get this over with.

Arty had a mid-morning appointment at the sperm bank, but said he'd could come in around two. Dr. Gibbs gave Arty the Xenotech address and said he looked forward to seeing him again, which was as true as saying he looked forward to having his hemorrhoids removed with a rusty pair of pliers.

As an enticement, and in lieu of actually signing Dr. Gibbs to an employment contract, Jerry Landis had provided him with a nice office and a private parking space at the Xenotech facility. Landis had a sign with DR. L. GIBBS on it placed in front of the parking spot and a similar nameplate on his office door, playing nicely on Dr. Gibbs's insecurity. Just driving into One Biotech Center and pulling his car into the personalized parking space gave Dr. Gibbs a feeling of accomplishment. Jerry Landis knew that trivial little perks like that had tremendous psychic value to people like Dr. Gibbs, and they cost a lot less than actually paying a good salary, so it was, in the vernacular of the business world, a win-win situation.

Dr. Gibbs had a few hours to kill before Arty arrived, so he made some calls in an attempt to find out about the feasibility of a testicular transplant. The first few doctors he spoke with scoffed at the notion so he decided to look for someone whose ideas didn't conform with those of the medical establishment, a person who perhaps had lost his or her medical license. The woman at the Board of Medical Examiners was surprisingly helpful, providing Dr. Gibbs with a lengthy list of defrocked urologists. One by one he called these urogenital professionals; some of their numbers had been disconnected, others were too bitter to speak. But not Dr. Vines. He was keenly interested in what Dr. Gibbs proposed, not only because there was good money involved but also because he felt he had been wrongly stripped of his medical license and he still liked trying things that hadn't been tried before.

Dr. Gibbs eventually got around to asking the delicate question. Dr. Vines giggled inappropriately and said, "Yeah, they took my license. But it turned out to be a blessing." There was something about the giggle that kept Dr. Gibbs from asking why Dr. Vines had lost his license. Instead he asked what the doctor was doing now. "I'm the founder and director of the Castro Valley Life Extension Institute and Spa." He went on to explain that prior to being drummed out of the ranks of the board approved, he had been investigating an area some people were calling "andropause" or "viropause"—the male equivalent of menopause. "It's an interesting area," he said. "Some think it may be the fountain of youth. Anyway, after the board finished its inquisition, I founded my institute and have been very busy ever since."

Dr. Vines explained that he was treating men in the forty-and-over set with hormone cocktails consisting of testosterone, dehydroepiandrosterone (DHEA), melatonin, and human growth hormone (hGH). He said baby boomers were refusing to take the aging process lying down and were fighting back with the hormone treatments he was providing.

Dr. Gibbs knew hGH was harvested from the pituitary glands of human cadavers and was quite expensive. He also thought it was regulated. "I thought you needed a prescription for some of that stuff," Dr. Gibbs said. There followed a silence on the line. Dr. Gibbs immediately realized his comment might have a chilling effect on the disgraced urologist and if he wanted help from Dr. Vines he had to smooth things over. "What I meant by that was I think the FDA and the Board of Medical Examiners are a pain in the ass."

"Amen to that," Dr. Vines said, his tone acrid. "Sorry bunch of bastards, telling me what I can and can't dispense. Well, I showed them. Before they started the hearings on my matter I stockpiled a fucking warehouse of the stuff."

"Good for you," Dr. Gibbs said. "Now the reason I'm—"

Dr. Vines interrupted. "Say, lemme ask you, Doctor. How's your angle of erection?"

"My what?" Dr. Gibbs asked.

"Your angle of erection. How good's your woody? That's a big part of my business. If your horn's not looking up the way it used to, I guarantee I can fix it. It's simple, really. As we age the body stops producing the hormones it did when we were young."

"I see your point," Dr. Gibbs said. "But the reason—"

"I'm telling you, the pharmaceutical companies have come up with some unbelievable stuff. You ever heard of prostaglandin E1?"

"No, can't say that I have," Dr. Gibbs said.

"Give you a hard-on that'll last an hour. There are a couple of others called papaverine and phentolamine. Just inject it and *boing*! You're in business."

Dr. Gibbs blanched. "You inject it? Where?"

"Where do you think?" Dr. Vines asked. You could almost hear his demented smile.

Dr. Gibbs didn't want to think, not about jamming a hypodermic into his johnson.

"What about your maximum ejaculatory distance? I bet that's not what it used to be either," Dr. Vines said. "But let me tell you, I got men, older than you I bet, who are shooting close to five feet! That's better than a horny teenager. You should see the looks on their faces!"

Dr. Gibbs saw a grotesque image of middle-aged men with their yardsticks out. He began to grow uncomfortable with the direction of the conversation. He had to get it back on track. "Dr. Vines, I'm sorry to cut this short, but let me ask you, if I manage to secure the gonad, are you willing to transplant it?"

"Ready, willing, and able," he said.

Merle Grimes was released from the Deckern County Psychiatric Hospital not so much because he had recovered but rather because he didn't have the money to pay the bills any longer. He also didn't appear to pose a danger to himself or the community. Merle was mostly in a catatonic state, though periodically he became animated and made barking and screeching noises that were remarkably like those of baboons. The mental health professional at the facility told Merle's cousin Billy Bob that it was a rare conversion disorder he called hysterical neurosis. The more accurate diagnosis would have been post-traumatic baboon attack syndrome, but such a diagnosis didn't exist, at least not yet.

All of this led Billy Bob to organize a fund-raiser for poor Merle. He contacted all their cousins and, despite company regulations to the contrary, invited them all to the Xenotech facility for a B.Y.O.B. barbecue. The turn-out was tremendous despite (or perhaps because of) the fact that the rumor mill had created some wild tales about what exactly went on in those mysterious woods. Cousin Frank brought a couple of jumping mules for the pony ride and cousin Betty brought her cotton candy machine and a ten-pound sack of sugar. Others brought venison tenderloins, possum sausages, and rack of racoon (small but gamy).

Merle was propped up in a folding chair with a plastic bucket in his lap. Billy Bob taped a hand-lettered sign on the bucket that said, DONATIONS PROUDLY ACCEPTED. He started things off with a one-dollar bill and two nickels. Throughout the afternoon Merle's cousins passed by and put a little money into the collection bucket. Each time they did this, Merle would make a baboon noise. The drunker they got, the more money they put in and the more noise Merle made. At one point, second cousin Roy drew a line in the dirt about eight feet in front of where Merle was seated. The kids lined up and attempted to bank coins off Merle's chest into the bucket. As the day wore on, everyone was having a grand time, with Merle providing the lion's share of the entertainment.

Roughly an hour into the fundraiser, something stirred in the woods surrounding the grounds. The baboons were curious about the peculiar calls coming from the clearing. They didn't know what to make of it, just as none of Merle's cousins would have known what to make of what was going on out in the woods. In fact, even the biologists working at Xenotech's Biomedical Research Center of the South would have been shocked to know what their work had led to.

In the wild, assuming they are not pregnant or suckling, adult female baboons enter the estrous phase for one week out of every month. During the first few days they mate with sub-adult males and during the last few days with the dominant males. The gestation period for a baboon lasts between five and eight months. They typically have only single births, though twins are born occasionally. All of that works wonderfully in nature and keeps the number of baboons in line with what their ecosystem can support. But in captivity, handled with care by geneticists, miraculous things are possible. And miraculous things is what Jerry Landis had in mind.

Years earlier, when he raised the capital to start the baboon farm, Jerry Landis learned all there was to know about the animals, and he told his scientists exactly how he wanted them changed. Their first, and easiest, task was to begin breeding the animals for size. They did this because the organs of a normal baboon aren't large enough to support the function of an adult human. Baby Fae received the walnut-sized heart of a young baboon, but such an organ would not have been any use to her parents. The scientists next tinkered with shortening the gestation period. The geneticists managed to get it down to four months, thus allowing each fertile female to deliver nearly three times a year. Finally they began invitro manipulations which guaranteed multiple births. When the scientists were done, a single female was able to produce up to a dozen young annually, up from only one or two. With the special veterinary care they received and the plentiful food supply, the baboons thrived.

The reason for all this genetic manipulation was simple. Once it became obvious that organ transplants were feasible, Jerry Landis knew it was inevitable that the process would be perfected—that's just how medical science worked. And once it was perfected, it was equally obvious that the supply of transplantable human organs would never meet the demand. That was the irony of the science; the more successful it was, the more it was in demand. And the more demand there was, the fewer number of people could benefit from it due to the increasing supply problem.

But why baboons? Genetically speaking, humans differ from one another by about .1 percent. Chimpanzees differ from humans genetically by about 1.5 percent, which means their DNA is fifteen times more different than human DNA than individual human DNAs are from one another. Still, chimps are the animals most closely related to humans genetically and thus they're the best animal for man to turn to for replacement parts. However, seventeen years ago chimpanzees were on the fast track to endangered species status and acquiring them was becoming expensive and involved more hassle than Jerry Landis felt they were worth. So he turned to baboons, our genetic second cousins. Baboons are roughly 5 percent different from humans, which means their DNA is about fifty times different from human DNA—a significant difference, but nothing compared to the swine–primate DNA difference.

Because of size and marketing considerations, most of the world's current xenografting research was focused on swine. Biotech corporations were in a rush to create the perfect transgenic swine organs for transplanting into humans. They chose pigs because: (A) they mature rapidly; (B) they have a short (114-day) gestation period; (C) they produce large litters; and (D) their organs are the right size and are anatomically suited to human function.

An equally important factor that pigs bring to the table is marketability. Marketing specialists found that consumers had what they called a high "gag factor" when it came to the notion of slaughtering primates for spare parts. However, since pigs are already raised for slaughter, the gag factor regarding the harvesting of their organs is almost nil. The downside of raising pigs for parts, as Jerry Landis saw it, was twofold. First, swine organ rejection would be more difficult to overcome because the genetic difference was so great. Second, the world pig population was already near 850 million. Hell, in the next ten years or so, everybody and his brother could have a transgenic pig farm.

But if—many years ago—you'd had the foresight to begin breeding large baboons, then you had two distinct advantages. The first was that baboon organ rejection should be easy to overcome (relative to swine organ rejection), and once you created the baboon organ antirejection drug you would have an absolute corner on the market because you would be the only one with the parts and the appropriate immunosuppressant.

The original idea was to keep the population steady around ten thousand, but the genetic alterations in conjunction with the almost unlimited food supply had resulted in a population boom. There were now nearly fifty thousand of the huge baboons spread out over the ten-thousand-acre compound. They lived in troops of nearly five hundred, almost ten times the size of an average troop on the African savannah. Unfortunately, the scientists weren't fully aware of the magnitude of the overcrowding, thus they had neither arranged to limit reproduction nor increased the food supply. So, as the number of baboons per acre increased, the normally cooperative and social animals became increasingly violent as they fought over the limited resources.

But right now the baboons were more curious than anything else. Drawn by the peculiar barks and hoots and screeches Merle was making, about a hundred of them gathered along the tree line that surrounded the grounds. There they listened and wondered what was going on. What unspeakable things could force one of their own to make such noises?

Cousin Roy triggered the whole thing when he bounced a fifty-cent piece off Merle's sole remaining front tooth, causing Merle to let out a sharp yelp. To the baboons, it was a cry for help. And one of the few things the Xenotech scientists hadn't bred out of these large primates was the instinct to help one of their own when in distress. Their black lips peeled back to bare their dangerous canines, and thirty high-ranking males led the charge—bountiful, thick shoulder manes exaggerating their already substantial stature. Several dozen sub-adults and juveniles followed, vicious and enthusiastic and hoping to climb in the social ranks based on their performance. The ground rumbled as ten thousand pounds of muscular quadruped charged into the clearing.

Billy Bob was the first to see them. He pointed but couldn't speak. He could, however, run like hell. Women grabbed their babies and fled, screaming, into the security building. Several of the dominant husbands—ex-college football players for State, Southern, and Ole Miss—ran bravely out to engage the oncoming baboons. It looked like homecoming kickoff on the Planet of the Apes. The men didn't stand a chance. The huge primates brushed past them as if they were weeds. But the baboons weren't intent on harming the people. They were simply going in to get Merle, and the closer they got, the more Merle barked. This of course set up a vicious cycle.

In the midst of all the noise, two of the larger males snatched Merle from his chair, spilling his mental health fund of forty-eight dollars and seventy-six cents onto the ground. Several of the sub-adults grabbed picnic baskets and ice chests filled with beer and wine coolers. Some of the juveniles (the baboons, that is) were screeching and jumping up and down on the hoods of the pickup trucks while others reached in and took the shotguns from the racks. The baboons' mission to save Merle ended as quickly as it had started. The entire troop withdrew into the pine forest and disappeared. That night, Merle was deep in the woods in consort with an adult female. As she used her rough fingers to part his hair and remove bits of grass and dead skin, Merle sipped a raspberry wine cooler and looked quite satisfied.

❈   ❈   ❈

Three days had passed since Georgette had gone to the abortion clinic and she was still ashamed. She didn't know how to tell Paul what she had done. But she knew she had to tell him; she owed him that much. He was understanding and supportive, wasn't he? And he loved her, didn't he? Besides, she hadn't actually had the abortion; she had only considered it. Keeping the fetus wasn't a capitulation to the anti-abortion community; Georgette had simply exercised one of the choices she was glad to have. And she wasn't really worried that Paul would hold against her the mere fact that the thought had crossed her mind. She was worried about something else. She was worried about her motive for *not* getting the abortion. She worried that keeping the fetus was nothing more than pure selfishness. Like a common breeder, Georgette wanted a child the same way you might want a new television or a new car. A child was something to love and something that would probably love you back, at least until the teenage years. Children could be a wonderful source of entertainment and pride. They were like talking pets, except you could never count on a pet to take care of you in your dotage.

To Georgette the argument that *not* having children was selfish was arrant nonsense, on par with the notion that having an abortion was playing God. Weren't those people familiar with the Book of Genesis? Wasn't *creating* life a lot more God-like than terminating one? Having a child, it seemed to Georgette, was the ultimate act of selfishness. It would be different, she thought, if the world was a decent and just place. But bringing a child into a world gone as bad as this one—with no signs that things would ever improve—just so you could enjoy its company was, on reflection, difficult to justify. Sure, she and Paul would love the child and do all they could to see that its future was secure—it was the least they could do given that the child had no choice of whether to be born in the first place. But they couldn't guarantee the child wouldn't be stricken by any of the horrors that plagued human existence. In fact, they couldn't guarantee anything, except that they wanted a child. What could be more selfish?

Of course that whole argument assumed selfishness was a bad thing. Maybe it wasn't. Maybe some types of self-indulgent behavior were good. Maybe . . . maybe not. Why bother Paul with all this? Georgette thought. She was going to have the child. Paul would be happy, and the baby, well, the baby would just have to take its chances. It wasn't a perfect world.

"What about the tenth?" Paul asked. He was holding a calendar.

Georgette was startled. She hadn't heard Paul come into the room "The tenth what?" she asked distractedly.

"For the wedding. How's the tenth?"

"Oh. Sorry, I was thinking about something else," Georgette said. "Let me see the calendar." She looked at the tenth before the problem occurred to her. "That's no good. The band's booked on the tenth."

"Damn, I thought we had it." Paul turned to leave, then stopped. "Sweetheart, are you okay? You've been acting preoccupied the last few days."

This was Georgette's chance to tell Paul what she had done, or almost done. She could tell him all she'd thought about, ask him if he thought something was wrong with her. It wasn't good to keep secrets like this, was it? "Well . . ." she said tentatively. "The other day—"

And then the phone rang. "Hold that thought," Paul said. He picked up the phone. After a few seconds Paul looked stunned, and for a freakish second Georgette wondered if someone from the abortion clinic was calling to see if she had changed her mind. She couldn't tell if Paul was getting good news or bad, but he was definitely getting news. Finally, Paul spoke. "Sure, Tuesday's fine," he said. "I'll be there." And then he hung up, looking rather pleased with himself.

"Be where?" Georgette asked.

"Jerry Landis's office. He got my letter and he wants to talk."

❊   ❊   ❊

"Varicoceles is a condition in which the veins in the spermatic cord enlarge and feel like a bag of worms." Dr. Gibbs closed the book he was reading, then delicately adjusted himself. He was in his office boning up on interesting testicle facts in preparation for his meeting with Arty, who was due any minute. There was nothing in the literature about testicular transplants, but Dr. Vines had made it sound completely plausible. He said it was just a matter of tapping the new vas deferens into the existing seminal vesicles and making sure the new gonad had a blood supply. From there, Dr. Vines said, the existing prostate, Cowper's gland, and urethra would supply the semen and function as the delivery system. Dr. Vines pointed out that the sperm from the new testis would not be that of the new owner. Dr. Gibbs said he understood. He had tried to explain that to the recipient but, he told Dr. Vines, the customer wanted what he wanted and in his experience it was best to operate under the assumption that the customer was always right.

A crashing sound at the door startled Dr. Gibbs. He imagined it was Arty arriving and losing control of his motorized wheelchair. He imagined further that Arty was now flailing on the floor like a wounded bandicoot. Dr. Gibbs stood and went to help, but before he got to the door it exploded open and he was face-to-face with the biggest tattooed son of a bitch he had ever seen.

"Hey, Doc," Arty said from his wheelchair. "I'd like you to meet my friend, Bonedigger."

The biker grunted something and forged into the office, moving furniture as he went so Arty could wheel his chair in without crashing into anything else. "I hired Bones here to be my chauffeur," Arty said. "Mass transit just wasn't getting me around fast enough to do all the deals I've got going."

Dr. Gibbs noticed the tiny helmet on the head of the huge chauffeur. The thing was so small in relation to the head that it almost looked like a hatch into Bonedigger's head. The biker's ensemble was completed with leather chaps, a denim vest, and heavy black boots. Arty explained that ever since he learned there was a black market for human organs, he'd been shopping himself around. He had been thrilled to find that selling solid organs paid much more handsomely than selling fluids and participating in experiments.

Dr. Gibbs kept an eye on Bonedigger while Arty discussed his improving financials. It was only when Arty stopped talking and Dr. Gibbs looked at him the second time that he noticed the eye patch. The doctor pointed at it and asked what happened.

"Aaaarrrggghhh." Arty did his pirate imitation. "You're gonna love this, matey. I found myself an ophthalmologist who needed a cornea quicker than the blink of an eye bank," he said. "Negotiated a great deal too, including the patch." Arty struck a pose. "Sort of makes me look like the Hathaway Shirt guy, don't you think?"

"Yes, quite handsome," Dr. Gibbs said. Looking at the little one-armed, one-legged, one-kidneyed, one-eyed man, Dr. Gibbs wondered how he was going to broach the subject of the one nut. He sighed and began to long for the good old days when he flew to Calcutta for parts. He turned to go back to his desk. Bonedigger was rummaging through his drawers. "Hey! What're you doing?" Dr. Gibbs asked.

"Just lookin'," Bones replied. "The hell you gonna do about it?" The biker had a look about him that the doctor had never seen before. Dark rings collared small bloodshot eyes set too close together for most primates. Crumbs of some sort nested in his pork chop-size sideburns.

"Fellas! C'mon," Arty said, "it's not my habit to intrude, but we're here to talk business."

"Sorry," Bonedigger said. "I was just lookin' for something to do this with." He pulled a small plastic bag of dirty white powder from his pants, his home-cooked crank. He dipped a long filthy fingernail into the bag, then jammed it up a nostril.

"Fine," Dr. Gibbs said, surrendering to the madness.

"Why don't we talk business?" He gestured for Arty to sit, but of course he already was. Bones sat next to him.

"Now, Doc," Arty began, "on the phone you said you were interested in something I still had two of. I hope it wasn't a cornea." He gestured at his eye patch.

"No," Dr. Gibbs said, "it's . . ." Bonedigger suddenly hit himself on the back of the head and blinked furiosly. After a moment he made a rude noise that began somewhere deep in a troubled sinus. ". . . more delicate than that." Dr. Gibbs had decided he wasn't going to let Bonedigger distract him anymore. He was just going to throw the question out there and see what happened. "Arty, I've got a patient in need of a testicle."

"Whoa!" Arty accidentally hit the joystick on the wheelchair and he lurched sideways, hitting one of Bonedigger's boots and spilling into his lap. "You're right, I do still have two of those," he said.

"Two what?" Bones asked as he put Arty back in the chair.

"Balls," Arty said.

Bones stood up. "Hell, I got two balls." He pulled down his pants to back up his claim. They were, in fact, two very large balls. They appeared to be nearly the size of jumbo hen's eggs.

"Yes, indeed you do," Dr. Gibbs said. "But I'm afraid my client hasn't got enough room in his scrotum for one of those. Sorry."

"I wasn't offerin' anyway," Bones said. He pulled up his pants and sat back down.

"Doc, here's the problem," Arty said. "I been making steady money at the sperm bank with these babies, not to mention the job satisfaction." He winked at Dr. Gibbs. "So if I part with one I need to know that I'll still be able to deliver the goods, otherwise my price goes up."

"Absolutely," the doctor said. "Your other testis will actually compensate and you'll produce the same amount as you used to." Dr. Gibbs made this up just to get the deal done.

"Fair enough," Arty said. "What're you offering?"

Jerry Landis had authorized Dr. Gibbs to go as high as fifty thousand dollars but said he could keep the difference if he got one for less. Based on his extensive organ experience in India, Dr. Gibbs arrived at what he thought was a fair price. "How's seventy-five bucks sound?"

"Not good," Arty replied. "What do you say we double that?" Arty turned and winked at Bonedigger.

Dr. Gibbs looked shocked. "A hundred fifty? Whew! I don't know, Arty, there are a lot of nuts out there."

"Doc, I'm firm on that," Arty said. "Not a dollar less, plus it comes with a guarantee. You don't like it, you can bring it back."

Dr. Gibbs refused to allow that image to form in his head. Instead he smiled. "Arty, you got a deal."

Arty slapped his hand on his armrest. "Now we're talking!"

9

Paul was on his way and he was taking his time. He wanted to savor every moment of the trip to Jerry Landis's office. And what better way than taking the bus again? In truth Paul was taking the bus because Georgette needed the car to go meet with caterers. Still, he liked that it felt as if he were rewriting an old scene, this time to favor *his* character instead of the bad guy. Paul intentionally sat in the same seat in the back of the bus where he had sat twenty-three years earlier. And just as intentionally he wasn't wearing a suit; Paul intended to show Jerry Landis very little respect this trip. Paul was shot through with confidence and looking forward to confronting the son of a bitch who had used that naive young boy for a cheap PR photo op. The man who destroyed wilderness for profit and who, more importantly, had killed his father. And this time, instead of a twenty-page proposal, Paul carried a different document, one that Jerry Landis could throw away if he liked but one which he'd have to deal with either way.

Paul had not seen Jerry Landis in person since 1978. The bastard hadn't attended any of the legal proceedings surrounding Fred Symon's death, opting instead to send his lawyers. Paul wondered if today Jerry Landis would finally apologize for what he had done. But, for a couple of different reasons, Paul decided not to bring that up. First he wanted to see if Jerry Landis would volunteer an apology, and second Paul wanted the meeting to be about business. He didn't want to sidetrack onto personal issues. If Landis didn't apologize today, Paul would simply keep hounding him until he did.

As the bus exited the freeway it looked for a moment as if Paul might not live to see Jerry Landis because the idiot backing up on the shoulder of the road suddenly pulled backwards into the path of oncoming traffic. It was a Buick roughly the size of a Sherman tank. The driver, having overshot his exit, apparently felt everyone else had just better get the hell out of his way as he backed onto the freeway. The bus driver cut sharply to the right, almost pitching down a sharp incline onto the frontage road twenty feet below. Paul watched the six-car pileup behind them and wondered what color paint ball Georgette would have proposed for the offending Buick. Lobster red? Nah. Taupe? Doubtful. Livid violet? Perhaps.

A few minutes later the bus stopped across the street from the parking lot outside the gleaming high-tech tower that was Xenotech, Incorporated. It was only a mile from the old Landaq headquarters. Paul grabbed his file folder, exited the bus, and headed for the tower.

After seven cups of bad coffee the security guard was on edge. He eyed Paul with suspicion from the moment he entered the building. Most of the visitors to Xenotech were scientists or weaselly-looking venture capitalists, most of whom could be described as average in size, but this guy was huge. His arms were sculpted and straining his short sleeves. Paul looked like he could do some damage if he wanted.

As a college linebacker, Paul had a good career, but he wasn't drafted by any NFL franchise, though the 49'ers did invite him for a tryout. Paul declined, opting instead to take his fund-raising position with the United Citizens lobbying organization, his logic being that he

wanted to help the world become a better place and—
at the same time—he felt it was unlikely he'd blow out
a knee in an office environment. Besides, the savage aspect of football had never appealed to Paul the way it
did to some of the guys he had played with. Up until
college Paul had always been so much bigger than the
players he opposed that he never felt the game was very
violent. Playing Pac-10 ball changed his mind about that,
and the thought of the NFL flat scared him. Paul was
big, not dumb.

As Paul approached the security-and-information
kiosk, the guard's suspicion morphed into raw fear. What
if this big son of a bitch was one of those crazy animal
rights people? The guard reached for the phone to call
for backup but it was too late, Paul was already upon
him, towering over the desk like an avenging angel. "Hi,"
Paul said. "I've got an appointment with Jerry Landis."

Thank God, the guard thought. Dying at the hands of
some eco-terrorist while making minimum wage was not
exactly how he wanted to leave the world. Still, the guard
stayed out of Paul's reach as he made a call to verify his
claim. Once he got the okay, he sent Paul up to the top
floor. As the elevator doors closed behind the intimidat-
ing visitor, the guard thought to himself that maybe it
was time he switched to decaf.

Paul last saw Jerry Landis when Landis was a healthy,
robust young man, six years before he was diagnosed
with Werner's syndrome. So Paul was surprised at the
wizened old coot who shuffled out from behind the desk
to greet him with a warm handshake. "Mr. Symon, please
do come in. It's a pleasure to see you again after so
long," Jerry Landis said. Of course what he meant was,
*I wish you'd curl up and die like your old man, you
pissant letter-writing son of a bitch. Whir-pffft whir-pffft
whir-pffft.*

"Thank you, Mr. Landis. I appreciate your seeing me
on time this go-around." Paul was surprised on a couple
of counts. First was the unexplained mechanical sound
issuing from Jerry Landis's abdomen—that was new since

the last time they had met. The second surprise was how old Landis looked. Paul couldn't help but stare and wonder what the hell happened. Maybe these were the wages of murder and eco-insensitivity. Paul hoped that whatever caused this was as painful as it was unappealing.

Jerry Landis knew his appearance had thrown Paul, but he wasn't going to address that. Better that Paul be confused and curious and kept off guard. "Would you like coffee, juice, anything?" *I'd happily serve you some arsenic, you rat bastard pain in the ass.*

"No thanks," Paul said, "I'm fine." *How about an apology, asshole? I've been waiting twenty years for that.*

Jerry Landis smiled and took his seat behind his desk while Paul looked around the finely appointed office. Pictures and awards covered three of the four walls, the fourth being the imposing monument of books. The desk was covered by thick sheafs of legal and scientific papers and what appeared to be a complete set of human organs modeled in plastic. Glancing at the computer monitor, Paul saw a spreadsheet which suddenly winked out and became a screen saver showing the familiar double helix of human DNA rotating in a star field.

"So you grew up and played ball at Cal," Jerry Landis said out of nowhere. "I remember that interception you made against Washington your senior year." *I just wish one of those big Husky bastards had taken your head off so you never would have darkened my doorstep.* "Yes sir," Jerry Landis said, "that was one hell of a run."

Paul nodded modestly at the memory. He had made an unbelievable one-handed grab and powered his way sixty yards up the field for the game-winning touchdown. "That was a long time ago," Paul said. "Were you at the game?"

Jerry Landis looked up from adjusting the battery pack on his L-VAD and saw that Paul was waiting for a response to something. "I'm sorry, did you ask me a question? My hearing's not as good as it used to be."

"It's not important," Paul said rather loudly.

"I'm looking into cochlear implants," Jerry Landis said. "It's truly amazing what they can do these days."

"Yes sir, it is," Paul said matter-of-factly. He leaned forward, toward Jerry Landis. "The question is whether we should do things just because we're able to."

"Ahhh yes." Jerry Landis tapped his index finger on the sheet of paper directly in front of him. "So you said in your letter." He picked up the letter and glanced at it. "If I understand correctly, your position is that our research here is, how did you say it?" Landis put on his reading glasses and scanned the letter. " Undermining natural selection.'" *Whir-pffft whir-pffft whir-pffft.*

Paul nodded. "Not just Xenotech, all the biotech companies. A lot of people in the area of population studies argue that in order to achieve an optimal sustainable population—"

"Let me tell you what disturbed me most about your letter," Landis interrupted. *You pig-ignorant, short-sighted piece of shit.* Jerry Landis looked seriously disturbed as he leaned across the desk toward Paul. "Quite frankly, it smacks of eugenics." He squinted, giving Paul a disapproving sideways glance. "You're not connected in any way to the Colonist Fund, are you?"

"The what?"

"The Colonist Fund," Jerry Landis said. "They financed Nazi eugenic projects in the forties. Today they concern themselves with worries about minorities lowering the overall intelligence level of the population and other morally reprehensible positions. They advocate sterilization of minorities on welfare, that sort of thing."

"Oh, so now I'm a neo-Marxist Malthusian, is that it?" Paul asked with a derisive laugh. "I've never heard of your Colonist Fund," Paul said calmly. *You infectious, slug-hearted bastard.* "Resorting to bush-league rhetorical devices is a fairly pathetic tactic, Mr. Landis, and it's got nothing to do with the merit of my argument." Paul felt the urge to reach across the desk and jam all those plastic organs up Jerry Landis's arrogant ass. But instead he just smiled. "There's no connection between my position and this Colonist Fund," Paul said. "Though I understand why someone like you would say something like that." Another smile. *Just wait, you imperious scumbag. Have I got a surprise for you.*

Jerry Landis squinted his bad eyes and nodded suspiciously even though he knew Paul had never heard of the Colonist Fund. He knew this because he had just made it up. But he also knew that Paul saw himself as an egalitarian. Landis hoped Paul would stop his attack on Xenotech's research if he thought there was any hint that his position had racist or Nazi overtones. And that's all Jerry Landis wanted, a brief respite while Paul looked into this Colonist Fund business. If the Xenotech researchers were closing in on the solution to the baboon organ rejection problem, the last thing Jerry Landis needed was an interruption. That's why he had invited Paul in for this chat.

But it looked like Paul wasn't falling for it.

Until now, all of Landis's projects had simply been business deals. Not only that, but business deals Paul couldn't have stopped if he'd wanted to. It didn't matter who Paul had voted for or how many people he got to sign his petitions; the fix was in. But this was different. First of all, while the xenografting research started off as just another business deal, it had become a matter of life and death—specifically Jerry Landis's life and death. Secondly, this was something Paul might actually be able to stop, since several branches of the federal government were starting to talk about regulation.

The dreaded *R* word. Landis had been around the track enough times to know that if so much as one federal agency began regulating xenografting he'd be dead and buried before a sub-committee could agree on the first breakfast menu. Jerry Landis knew this because he had recently acquired an FDA document proposing unimaginably strict guidelines over potential breeding colonies for xenograft animals. So if Paul got around to copying his letters to these agencies, Landis could be dead meat.

"Let me try this from another angle," Landis said. "You say what we're doing undermines natural selection."

Paul nodded.

"But how can that be?" Landis asked. "I mean, if humans are simply another species of animal—which, I believe, is your position—then anything we do is simply a part of nature. And if we do something that results in the extinction of our species, that's natural selection just the same as if we did something that favored our species over another. So we're not undermining the process, Mr. Symon, we're simply a part of it." Jerry Landis held out his hands as if he were delivering the truth.

Paul shook his head ever so slightly. "The difference, Mr. Landis, is that most animals operate on instinct while humans are supposed to operate on intellect. So *we* have a choice to make that other animals don't have. And if we make the wrong choice, which is what you're doing, then we undermine the process and we unnecessarily increase the odds of our extinction."

Jerry Landis made little spurning sounds with his mouth, dismissing Paul's argument. He gave up on debating Darwinist theory and returned to his earlier angle, despite the fact that Paul didn't seem to be falling for it. "Mr. Symon, as a firm believer in the First Amendment I will defend your right to say whatever you want in opposition to my business interests, but this . . ." He pushed Paul's letter away from him as if it were contagious. "This is so offensive, so unlike you, quite frankly, that I had to invite you in to see if you understood what you were saying." Jerry Landis assumed the countenance of a disappointed parent. "I was afraid you'd been duped by the people at the Colonist Fund." *Now get the fuck out of my office, you insignificant, witless cretin.*

Paul stood suddenly and leaned across the desk, looming over the aging entrepreneur. "Mr. Landis, I don't know anything about your Colonist Fund and there's nothing in my position that can be construed as racist. The long-term survival of humans on this planet depends on the rate of our resource consumption, and rich, white, first-world babies are far worse offenders than third-world babies, so the racism argument just doesn't hold. The point is we have already overpopulated the planet and the biotechnology industry serves only to make the problem worse. And I want to know what you are going to do about it!" Paul slammed his hand onto the desk with tremendous force, shattering the plastic pancreas, islets of Langerhans and all. The violence stunned both Paul and Jerry Landis. But Paul didn't let it show.

Whir-pffft whir-pffft whir-pffft "I didn't mean to imply anything, Mr. Symon. I was just curious. It's just that, after reading all your letters over the years I felt I knew you, that's all. I was just looking for an explanation." Landis decided to take a new tack. "Mr. Symon, I'm going to be frank. Let me tell you the real reason I'm pursuing this xenograft research." Landis took a deep, dramatic breath and gazed out the window for a moment before continuing. "Have you ever heard of Werner's syndrome?"

Paul shook his head disinterestedly.

"Well, I have it, Mr. Symon, and as a result, I'm dying."

"Aren't we all," Paul said flatly.

"Yes, but I'm dying twice as fast as everyone else. That's why I look this way. Werner's syndrome is a disease of accelerated aging. They don't give me another year."

"Well at least you have the time to get your affairs in order," Paul said. "Some people don't get that luxury." *Like my dad, you murdering son of a bitch.*

"Yes, well that's true enough," Jerry Landis said. "But my point is that the genie is out of the bottle, Mr. Symon, and there's no putting him back. The science is here, as is the demand. It doesn't matter if Xenotech or someone else does it. The point is, it's going to be done and there's nothing you can do about it." *You sanctimonious, worm-ridden prick. Whir-pffft whir-pffft whir-pffft.*

Paul didn't like being told there was nothing he could do about something. It was bad enough when Georgette said it, but he wasn't going to take it from someone like Jerry Landis, dying or not. But what could he do? The man was right, the genie was out of the bottle. As Paul considered his response he went to the far side of the room to retrieve the pancreatic duct, which had flown farther than any of the other plastic parts. Paul was crossing the room when he noticed a photograph on the far wall. It was only one of many but it caught his eye. It was the photo of himself as a young boy handing over his proposal to a smiling, and much younger, Jerry Landis. It wasn't a fond memory.

"Now, Mr. Symon, I know you're disappointed," Jerry Landis said, "but be realistic. Trying to prevent xenografting would be like trying to stop the space program after *Sputnik*. It's simply not going to happen." He looked at his watch. "And now, I'm afraid I've got to end this meeting as I'm scheduled for some delicate surgery in the morning." *You've wasted enough of my precious time, you festering sack of pus!*

Paul knew what he had to do and he was going to relish doing it. He wasn't going to let Landis win again, not without a real fight. He went back to the chair where he'd been sitting and picked up his file. He pulled out some documents and looked Jerry Landis in the eyes. "You may be right. Maybe there's nothing I can do to stop it." Paul smiled. "But, as you know, I'm willing to try."

Jerry Landis caught a glimpse of the documents. They looked like organizational charts and, in fact, they were. They were from the Department of Health and Human Services, of which the Public Health Service was a part, of which the Food and Drug Administration was another part. Paul got them from the FDA web site. "Let's see," Paul said, reading from one of the charts. " 'Center for Biologics Evaluation and Research, Bradley M. Fairly, director. Office of Regulatory Affairs, Office of Enforcement, Stephen F. Shirley, director.' " Paul turned the page. "Here's a good one, 'Office of Establishment Licensing and Product Surveillance . . .' "

Whir-pffft whir-pffft whir-pffft. Jerry Landis tried to remain calm, but it wasn't easy. Paul was threatening him with bureaucrats, but he might as well have been pointing a gun. *You cocksucker!* Landis started to do the math on bribing his way through these various federal offices, a task he once had the mental capacity to do on the fly. But his doddering brain was no longer capable. Landis would have to find an easier way to deal with the problem.

". . . 'Division of Bioresearch Monitoring and Regulations, Mary M. Drew, director.' How about the Office of Compliance within the Center for Devices and Radiological Health or the Division of Transfusion Transmitted Diseases? Can you believe some of these? Here's a Division of Monoclonal Antibodies, whatever that is," Paul said. "Your tax dollars at work, huh, Mr. Landis? Here's the Center for Drug Evaluation and Research, Office of Compliance, Victor A. Thomas, director . . ." Paul was only halfway through the documents and this was only the FDA. There were similar offices at the CDC and the NIH and they both knew it.

Jerry Landis pulled his checkbook from his coat pocket. "What do you want, Mr. Symon, money? Is that it? That's what this is all about, isn't it?" *You nickel-and-dime schmuck.*

Money? You think I want money? How about I want my father back? "I'm not after money, Mr. Landis," Paul said. "What I want is for you to do the right thing, and I think you know what that is."

Jerry Landis stood abruptly. "Mr. Symon, do what you have to do. I will do likewise." He gestured at the door. "Now if you don't mind." *Get out of my sight, you greasy pig fucker!*

Paul was hesitant to leave. He was enjoying this but he knew he'd made his point. "Thank you for your time, Mr. Landis," Paul said. "It was nice to see you again." He handed the FDA charts to his nemesis. "Feel free to throw these out if you like." Paul turned and walked calmly out the door, closing it behind him.

Whir-pffft whir-pffft whir-pffft. Jerry Landis hurled the sheaf of papers at the door. Then he sat down and began reassembling the pancreas as he considered his options. He certainly couldn't pay off these bureaucrats one by one; the time and expense would be prohibitive. Perhaps he could buy the head of each of the agencies. But what if—as hard as it might be to imagine—one of them couldn't be bought? This wasn't a perfect world, after all. As he put the last pieces of the pancreas together he realized the solution was unavoidable. Jerry Landis had to take the path of least resistance. He would simply have to kill Paul Symon.

Mr. H. Wayne Grigsby called his wife and told her he'd be working late again. Of course she knew he was just sitting there swilling scotch, but she didn't care—better than the mean bastard coming home and torturing her. She often wished he'd just have an affair so she could catch him and drag his ass into divorce court but such was not her luck. Single-malt scotch and the family business were all that seemed to interest Mr. Grigsby anymore.

The family business, Grigsby Research Equipment, manufacted what they called biomedical research appliances. It had been doing so for sixty years. The company motto was "Quality vivisection devices for three generations." Sensitivity was not the strong suit in the Grigsby gene pool.

H. Wayne Grigsby's spacious office was a veritable museum of the sadistic playthings the company had designed and manufactured over the years. On the walnut credenza behind Grigsby's desk was a clever stainless steel restraining device used to restrict the movement of rhesus monkeys with special leather emphasis placed on their heads. There was an old wood-and-copper electroshock gizmo that his grandfather had designed for an experiment involving wet dogs. There was a catapult-like mechanism devised to slam rabbits headfirst into a brick wall, the point of which had long been forgotten. In addition to these fine instruments of science, there were many others. Depending on your point of view the office was either a chamber of horrors or a monument to man's ascendancy over the rest of the animal kingdom.

Mr. Grigsby liked to be at the office late at night so he could go into the laboratory after everyone else was gone. After several drinks he enjoyed wearing the white lab coats and doing experiments of his own design; it gave him a much-needed feeling of superiority. Sometimes he used an animal that was already in the lab, other times he went to a twenty-four-hour pet store that was nearby. H. Wayne Grigsby, it could be said without fear of contradiction, had a heart like a bone.

It was eight-thirty when the last of the custodial staff left. The old articulated hinge slowly eased the door shut behind the last janitor, but just before it closed a gloved hand reached from out of the darkness and caught it.

In his office, Mr. Grigsby went to the bar and again filled his tumbler with scotch and ice. Keeping a giddy eye on his drink, he left the office and weaved his way down the hall toward the laboratory. The ice in his glass tinkled like a delicate cowbell, warning all the little animals that he was coming. He stopped at the gunmetal-gray door and gulped some hooch to steel him for the tasks ahead. Once inside he slipped into one of the long white lab coats and put his hands into the pockets, posing the way he imagined an animal experimenter might. He crossed to the rows of cages on the far side of the room and leaned down to taunt a small cat.

That's when the lights went out, confusing the inebriated vivisection executive. He straightened up and waited for his eyes to adjust to the darkness. H. Wayne Grigsby then heard what sounded like the door being locked. A second later the lights came back on, flooding his dilated pupils with several hundred watts of pain. He shielded his eyes against the brightness and heard a strangely muffled voice. "On your knees, asshole."

Grigsby gulped the last of his scotch and did as he was told. On the floor, he peeked between his fingers and saw a very large dog standing on its hind legs. Actually, it was a large person wearing a frightening and grotesque dog mask, which resulted in the muffled voice.

"What do you want?" Grigsby asked.

"Shut up," the dog said, "or I'll staple your fucking mouth shut." The dog walked over to the kneeling H. Wayne Grigsby and kicked him in the kidney region. "Tell me what you know about the rights of animals."

Christ Almighty, Grigsby thought, his nightmare was finally coming true. Ever since Peter Singer got *Animal Liberation* published in 1975, Grigsby Research Equipment had become a magnet for every animal rights nut west of the Rockies. Grigsby took a defiant and vaguely inaccurate stance. "We're doing medical research here," he said. "The rights of animals are secondary to the rights of humans."

"Wrong answer," the large dog said before kicking Grigsby solidly in the head. While H. Wayne was unconscious, the dog strapped him into one of the company's new primate-restraining devices, one that Grigsby thought would sell quite well at the upcoming Vivisection Expo in Anaheim. When H. Wayne came to, his eyes were wide open and he couldn't shut them no matter how hard he tried. He didn't know how long they'd been that way but it felt like his contacts had fused completely to his dried eyes. Despite the fact that his eyelids had been duct-taped wide open, H. Wayne Grigsby couldn't see his tormentor at the moment.

"Where the hell are you?!" Mr. Grigsby said. "My eyes are drying up!"

"Not a problem," the dog said. "I'll take care of that in a second." The dog stepped into view holding a large container of U.S. Petroleum machine lubricant. "But first, let's talk about equal consideration." The mutt said this while scooping up a pawful of the crude product. "Would you agree that animals have the right to equal consideration as humans?"

Unfortunately for Mr. Grigsby, alcohol had a tendency

to make him belligerent, so it was really the scotch talk-ing when he said, "No, I don't agree. Fuck you!"

The caged animals were upset by Mr. Grigsby's screams. Even though it was a simple eye irritancy test, Grigsby made such a fuss you'd have thought someone had injected a herpes virus directly into his brain, much the way scientists did to those mice in Cambridge back in 1984.

"Let me ask you again, in case you misunderstood me the first time," the dog said. "Where do you stand on animal rights?"

Staring out through the machine lubricant, everything was a blur to Mr. Grigsby. His conjunctivae were swelling and they were beginning to discharge a fluid of some sort. On the upside, the dryness wasn't such a problem anymore. Certain that he was going to be killed by this sadistic mongrel, Grigsby damn sure wasn't going to say what the dog wanted to hear. "They don't have any fuck-ing rights!"

"Not in here, they don't," the dog said. "You're right about that."

Grigsby knew about organizations whose members concerned themselves with the welfare of animals. The Society for the Prevention of Cruelty to Animals (SPCA) and People for the Ethical Treatment of Animals (PETA) were both nonviolent fund- and consciousness-raising groups. Then there was the Animal Liberation Front (ALF), a somewhat more radical outfit, akin to the envi-ronmental group EarthFirst!, whose members took more direct action against those they considered transgressors. These were the sorts of people who frequently staged protests outside Grigsby Research Equipment and occa-sionally got inside to free some of the animals. Grigsby figured he was being ALFed.

Grigsby also knew there were organizations out there that supported animal research. Just the other day he had savored a full-page magazine ad for a group calling itself Americans for Medical Progress Educational Foun-dation, "helping the public understand animal research in medicine." The headline of the ad read "You can't be for AIDS research *AND* animal rights!" Fuckin' A, Grigsby had thought, but where the hell were these people when he needed them?

The dog pulled a tray of syringes from one of the cabinets. "You probably can't read the label on this, so allow me," the dog said. "It's soman, a liquid nerve agent. Same stuff you sold to those researchers in San Antonio. You may recall they conducted an experiment on the neuro-behavioral effects of repeated sublethal soman exposure in primates." The dog put the tray down and prepared one of the syringes. "I'm going to do a little follow-up research, if you don't mind."

Before the night was done, H. Wayne Grigsby had helped expand the body of scientific knowledge by participating in several other experiments. After the one involving an anti-infection vaccine given as a treatment for severe burns the dog explained how skin grafts could make Mr. Grigsby's face almost as good as new. The last experiment was designed to see how the brain perceived parts of the body. It was based on a study done at UC San Francisco, where eight adult owl monkeys had their fingers amputated. When it was over, H. Wayne Grigsby reluctantly agreed that animals did, in fact, have rights.

Although still strapped in the restraining device and nearly blind from the irritating machine lubricant, H. Wayne Grigsby could tell the dog was letting all the animals out of their cages. But he couldn't see what the dog wrote on the chalkboard before leaving. And even if he could have read it, he wouldn't have understood. All it said was "¡Terra tuebor!"

Dr. Gibbs was anxious. He was standing in front of One Biotech Center waiting for Arty to arrive. He hoped his one-eyed testicle supplier wasn't having second thoughts. If he were, Dr. Gibbs would have to pucker up and kiss his Xenotech career good-bye. He looked to the far end of the long driveway that curved through the unnaturally landscaped property hoping for a sign of his donor. In the distance a machine of some sort was making an ungodly amount of noise. Dr. Gibbs hoped it wouldn't interfere with Dr. Vines's ability to concentrate during the operation—assuming there was an operation.

He looked to a window on the fourth floor behind which Jerry Landis was being prepped for the ground-breaking testicle surgery. It was a small room down the hall from where the surgery would take place. Jerry Landis was wearing a green surgical gown and a dreamy smile as an attentive nurse carefully shaved his withered private parts. In the chilled room his old scrotum had contracted to the texture of possum flesh, wiry hair pointing outward like arthritic fingers. Even with her years of experience the nurse doubted her ability to render hygienic this hideous fleshy moonscape.

Down the hall was the state-of-the-art operating theater with its disinfected white tile and sterilized stainless steel. And, with the exception of Dr. Vines, it was being manned for today's operation by some of the Bay Area's top people. Jerry Landis's money made sure of that.

Down below, Dr. Gibbs was about to go back inside and call the police to complain about the noisy machine which seemed, incredibly, to be getting even louder. Then he saw Bonedigger on his Harley and he made the connection. He wondered if the idiot liked the noise because he was so stupid or if the noise had made him that way; it was a chicken-or-the-egg sort of thing. Then it struck the doctor: Where the hell was Arty? Perhaps the tattooed chauffeur had driven off without his boss. All Dr. Gibbs could do was wait and see if the knucklewalker on the bike had any answers. But instead of answers, what Bonedigger had was a backpack. And sticking out of the top of the backpack was Arty's head, the black patch still dotting his eye. Dr. Gibbs wondered if the cranked-up biker had broken Arty's two remaining limbs to stuff him in there, never imagining that the truth was much worse.

"Hey, Doc!" Arty said, chipper as ever. "Sorry we're

late. I wanted to change my dressings before coming over."

Bonedigger took the backpack off and handed it to Dr. Gibbs, who took it like a full sack of groceries. Cradled in his arms, Arty's face was uncomfortably close, his breath malt-liquorish. Dr. Gibbs backed his head as far away from Arty as his neck would allow. "Dressings?" Dr. Gibbs said. "Like for a wound? What happened?"

Arty craned his head to look at Bonedigger. They both broke into semi-drunken smiles. Then, simultaneously, they said: "Construction accident!" They both laughed, and Bonedigger put one of his dirty hands in the air for a high five. A moment passed before he realized Arty wouldn't be able to accommodate him, so he settled for a pat on the head. As Bonedigger parked his hog in the handicap spot, Arty explained to an incredulous Dr. Gibbs how he had lost his last two limbs. Dr. Gibbs almost dropped Arty when he got to the part about the circular saw. Arty said that he was uncomfortable with his lack of symmetry, having only a left leg and a right arm. Also, his accidental death and dismemberment policy was about to lapse so, instead of paying another premium, he'd opted for another construction accident and a final insurance payoff. "I feel much more balanced now," Arty said. "By the way, if you ever need someone handy with a circular saw . . ." He nodded at Bonedigger.

Dr. Gibbs was now holding Arty at arm's length, and he noticed a moist reddish brown splotch forming on the backpack approximately where the right arm had been. "I'll keep that in mind," Dr. Gibbs said, tossing Arty back to Bones. "Now can we go inside? They're waiting."

After shaving Jerry Landis clean, the attractive nurse plugged him into an IV of lactated Ringer's. "I'll be back for you in a few minutes," she said. "We're almost ready." Dr. Gibbs watched the nurse leave, longing to be shaved himself.

"Doctor," Jerry Landis said. "Come here. I have something important to tell you." Gibbs turned and looked at his aging mentor. He felt sorry for him. He looked so ancient and feeble. It made Dr. Gibbs angry. Werner's syndrome was killing the man who had promised him a future, the man who repeatedly called him Doctor in front of others. Dr. Gibbs loved Jerry Landis and wished he could help him in some way. "There isn't much time," Jerry Landis said. "Listen carefully to what I have to say. Everything we're doing depends on it." His voice was weak.

Dr. Gibbs nodded. "I'm listening."

"There are two very important things you must do if we are to make our mark in history," Jerry Landis said in a voice that entranced the doctor. "If you fail, there will be no Xenotech and you will have to start over again. Do you understand what that means, Doctor?"

Dr. Gibbs remembered the gamy stench of the spoiled eyeballs in the warehouse. He knew he didn't want to start over again. "Yes, I understand," he said. "What do you need?"

Jerry Landis made a noise that didn't resemble language. The nurse had given him a dose of Robinal so he wouldn't drool all over the anesthesiologist during the operation and now his mouth was so dry he could barely speak. He mustered some saliva, then managed some words. "Now, first, do you remember the man I told you about? Mr. Symon?"

"Yes, of course. The activist." He spit the word out as if it tasted bad.

"Yes," Jerry Landis said. "I need him taken care of." He looked to Dr. Gibbs to see if his meaning had been lost or misconstrued.

"Yes sir, I understand. What's wrong with him?"

Jerry Landis looked dismayed that the meaning had, indeed, been lost. "He has threatened to ruin us, Dr. Gibbs, to bring our work to a halt. We cannot afford that. Do you understand?"

Dr. Gibbs was suddenly afraid that he did, but he was holding out a little hope that he was wrong. "I'm not sure I do, sir. How can he ruin us? You said he was just a crackpot."

Jerry Landis reached over and gently took Dr. Gibbs by the arm. His grip was firm and fatherly. He pulled Gibbs close and looked deep into his eyes. He spoke very calmly. "Listen to me. If you are to have a future at Xenotech, you will see to it that young Mr. Symon does not cause us any trouble. Do you understand?" His voice was soothing. It was a guiding light the doctor knew he had to follow. He was mesmerized.

"Tell me what you want me to do," Dr. Gibbs said.

Jerry Landis pulled him closer still and spoke gently into his ear. "I want you to kill him."

Dr. Gibbs could only nod; a vague sense of duty embraced him.

"The second thing I need may be more difficult," Jerry Landis said.

"It's time," the nurse said as she entered the room. She carried a syringe which she plunged without warning into the patient's left buttock. The intramuscular morphine made Jerry Landis feel better about everything from his future to the color of the ceiling. Another nurse entered the room and helped put Landis onto a gurney.

"Be careful," Dr. Gibbs said. "He's frail."

As they rolled Jerry Landis down the hall Dr. Gibbs followed like a lamprey attached to the side of a shark. "Sir, what's the second thing? Tell me what to do."

Landis put a finger to his lips. "Not here. Wait until we're alone."

They wheeled Landis into the OR and transferred him onto the operating table.

"All right," Dr. Gibbs said. "I'll be right back. I have to go get ready." Since he was going to be leading the testicle-harvesting team, Dr. Gibbs went to the next room to put on his scrubs and surgical mask. He dressed in a hurry. He wanted to talk to Jerry Landis before they put him under. He had to know what the second thing was.

Two attendants wheeled Arty into the operating room and prepared to move him to his table. They grabbed the sheets and lifted, but failing to compensate for his lack of legs, they spilled Arty, buck naked, onto the floor. "Whoa!" he said as he landed on his fresh leg stump. "Umpf!" It looked like it would have hurt, but the morphine softened the blow. Arty was a sight like few had ever seen: a naked pink torso with a smiling pirate's face at one end and hairless genitalia at the other. Even Dr. Vines gasped, and he had seen some pretty weird things in his checkered career. The nurses and attendants scurried to get Arty onto the table. They quickly administered three cc's of Fentanyl, then a syringe full of milky white Propofol, a fine sedative hypnotic. Arty was happier than he'd ever been. He began to dream of the orphanage.

They strapped Jerry Landis to armboards and medicated him in a similar fashion, then they placed a pulse oximeter onto his index finger and attached the other monitoring devices. Then he took his first breath of vaporized isoflurane, about 2 percent mixed with a forty-sixty oxygen–nitrous oxide blend. It was very nice. *Whir-pffft.*

Dr. Gibbs entered the operating theater, his surgical mask tied tight. He went to Jerry Landis and leaned down to speak to him. "Sir, what's the second thing?"

Jerry Landis's voice was thick with narcotics. "It's important," he said. *Whir-pffft.*

"I understand," Dr. Gibbs replied, "but what is it?"

Jerry Landis looked deep into Dr. Gibbs's eyes and then surrendured to the gas. *Whir-pffft.*

Paul slapped another puppy onto the wall. "How does that look?" he asked.

"Like Walt Disney's last nightmare," Georgette said. "You're putting them too close together."

Paul looked wounded. "Sorry. I guess I need closer supervision." He began to spread the puppies around but held out little hope that his supervisor would be much help. Georgette was watching him but Paul knew her mind was elsewhere.

"What about Rene?" she said. "It works for a boy or a girl."

"So does Moon Unit," Paul said. "But that's no reason to choose it."

"Be serious," Georgette snapped. "We are talking about our child."

Paul looked down from his perch on the ladder, amused at the attitude he was getting. "Two weeks ago you were calling this our embryo's room," he said, smiling.

"Yeah, well . . ." Georgette hesitated. "Things change." No one was more surprised about Georgette's change of heart than she was—and certainly no one was more embarrassed. There was no intellectual justification for this sudden philosophical U-turn. It was the ideological equivalent of turning the wrong way onto a one-way street and Georgette knew it. She'd be the first to admit she deserved to be shot with a paint ball because, at some point when she wasn't paying attention, Georgette began feeling mushy about the child thing. She hated herself for it but there was no denying she felt motherly. Georgette didn't know why it happened but she was ready to blame it on hormones, thereby absolving herself of personal responsibility.

Earlier in the day Paul and Georgette had discussed Paul's meeting with Jerry Landis. Paul prevailed on Georgette to help him write a letter to the FDA regarding the research going on at Xenotech. She agreed to help only if she was allowed to include examples of Jerry Landis's prior acts of eco-irresponsibility, a condition to which Paul acceded. And even though she asked nicely, Paul refused to let her fabricate any new ones. Their letter addressed a concern shared by many that xenografting could lead to problems far worse than a shortage of transplantable organs, namely, a plague. The argument was that animal viruses that were benign in their natural hosts might become uncontrollable, primitive, impervious killers when transplanted into a host of a different species. Many believe AIDS originated when an African villager ate a monkey that carried the virus. Catastrophic ebola outbreaks have occurred after people have been scratched or bitten by infected chimpanzees. Just for good measure, Paul and Georgette also included a paragraph on the bovine spongiform encephalopathy–Creutzfeld-Jakob disease controversy. These were all fears the FDA was aware of, but a well-researched letter (especially one that managed to get prior acts of eco-irresponsibility admitted into evidence) was sure to trigger some sort of bureaucratic movement, however glacial that might be. They addressed the letter to the special assistant for investigations at the FDA, and cc'd to a dozen other federal departments, agencies, and offices.

After mailing the letter, Paul and Georgette moved on to the interior decorating portion of their day. The puppy decorating scheme was a compromise. The jet fighters were too macho, and pink with blue trim was too dainty. Paul had argued rather forcefully for the latter, saying the colors were womblike and would make their son's transition into the world less jarring. Georgette felt their daughter needed to be surrounded from the start by symbols of achievement and soaring flight so she'd have a foot up on those who tried to saddle her with traditional female limitations.

The wedding date issue was currently out of their hands. A week ago they had sent a new list of possible dates to their "critical invitees" and were waiting for word back on that. The dates on the list were either very soon or a long way off and were designed to accommodate the availability of the facility, the schedules of parents, their closest friends, the band, and a caterer.

"I think we've got enough puppies up there," Georgette said finally. "Let's start painting the baseboards." She began to unfold an old sheet to use it as a drop cloth.

"I've got a better idea," Paul said as he descended from the ladder. Georgette suddenly felt something surrounding her. It was Paul snaking his arms around her from behind. He sneaked his hands under her T-shirt and cupped Georgette's wondrous new breasts. "Have I mentioned lately how much I love you?" he said.

Georgette snuggled backwards into Paul's embrace. "No, but I'm willing to listen."

Thanks to the gym shorts Georgette was wearing, Paul's hands were gliding over some very sensitive areas, and Georgette was feeling quite responsive. Paul kissed her neck and she closed her eyes and leaned into it. Hoping to encourage more unprincipled behavior, Georgette turned around to face Paul but she didn't let go of the drop cloth. She began to spin slowly as Paul continued nuzzling her neck. Soon they were cocooned in the soft cotton sheet and Georgette was stepping out of her gym shorts. They hopped a few feet to their left and dove onto the futon, which, fortunately, was strong enough to withstand the considerable force. Georgette soon had

Paul undressed and excited. They were thrashing about, panting and giggling, when Paul suddenly stopped cold. "Wait a second," he said, sitting up suddenly.

"No," Georgette replied, pulling him back down. But it was too late. The momentum was gone, a new excitement replacing the old. Paul sat up again, thinking. Georgette sighed. "Xenotech is trying to solve the cross-species organ rejection problem for baboon organs, right?"

"So you said," Georgette replied. "But I've got to tell you, discussing baboon organs isn't as much of a turn-on for me as it is for some girls."

"This is horrible," Paul said.

"I'm sorry. Call me old-fashioned."

"Sweetheart, it doesn't make any sense."

"So little does anymore," Georgette said.

"It doesn't make any sense to solve the baboon organ rejection problem unless you've got baboons to supply the organs," Paul said. "And you'd need to have a lot of them to make it economically feasible."

Georgette stopped her kissing. She suddenly understood what was so horrible. "And if they create a workable immunosuppressant, they slaughter the baboons," she said.

"We've got to do something," Paul said.

"We were doing something great until all this came up," Georgette said. "Of course it wouldn't save any baboons . . ." Her voice trailed off.

"We've got to find out where the baboons are and—"

"And what?" Georgette asked. "Write another letter?"

Ever since the testicular transplant Dr. Gibbs had been worried. Truth be told, he was worried prior to the surgery, but it was only afterwards that he finally was struck by the magnitude of what Jerry Landis had asked him to do. And, as if that weren't bad enough, there was the question of "the second thing." The mysterious task Jerry Landis had said might be even more difficult than the first. And now, after being summoned by his boss,

Dr. Gibbs worried that Jerry Landis would take away his office and his parking space when he admitted he hadn't yet "taken care of" the Paul Symon character. The fact was, Dr. Gibbs knew he had to obey the strange old man if he wanted a future at Xenotech—and he did, indeed, want that. But he had waited to see if Jerry Landis would survive the surgery before actually setting out to kill Paul Symon.

But Jerry Landis did survive, and it was impossible to say who was more surprised: Jerry Landis himself, who suddenly felt like a twenty-year-old; Dr. Gibbs, who never thought the transplanted testicle would take; or Dr. Vines, who didn't think the patient would even survive the anesthesia, which explained why he demanded his fee up front.

But Jerry Landis was living proof that three testicles and a good hormone treatment could go a long way toward keeping you young and virile, or at least toward making you feel that way. Based on the theory that the young heal faster than the old, Dr. Vines had started the intensive hormone treatments as soon as it was clear that Landis would, in fact, regain consciousness. Dr. Vines had adjusted his usual prescription to suit the needs of his unusual patient. He went with a slightly lower dosage of human growth hormone (since it was contraindicated for diabetics) and he doubled the normal doses of melatonin and dehydroepiandrosterone. He stayed with the standard measure of testosterone, assuming that the extra testis would provide its own little boost.

The results were impressive. Within days, Jerry Landis was undergoing a remarkable transformation. His skin, once thin and papery, became supple and resilient. His energy level soared and his mind was more facile than it had been in years. Joints that a week earlier had ached with arthritis were suddenly pain free and capable of a range of motion Landis hadn't experienced since high school. Best of all, as far as Jerry Landis was concerned, was the awakening of his long-dormant libido.

And now that Jerry Landis was in full recovery, Dr.

Gibbs began to wonder how he would commit the crime that would keep his career on track. He had killed before, but only by botching kidney harvests in Calcutta, and Dr. Gibbs felt it was unlikely he could coax Mr. Symon onto an operating table. Perhaps Mr. Landis would have a suggestion.

When Dr. Gibbs arrived at the office, Jerry Landis was nowhere to be seen.

"Hello?" Dr. Gibbs said.

A voice responded from behind the desk. "Down here."

Dr. Gibbs found Jerry Landis on the floor doing push-ups. "Almost done," he said. Dr. Gibbs watched him do five more before he sprang to his feet. *Whir-pffft whir-pffft whir-pffft.*

"It's a little soon after surgery for calisthenics, isn't it, sir?"

"Bullshit. I feel fantastic!" Jerry Landis said. "I'm thinking about investing in that Castro Valley Life Extension Institute. That Dr. Vines has a damn good product."

"Yes, sir. I'm glad it's working out."

Landis opened the top drawer of his desk and removed an adhesive testosterone patch. He unbuttoned his shirt and stuck the patch onto his stomach. Dr. Gibbs could see from the red rings and the adhesive residue tangled in the hair on his belly that this wasn't the first patch Jerry Landis had used. It appeared he was self-medicating. "Did Dr. Vines prescribe those patches?"

"Ha! You caught me," Jerry Landis said. "No, the little quack said I was getting enough testosterone from that concoction of his plus the transplant, but I thought he was wrong so I asked for the patches. When he refused I called a friend at Applied Hormone Technology and got a whole damn case. And if that pissant Vines doesn't like it, I'll kick his little ass from here to Oakland." He held up his fists and began to bob and weave and throw punches.

The hormone treatment, in addition to improving Jerry Landis's appearance, had made him surprisingly aggressive and frightfully mercurial in his moods. "So let me ask," Jerry Landis said, "have you taken care of that problem I asked you to?" He threw a combo at his unseen foe.

Dr. Gibbs backed out of Jerry Landis's reach. "I'm still looking into it, sir. I didn't think you'd want me to rush into something like that."

Jerry Landis nodded. "You're right. You should be careful; it could have consequences." *Whir-pffft whir-pffft whir-pffft.*

"Exactly, sir," Dr. Gibbs said. "We need to consider the consequences."

Jerry Landis threw a knockout right hook, then turned and spoke as if addressing a child. "No, we don't need to consider the consequences, we simply need to make sure we *avoid* any. Now, do you remember I told you there was something else I needed? Something important?"

"Yes, sir. Maybe that's what I should start on." Dr. Gibbs watched as Landis fell to the floor and did another fifteen push-ups. When he finished he sat cross-legged on the floor and patted a spot on the carpet next to him, inviting Dr. Gibbs to sit. The doctor slowly lowered himself down and sat.

Jerry Landis scooted over close to Dr. Gibbs and put his arm over his shoulder. "I owe you a great debt, Doctor. Last night I had an orgasm that would have blinded me two weeks ago." He leaned over and spoke conspiratorially. "If my tape measure's right, it went nearly three feet."

Dr. Gibbs looked ill at ease. "That's something, sir. Thank you for sharing that."

Jerry Landis stood and crossed to the wall of books. When he turned back to face Dr. Gibbs, his waggish smirk had given way to a more troubled countenance. Dr. Gibbs remained on the carpet. "Doctor," Jerry Landis said. "I was visited again last night. By the golden light." He seemed almost ashamed, as if he wasn't worthy of what had happened to him. "The warm hand of the

Lord was upon my shoulder and the truth was revealed to me." There was something about Jerry Landis's eyes that took Dr. Gibbs hostage. The man's voice bound and gagged him where he sat. At times like this the doctor could only listen. "Do you understand what we are trying to do here at Xenotech?"

Dr. Gibbs's response was best described as a bovine stare.

"It's very simple. We are doing miracles." Jerry Landis chose his words carefully. His voice was rich and deep and certain. "What you and Dr. Vines did was miraculous." He cupped his hands as if holding a precious liquid. "The way you took that life-giving organ from that other man's body and put it into mine . . . I wish I had your gift, Doctor, but even all my money cannot buy something so rare."

These words had enormous emotional impact, just as Jerry Landis suspected they would. Dr. Gibbs was deeply moved that someone would say such things about him. His parents had been demanding but never encouraging, and he knew his former classmates snickered about his background. In fact, no one had ever paid Dr. Gibbs a compliment about his abilities, until this very moment. Jerry Landis knew his secret broken bone. The doctor struggled against the emotion and spoke. "Thank you, sir."

Jerry Landis waved off the gratitude as he went to his desk drawer and removed another testosterone patch. He stuck this one on his arm and rubbed it as he spoke. "Doctor, last night I was reading about children with Hutchinson-Gilford syndrome. Progerics, as they're called, usually die of a heart attack or a stroke by the time they're eighteen, makes Werner's syndrome seem like an endless tea party. But now there's something called telomere theory that may explain why they age so quickly, has to do with telomeres and chromosomes and fibroblasts . . . I don't know that I completely understand it. The point is, as I read this, I was bathed in the golden light and everything suddenly became clear in my mind.

The xenografting, the immuno-suppressive drug research, the life-extension hormones, telomere theory . . . Don't you see? This proves we are on the right track."

Dr. Gibbs wanted to see because he believed Jerry Landis knew things that few others did. But the non sequitur he'd just served up didn't make a goddamn bit of sense to Dr. Gibbs.

"We have found what Ponce de Leon was searching for," Jerry Landis said. "He was just at the wrong place at the wrong time. Don't you agree?"

It was at times like this that Dr. Gibbs wished he had paid more attention during history class. Who the hell was Ponce de Leon and what did he have to do with biotechnology? Was he a sixteenth-century scientist? The name had that vague familiarity, like Copernicus and Galileo. He had once known who they were but he had long since forgotten. And up until this point, none of it had ever come back to bite him on the ass.

"Doctor, I believe transgenic baboon organs and the proper immunosuppressive drugs might just be what flows from the fabled fountain of youth. And *that*, Dr. Gibbs, would indeed be a miraculous thing."

"I see what you mean," Dr. Gibbs said.

Like all effective speakers, Jerry Landis knew his audience. He understood the rhythms of a good sermon. He knew how to toy with the emotions of his listeners and how to work them up to the point they would be willing to do whatever he asked. "Doctor, many years ago I heard about a biotechnology company called FuTrans. They were one of the first companies to look into ways to use animal organs for human transplants," Jerry Landis said. "It was controversial at the time and the company was behind schedule and running out of capital when I went to look at their facility. The first thing I saw when I walked into their laboratory was three pig hearts attached and functioning on the shaved necks of some surprised-looking baboons. Later, I watched as they transplanted a pig heart into the chest of another baboon and I saw one of nature's pure wonders."

Jerry Landis began talking about the wonders of the autoimmune system. When an untreated organ from a pig is transplanted into a primate, the primate's immune system sends B cell antibodies to attach themselves to the endothelial cells lining the blood vessels of the transplanted pig organ. After these antibodies attach to the transplanted organ, they form an enzyme that attracts a deluge of one of the most powerful weapons in the immune system, the complement proteins—the body's border patrol, a group of about thirty proteins that search for illegal aliens. The complement proteins cascade onto the organ, stabbing holes in the membranes of the endothelial cells and, along with the white blood cells, disrupting the endothelium so the blood clots in the vessels. Within minutes the transplanted organ becomes black, swollen, and clogged with congealed blood.

This, as they say, is incompatible with life.

Landis shook his head as he recalled the story. "They were testing cobra venom factor as an antiplatelet aggregator along with cyclosporine A to see if it would retard the rejection. Needless to say, it failed. But once you understand the *process*," Landis said, "once you understand that, you can begin looking for a way around it."

Two weeks later Jerry Landis bought the company. After the deal was done, he walked into the conference room at FuTrans and made an announcement to the gathered scientists and executives. "Ladies. Gentlemen. I believe we have the ability to solve the problem of xenografting. I am therefore investing fifty million dollars in further research and development." The scientists cheered their savior. Excitement and enthusiastic applause rolled like a wave over the room. "But!" Jerry Landis continued. "We are changing the focus from pigs to baboons."

The scientists' enthusiasm subsided. One of them tentatively raised his hand. "But there aren't enough baboons," he said.

"You let me worry about that," Jerry Landis said.

"What about the gag factor?" another one asked, referring to their marketing surveys. "How are we going to get people past that?"

Dr. Gibbs was staring up from his seat on the floor as Jerry Landis told the story, an apostle at the feet of his messiah. "Do you know what I told them, Dr. Gibbs? Do you know what I said about their gag factor research?"

Dr. Gibbs shook his head no.

Jerry Landis continued, speaking calmly, evenly. "I said, 'The gag factor exists only when answering marketing survey questionnaires.'" His voice dropped to a near whisper. "When it becomes a matter of life or death, they will always choose life. And it doesn't matter if they have to kill their next-door neighbor or a fucking monkey."

In the deepest recesses of his soul, Dr. Gibbs knew Jerry Landis was right. Now he wanted only to know what the second thing was he had to do for this wondrous man who had seen the future and was willing to share it with him. Jerry Landis rubbed his testosterone patches like lucky charms. "I renamed the company Xenograft, Incorporated, and for the next fifteen years I directed and redirected the research efforts until we hit upon what is now considered the most likely solution to the xenografting problem. The transgenic animal."

Dr. Gibbs actually knew about this. Most of the companies involved in xenograft research were in a race to perfect transgenic pig organs. The way he understood it, human organs were protected from the body's vigorous complement protein system (primarily C3b proteins) by membrane cofactor proteins (MCP) and decay accelerating factor (DAF), the so-called shield proteins. DAFs block C3bs from forming the enzyme that causes the C3b cascade. MCPs work with another enzyme to cleave and inactivate the C3b.

Normal animal organs do not have MCP or DAF and are thus hyperacutely rejected when placed in the human body. What the transgenic swine people decided to do was to take eggs from sows and inject them with human genetic material before putting them back for gestation.

The eggs incorporated the human genes for MCP and DAF into their own DNA and the piglets were born with the ability to produce human shield proteins.

For some reason, Dr. Gibbs recalled that the first transgenic pig was named Astrid.

The researchers selected the piglets that produced the greatest amount of shield protein and bred them with one another. After repeating this process for several generations, they hoped to have genetically altered swine organs that would not trigger the C3b attack when transplanted into humans. Then it struck Dr. Gibbs. "Did you say transgenic *baboon* organs?"

"Yes. I started a baboon farm many years ago."

"A baboon farm?" Dr. Gibbs asked.

"A special breeding facility in Deckern County, Mississippi. That's where the transgenic baboons are. And don't worry about organ size, we've taken care of that too."

Dr. Gibbs knew he was in the presence of greatness. Only a prophet could have seen so far ahead and connected so many of the dots in a puzzle that had escaped solution for so long. "Have you ever considered the liver, Dr. Gibbs?" Jerry Landis started to count on his fingers. "Hepatitis. Billiary obstruction. Hepatoma. Cirrhosis. Gilbert's disease. Metastatic cancer. Blunt force trauma. Penetrating trauma. Parasitic infection, and on and on. Hell, there must be fifty ways to lose your liver. And when someone loses their liver, Dr. Gibbs, they need a new one because otherwise . . . They. Will. Die. Some of them will find a new one through the Organ Procurement Network, but that line is long and it moves slowly. And after they've been at the end of that line for a while . . . they will come to us." *Whir-pffft whir-pffft whir-pffft*

Dr. Gibbs's eyes were fixed and dilated. He sat on the floor listening to the prophet speak and was spellbound by a presence beyond his ken. Jerry Landis fell to his knees, came face-to-face with Dr. Gibbs, and spoke with remarkable clarity. "You must keep in mind that these events which appear to be medical in nature are nothing more than transactions. This is business and we are selling a rare commodity, Dr. Gibbs, and it isn't organs. And it's not a surgical procedure and it's not immunosuppressive drug therapy." The following words came softly and with reverence: "The product," Jerry Landis said, "is life itself." He paused to let that sink in. "You might charge a hundred thousand dollars for a mere organ, but life? That's worth some money, if you think about it. Life's gotta be worth ten times that." People will come to us when they are running out of *life* and we will sell them more of it. And for that they are willing to pay dearly.

Jerry Landis took Dr. Gibbs gently by the hand and helped him to his feet. He maintained his tone of serenity as he spoke. "The rich will pay because they have the means," he said. "The not-so-rich will turn to their families and their churches and their government. And they will have bake sales and car washes and entitlement programs and they will raise the money to keep one another alive. I promise you they will do this."

Dr. Gibbs was so much putty. He knew Jerry Landis was right and he wanted to be a part of Xenotech, Incorporated when it took over the world. He was ready to get out and do whatever Jerry Landis wanted. He just had one question. "What is the second thing?"

Jerry Landis put his hands on Dr. Gibbs's shoulders and looked into his eyes. "You are the best in your profession and it is because you are a doctor and you have a rare gift. I need you to go and procure organs for me."

"Anything," Dr. Gibbs said quietly. "What do you need?"

"Doctor," Jerry Landis said, "bring me uteri."

There followed a pause as Dr. Gibbs silently mouthed *you-ter-I*. "Uteri, sir?" Dr. Gibbs said. "I don't know what that is."

"It's plural for *uterus*," Jerry Landis said. "And if I am to fulfill God's will to go forth and multiply, I will need uteri."

Dr. Gibbs wondered if the man wanted to have a uterus transplanted into himself so he could have his own children or if it was something somehow more twisted than that.

"Doctor, I need industrious young women who are in challenging situations."

Dr. Gibbs shook his head. "Sir?"

Jerry Landis looked the doctor straight in the eyes. "I'm looking for desperate and willing young women, preferably attractive," he said.

Dr. Gibbs slowly raised one of his hands. "Let me see if I understand, sir . . ."

"We do not need to understand God's will in order to fulfill it," Jerry Landis said. "Just bring me girls of childbearing age, Doctor, and you will be part of history." Jerry Landis took the hand that Dr. Gibbs had raised and rubbed it over the testosterone patch on his stomach. "Now do you understand what we're trying to do here at Xenotech, Dr. Gibbs?" *Whir-pffft whir-pffft whir-pffft.*

The biggest surprise that Saturday evening was that Mr. Lemsling was alive at all. After three days buried in his landfill he was severely malnourished and dehydrated. The only reason he hadn't drowned in his own vomit was that he finally managed to spit the disposable diaper out of his mouth.

The homeless woman who found him had nearly died of shock herself. She was scouring the dump looking for food when she saw a human head on the ground. That frightened her pretty bad, but when the eyes opened and the head called out to her, the woman ran screaming from the landfill. The police arrived shortly thereafter and dug the garbage mogul out of his predicament.

Lance Abbott, who had been following the Lemsling story since he first heard about it on the radio, arrived at the dump just in time to hear Mr. Lemsling swear on his beloved mother's grave that he was going to spend his entire personal fortune, if necessary, to pay to have every recyclable item in each of his landfills extracted and disposed of properly. Moments before that, without the slightest bit of police coercion, Mr. Lemsling had confessed to a bevy of fiscal and political shenanigans related to some creative financial arrangements made with several members of the County Solid Waste Subcommittee. He seemed quite sincere about the whole thing.

Suddenly, Mr. Lemsling began to scream. "There's something in my pocket! There's something in my pocket!" He blinked wildly and stuck his tongue out for no apparent reason.

The cop who had been taking his confession reached, with gloved hands, into Mr. Lemsling's wet shirt pocket and pulled out a soggy piece of paper. He looked at the handwritten note. "The hell is this?" the cop said. He couldn't make head nor tails of it.

"Listen!" Mr. Lemsling yelled. "You hear the mergansers?" He began to imitate them.

The linguistically challenged cop showed Lance the note. "You speak French?" he asked.

"*De mal en pis.*" Lance shrugged. He looked at the note. "But that's Latin. Can't help you there."

"Oh," the cop said. "Who speaks Latin anymore?" He tossed the piece of paper on the ground, then tucked Mr. Lemsling into the back of the patrol car and drove away. Lance picked up the note and looked at it. He didn't know what it meant but he recognized the handwriting and the words and he was beginning to get curious about both.

The soggy piece of paper said, "!Terra tuebor!"

Dr. Gibbs's to-do list was short but stout: (1.) Kill Paul Symon; (2.) Pimp for Jerry Landis. And although resolved to do both, Dr. Gibbs had decided to ease into the muck instead of doing a swan dive. First he approached Mr. Landis with the idea of hiring a third party to do the killing, selling it as a way of distancing themselves from the act. Jerry Landis, a longtime Republican and admirer of Richard Nixon, concurred and authorized a respectable slush fund for the doctor to use for both items on his list. As usual Dr. Gibbs was entitled to keep any change left over.

The doctor had heard that mercenaries sometimes advertised vague services in magazines like *Soldier of Fortune* but upon reviewing the latest issue at a local newsstand he found no such thing. Dr. Gibbs spent the next several nights cruising bars on the outskirts of Oakland, where he hoped to find a Raiders fan who might be willing to take the job. He had seen these people on television for years and thought that they looked and acted the part. Unfortunately, soft, fleshy, balding men with no tattoos tend not to fare well in Oakland Raiders bars, so Dr. Gibbs was lucky that he had the slush fund with which to buy numerous rounds of drinks. Certainly these were frightening people—it was the first time the doctor had seen a tattoo on the inside of a lip that didn't belong to a horse. And while there was plenty of talk about how so-and-so had killed one rat bastard or another, there were an equal number of tales about how the same people had avoided doing serious time by "rolling over" on accomplices. In the end Gibbs didn't find anyone at the bars who provided him with the comfort level he needed to move forward on the project.

Dr. Gibbs was walking to his car in the parking lot of the Pirate's Pit in Alameda when something exploded, or so he thought. In fact, it was just a motorcycle starting, but not just any motorcycle. It was a cretinously loud motorcycle, just like the one Arty's chauffeur rode. And suddenly, Dr. Gibbs had the answer to his question.

The next day he drove over to the Los Trancos Trailer Park. He was going to drop in on Arty, see how he was doing after the testicle operation, and ask about the whereabouts of his big friend, Bonedigger. When he arrived at the trailer park, Dr. Gibbs realized he didn't know Arty's address. So he started looking for the Harley, thinking that once he found Bonedigger, he could find Arty since Arty said that he and Bones lived in the same trailer park. But since the Harley was nowhere to be seen, the doctor decided to speak to one of the locals.

When he saw a buxom young woman sitting by herself in front of a double-wide he parked his car.

The woman's trailer was elevated a couple of feet higher than most of the others in the park, and brown wooden latticework encircled the space underneath the trailer, making a sort of corral. It was only when Dr. Gibbs got closer that he noticed the eyes peering through the latticework. There were sixteen in the little diamond-shaped spaces and there were lots of little fingers poking through as well. That's when he realized they were children, eight of them. "Excuse me," Dr. Gibbs said. "I'm looking for—"

There was a sudden commotion behind the latticework as two of the children began to fight like small dogs. The woman turned and screamed, "You kids don't cut that crap out, I'll turn that hose on you again!" The children hushed instantly and a small cloud of dust drifted from under the trailer as all the fingers and eyes suddenly disappeared. "I'm sorry," the woman said. "They're a handful."

Dr. Gibbs wasn't sure what to say. "Is this a . . . day care center?"

"Don't I wish!" the woman said with a laugh. "At least that way I'd make a little money for doing this."

Dr. Gibbs guessed she was of Italian descent, late twenties, Rubensesque with dark wavy hair curling half-way down her back. She had a welcoming smile and plenty of bosom. If this woman had given birth to even half the children under the trailer, she looked remarkably well preserved. "So, those are all yours?" Dr. Gibbs asked, trying to sound as if that could somehow be a good thing.

"All but two," she said. "I'm sitting for my friend, Thelma. She went to get our checks." They had a short discussion of the welfare state. She didn't like it, but welfare provided better than minimum-wage jobs did, so the choice was essentially made for her.

"Well, good luck . . ." Dr. Gibbs said, not knowing what to call her.

"It's Melanie," she said. "Are you looking for a space here?"

"No, I'm not, but maybe you can help me. I'm trying to find a man who drives a very loud motorcycle, I think it's a Harley." Dr. Gibbs held his hands up as if they were on the hand grips of the chopped-out bike. "Like the ones in *Easy Rider.*"

Melanie knew the bike. "You're looking for Bonedaddy?"

"Bone*daddy*? I thought it was Bonedigger," Dr. Gibbs said.

"It's both to me. Bones fathered number four down there." She pointed at an unfortunate-looking child underneath the trailer. "What do you want him for? He owes me a lot of child support. You're not a process server, are you?"

"No. I want to talk to him about a job."

"He's not much for regular employment," Melanie said. "You got a job for me? I'd love a job that pays better than minimum wage."

And just like that the day took a bright turn for Dr. Gibbs. With great enthusiasm Dr. Gibbs lied to Melanie about the wealthy widower who wanted children but not a wife. The man was willing to pay ten thousand dollars plus all medical expenses to any woman willing to have his child. Equally enthusiastic about the prospect of providing a child for a lonely old man, Melanie asked if the ten grand would be paid up front. The doctor explained that the deal was half up front, half on delivery, so to speak.

"How many children's he want? I bet my friend Thelma would sign up. But this man's got to sign an agreement that he's gonna take care of 'em. I don't think there's any more room under the trailer. And he can't report the income."

Dr. Gibbs improvised some representations and warranties regarding payments, 1099s, anonymity, and screening for STDs. He also invited Melanie to discuss the matter with her friend. They were making arrangements to finalize the deal when thunder shook the sky, which seemed odd on such a sunny day. "Sounds like Bones is home," Melanie said. She gave Dr. Gibbs directions to Bonedigger's trailer. Gibbs said he'd be in touch about their deal and headed back to his car. Dr. Gibbs found Bonedigger's place on the other side of the trailer park. The ground between Bone's and Arty's looked like an abandoned construction site. Splintered two-by-fours, some with reddish brown stains, were piled haphazardly near a rickety wheelchair ramp. Dr. Gibbs made his way through the damaged lumber to Bonedigger's door and knocked. As he waited for a response, standing on the blue plastic milk crate that served as the staircase, he could hear the television inside. Curious as to the biker's taste in daytime TV, Dr. Gibbs leaned his ear close to the door to listen. The voice seemed familiar, but it didn't sound like a game show or a soap, it sounded more like—

WHAM! Bonedigger threw the door open and nearly took the doctor's head off. Gibbs landed near the pile of two-by-fours, the nasty gash on his forehead adding confusing new DNA evidence to any insurance fraud investigations that might come this way. Bonedigger, three feet of heavy chain dangling from his right hand, stood in the doorway staring down at the dazed doctor. "Whaddya want?"

Dr. Gibbs groaned. The sight in his right eye seemed diminished and there was a loud ringing in his ears. He pulled an old tissue from his pocket and applied pressure to his wound. "I don't know if you remember me . . ."

"I remember," Bonedigger said. "You're the guy bought one of Arty's nuts. I told you I ain't interested in that."

"No, that's not why I'm here," Dr. Gibbs said. "Could I come in for just a minute?"

As he went back inside, Bonedigger mumbled something about not getting too much blood on the furniture. Dr. Gibbs used his unbloodied hand to steady himself as he made his way through the lumber, up the milk crate stairway, and inside to the sofa. He was surprised by how neatly kept the trailer was. When the ringing in his ears subsided Dr. Gibbs could again hear the familiar voice on the television. It was Oprah. Today's show was "I Love My Big Family." It featured a collection of breeders whose relentless couplings had resulted in families of fifteen or more children. These people were stunning examples of asymbiotic recklessness and a perfect illustration of the hyper-romanticization of human life that had become commonplace in America in the waning years of the twentieth century. Such unwarranted rhapsodizing about the collection of cells that constitutes *Homo sapiens* led naturally to parading these kinds of idiots past the brief window of fame that is the television talk show. Such celebrity—compounded by the congratulatory treatment heaped upon them during the program— not only validated, but foolishly rewarded, this sort of behavior.

However, Dr. Gibbs was unaware of all this so he sat on the sofa in search of some small talk. "So, uh, Bonedigger. That's an interesting name," Dr. Gibbs said. "How'd you get it?"

Bonedigger glowered at the doctor for a moment before standing and going to a closet. "It's none of your fucking business," he said as he reached for something in the back of the small storage space. What he grabbed was long, and even from the shadows, Dr. Gibbs could tell it was made of metal. The doctor feared for a moment that Bonedigger was getting a rifle but, to his relief, it turned out to be a badly tarnished trombone. Bones said it was a memento from his first felony—it seems he got his nickname after killing a trombone player about ten years earlier.

Dr. Gibbs nodded slowly as he imagined a jazzman sneaking around with the wrong woman. He assumed a jealous husband had hired Bones to do the guy in. As Dr. Gibbs conjured this sordid tale of infidelity and murder for hire he inadvertently picked at the dried blood on his face. "Well, I see where the 'bone' comes from.

I mean, trom*bone*, right? But what about the 'digger' part?"

"Somebody had to bury the son of a bitch, didn't they?" Bonedigger pursed his big lips and blew into the mouthpiece, causing the trombone to bleat like a cloned sheep. Then he looked at his visitor. "Now I'll ask you again. Whaddya want?" he said.

The vision in Dr. Gibbs's right eye suddenly returned and—just as suddenly—he could see how good things were going for him. Except for the nasty gash on his head, the day was turning out better than he had any right to expect. He had come here hoping only to gauge the possibility of approaching this tattooed nitwit about solving the Paul Symon problem. Now, after being at the trailer park for less than an hour, he had found both uteri and an experienced killer. The gods were surely smiling on him. Dr. Gibbs sat forward on the sofa to convey conspiracy. "Well," he said, "I know a man with a problem and he wants the problem . . . *solved*." Dr. Gibbs had no idea how well Bonedigger picked up on such subtle shadings as the way he had hesitated before saying "solved" the way he did, but apparently he picked it up well enough.

"No problem," Bonedigger said. "How much?" He picked at something thick and yellowish between his teeth which he then wiped off on one of his curly pork chop sideburns.

How much, indeed. Dr. Gibbs hadn't thought about that. He had no idea how much to offer. The truth was Dr. Gibbs really didn't want this Paul Symon guy dead but, at the same time, his craving for a piece of Xenotech, Incorporated sufficiently outweighed his scruples so he had to offer something. Even after taking into account Melanie's and Thelma's childbearing fees, Gibbs still had thirty thousand dollars to work with. He felt certain Bonedigger could be had for less than that. But how much less? Offer too little and the guy might get insulted and start looking for a new nickname: "You can call me Doc." Offer too much and his own profit margin shrank.

Bonedigger coaxed another wounded animal noise from the trombone, calling Dr. Gibbs back from his thoughts. Sensing impatience, Dr. Gibbs decided the best idea was just to ask about pricing. "What did you get for doing the trombone player?"

"The fucking trombone," the biker replied. "Plus the nickname." It turned out Dr. Gibbs's tale of cuckoldry was all wrong. The way Bonedigger told it, the trombonist had been playing for spare change, offering J. J. Johnson's oeuvre to the passersby on a sidewalk in front of a bar where Bones (or Spanky, as he was known at that point) was drinking and selling crystal meth. The performer was taking a break after finishing an awkwardly improvised ending to "Night Flight" when he drained his spit valve, inadvertently wetting the seat of Spanky's bike. Drunk, on speed, and enraged, the biker attacked the horn man and broke his neck like a toasted bread stick. The memory made Bones chuckle fondly.

"I see," Dr. Gibbs said. He looked at his tissue and saw that he still hadn't checked the flow of blood.

Bonedigger stood and motioned for Dr. Gibbs to follow. They went into the kitchen area, which resembled a laboratory more than anything else. A series of beakers, Bunsen burners, and valves connected by Pyrex tubing added up to a fairly sophisticated, if boutique-sized, speed factory. "Want some crank?" Bonedigger asked.

Dr. Gibbs shrugged noncommittally and watched as his host snorted a long, thick line of the sparkly white powder. When Bonedigger handed him the straw, Dr. Gibbs decided to take a walk on the wild side. "Well, when in Rome . . ." he said before going down on the line Bones had left behind. The burning sensation in his sinus lasted only a few seconds. A moment later Dr. Gibbs began to feel an affinity for the large biker. He started to feel good about Melanie and her plentiful bosoms. Next he got a warm feeling about her uteri. He also began to feel good about the Paul Symon problem, and then he started to talk and talk and talk.

He told Bonedigger about his childhood and his parents' expectations and how he ended up in a Haitian medical school. He told glorified versions of his experiences in India and Hong Kong and how he had come to meet Jerry Landis and had learned about the science of xenografting and how the company had a baboon farm down in Deckern County, Mississippi, and how this Paul Symon character was threatening to ruin everything and . . .

"I got an idea," Bonedigger said, hoping to shut the chatterbox up. "Give me twice what you gave Arty for his nut."

"Three hundred bucks?" Dr. Gibbs couldn't help but look surprised at such a low number.

"Yeah, the problem's this Symon guy, right? He's got two balls, right? Give me one-fifty for each *cojone*."

Dr. Gibbs did the math in his head, the result of which was a very handsome profit. The combined euphoria from the speed and the easy money made him feel generous. "I tell you what," Dr. Gibbs said. "Throw down some more of that crank and I'll make it five hundred."

It was just past four in the afternoon when Jerry Landis peeled the backing off the testosterone patch. He was about to slap it onto his stomach when suddenly he had another notion. He closed the door to his office. Then, leaning against the door, he dropped his pants and stuck the new patch directly onto his bulging scrotum. *Whir-pffft whir-pffft whir-pffft.*

After several weeks on Dr. Vines's hormone program Jerry Landis looked and felt like a new man. His third gonad was functioning beautifully, and he could hardly wait to meet these women with whom Dr. Gibbs had made arrangements. He did, after all, have a mission to fulfill. His outward glow notwithstanding, Jerry Landis was still suffering from Werner's syndrome—but until the disease dragged him into the dark hole of death Jerry Landis would continue taking care of business, which, these days, consisted of monitoring the progress of his two groups of researchers.

In the past, when told that the Xenotech scientists were not making any discernible headway in solving Werner's syndrome, Jerry Landis had been disappointed but had encouraged his charges to persist and to be creative in their search. But these days that same report just got him pissed off. Under the influence of the hormones, Jerry Landis had begun dropping by the company's research facilities on a daily basis to let them know, in surprisingly aggressive terms, that he was still waiting for a goddamn cure.

The scene was equally tense in the other lab despite the fact that those researchers were making demonstrable progress with the transgenic baboon organ and antirejection drug projects. In the past three weeks there had been two major breakthroughs with the antirejection drug, and as always, that had triggered the shipment of another of the huge primates from the baboon farm. Next came the delicate matter of finding what was nervously referred to around Xenotech as a volunteer into whom the baboon heart could be transplanted. So far none had been found.

After pulling his pants up, Jerry Landis planned to go to the labs for this afternoon's stern reminder that he was still the boss and was damn sure expecting a cure for all the money he was pouring into this place. But his plans took an unexpected and ugly turn when his secretary buzzed him to say that a Mr. Alex Luckett from the Food and Drug Administration was here to see him.

Whir-pffft whir-pffft whir-pffft . . . Jerry Landis suddenly felt ill. Why the hell was the FDA here? "Does he have an appointment?" he asked his secretary.

"He's from Washington," she said. "Thinks he doesn't need an appointment."

"Stall him," Landis said. He considered the possibilities. Maybe it was a friend playing a practical joke. No, the few friends he had knew better than that. Around One Biotech Center the FDA was not considered good comedy material. This had to be the real McCoy. But why? Xenotech had a sterling reputation for meeting federal paperwork requirements. Jerry Landis had personally signed off on the latest investigational new drug application. Maybe there was a problem with someone on their Institutional Review Board, a conflict of interest matter that could be solved without impeding research. No, they'd simply send a field investigator out for that. Then it hit him. That goddamn Paul Symon. The bastard sent his letter.

Bzzzzz. "Sir, Mr. Luckett is waiting."

"Yeah, all right," Mr. Landis said, "send him in." It occurred to him that there was, as yet, nothing to worry about. The FDA knew exactly what sort of research Xenotech was doing. It wasn't involved in any illegal activities, at least none over which the FDA had jurisdiction. It was probably just some bored bureaucrat doing routine follow-up to a letter from a concerned citizen.

Mr. Luckett was in his late fifties, a bit overweight, and had a large mustache that lent him the aspect of a walrus. Mr. Luckett had worked his way slowly up the FDA ladder, filling voids left by the death or retirement of those above him. He wore a charcoal gray suit the cut of which was best described as mechanical.

"Come in, Mr. Luckett. I'm Jerry Landis, how can I help you?" He herded the FDA man toward the chair opposite his desk. But Mr. Luckett remained standing as Jerry Landis sat.

Hovering near the chair, Mr. Luckett eyed his host with disdain. "Cut the crap, Mr. Landis. You and I both know I'm about as welcome here as two pints of ebola virus. And the last thing you want to do is help."

Jerry Landis took this as a bad sign. Sure, it was all true, but what kind of person just came out and said it?

Mr. Luckett, in addition to having little fashion sense, had little use for these sorts of duplicitous niceties. No one wanted to help him. He knew that. Mr. Luckett's was a thankless job that offered no glory and only a modest income. That's almost certainly why his wife had left him. Okay, so maybe he wasn't a great dresser and as a conversationalist he was slightly less adept than Marcel Marceau but, dammit, what he did was important. And even if the job wasn't as glamorous as, say, something over at the Department of Agriculture, he still had the power to move important new drugs into phase three testing and then into the marketplace. And if you wanted to fuck with Mr. Alex Luckett with phoney How are you's and What can I do to help's, well then he could also put your project on "clinical hold" and bring your company to its goddamn knees. If he had nothing else, he had that power and he wasn't afraid to use it.

As the FDA man dropped his briefcase into the chair Jerry Landis smiled and struggled against his urge to come across the desk and break the bridge of this fucker's nose. Of course since starting the hormone treatments he struggled against that same urge a dozen times a day. The difference this time was that Jerry Landis was thinking seriously about surrendering to it.

Mr. Luckett was looking at the plastic organs and the documents on Landis's desk, trying to read upside-down memos. "Mr. Landis, do you know why I'm here?"

"Quite frankly, no. I don't think you'd bother coming out here about the latest IND application or our review board. And you've had our research protocols on file so long that, if they were the problem, we'd have heard from you years ago." Jerry Landis covered a mildly inflammatory memo with the plastic pancreas. "So why don't you just cut to the chase?"

Mr. Luckett sneered. "My job is to assess risk, Mr. Landis. When a company is developing a new drug it is my job to weigh the potential risks against the potential benefits."

"I'm familiar with the FDA's charter," Jerry Landis said. "Exactly what office do you report to over there?"

Mr. Luckett handed over his business card. "I'm with the Center for Drug Evaluation and Research. We report to the Interim Deputy Commissioner for Operations, who reports to both the Director of the Center for Biologics Evaluation and Research and the Director of Enforcement. They, in turn, report to the Office of Chief Counsel at the Division of Bioresearch Monitoring, which reports to the Acting Special Assistant for Investigations. She reports directly to the Commissioner of Food and Drugs. That's in the Office of Operations. There are also horizontal reporting requirements that require us to inform people in the Offices of Policy, External Affairs, and Management and Systems as to our field investigations. Does that answer your question?"

"More or less," Jerry Landis said. The answer was that this charcoal gray slug was buried so deep in the bureaucracy that he could close down Xenotech, Incorporated with one negative report before anyone noticed he had no good reason for doing so. "But I still don't understand why you're here."

"I'm here, Mr. Landis, because your research makes me uncomfortable."

"Uncomfortable?" Jerry Landis couldn't believe it. The FDA had a million standards by which to judge biotech companies, but unless it was a recent addition to the list, personal comfort level wasn't one of them. "Uncomfortable in what way?" he asked.

Mr. Luckett picked up the model kidney and popped it open as he spoke. "Have you ever heard of Mary Baker Eddy?"

Jerry Landis flipped through his Rolodex. "Mary Baker Eddy? Isn't she the Deputy Commissioner for the Division of Clinical Pharmacology?"

"No, you're thinking of Rene Magritte, and she's Policy Co-coordinator over at the Division of Microbiological Studies now," Mr. Luckett explained. "Mary Baker Eddy isn't with the FDA."

"Is she at CDC?" Jerry Landis asked.

"No," Mr. Luckett said peevishly. "And she's not at NIH either."

"Oh, then I don't think I know her," Landis said. "I take it she has something to do with your . . . lack of comfort with our research?"

"You could say that," Mr. Luckett said as he snapped the kidney back together and returned it to the desk.

"I still don't understand," Jerry Landis said. "Did this Mary Baker Eddy contact you about us or something?"

"No. She's dead." Mr. Luckett opened his briefcase and produced a sheet of paper. "But we did hear from a Mr. Paul Symon." He waved Paul's letter in the air.

Christ, this was getting worse by the second, Landis thought. He assumed a defiant attitude. "Well, I can guarantee you that Xenotech, Incorporated had nothing to do with Ms. Eddy's death no matter what Mr. Symon says in his goddamn letter."

"I'm sure you didn't," Mr. Luckett said.

"Well then what the hell does Mary Baker Eddy have to do with the price of tea in China?" Jerry Landis blurted. He was losing his patience. He wondered if attacking an FDA employee was a federal offense or just a run-of-the-mill assault charge.

"Mary Baker Eddy was the founder of Christian Science," Mr. Luckett said. "She died in 1910."

Jerry Landis held his hands out, palms up, and shrugged his shoulders in the internationally recognized gesture of "I have no fucking idea what you're talking about."

"I am a Christian Scientist, Mr. Landis. I believe prayer heals sickness, not conventional medicine, and certainly not the procedures *you* propose. And that is why your research makes me uncomfortable."

Jerry Landis was dumbstruck. He was staring at Mr. Luckett and there were things he wanted to say, but nothing seemed to be coming from his gaping mouth.

Mr. Luckett took the opportunity to expound further. "You see, Jesus's healings were not miraculous interruptions of natural law but the operation of God's power or spiritual law." Mr. Luckett gestured at Paul's letter to the FDA. "And what you propose to do with your baboons is an affront to spiritual law and therefore I am unable to write a favorable report on behalf of your research."

"I see." *Whir-pffft whir-pffft whir-pffft.* On a scale of one to ten, with ten being most disastrous, this rated about three million. Of all the deals in Jerry Landis's life, Paul Symon was about to stop the only one that actually mattered, the one that might keep Jerry Landis from death. Although there were many reasons to panic, Landis remained calm. "Let me ask you, isn't there something in the First Amendment about separation of church and state? That hasn't been repealed, has it?"

"What the First Amendment does," Mr. Luckett said, "is allow me to practice the religion of my choice. The fact that I'm able to practice it more effectively at my current job is just one of those funny things in life." He smiled a Christian Science smile.

Failing to find the humor in this, Jerry Landis quickly conjured three plans of action, all of which had proved effective at various points in the past. He trotted out the first. "Mr. Luckett, have you ever heard of Werner's syndrome?"

"Can't say that I have. But my bet is, you've got it."

"I'm afraid so, and they don't give me more than a year to live."

"Well then I hope you have someone praying for your health because otherwise, as far as I'm concerned, your death is God's will."

Good Lord, Landis thought, Christian Science was nothing more than natural selection with a side order of prayer. So much for plan one.

"I'd pray for you myself if there wasn't an obvious conflict of interest," Mr. Luckett said.

Ignoring the political consultant's creed that one should never underestimate the power of a cash bribe, Jerry Landis decided to skip plan two and move directly to plan three. He picked up his phone. "I'd like you to meet with my head of research," he said. "Let him tell you about what we're doing. Maybe he can change your mind." He held up his hand just as Mr. Luckett was about to object. "Yes, hello, Dr. *Taylor*, it's Jerry Landis. Could you come to my office, please? Yes, that's right. Another demonstration."

"There's nothing this Dr. Taylor can say that will change my report," Mr. Luckett said.

"Please, indulge me. You know how important this research is to the company. At least allow us to do our presentation before you shut us down. Think of it as a dying man's last wish." Jerry Landis noticed Mr. Luckett glancing toward the bar. "Would you like a drink? C'mon, it's the end of the day and it's going to be a few minutes before Dr. Taylor gets here. Besides, there's no reason we can't be civilized about this."

Mr. Luckett hesitated, his eyes narrowed. "Tea," he said.

"Tea," Jerry Landis repeated. Great, he thought, not only a Christian Scientist but a devout one. "I hope you don't mind if I have a bourbon." Jerry Landis poured himself a double.

About halfway through their drinks, Dr. Taylor entered carrying some documents. He looked apprehensive. "Sorry I took so long. I had to go to the other lab to find something."

"And I trust you found it," Jerry Landis said, smiling.

"Yes sir. No problem," he said.

"Good, then let's get started," Mr. Landis said. "But first, why don't you freshen up our guest's drink? Mr. Luckett is having tea."

After fixing Mr. Luckett's tea, Dr. Taylor launched into a discussion of the origins of cross-species organ transplants. Fifteen minutes later, he was talking about how Dr. Robert Michler at Columbia Presbyterian had transplanted half a dozen cynomolgus monkey hearts into six baboons with an average survival time of six months. That's when Mr. Luckett's expression changed from indifference to mild concern, though not about the monkeys. His right hand reached up to rub the left side of his chest. He tried to take a deep breath but could manage only a shallow gasp. A moment later he became visibly distressed.

Seeing this, Dr. Taylor stopped. "Are you all right, Mr. Luckett?"

The remainder of Mr. Luckett's tea splashed onto the carpet as he dropped his cup. Jerry Landis rushed over and grabbed his arm.

"Dr. Taylor, call Dr. Gibbs right away!" Jerry Landis turned to Mr. Luckett. "What's wrong? Are you in pain?"

Tiny beads of cold sweat formed on Mr. Luckett's

brow. He labored to take a breath. "Hard to . . . describe. Heaviness . . . discomfort."

Dr. Taylor was on the phone. "Dr. Gibbs, come to Mr. Landis's office, stat! And bring your bag." After hanging up, he helped lay Mr. Luckett down on the sofa. Hovering over Mr. Luckett, Jerry Landis turned to Dr. Taylor and whispered urgently, "Angina pectoris?"

"The dyspnea's certainly classic and his skin color fits." Dr. Taylor turned to Mr. Luckett. "The discomfort is radiating into your neck and arms and jaw, isn't it?"

Mr. Luckett looked like a frightened child, eyes wide and searching for help, as he nodded yes to all the questions. "Please do something," he said.

"We've sent for the staff physician," Jerry Landis said.

As if on cue, Dr. Gibbs burst into the office. "What's going on?!"

"Myocardial infarc!" Jerry Landis said, though it would be diagnosed differently by qualified heart people.

Mr. Luckett struggled to speak. "Call nine-one-one," he said, forsaking his faith. "Now."

Dr. Taylor slipped the tensiometer's pneumatic cuff onto Mr. Luckett's arm and pumped it tight. Dr. Gibbs listened intently to the information supplied by the stethoscope. A moment later the doctors exchanged a damning glance, shaking their heads.

"What's wrong?" Mr. Luckett asked. "Tell me."

Leaning down, Jerry Landis placed his hands on the doctors' shoulders, halting their activities. He then looked down at Mr. Luckett and spoke calmly. "I'm afraid you're having a severe heart attack. Your coronary artery is probably blocked, your myocardium is starving for oxygen. Necrosis has already begun, that's irreversible damage to the myocardial tissue."

Mr. Luckett felt nauseous and was sweating profusely. "Can't you do something?"

Jerry Landis leaned closer. "Would you like us to pray?" he asked gently.

Mr. Luckett shook his head no as he looked up hopefully at the men lingering above him. Had he not been under the impression that he was dying, Mr. Luckett probably would have noticed that Dr. Taylor was wearing a name tag that said "Dr. Putnam." He labored to catch his breath. "Ambulance," Mr. Luckett said.

Jerry Landis pulled a syringe from Dr. Gibbs's black bag. "There's really no point in that, I'm afraid. The necrosis would require a new heart, but there's such a shortage of human organs that, well, I'm sure I don't have to explain it to you." He held the syringe up to the light and tapped the air bubbles to the top. "This is going to put you to sleep," he said. "Just relax."

Within the minute Mr. Luckett was out and he dreamed he was dying. A calm came over the room. Jerry Landis turned to Dr. Gibbs and Dr. Putnam. He was all business. "Gentlemen, I believe we can call off our search for a volunteer."

Lately, Lance Abbott had become something of the Monday morning detective. After talking to the investigator at the scene of the BART tunnel accident, something started nagging at him. Then, after leaving Lemsling's landfill, Lance was convinced that something funny was going on. So he did a little research. In addition to Shart Lemsling and H. Wayne Grigsby, Lance learned of one additional "Terra Tuebor" victim. Her name was Edith Hazelquist, the president of the West Coast's largest retail fur chain, Furever Yours. A couple of months ago, according to a San Francisco Police Department report that Lance obtained, Ms. Hazelquist had been found in one of her cold storage facilities, alive but crudely scalped. She was tied up in a chair with half a dozen hungry minks clawing their way around in the pair of stretch pants she shouldn't have been wearing in the first place. The carnivorous little mammals had been forced to survive on the fat reserves of Ms. Hazelquist's copious thighs. The "Terra Tuebor" note was stuck to her bloody scalp like a bad rug.

In addition to the "Terra Tuebor" victims, Lance Abbott had compiled a list of unsolved and mysterious deaths which included the bifurcated man in the BART tunnel and several other, similar deaths in and around the Bay Area. The deaths were similar in that all the victims had been severely mutilated. There was, for example, the dolphin-unfriendly tuna boat captain whose hideously mangled body had been extracted from an industrial fish scaler. There was also a veal tycoon who had been run through an automated beef carcass cleaning system, leaving very little behind.

Although a few members of the press had written stories suggesting connections among a couple of these incidents, no one, including the dozen computer-aided law enforcement agencies within whose jurisdictions these victims had been found, seemed to have uncovered as much as Lance Abbott. And Lance hoped it would stay that way because his plan was to solve the series of crimes and return to Hollywood with the rights to the story. As the sole owner of a hot property, Lance Abbott would secure the role of the handsome organ procurement specialist turned crime solver, sort of a cross between Dick Van Dyke's *Diagnosis Murder* character and Jack Klugman's Quincy. The more he thought about it, the more he felt this was a great movie-of-the-week idea that could be used as a back door pilot for a series. Lance felt he'd be able to sell the idea to the networks as appealing to a younger demographic since Lance was both younger and better-looking than Klugman or Van Dyke. Of course he'd want to find a good writer (that is, one willing to work cheap) to do the script before approaching packaging agents.

But he was getting ahead of himself. First he had to solve the mystery of his two lists. Perhaps this latest victim would provide a new clue.

Lance was heading east on Interstate 580. He was just past the exit for the Lawrence Livermore National Laboratory, on his way to Altamont Pass, where, his police scanner informed him, there was a need for a coroner's wagon. Lance assumed he wouldn't find any human parts for resale there, but he was hoping for answers or—even better—a third act for his yet-to-be-written script. He turned off the interstate and was soon driving through the soft, round, golden hills of east Alameda County, home of the Central California Wind Farms, where thousands of wind turbine generators whiskered the hills, creating cheap, efficient, eco-friendly energy as long as the wind averaged a minimum of thirteen miles per hour. On his left was a group of two hundred vertical-axis turbines, their massive rotors spinning the giant curved aluminum blades and looking for all the world like the eggbeaters of the gods. Farther ahead on the right, on top of a knoll, were a hundred horizontal-axis wind turbines. Perched atop thirty-foot-tall towers, these huge tri-bladed high-density polyethylene propellers looked as if they might power the earth's rotation.

Leading to the top of the knoll was a dirt road where Lance saw a highway patrol cruiser and several sheriff's vehicles along with the coroner's wagon. He pulled in and parked. Walking to the scene he noticed two things. The first was the low-frequency *whomp-whomp-whomp* of the huge blades as they cut through the air above and around him. The second was that the ground was littered with the mangled bodies of a great many birds. It looked as if several species had fought a terrible battle here— the Battle of Altamont had a nice ring to it—and there hadn't been time to bury the dead. The truth was somewhat less thrilling than that: These birds simply had failed to negotiate the airspace between the whirling and not-so-eco-friendly-after-all blades of the wind turbines.

Lance watched his step as he crossed the battlefield and approached the group of men gathered around what he guessed was the victim. Assuming it hadn't blown away, Lance figured there was a "Terra Tuebor" note somewhere in the vicinity. The men were standing seventy yards from the only turbine generator in the wind farm that wasn't spinning. There was a crude scaffolding built up in front of the still windmill and one of the blades was a bloody mess.

When Lance reached the gathered men and looked

down, he saw the most disfigured human face he had ever laid his eyes on. It was almost folded in on itself, the ears nearly touching one another and the nose practically pushed out the back of the head. The rest of the body hadn't fared much better. It was badly distorted, having been split to the spine along the torso's midline like a butterflied shrimp. After Lance flashed his SCOPE business card, the authorities made a few Frankenstein jokes before answering his questions.

It seemed the victim, a man named Jonah Levin, was the Associate Director of Defense and Nuclear Technologies at the Lawrence Livermore National Labs, just down the road. The highway patrolman's theory was that Mr. Levin climbed up the scaffolding by the wind turbine. He assumed Mr. Levin was conducting some sort of energy experiment. The patrolman theorized that a strong gust of wind caught the scientist by surprise and pushed him into the path of the oncoming blade and the force of the impact hurled him seventy yards north to where they were now standing. "If those blades weren't so thick, Mr. Science here would've been split clean in two," he said.

Lance didn't say anything, but he was willing to bet that no one at the Livermore Labs would know anything about any energy experiments Mr. Levin was conducting. "Did you find any notes?" Lance asked as he looked around.

"What, like a suicide note?" one of the sheriffs asked with a laugh.

Realizing he had tipped his hand, Lance played dumb and decided not to go into the "Terra Tuebor" business. He didn't want to tell these guys his theory and risk losing exclusivity on the rights, so he grinned like an idiot as the cops talked about what a stupid way this would be to commit suicide. Still hoping to find a note, Lance walked over toward the wind turbine. He climbed up the scaffolding and looked at the still blades. He climbed back down and was walking back toward the group of men when something on the ground caught his eye. It was a dark piece of muscle or tissue of some sort. Lance bent down and, while pretending to tie his shoes, slipped the tissue into the cuff of his pants. He had a notion it might tell him more than it would tell the rest of the people gathered at the scene.

Lance then walked back to his car. He was disappointed there was no terrorist's note, but at least he hadn't come away empty-handed. Lance felt in his heart and his bones that he was onto something big. He planned to take the tissue to a friend for identification and then go back to his office and review the information that was in the "Terra Tuebor" file he had started.

There is, in certain circles of the pharmaceutical industry, the oft-told story of the British physiologist who, in 1983, after addressing the American Urological Association, stepped from behind the podium, dropped his pants, and proudly displayed his thoroughly erect penis. As wonderful an image as that was, it could have been improved only by having the man's colleagues crowd onto the stage for a closer look, which is, so the story goes, exactly what they did.

The stiff physiologist had been extolling the virtues of certain chemical relaxants capable of opening the blood vessels that feed the penis's inner chambers and result in a woody you could do chin-ups on. The physiologist exposed himself to his audience, as an old commercial spokesman used to say, "just to prove a point."

Upjohn, the pharmaceutical giant, was credited (or blamed, depending on your point of view) as being the first company in the world to sell a legitimate commercial erection-inducing substance. Called prostaglandin E1, the vasodilator had proven itself capable of producing boners of an hour's duration. According to urologists at least two other drugs, papaverine and phentolamine, were capable of the same feat. The bad news was it didn't come in pill form.

Pharmacia & Upjohn was now marketing something called Caverject Sterile Powder—alprostadil for injection.

Part of the text in their full-page ads read: "Priapism, a condition in which an erection lasts longer than 6 hours, was reported in less than ½ of 1% of all patients. Although rare and usually dose-related, it requires immediate medical attention. The most common side effect of Caverject is mild to moderate pain after injection."

Whir-pffft whir-pffft whir-pffft. Jerry Landis listened impatiently as Dr. Vines explained to him how it all worked. Finally he had heard enough. "Listen," he said, "these girls are going to be here in ten minutes, so just load your goddamn needle and shoot me." Dr. Vines shrugged and did as he was told. He took the hypodermic in one hand and Jerry Landis in the other. Then they shared a noticeable, respectful, moment before going forward with the needle. Eventually Dr. Vines poked it into the side of Jerry's skin flute and injected a few cc's of the miracle juice. Jerry Landis watched his johnson, waiting for something to happen. "How long before I'm in business?" he asked.

"Soon," Dr. Vines assured him. He disposed of the needle and packed his black bag, then cleared his throat. He appeared to blush slightly. "Uh, Mr. Landis, when the girls arrive, would you mind if I, uh, watched? Just in the interest of science, of course."

Jerry Landis looked up at the defrocked urologist. "Listen, you twisted little shit, in the interest of keeping your scrawny ass alive you better get the hell out of here."

"Yes, sir, I understand. It's just that I never . . . well, never mind." Dr. Vines slunk out of the office without further exposing his deviance.

Jerry Landis had mixed feelings about the coming attractions. Part of him hoped that tonight's proceedings would be bathed in God's golden light, thereby lending them a somewhat more spiritual ambience than they otherwise might have. The other part was hoping for a wild night of squat and gobble regardless of the lighting. Uneasy about his mixed feelings, and lacking the time to pray for guidance, Jerry Landis poured himself a double bourbon and stood at the window looking down at the parking lot, watching for his guests. He was there for a few minutes before he felt a rare tightening sensation in his pants. He saw no signs of life in the parking lot below so he took a healthy gulp of the whiskey and crossed to the sofa, where he sat and marveled at the sudden rigidity of his schvantz. *Whir-pffft whir-pffft whir-pffft.*

Dr. Gibbs was ten floors down, sitting in the dark lobby of One Biotech Center, fretting about his future while he waited for the taxi to arrive. After dealing with Mr. Luckett's little heart problem, Jerry Landis figured the FDA wasn't much of a threat, so he had told Dr. Gibbs to stop the contract on Paul Symon. Ever since then Dr. Gibbs had been trying to get in touch with Bones but he didn't have the biker's phone number and he was never at the trailer park when the doctor dropped by. His worst fear was that Bones would kill Paul, get caught, and turn state's evidence. Dr. Gibbs knew what sort of future awaited him in prison, and the prospect made him long for the good old days when the only blood on his hands was that of impoverished kidney vendors who had signed all the necessary waivers. The more he thought about his current situation, the more depressed he became.

However, before Dr. Gibbs reached the bottom of his pit of despair, the cab with Melanie and Thelma arrived. Dr. Gibbs felt his inside coat to see that the envelopes were still there. Each envelope had five thousand dollars in it, the down payment for services to be rendered— services which, according to the negotiated contract, had to include "the natural process of reproduction." In other words, no one wanted to go with artificial insemination, Jerry Landis for obvious reasons, Melanie and Thelma because they just wanted to do it and get paid. They figured the two of them could take care of business a lot faster than a room full of lab technicians. Besides, as Thelma had put it so eloquently during the final phases of contract negotiations, all of which had been conducted over the phone, "We both like doing it."

Dr. Gibbs went outside to greet the arriving ova. As he approached the cab's door, a pair of panties shot out the open window and landed at the doctor's feet. A moment later Melanie and Thelma spilled out of the back seat onto the sidewalk, giggling. They had been drinking.

This was the first time Dr. Gibbs had seen Thelma. She was taller than Melanie and had long, seriously bleached hair. Her short dress clung to her quite favorably, especially in light of her two children. As she lay giggling on the sidewalk next to the voluptuous Melanie, Dr. Gibbs had what would most accurately be described as impure thoughts. After helping the women to their feet he gave each of them an envelope. He wanted them to pay for the cab out of their own pockets. Dr. Gibbs tugged on his desperate little ponytail the way he always did when he was nervous. "Listen, Melanie," he said, "I've been trying to get in touch with Bonedigger. Do you know where I can find him?"

"No, he hasn't been around much lately," Melanie said as she dealt with the cabbie.

"I heard his bike the other day," Thelma added, "but I didn't see Bones."

The cabdriver couldn't break a hundred and Melanie had no intention of tipping the guy sixty bucks, so Dr. Gibbs ended up paying the whole tab. "Do you know where he hangs out or anything like that?" he asked as they walked into the lobby.

"You might talk to Arty," Melanie said. "They keep in pretty close touch."

Thelma skipped a few steps ahead of Melanie and Dr. Gibbs before turning and playfully lifting her skirt for a flash. "So, where's our date?" she asked with a horny giggle.

Dr. Gibbs's eyes weren't what they used to be, so in the dimly lit lobby he wasn't sure whether Thelma was wearing dark panties or none at all. "Uhhhh." The impure thoughts returned and short-circuited his cognitive processes for a moment. "Uhhh, upstairs." He called the elevator and told the trailer girls not to be expecting Brad Pitt when they got to the penthouse.

"Hey, the only reason we're here is to help this man have the kids he wants," Melanie said as she counted her money. "He doesn't have to be handsome."

Thelma looked shocked. "You didn't tell me he was ugly!"

Before Dr. Gibbs could say, "Have you ever heard of Werner's syndrome?" the elevator arrived and the guests of honor climbed aboard. As the doors shut Thelma yanked her skirt up again and winked at Dr. Gibbs. He could hear her giggling as the car ascended the shaft.

Jerry Landis was on his third double bourbon. He was still sitting on the sofa flexing his love muscle when the elevator doors opened. *Whir-pffft whir-pffft whir-pffft.* It was hard to say who was more pleased at what they saw. Landis couldn't believe how young, beautiful, and exotic the two women seemed. Melanie and Thelma were pleased not only that Jerry Landis wasn't extremely ugly but also because it looked like he wouldn't need a lot of coaxing. "Wow!" Thelma said. "That's quite a boner."

Jerry Landis blushed and modestly tucked himself away. He invited them to come sit with him while he told fantastic stories of the miracles produced in the laboratories he owned. He also talked about Dr. Vines's hormone treatments and how great he felt despite Werner's syndrome. The women marveled at how thick and lustrous his hair was and they squeezed his muscles. He boasted of an ejaculatory distance that was humanly impossible and offered to demonstrate his youthful urinary arc. To his credit, Jerry Landis didn't make any false claims about his skeletal condition. With Werner's syndrome came advanced osteoporosis and the severely compromised integrity of his bones. Not even the hormone treatment could help that.

"Now," Jerry Landis said to Thelma. "Tell me something about you."

Thelma smiled. "I'm not wearing any panties!" she said with delight.

"Do tell," Jerry Landis said with a wet smile.

"Is that the bar?" Melanie asked.

"Indeed it is." Jerry Landis poured drinks and soon the alcohol was talking, or singing actually. "I got my mojo workin', just won't work on you . . ." Since Landis couldn't carry a tune, his choice of blues over, say, opera, indicated that his judgment wasn't entirely impaired.

Melanie was dancing on the credenza with a drink in one hand and her bra in the other. "Hey!" she said to Jerry Landis. "What's your name? Mr. Gibbs never told us your name."

Landis, who was dancing on his desk, dropped his pants. "Just call me Tripod," he said.

Melanie leaned down to look at Dr. Vines's handiwork. "Hey, you've got three balls!"

Landis leered. "The better to love you with, my dear," he said. He began kicking the plastic organs off his desk. He held his hand out to Thelma. "Come on up here, sweetheart."

Thelma was both first and second. Melanie stood at the bar and watched in awe as Jerry Landis demonstrated a prowess she had only dreamt of. Finally, after several maneuvers that required more stamina than Thelma possessed, she fell onto the sofa, exhausted. Like a tag team wrestling partner, Melanie took over, proving both capable and inventive. Jerry Landis, for his part, was sowing more oats than International Harvester. He saw the golden light and felt its warmth as he did his righteous duty. He was being fruitful and trying to multiply and replenish the earth and subdue it. And since he knew it was not good for man to be alone, he felt doubly blessed to have both Melanie and Thelma. And something from the Book of Genesis came to his mind and he uttered it. "This is now bone of my bones," he said.

"You ain't just whistling Dixie," Melanie replied as she looked back over her shoulder at Jerry Landis. "But let's try something new." They realigned as if playing Twister and Thelma had called out "Left foot red!" And soon they were driving like a well-oiled machine. All Jerry

Landis needed was a little more traction and he'd be able to deliver once again. He reset his left foot and pushed very hard. Unfortunately, the angle at which he was now operating created far too much torque for his calcium-compromised tibia.

SNAP! His shinbone broke clean and tore through the skin. Melanie fainted dead away under him at the sight of the compound fracture. Thelma ran screaming from the room. Jerry Landis had never known such exquisite pain. And despite the fact that he could no longer push off with his left leg, he just kept pumping. "Thy will be done!" he cried.

Methamphetamine is a prototypic psychomotor stimulant which is neurotoxic to dopamine and serotonin systems and can cause irregular heartbeat, convulsions, and kidney damage. When smoked it can lead to pulmonary edema and dilated cardiomyopathy. When smoked *too much* it can produce diffuse vasospasm resulting in acute myocardial infarction, cardiogenic shock, and death. However, if it doesn't kill you, the behavioral consequences include vigorous euphoria, paranoid behavior, and extreme violence.

This was bad news for Paul because, as of yet, the meth hadn't killed Bonedigger. He was simply in an elevated state of agitation with a loaded .22 Colt Woodsman sitting on the passenger seat of his truck, right next to the peanut butter jar full of the white powder. Bones had stolen the gun three nights ago and had been on a meth jag ever since. He was restless, moody, and periodically manic. His intermittent hallucinations provided something for him to shoot at other than the relentless parade of bad drivers which seemed out to get him on the drive to the mall.

Bones had followed Paul here but had lost him at the entrance to the parking lot when the electric system in his truck suddenly gave out. By the time Bones got the truck resuscitated, he had lost Paul. For the next twenty minutes Bones cruised the seventy-acre plot of asphalt snorting speed and looking for the little blue car. When Bones finally found it he parked his truck and took his tool kit from the back. He walked over to the little blue car and felt the hood, still warm. Bones wedged himself underneath the car and searched for the brake line. He cut it and fluid dripped onto the asphalt. Bones then loosened all the lug nuts on the front right tire. He figured it this way: Paul would take the freeway home and one or both of these mechanical adjustments would be enough to cause Paul a serious, hopefully life-threatening, accident. Bones would follow him so that if the accident was inadequate or if Paul pulled over to see what was wrong before there was an accident, Bones would pull over to help. Then, hidden behind the car looking at loose lug nuts, he would kill Paul with a couple of head shots. It wasn't the world's most elegant plan, but in fairness, Bones had never done this before and he also hadn't slept in several days. Further, it had to be said, Bones just wasn't too damn bright to begin with.

He put his tools away and went back to the truck to wait. He was there for half an hour wrestling with paranoia and a dull pain in his kidneys before his victim returned. Bones slumped noticeably in his seat, not so Paul wouldn't see him but because it wasn't Paul. He had sabotaged the wrong car. Having failed to consider the possibility that there were hundreds of cars on the road just like Paul's, Bones hadn't thought to do anything clever like memorize his license plate number.

And now what? Some woman was about to drive off in a potential deathtrap of a car. What the hell was Bones supposed to do about that? He figured there was no point in telling her; she'd find out soon enough. So now he had to resume his search for Paul. He kicked at the fuse panel and coaxed the truck to life. Over the next forty-five minutes, Bones sabotaged another six blue cars, none of them Paul's. Bones realized this just as he was about to sabotage car number seven. But Paul got to the car first and a minute later he pulled out of the parking lot with Bones six cars back and pissed off.

Traffic was a nightmare, and as Bones weaved crazily up the boulevard after his target, his truck periodically conked out in the middle of intersections, forcing him to kick at the fuse panel with his biker boots, resulting in a spray of sparks and the smell of burning wire insulation. After the third stall, Bonedigger was mad enough to kill, which was fine, since that's what Dr. Gibbs had hired him to do. Unfortunately, the person he'd been hired to kill was now a quarter mile in front of him and getting away because of the truck's faulty electrical system. None of this improved the biker's disposition.

Up ahead Bones could see Paul's little blue car darting in and out of lanes. Fortunately Paul always used his signal when changing lanes, and this helped Bonedigger keep his eye on his target. The upcoming light turned yellow so Bones naturally accelerated. "Don't you pussy out on me!" he bellowed at the Volvo in front of him. But it was too late. The brake lights came on. "Goddammit!" The veins in Bonedigger's neck bulged as he gassed the truck and screamed at the top of his lungs, "I told you not to stop you stupidfaggotsonofabitch!" Accelerating madly, Bonedigger cut the wheels and leaned on the horn as he literally scraped past the Volvo on the right, taking a Swedish side mirror with him. "Dumbfuck!" he yelled at the fainthearted driver.

As he lurched through the intersection, Bones glanced in his rearview mirror to see if Volvo Boy had anything to say about the mirror incident. He didn't. When Bonedigger looked back to the road in front of him he saw the BART Express bus pulling away from the curb directly into his path. "Goddammit!" Bones was near his breaking point. He slammed on the brakes and reached for the gun. Somebody was going to have to pay for this. But the force of the sudden braking hurled the gun and peanut butter jar to the floorboard on the passenger side, out of reach. "Goddammit!" The truck stalled again and

Bones kicked wildly at the fuse panel and twisted the key until the Ford roared back to life.

He raced around the bus and suddenly the road opened up in front of him. Three lanes and no traffic for two hundred yards. So Bones gassed it. At this rate, he'd catch back up with Paul in no time. He was going about seventy when he saw the cop. Bones glued his eyes to his rearview mirror to see if the cop was going to pursue. Blue lights said yes. Now Bones had to make a getaway. But when Bones looked back to the road in front of him, all he could see was the dump truck going approximately two miles per hour. And at that point it was too late to do anything but hold on.

Dr. Gibbs was there when his boss woke up with a cast on his leg and a smile still on his face. "What happened?" Landis asked.

Gibbs explained how Thelma, after regaining her composure that night, had called and asked for help. Dr. Gibbs had rushed back to One Biotech Center and found Jerry Landis lying on the floor, unconscious, with the plastic organs piled up around the broken leg. The girls couldn't stand the sight of the compound fracture so, while waiting for Dr. Gibbs to arrive, they had tried, in vain, to cover it. But it turned out plastic organs aren't any good for hiding broken bones.

Dr. Gibbs got his boss to the hospital, where, with the help of a couple of pins, they set Jerry Landis's bone, wrapped his leg in a cast, and sent him home. Thanks to the copious amounts of bourbon in the biotech executive's system, he didn't wake up until the next day.

Since one aspect of having a left ventricular assist device was that Jerry had to take Warfarin, a blood thinner that's also used as a rat poison, everyone agreed it was a miracle that Landis hadn't bled to death. And the fact that he hadn't only served as further evidence to Jerry Landis that he was part of God's plan.

Now, two days later, Jerry Landis was back in his office, in a wheelchair with his broken leg sticking out like a battering ram in front of him. Despite this inconvenience and the constant throbbing in his leg, visions of Thelma and Melanie still danced naked in his head and Jerry Landis was feeling generous toward the man who had made it all possible. "Congratulations, Doctor," he said as he signed the employment contract. "You are now, officially, Xenotech's vice president of procurement." *Whir-pffft whir-pffft whir-pffft.*

It was an emotional moment for Dr. Gibbs. He had come a long way since being denied admission to even the most marginally acceptable medical schools in the States. After all the years of desperate and gruesome negotiations for people's organs and all the accidental deaths, he had done what many thought was impossible. He had made a positive vertical career move while in his fifties. And now he was receiving stock options from the most promising biotechnology company in the world. He hoped his parents were looking down on him, finally proud. "Thank you, sir. I'd just like to say—"

Suddenly there was a loud commotion in the outer office, cutting short Dr. Gibbs's acceptance speech. The secretary yelled something just before the door burst open and Dr. Putnam, Xenotech's head of research, rushed in. Clearly he wanted to blurt something out but instead he paused to compose himself.

Jerry Landis knew exactly what this was about. "Well?"

"Membrane cofactor protein and decay accelerating factor counts are holding at normal levels and there's no indication of a C3b cascade," Dr. Putnam said. "We're talking excellent cardiac function by echocardiography and no evidence of rejection."

Jerry Landis was skeptical. It sounded too good to be true. "What are you telling me?"

Dr. Putnam delivered the news with dignity. "We have created an immunosuppressant for transgenic baboon organs."

Whir-pffft whir-pffft whir-pffft. Jerry Landis froze, as if listening to the words echo off the office walls. This was the moment for which he had been waiting a very long time. Now that he understood it, Dr. Gibbs also was struck by the significance of the announcement, though he saw it more from the perspective of a man who had just received a trunk full of stock options than from a potential lifesaving point of view. Jerry Landis took a deep breath and cleared his throat. This wasn't the first time Dr. Putnam had come to his office to make such an announcement, though it was the first time he hadn't modified "created" with "we think we have." Still, Landis tried to control his emotions. "Well, let's go have a look, shall we?" He put his wheelchair in drive and whirred out the door with the two doctors following in his wake.

Because of the nature of Xenotech's research there was a complete operating theater on the fourth floor. It began as the room where they transplanted pig organs into monkeys, but as the xenograft research progressed, it had been transformed into a full-blown OR. However, unlike most operating rooms, this one included a heavy-gauge steel guide track in the ceiling. It was the sort of thing used at large animal hospitals. The guide track was anchored to structural beams and went from a pre-op room to the OR. The steel beam held an industrial trolley pulley which, via hoisting ropes, held a hoisting block with a big steel hook on the end of it. This mechanism was necessary for lifting the massive baboons onto and off of the operating tables.

Excluding the surgeries on swine and lower primates, there had been eight or so major operations done there, including Jerry Landis's testicle transplant. Down the hall from the OR was the recovery room, which is where Landis and the two doctors were currently heading. At this point Jerry Landis was having trouble containing his excitement. "Faster, goddammit!" he barked. Dr. Gibbs and Dr. Putnam jogged to keep up with their boss as he raced his electric wheelchair down the hallway. "How long has he been awake?" Landis asked Dr. Putnam.

"About an hour," Dr. Putnam replied. "Said he feels like a million bucks."

Jerry Landis slapped his left hand down on the wheel-chair's armrest. "Hotdamn!" They arrived at the recovery room and circled around the bed. Dr. Gibbs helped his boss stand so he could look down on the patient. "Well, well, Mr. Luckett," Landis said with a friendly smile. "Feeling better, are we?"

The FDA man looked up through a post-op haze. He had tubes sticking in his arms and up his nose. He tried to focus on Jerry Landis and soon there was a glimmer of recognition. Mr. Luckett reached over and touched Landis's hand. "What happened? Am I all right?"

Jerry Landis patted Mr. Luckett's hand. "You're fine. You just had a heart attack," Landis said, telling half the truth. It was true that Mr. Luckett was fine, but there had been no heart attack. Mr. Luckett had simply reacted to the extraordinarily high levels of epinephrine that his cup of tea had delivered to his system during the meeting a couple of days ago. Although epinephrine is normally an intravenous liquid, the boys in the lab had created a synthesized adrenaline in a crystal form that constricted small blood vessels and raised blood pressure to a fairly dangerous level. Those physiological symptoms combined with the power of suggestion (augmented by the fact that the people making the suggestions were authority figures, in this instance "doctors") led Mr. Luckett to believe he was, in fact, suffering a myocardial infarction that afternoon.

It had all come about so elegantly: After dosing Luckett with the epinephrine and putting him under with a sedative, the Xenotech transplant and harvest teams were notified that there was a new volunteer for the latest xenograft and drug test. Dr. Gibbs, meanwhile, was on the phone looking for a buyer for Mr. Luckett's perfectly good heart. He reached Lance Abbott, who had just what the doctor ordered. There was, on Lance's private data-base, a local industrialist whose unchecked fondness for pork roast and bacon had set new standards for athero-sclerosis and made him a perfect (if ironic) candidate for a pig's heart, if only the transgenic swine organs had been available. Mr. Luckett's blood type matched perfectly with the recipient, and before you could say "I left my heart in San Francisco," $250,000 was transferred to the proper account and the industrialist was airlifted from St. Francis Memorial to the rooftop helipad at One Biotech Center.

As per company policy, there was always a minimum of one of the transgenic baboons at the Xenotech facility. The three-hundred-pound old world monkey was anesthetized in the pre-op room, hoisted by the crane, and trolleyed into the OR, where the harvest team went to work. Meanwhile, the transplant team prepared Mr. Luckett for a median sternotomy. Over the course of the next several hours, Dr. Putnam and the transplant and harvesting teams pulled Luckett's heart and dropped it into the industrialist's chest. They took the baboon's heart and stuck it into Mr. Luckett's awaiting cavity. The industrialist's heart ended up in the trash. Total time from drugging Luckett to wheeling him into the recovery room: nine hours.

And now, though he was completely ignorant of what had happened over the past twenty-four hours, Mr. Luckett was so overwhelmed by the fact that he hadn't woken up dead he was misty-eyed. "You saved my life," he whimpered.

Landis feigned some modesty. "Well, it wasn't me, really. Dr. Putnam here performed the actual transplant," Landis said.

Mr. Luckett blanched. "Transplant?" His aspirations to leadership in the Church of Christ, Scientist were suddenly quashed. "I don't understand, you said there weren't any hearts."

Jerry Landis pointed an index finger to the ceiling. "I said there weren't any *human* hearts." Landis smiled as he let this sink in.

"Oh my God," Mr. Luckett said, wondering how he'd explain this to his friends back in the old reading room.

"That's right," Jerry Landis said. "You're being kept

alive by a transgenic baboon heart. That plus Xenotech's newest immunosuppressive drug therapy."

The true significance of this finally hit Dr. Gibbs. "Xenotech's newest and *highly marketable* immunosuppressive drug therapy," he said.

"Yes," Dr. Putnam said as if he had stock options of his own, "*highly* marketable."

At the moment Jerry Landis wasn't so concerned about the marketability issue. He was still reeling from the implication of the drug's success. It would allow him to delay his death long enough to find a cure for Werner's syndrome and that meant he would be able to wallow in the billions of dollars that would soon be flowing in. It was when *that* thought occurred to him that Jerry Landis considered the marketing consideration. "If only we could get FDA approval," he said wistfully. He sat back down in his wheelchair and wheeled over to the IV line that was dripping critical fluids into the FDA man's system. "Now, Mr. Luckett, as long as you continue taking our immunosuppressant, you'll be fine." Landis, understandably, left out the part about how extreme immune system suppression can lead to severe infection problems. "The only possible problem I can foresee is if, for some reason, the FDA decides to put a clinical hold on our research." To emphasize his point, Landis pinched the rubber hose that was dosing Mr. Luckett with the drug. The critical liquid stopped flowing.

"Mr. Landis," Luckett said as he eyed the dammed fluid, "I've been doing some thinking and, quite frankly, especially after your demonstration, I must admit I'm no longer uncomfortable with what you're doing here at Xenotech. In fact, I can see how absolutely vital it is."

Jerry Landis let go of the rubber tube and the liquid once again flowed.

"As a matter of fact, my report will *demand* FDA fast track approval," Luckett said.

"That's tremendous news," Jerry Landis said. He looked to the doctors, who couldn't have agreed more.

The FDA man narrowed his eyes. "I've only got one question," he said.

"I'm glad to answer any questions you have," Jerry Landis responded.

"What about stock options?"

Suddenly the room filled with the sound of silence. No one was quite sure how Jerry Landis would take such a brazen inquiry. Finally, Landis broke the tension with an infectious chuckle. The jovial mood spread quickly and soon everyone was laughing so hard it became necessary to put the oxygen mask on Mr. Luckett to insure he lived long enough to write his report. After catching his own breath, Jerry Landis explained how the stock options worked and how many he could let Mr. Luckett have for his trouble, and a few moments later everyone was shaking hands and reminiscing fondly about the awkward moment of silence that had followed the brazen inquiry.

Later, back in his office, Jerry Landis told Dr. Gibbs to contact the Deckern County facility and have them send another baboon immediately. He also told Gibbs to find another volunteer, this time a real one, one whom Mr. Luckett could cite in his FDA report. "We need one more test with the new drug therapy before we take it to market."

Dr. Gibbs agreed and said he would get on that immediately.

"Oh," Jerry Landis said, "and tell them to start rounding up about five hundred more of those damn monkeys." He winked at Dr. Gibbs. "It's harvest time."

Billy Bob was in the big truck. He was on his way to check the baboon trap so he could ship one of the old world monkeys out to San Jose like he'd been told to do. He had no idea what they did with these huge primates out there in California. He knew it had something to do with medical research. He imagined they were used for drug testing or maybe for teaching medical or veterinary students how to make incisions and then sew them back up. Billy Bob figured they did whatever they did and then gave the baboons to a zoo or something, which would explain why he had to ship a new one out there every so often. In his worst nightmares he never imagined they were simply being killed for experimental organ transplants.

But now that he'd been told to round up five hundred of them and await further instructions, Billy Bob began to wonder what the hell was going on. There was something about the combination of medical experiments and the instructions to gather together a large group of living subjects that made even Billy Bob uncomfortable. But it was his job and he was damn proud to have one, so he'd just get on with doing whatever he was told to do and try not to think about what it all meant. "Mine is not to question why" might have been his motto. It sounded better than "I was just following orders."

The only difference this time was that they instructed Billy Bob not to send any of the dominant males. They wanted only females, juveniles, and sub-adults. Though they didn't tell Billy Bob, the problem was that the organs from the giant males were simply too big to transplant into humans. The smaller baboons, however, were ideal.

As Billy Bob guided the big truck through the piney woods he wondered how in hell he was going to do it. Catching one of the huge, genetically altered baboons wasn't really that difficult, but five hundred? He'd have to think on that a while.

To catch them one at a time Billy Bob used a trap that he built himself. The design was copied from the classic Havahart traps, the shoe box–shaped aluminum traps that were good for catching squirrels and racoons. There was a door at each end of the trap and a pressure plate in the center of the caged area which, when stepped on, caused the two doors to slam shut. When Billy Bob inherited his job as head of security, somebody had explained that one of his duties was to capture and ship a baboon to the home office in California every now and then. However, he failed to tell Billy Bob about the tranquilizer guns, so when the time came, Billy Bob came up with his own method.

Back in high school Billy Bob had been a below-average student in everything but metal shop, where he was top of his class. At his tenth high school reunion, Billy Bob's guidance counselor commented that when he thought back on all the crap Billy Bob had failed to learn in high school, he marveled that Billy Bob could think at all. However, if you measured intelligence by one's ability to catch mutant baboons, Billy Bob was a genius.

When the time came, Billy Bob got some half-inch steel plate and his welding torch and built his own giant Havahart baboon trap. It was, necessarily, larger than the original model. In fact, it was about the size and shape of a Volkswagen van without the wheels. Billy Bob would cart the trap into the woods on the back of the large flatbed truck and drop it at the edge of a clearing. He would cover the pressure plate with onions, peaches, eggs, and alfalfa and then camouflage the outside with branches, fooling himself much more than the baboons.

Because of their high cognitive function the baboons learned very quickly that this giant steel box with the branches leaning against it wasn't a good thing, so Billy Bob was forced to leave the trap in a different troop's territory each time. Driving all over the huge compound was a pain in the ass, but it was the only thing that worked.

Billy Bob parked the truck about a quarter mile from the current trap location. He would walk the rest of the way. If he hadn't already caught one of the great baboons and one was considering the bait, he didn't want to scare it off with the noisy vehicle. Besides, strolling through the woods on the crunchy carpet of pine needles was something he had always enjoyed, a little communion with the woods and the creeks. During his lifetime Billy Bob had noticed a dramatic decrease in the amount of undisturbed pine forest available for such communions. His cousins in the timber business told him it was because demand for wood and paper products kept increasing as the population grew. He sometimes worried that one day there wouldn't be any pine forests left for these walks.

In any event, Billy Bob was still a long way from the trap and was enjoying his stroll in the woods when he suddenly stopped. Up ahead he saw one of the baboons. No, there were two of them, a mother and a baby whose furry little ears stuck out comically from the side of his head. The baby's fur was much darker than the silvery-brown of the mother, but that would change in the coming months. The baby's short muzzle was wrinkly and puckered like an old man without teeth, not elongated like the adults. The little baby was pulling on his mother's hand. Billy Bob didn't want to approach for fear of spooking the mother into a protective attack but, after a minute, he noticed that the mother wasn't moving. The baby sat next to her, pulling at her hand as if to get her to do something. When Billy Bob crept closer he saw that the baby was distressed.

And then he saw why.

The mother was dead. The baby didn't understand this and so he kept tugging on her large hand, trying to get her to hold him. After tugging on her hand and getting no response the little baboon slumped sadly and made a crying sound. Billy Bob crept a little closer and *SNAP!* He stepped on a dry branch, sending the baby baboon scurrying into the weeds, scared and unprotected. Billy Bob couldn't see any others, so he approached, shooing away the flies that were beginning to gather. He saw a single gunshot wound in the mother's chest. "I'll be a monkey's uncle," Billy Bob said. The baboon had been shot to death.

What Billy Bob didn't know, aside from the fact that he was more like a monkey's cousin than an uncle, was that there were many more dead baboons throughout the ten thousand-acre compound. He only knew about this one and the scared little baby that was now peering out through the weeds. Billy Bob tried to call him out from the tall grass, but he wouldn't come. He just kept looking at his mother. Suddenly the baby baboon looked straight at Billy Bob and their eyes connected. Something basic in the man stirred as he looked into the poignant brown eyes of the motherless child. His mother was dead and his father had abandoned him. He would probably die of hunger, alone, frightened, and confused. The baby took a shallow breath, then let out a small sigh as he looked back to his mother. Billy Bob felt profoundly sorry for him. He looked so human and so sad.

Paul and Georgette were waiting for the other shoe to drop. Everything else had suddenly come together. The guests, the band, and the caterer had all agreed to hold three weekends free for forty-eight hours while Paul and Georgette tried to secure the place in the redwoods. But the Penumbra, as the place was called, was a tough ticket. Fortunately, Georgette was getting tougher as she grew more pregnant. She wanted to get married and so she began hounding the manager of the place. She finally badgered the man into admitting that a few couples had made reservations without benefit of a deposit. Georgette immediately sent a money order and demanded one of the weekends. The manager said he had to give the other couples the chance to put down deposits and if any of them didn't make the deadline the place was Georgette's.

In the meanwhile, Paul was beginning to have doubts about his ability to find Xenotech's baboon-breeding facility. He knew it existed but had no idea where. Paul felt like an idiot. He imagined Jerry Landis smirking as he gave someone the go-ahead to begin the slaughter. It was the same smirk he'd had on his face as he tossed Paul's proposal into the trash. Paul imagined Jerry Landis had smirked that way after the jury delivered its verdict in the Cel-Tech civil trial. Paul wanted personally to wipe the smirk off the bastard's face. Paul had been hiding behind his voting record for too long and too many acres of forest had come down and too many waterways had been fouled and his unwillingness to do anything was starting to gnaw at him. Something had to give. Soon.

Paul had left messages all over Europe, South Africa, and the United States—Animal Liberation, Auckland Animal Action, and Animals Australia; Keele Animal Rights Society and Cambridge Animal Rights in jolly old England; Front for Animal Liberation and Conservation in South Africa; Gaia in Belgium; Lega Antivivisezionista and Lega Italiana dei Diritti dell' Animal in Italy; Les Cahiers Antispecistes in France; NOAH Organization in Norway; the Swedish Society Against Painful Experiments on Animals (Uppsala Branch); the Student Organization for Animal Rights at the University of Minnesota, and many others.

The Internet was a wondrous thing inasmuch as it allowed you to communicate with people all over the world, but if those people didn't have the answer to the question you were asking it just added to your phone bill.

Having exhausted the animal rights web sites, Paul ran a Boolean search for "earth" and "ecological disaster." He clicked on the first result of the search. It was a web site consisting of nothing more than a brief essay:

FROM ZERO TO A BILLION IN SIXTY SECONDS
(with all due respect to Jonathan Swift and his Modest Proposal)

In 1798, before we had one-sixth of the human population we have now, the Reverend Thomas Malthus—England's first professor of political economy—published his famous *Essay on the Principle of Population.* Malthus noted that human population grows at a geometric rate (2-4-8-16-32 etc.) while food production increases only at an arithmetic rate (2-4-6-8-10 etc.). In other words, according to Malthus, the world's food supply eventually would be unable to match the geometric rate of human population growth which occurs when no human action is taken to limit reproduction. "The power of population is so superior to the power of the earth to produce subsistence for man, that premature death must in some shape or other visit the human race," were Malthus's exact words.

Now, Evolutionists and Creationists agree that at some point in the past there were no humans on the planet. According to one popular school of Christian thought that point was roughly six thousand years ago. According to Evolutionists *Homo sapiens* evolved from Neanderthal man somewhere around 38,000 B.C.

In any event we can agree that at some point between six thousand and forty thousand years ago, there were no humans on planet Earth.

During the period of time from the dawn of humanity (whenever that was) to the year 1830, human population went from zero to one billion. In other words, it took somewhere between six thousand and forty thousand years for human population to reach one billion. It then took a mere one hundred years (from 1830 to 1930) to add a second billion people to the earth. It then took only *sixty* years (from 1930 to 1990) to add not just the next *one* billion, but an additional *three* billion people to the planet. At this rate of population growth, we will add another billion in just 11 years. U.N. projections issued in 1990 show the world population increasing from our current 5.75 billion to 6.2 billion in the year 2000 and 8.5 billion in 2025. At that rate, the world's human population will be 128 billion by the year 2155.

If you think traffic's bad now, just wait.

According to International Planned Parenthood Federation, every year another 95 million people are born to a world ill-prepared to support them. According to Zero Population Growth in Washington, D.C., one hundred million Africans do not consume enough food to maintain an active-working life due to the effects of overpopulation. According to environmental groups, 100 acres of rain forest are destroyed every *minute* to meet demands for forestry products and to create pastures for cattle grazing.

According to others, there's nothing to worry about.

In *Man and His Environment,* author Ansley Coale noted that if human population were to grow at current rates for another six hundred to seven hundred years, every square foot of the surface of the earth would contain a human being; if it were to expand at the same rate for twelve hundred years, the combined weight of the human population would exceed that of the earth itself, and if that growth rate were to continue for six thousand years—a very short period of time in terms of biological history—the globe would constitute a sphere whose diameter was growing with the speed of light.

Just try to imagine the cost of a three bedroom apartment in New York at that point.

Paul Ehrlich, author of "The Population Bomb," and Gretchen Daily study human population dynamics at Stanford's Center for Conservation Biology. In their 1992 paper, "Population, Sustainability, and Earth's Carrying Capacity," they argued that "our current population of 5.5 billion is being maintained only through the exhaustion and dispersion of a one-time inheritance of natural capital including topsoil, ground-water, and biodiversity. The rapid depletion of these essential resources, coupled with a worldwide degradation of land and atmospheric quality indicate that the human enterprise has not only exceeded its current social carrying capacity, but it is actually reducing future potential biophysical carrying capacities by depleting essential natural capital stocks." In other words, our unchecked population growth combined with our rates of resource consumption are leading humankind toward a dismal future.

Others say such predictions are baseless pessimism.

Malthus argued that if human beings failed to limit their reproduction, *nature* would provide checks on human population growth. According to Malthus those checks are famine, war, and disease.

Some say that Malthus failed to take into account that technology could allow us to increase food production. And, indeed, the agricultural biotechnology industry *has* helped us increase the output of food-per-land-unit. In fact we've done such a good job of overcoming the "famine check" that only thirty-eight thousand children die each day from lack of food and water. And some argue that there is, in fact, plenty of food in the world, suggesting that those children are dying from a simple distribution problem and not malnutrition.

Malthus also failed to take into account the rash of peace treaties and nuclear arms accords that man has engineered (understandable in light of the fact that he also failed to anticipate nuclear weapons). Sure, the IRA still fights with the English, and the Jews and the Palestinians refuse to stop killing one another, and occasionally a hundred thousand Rwandans are massacred by Tutsis (or vice versa, I forget), but all the deaths in these types of wars just don't amount to much relative to the number of humans born each day.

Thus, according to Malthusian theory, the only check remaining to prevent mankind from destroying itself through overpopulation and exceeding the planet's carrying capacity is disease. But the biotechnology industry, motivated by profit and the human desire to live longer and longer, is hard at work solving that problem.

The point is we can't have it both ways. The notion that technology will solve all of the problems we create is a foolish one given mankind's history. We can either have *fewer* people with longer (and higher quality) life spans or *more* people with short, nasty, and brutish ones. But we have to make the choice now and the former choice seems better than the latter.

"Hard to argue with that," Georgette said, startling Paul. He hadn't noticed that she had been reading over his shoulder for the past few minutes.

"That's an interesting comment for a pregnant lady," Paul said.

"Hey, I'm only having one. I believe that's within acceptable zero population growth guidelines." Georgette pointed at the uniform resource locator. "What the hell does h-t-t-p mean anyway?" she asked as Paul drove down the info superhighway to the next search result.

"Does it matter?" His curt response reflected his increasing frustration. It had been several days since Paul had left his messages at the web sites and now he was discovering that no one knew where the baboon farm was.

"Let's go to Bianca Troll's Smut Shack," Georgette said, trying to lighten the moment. She was worried that Paul's degree of concern was inching uncomfortably close to obsession. Besides, she thought the Smut Shack sounded like some innocent fun that might lead to some sex. And right now she thought Paul could use a little of that. She knew she could.

"Maybe when I'm through," Paul said flatly. He linked from NORINA (a web site dedicated to alternatives to laboratory animals in teaching) to something called Stop the Slaughter at bushmeat@biosynergy.org. When Paul read that the Bushmeat Project was established to stop the 1,500 bushmeat hunters who were alleged to be supported by the timber industry infrastructure, the sign popped into Paul's head again.

ACRES OF RAIN FOREST REMAINING: 497,229,000

The text said the bushmeat hunters killed and butchered more than two thousand gorillas and four thousand chimpanzees in the forest region of west and central Africa that year. That was four times the number of gorillas on Rwanda's Mount Visoke and ten times more chimpanzees than live near Tanzania's Gombe Stream. People, it turned out, were eating more great apes each year than were now kept in zoos and laboratories in North America.

Paul shook his head and wondered if anything could be done to save mankind from itself. Didn't anyone else see what was going on? Was Paul simply oversensitive or was it something else? It seemed to Paul that during the course of his lifetime the world had changed mostly for the worse and that people had simply lowered their standards to meet the level of the madness. Over the past three decades, things had become so much more complicated and people so much busier that no one had the time or energy at the end of the day to try to separate ecological facts from corporate spin.

And, of course, the planet was getting more and more crowded every day. Crime had grown disproportionately in relation to the population so that now people were happy when the increase in violent crime was simply kept under a certain percentage. The poor cops were so busy trying to keep up with multiple murderers and child rapists that they didn't have time for mere assaults with deadly weapons, let alone crimes against property.

Industrial pollution was so flagrant, overwhelming, and relentless that most people were paralyzed just trying to figure out where to send their money to slow it down, only to find out that just ten cents of every dollar went where it was supposed to go, with "administrative costs" taking the rest.

Those who really cared were so preoccupied trying to deal with large, serious issues that they didn't have time to say anything about the small-scale stuff like all the idiots tossing cigarette butts out their car windows. And the citizenry had grown so accustomed to corrupt government that they didn't even care that senators and congressmen who got caught pants-down-red-handed-with-the-smoking-gun-in-their-hand-in-the-soft-money-cookie-jar got re-elected Speaker of the House or retired with full benefits at taxpayers' expense. There were too many other things to worry about, like does my house have lead paint on the moldings, or radon gas seeping in through the crawl space, or asbestos in the attic, or does my kid have attention deficit disorder and does he need Ritalin or is the teacher just lazy and how is he going to get into a good pre-school so he can get into a good elementary school so he can get into a good prep school and on and on and on?

Paul remembered his favorite scene from *Grand Canyon,* where Steve Martin's character, who had been shot during a robbery, was told by another character that he was lucky to have lived. Martin's character bristled at the notion. He pointed out that winning the lottery was lucky, not getting shot. He said the notion that he was lucky was a perfect example of how low everyone's standards had sunk.

Paul found no answer to his baboon query at the bush-meat web site so he linked to Primate Info Net and then to the International Primate Protection League. There he found a message from someone at the University of Texas who had some information that looked useful. The student, whose screen name was Trophonius, said there was a place in San Antonio called the Southwest Foundation for Biomedical Research. They had nearly three thousand baboons at their facility. It was the largest known captive population of the old world monkeys. But, Trophonius said, he had infiltrated the facility and found the baboons to be of normal size and therefore of limited use to anyone trying to solve the human organ demand problem.

Paul thanked Trophonius for the information and signed off. He was ready to face the fact that he wasn't going to find the baboons, that he was going to have to stand by as they were slaughtered. He looked as defeated as a dream that wants to die. Georgette was worried. Paul was taking this much more personally than any of the other causes he had ever pursued, which wasn't to say Georgette didn't care about the baboons. She just felt that stewing in front of a computer (especially one as slow as theirs) could only add to Paul's frustration.

"Hey, let's take a break, maybe go finish decorating the baby's room," she said. "I think maybe it could use a few more carefully placed puppies on the walls."

"Maybe you're right," Paul said.

"Of course I am," Georgette replied. "Let's get busy." She started to leave.

But Paul just sat there, staring at the computer. "Maybe all this letter writing and petition signing and voting is nothing more than a pacifier, a waste of time to give me the impression that I'm doing something worthwhile. Maybe I actually ought to be *doing* something." Paul signed off the Internet and turned the computer off. He rubbed at his tired, dry eyes.

"Like what?" Georgette suddenly felt an odd, tingling sensation on her scalp. She'd never known him to have doubts. She wondered what idea Paul was entertaining.

Paul swiveled in his chair and looked at Georgette. "Like . . . I don't know. That's probably why I do what I do. I can't think of anything else." Paul got up, brushed past Georgette, and went into the garage. There, he opened up a large box containing hundreds of files. In the files were all the letters Paul had ever written to anyone regarding his causes. There wasn't a single significant victory represented among them.

Georgette didn't like Paul's mood. But there was nothing she could do to snap him out of his funk so she went to the kitchen and made some tea. As it steeped, the phone rang and Georgette answered. She listened for a moment, her jaw growing increasingly slack on its hinges. "Oh my God," she said finally.

Paul had heard the phone ring from the garage but hadn't given it a second thought until Georgette appeared in the doorway. The expression on her face was one Paul had never seen before. It looked as if someone had told Georgette not only where the baboon farm was but that they had already begun the slaughter. "What is it?" Paul asked. "Was it about the baboons?"

"No. The wedding's Saturday."

Paul blanched. "Good Lord."

Dr. Gibbs pulled into the Los Trancos Trailer Park hoping for a couple of things. First he hoped to talk to Arty about his newest and, he hoped, his final proposition. He expected this would be the hardest sale he'd ever attempted. After all, it's one thing to sell a kidney or a testicle when you've got two of them, it's something else altogether when you start screwing around with the heart. Add to that the notion of having a genetically altered baboon heart plunked into your chest—just to see if it works—and, well, even someone as peculiar as Arty might balk. But Dr. Gibbs had to ask. His future depended on it.

Secondly, he hoped to run into Bones to call him off the Paul Symon deal; now that they had the FDA in their pocket, there was no need to kill him. However, when Dr. Gibbs arrived at Bonedigger's trailer space all he saw was a pile of smoldering rubble where the trailer used to be. As he poked around the ashes, he kicked at something which turned out to be the blackened trombone. A moment later he heard Arty's voice coming from next door. "Bones? Is that you?"

"No, Arty, it's me, Dr. Gibbs."

"All right! Doc! Come on over!" He sounded thrilled

to have a visitor. Dr. Gibbs opened the trailer door and saw the little one-eyed guy propped up in the corner of the sofa, smiling as if he owned the world. "Man, am I glad to see you!" Arty said. It looked like he hadn't shaved in a while and it smelled like he hadn't showered lately either.

Dr. Gibbs asked about what happened next door. Arty said Bones apparently had failed to turn off one of his Bunsen burners when he left to go somewhere. The crank lab had exploded and the trailer burned down. "Well, I'm glad you're all right," Dr. Gibbs said, and he meant it. He liked Arty, liked his positive attitude, his willingness to take chances. He especially liked the way that Arty kept coming through for him. "Listen," Dr. Gibbs said, "the reason I came over is I couldn't get you on the phone."

Arty explained that he had been home when the doctor called but, owing to his limbless condition, he couldn't really move. And even if he could move, he couldn't have picked up the phone to answer. "I've been thinking about getting a hands-free unit," Arty said, "but I haven't gotten around to it." In fact, Arty hadn't got around to much lately since his chauffeur had disappeared shortly after delivering him to One Biotech Center for the testicle operation. A Xenotech employee had taken Arty home afterwards, and since then, Melanie was the only person Arty had seen—and it was just dumb luck that that happened.

Melanie came by the day after she and Thelma had fulfilled their contractual obligations with Jerry Landis (which happened to be the same day Bonedigger was out making his first attempt on Paul's life). Melanie had been looking for Bones that day, and during a pause in her screaming through the door for Bonedigger to bring his big, sorry ass outside to talk to her, she heard Arty yelling from inside his own trailer. Arty told Melanie he hadn't seen Bones since the operation, and since Bones had been acting as Arty's arms and legs, he asked Melanie if she could take over until Bones came back. "I don't know, Arty, I got all those kids to deal with," she had said. "You think you'd be all right under my trailer?"

"I'm willing to pay," Arty said. "But I'm staying in my own trailer."

Always on the lookout for additional income streams, Melanie accepted. She fed Arty, took him to the bathroom, and changed the channel on the television every now and then. She dropped in every day or two, tending him like a finicky plant. Arty couldn't have been happier with the arrangement, except for one thing. "Listen, Doc," Arty said. "Melanie hasn't been here in two days and the last thing she gave me before she left was this Big Gulp." His one eye glanced down at the plastic sixty-four-ounce cup that had a long curly straw snaking out of the top. "Could you do me a favor and carry me down to the john?"

Dr. Gibbs nodded. He figured performing such a kindness might put him in a better bargaining position when he began negotiating with Arty. So he picked Arty up and went to the bathroom. What Dr. Gibbs failed to consider was the extent of the kindness he had offered. It was only when he arrived at the toilet that it occurred to him exactly what he'd have to do.

"Don't worry about me," Arty said. "I'm not what you'd call modest. Just drop my drawers and prop me on the pot. But you've got to hold me up; otherwise I just fall over." He laughed. Arty was wearing gym shorts, the legs of which had been sewn closed. The shorts looked like an ill-fitting cotton shower cap and they popped right off with a gentle tug from Dr. Gibbs's careful hands. Arty wasn't wearing any underwear, and the doctor couldn't help but notice how strange the still-shaved scrotum looked with only one gonad in it. Dr. Gibbs lowered Arty onto the throne and began breathing through his mouth. After they had been there a while, the doctor offered a medical opinion: "Arty, you should consider getting more fiber in your diet."

"Thanks, Doc, I'll keep that in mind," Arty said. A moment later Arty was done. Using one hand to keep

Arty atop the toilet seat, Dr. Gibbs bent down to grab the shorts with the other. "Whoa there, Doc, aren't you forgetting something?" Arty glanced at the toilet paper. "Just tilt me to the side," he said. "And be gentle."

Dr. Gibbs's fondness for his little pirate friend was waning, but he forged ahead, all the while fantasizing about stock options and the view from his office at Xenotech. When the unpleasantness was over, they returned to the living room and Dr. Gibbs propped Arty back in the corner of the sofa. "Doc, I really appreciate your help with that," Arty said. "Now, what did you want to see me about?"

Dr. Gibbs stiffened his neck and sat up straight. "Arty, I've got another proposition."

Arty's face lit up. Despite the fact that he had made so much money in the past six months that he hardly knew what to do with it all, he still wanted more. He hoped eventually to have enough money to build a new dorm building for the kids at the orphanage. "Doc, funny you should say that. I was thinking about calling you with an idea myself. See, I read somewhere that you can actually *farm* your liver, just cut a slice out every now and then, slip it into whoever needs a new liver and the damn thing grows back like a lizard tail. Is that true?"

Dr. Gibbs nodded. "More or less, but it's very painful and rather dangerous. I mean, it's major surgery, Arty, and the risk-to-return ratio is unfavorable."

"Oh." Arty looked disappointed. "Well, let's hold off on that and hear about your idea."

"Arty." Dr. Gibbs said this very gravely. "Xenotech has reached a critical point in its research and we're looking for someone with the courage to help us take the next step. A step that could benefit all mankind."

"Well, call me Captain Courageous," Arty said. "You want some brain tissue or what?"

"No, we want to put a baboon heart in you."

"A what?" Arty nearly tipped over.

"We'll pay you two hundred thousand dollars."

"Whoa! Now we're talkin'!" Arty would've slapped a

hand on something if he still had one. But, as he was nothing more than a torso with a head, slapping anything was out of the question. Nonetheless, his brain told the muscles in his body to try to move one of his phantom arms, and in so doing, Arty tumbled off the sofa. "Whoa!" He landed headfirst. After Dr. Gibbs put Arty back on the sofa they began their negotiation. When it was done, Arty had arranged for the biggest payday of his life. He would receive a fee of $250,000 for having the baboon heart transplanted into himself, half up front and the other half payable on the day of the surgery. He would make a minimum of $100,000 from the sale of his own, perfectly good, heart on the open (black) market, with Xenotech paying Lance Abbott's fee separately. Finally, he would receive two hundred thousand shares of re-stricted Xenotech stock, which was currently selling for a skinny $2.80 a share. Not counting the stock, it worked out to a guaranteed minimum of $350,000 for Arty. The only thing *not* guaranteed was Arty's survival.

Two days later Arty was on his back, staring up at the bright lights over the operating table in the OR where he had given up his testicle to Jerry Landis not too terri-bly long ago. In the next room a team of harvest surgeons had one of the juvenile transgenic baboons on an op-erating table, its chest splayed open like a blooming flower. On the table next to Arty was a venture capitalist whose ticker was sicker than the man was rich. He had won the bidding war for Arty's heart for $135,000, raising Arty's up front take to $385,000. It was an excellent tis-sue match.

Dr. Putnam approached his patient. "Hello, Arty. Are we ready to make a little history?"

"You betcha!" Arty said, delirious on Fentanyl. "Where're those rib spreaders? Let's get crackin'!" He cackled.

Dr. Putnam nodded to the anesthetist, who gassed the little pirate with the wondrous vaporized isoflurane. After a few moments Arty's mouth moved as if to say something sweet, then his one eye eased shut and Dr. Putnam held out his hand and asked for the sternal saw.

The man dressed in black squinted after asking the question, as if testing its resolve. The tension was thick as the silent crowd watched the second man turn to look at the woman. "I do," he said.

The man in black smiled. "Then with the power vested in me by the state of California, I now pronounce you husband and wife," he said. And with that, two people were married. "You may now kiss the bride." The act was outrageous. It wasn't some pro forma wedding kiss where the couple does it to close the deal, the kind of kiss that has all the passion of a notary public's seal. The happy couple finally came up for air, prompting the man in black: "Ladies and gentlemen, it is my pleasure to present to you for the first time in public Mr. and Mrs. Paul Symon!" The crowd stood and cheered as Paul and Georgette beamed out at their friends and family. Georgette's smile was contagious; it sparkled like the diamond in her nose. She burned like a bride.

After another kiss, the bagpipe-zither combo played a nice mid-tempo arrangement of "Something So Right" as the recessional. Georgette was showing more than she had hoped but she was unconcerned. Escorted by Paul, she waddled down the aisle six-and-a-half-months pregnant, happier than she'd ever been, her free arm resting on top of her swelling belly. Georgette had gone from feeling completely clinical about her pregnancy to feeling like Earth Mother the Giver of Life. And she wouldn't apologize for these feelings even if confronted with how they betrayed her former position. Georgette knew now that a miracle was occurring inside her and woe be unto anyone who challenged her on the issue.

Paul certainly wasn't going to do it. He preferred this over the alternative. When he secretly saw Georgette gently running her hands over her stomach and whispering to the child within he felt something he'd never felt before. He felt connected and completed and poetic.

And now, as he escorted her down the aisle parting the sea of smiles, he was warm and content and focused by his love for his family and his friends. The world's problems would have to wait.

The reception was an unusual gathering, taller on average than most wedding reception crowds because of Paul's and Georgette's athlete friends. There was also a retro hippie/new age contingent—hairy-legged, braless women in flowing tie-dye dresses and men who were weirdly comfortable wearing sandals despite how bad they looked. Stereotypical as it seemed, these were their activist friends, fellow Save the Rain Forest proponents and No Nukers. Mingling with the jocks and the tree huggers was a pod of aunts, uncles, and cousins. And, of course, parents. Georgette's mom and dad were there, as was Paul's mother. "Your father would have been so proud," she said as she gave Paul a big hug.

"I hope so," Paul said. Paul missed his father. It had been twenty years since he died, but Paul's memories were vivid. Fred Symon was a big, friendly guy and he was devoted to his wife and only child. He had a prickly sense of humor and he liked to tickle people. Just thinking about that made Paul smile. Paul remembered, as a very young boy, being in a park, sitting underneath a larch tree with his dad. Together they played some long-forgotten game that involved peeling the layers off a pinecone. Then they laid in the grass and looked up at the tree's green canopy. Paul didn't remember his dad saying anything lyrical about the tree but it came to him nonetheless. Paul hoped to share similar moments with his own son—not only for his son's benefit, but in an attempt to recapture the time he had with his own father.

Paul's mom stepped back and regarded her son and daughter-in-law. She took a dramatic deep breath, closed her eyes for just a moment, and then said, "I feel like I've completed my cycle," she said.

"Mom, you sound like a salmon," Paul teased.

"Oh, hush!" she said. "Just let me enjoy this without any of your smart comments." She spread her arms and gazed around. "I can't believe how beautiful this place is."

The Penumbra was built in a ten-acre stand of old growth redwoods on the coastal side of Marin County, across Tomales Bay from the Point Reyes National Park. In addition to the main house there were several guest houses and a cabana, all surrounding a natural hot spring. There was a spacious outdoor entertainment area with a large flagstone barbecue pit, a bar service area, and a gazebo big enough to hold a septet. The wedding ceremony was held farther back on the property where an amphitheater had been built among the huge trees on a gently sloping hillside. It was a beautiful place for a wedding and especially appropriate for a whole-wheat ceremony like this one.

The Penumbra was part of the Headwaters Forest—sixty thousand pristine acres with half a dozen magnificent old growth redwood groves. Ironically, a significant portion of the Headwaters was owned by Conifer Lumber, which recently had been bought by an investment group headed by Jerry Landis that was ready to start cutting down the trees. Worse, a state senator was doing her best to see that the logging could start the following week. The senator, who, perhaps predictably, had received large (yet soft) campaign contributions from Conifer Lumber, had recently struck a deal that would, as the senator's publicist put it, "strike a balance between economic and environmental concerns." The publicist failed to note, however, that the balance was tilted heavily in favor of the economic concerns, especially those of her boss. The deal was simple: In exchange for $250 million from the federal government and another $130 million from the state, Conifer Lumber would turn 7,500 acres of its own property into a wildlife and recreation preserve. In addition to the $380 million payoff, the government would allow Conifer to start logging the remaining 52,500 acres immediately. It surprised no one that none of the old growth redwood groves were protected.

And that explained why, at the head of the reception line, next to the book where the wedding guests were signing in, there were two petitions—one designed to prevent the logging in the Headwaters Forest and one to have the senator recalled from office for breaching the public trust. Paul considered it a minor victory that he was able to continue fighting Jerry Landis's evil empire while celebrating his wedding.

The most frequently repeated story at the reception was how Paul and Georgette first met. They knew of each other from Bay Area sports pages but they didn't meet until they both attended a protest at Marine World. They were protesting the exploitation of marine mammals as entertainment for terrestrial mammals. Theatricality was the guiding principle at this particular protest, so Paul was dressed as a sperm whale while Georgette was a placard-carrying bottle-nosed dolphin. They fell for each other at first sight, and Paul spent much of the day mimicking aquatic mammal mating calls. After a long day of demonstrating, Georgette invited Paul back to her place, where, still dressed in their foam rubber marine mammal costumes, they made love all night long as only young athletes can.

At the end of the final retelling of this story, Georgette placed her hands on her swelling belly and made a sperm whale joke. In the gales of laughter that followed, she and Paul made their exit. As they ran the gauntlet of birdseed-throwing friends and relatives, Paul's cousin Richard, who, up to that point, had refrained from any lewd behavior, emerged from the crowd and dropped his pants, mooning the happy couple. As they passed by, Georgette smacked Richard on the ass so hard he would still be able to see her handprint the next morning. The crowd cheered, and Georgette took a quick bow before ducking into the car.

In front of the newlyweds was a ninety-minute drive to an eco-friendly bed-and-breakfast near Calistoga. There Paul and Georgette would leave the world and all its troubles behind for a few days of wine, mud baths, and intimacy. Then, refreshed and satisfied, they would return to the battle and the search for the baboon farm. Paul was at the wheel, heading toward Petaluma, when he took his eyes off the road to look at his wife. "Have I mentioned how much I love you?"

Georgette smiled. "If you really mean that, you'll keep your eyes on the road and get us to that B-and-B so you can prove it." She reached over and started to rub Paul's thigh. "Drive, Romeo, drive," Georgette said. Paul accelerated, so aware of his keen attraction to his pregnant wife that he had to make an adjustment in his pants.

They had been on the road about twenty minutes when something came out of the woods onto the road ahead of them. It was a large truck pulling out from a dusty logging road, threatening to ruin their honeymoon. It was one of Conifer Lumber's logging trucks. It was carrying what looked like a seven-hundred-year-old redwood—a beautiful, magnificent, and sad testament to a dying planet. One of the world's oldest living things, one of its most extraordinary life-forms, cut down and dragged out of the woods like an escaped convict. And for what? Paneling? Roof shingles? That didn't matter to the loggers because they had big families with lots of children to feed. So they cut it down for the money and now they were parading it through Marin County at about twenty miles an hour, as if they had killed some giant beast and they wanted to show the world what they had done. A blood-red flag waved from the end of the huge tree, as if it had been killed while trying to surrender. The flag waved in Paul's face, taunting him, and once again the sign flashed in Paul's head.

ACRES OF RAIN FOREST REMAINING: 328,631,000

The trees screamed and cracked, and Paul's emotions did the same. That murdering son of a bitch Landis had found a way to fuck up his honeymoon. Goddammit, Paul wanted to find that aging asshole and break his wrinkled neck. Right now it seemed to Paul that Jerry

Landis was responsible for everything wrong with the world.

Paul looked over at Georgette. There was something he had to tell her. He'd been wanting to tell her for a long time but he either didn't know how or he just couldn't bring himself to do it. And now, even though it was too late, Paul was wondering if he should have told Georgette before he asked her to marry him. Yeah, it would have been the right thing to do, he thought, but he was afraid that what he had to say would scare her off. And Paul couldn't withstand a blow like that. He couldn't live without his G. She was the only thing right about the world. But instead of trusting Georgette, and telling her what was wrong, Paul kept hoping she would just see it and would get him the help he needed.

For months, Paul had been worried that something was very wrong with him. Not physically, but mentally. He didn't seem to see the same world that others did. He saw a place desperately in need of help and which seemed to be getting worse by the minute. And no one else appeared the least bit concerned about the state of things—not the political state, that was a hopeless matter, obviously—but the simple, physical state of the planet where they lived.

Paul wanted to tell Georgette that he was scared. He was afraid that he was going to be overwhelmed trying to fix everything. And what would happen when he snapped?

For years Paul was so focused on trying to stop the spread of nuclear power and whatever Jerry Landis was up to that he didn't even notice all the small things that were now driving him insane. But the years passed and the nuclear power plants all got built and Jerry Landis never slowed down and now every little thing that people did provoked a nasty, dark side of Paul that Paul didn't like . . . People throwing cigarettes from their cars; people whose entire universe of entertainment relied on the combustion of hydrocarbons: jet skis and power boats disrupting the serenity of beautiful lakes; dune buggies and off-road motorcycles defacing the desert; fathers who spent more time playing golf than they spent playing with their children; women who felt it was their right to smoke while they were pregnant . . . It was all Paul could do to drive to the grocery store, shop, and return home without going postal on one idiot or another about any of a dozen infractions of Paul's Code of Life.

What the hell was wrong with him? He was afraid of where this was going. Paul used to see himself simply as a concerned and active citizen. But he was beginning to feel like a crackpot of Kaczynskian proportions. Paul wished he could turn his anger into action. He wished he had the capacity for wrath.

There must be something wrong with me, Paul thought. It's like I don't belong here. What's wrong with me? Am I an alarmist nitwit? Is there no reason for concern? Is the Cornucopian Myth not a myth after all? Will the earth spontaneously generate endless amounts of food and fuel for the billions to come? Will it magically absorb all the poisons people produce? Or will it turn out that pollution is really a myth?

For a long time the only explanation that made any sense to Paul was that he was right and everyone else was wrong. But now, after four decades of trying to make things better in the world around him—while largely failing at the task—Paul was beginning to think that the simpler explanation was the more likely one. Besides, who was Paul to think he knew more than everybody else? If he was so smart, how come he couldn't change anything? The old explanation just didn't work anymore. The more realistic interpretation of things was that Paul was wrong and the rest of the world was right. Paul just hoped Georgette could help him deal with that.

Georgette had no idea of the depth of Paul's distress. She never *had* known but that wasn't her fault. Paul tried to explain it a dozen times and Georgette had listened and thought she understood. But she didn't, because Paul didn't have the words to express his rage. Maybe the words didn't even exist. He sometimes worried that one day he would just go mad.

"I've got an idea," Georgette said. "Let's get this guy to pull over. When he does, we'll drag him out of the cab and nail him to the tree."

Paul tapped at the steering wheel as he considered the option. "Nah," Paul said, "it's too late to save that tree. Crucifying the driver wouldn't help."

"No, but it might make you feel better," Georgette said.

"No, I bet committing murder on your honeymoon tends to put a damper on the mood."

"I said we'd *crucify* him, not kill him. Geeze, what do you think I am, crazy?"

"Crazy enough to marry me," Paul said, hoping the flip comment would make him forget his anger. "I figure you're crazy enough to do damn near anything."

"You have a point," Georgette said. "Okay, let's shelve the crucifixion idea and just try to save the honeymoon." She turned on the radio, hoping to find a distraction. The country songs were too sad. The pop was too stupid. And they couldn't understand the rap. So she settled on an all-news station.

". . . as the Journal of the American Medical Association is known, today released the results of a study by scientists at the University of Washington. The report concludes that consumption of large amounts of green tea may be linked to high rates of liver cancer. The scientists warned . . ."

Georgette made a quick mental note to switch to chamomile.

Paul wasn't listening to the radio. He kept looking for a chance to pass the slow-moving truck, but the winding, narrow county road wouldn't allow it. He wanted to get away from this tree, which reminded him of Jerry Landis, which reminded him of the baboons he knew were out there somewhere and which he knew were going to die. He wanted to forget about all the things that were wrong with the world and about which he could do absolutely nothing. He wanted to be left alone with his wife and not be bothered by his conscience. But Paul was in a no-passing zone. He'd be forced to follow the dead redwood, as if he were next of kin in a funeral procession.

As Georgette wondered about how much green tea she had consumed in her life, Paul considered his choices. He could follow the truck at a mind-numbing twenty miles an hour, all the while staring at the seven hundred rings of the dead tree, or he could try a death-defying pass on the inside of a blind curve, or he could pull over and wait.

Georgette decided to start drinking coffee again and returned her attention to the radio. ". . . press secretary said he was shocked that the Supreme Court had ruled that a sitting president must respond to civil lawsuits regarding sexual harassment. Turning now to the financial report, Menlo Park–based Xenotech, Incorporated announced that they have received FDA approval for a trial of their new immunosuppressant as well as the transgenic baboon heart they have developed. This follows on the heels of the British government's approval of continued transgenic swine research. Xenotech filed their investigational new drug application only nine days ago, and in a highly unusual move, the FDA said they expect to give Xenotech immediate approval to move to phase three studies, allowing them to perform almost unlimited xenografts if the first transplant is a success. Xenotech closed Friday up two and five eighths, and analysts predict . . ."

The honeymoon was over.

Georgette turned the radio off and they drove in silence a while before Paul finally said it. "That bastard already knows it works," he said. "They wouldn't make that announcement unless they knew. There's too much money at stake. This trial's just for the record and then they start killing the baboons." Georgette stared into the darkness. She didn't know what to say. Paul pulled the car to the side of the road and watched as the tree disappeared in the night. He stared straight ahead, his rage welling, caught in his throat. "I don't know what to do," he said.

Georgette reached over and took Paul's hand. "I'll tell you what we're going to do," she said. "We're going to find those baboons."

The mysterious building had been on the property for two years, unoccupied, the interior incomplete. Thick wires sprouted from recessed electrical boxes like Technicolor ear hair awaiting connection to unusual machinery. Contractors had come to finish the work only in the last two months and no one else was allowed inside. The building was larger than the others on the property, about eight thousand square feet total. It had a sophisticated industrial plumbing design, including an intricate commercial draining and fluid-recycling system. As the interior took shape it began to give the impression of something out of modern Japan or Detroit, almost like an automobile assembly line.

There was a series of complex, computer-controlled robotic arms and hands, some capable of performing tasks of remarkable strength, others designed for tasks of incredible sensitivity and dexterity. The tactile array sensors located on the hands sent staccato signals of constant digital information to a mainframe regarding pressure the gripping mechanisms were exerting at any given nanosecond. This allowed for adjustments so minute the hands might as well have been those of a surgeon.

Cameras mounted on the robotic arms allowed for recording and visual display at a main command console located in what looked like a television production control room. Technicians were in the process of fine-tuning the lighting equipment and the wall of high-definition video monitors. There were a dozen large wooden crates standing in the center of the main room waiting for all the other work to be finished. A shipping manifest on one of the crates indicated the machinery inside had been manufactured to extremely high tolerances in Hamburg, Germany. The crates were quite heavy, and if you peeked inside and the light hit just right, you could see the glint of stainless steel.

Arty's eye was stabbed by the flash from a photographer's camera. He was lying in an acrylic incubator propped up at a forty-five-degree angle for easy viewing. His surgical gown was on backwards, thereby exposing the draining tubes protruding from his midsection as well as the fine stitchery that kept his chest closed.

A television reporter called out, "Arty, how're you feelin'?"

"Groovy!" he said, smiling as if he'd just won the center-of-attention lottery.

Dr. Gibbs had called the press conference to announce the success of Xenotech's first FDA-approved xenograft, and Arty was on prominent display, his smiling little pirate head swiveling toward each request for a photograph. The auditorium at One Biotech Center was packed. The front half of the room was filled by a frantic crowd of over two hundred print and electronic media journalists from around the world. Filling up the seats at the back of the room were several dozen discolored and sickly looking potential organ recipients and their immediate families. All around the auditorium there were video monitors showing the Xenotech logo.

Jerry Landis was at the podium, looking fit and vigorous thanks to the good news and the ongoing hormone treatments. The muscles in his arms were full and round and his broken leg was almost healed. He had two testosterone patches glued to his scrotum, and every time one of his hands disappeared from the side of the podium it was a safe bet he was massaging himself.

Dr. Putnam and the rest of the medical and research staffs stood in the background, grinning more like proud parents of an honor roll student than a group of scientists who had just overcome one of nature's most potent forces. Mr. Luckett stood in the center of the crowded stage, playing with his big mustache, happy to be alive and lending FDA approval.

"With this momentous announcement, Xenotech, In-corporated ushers in a new era of medicine," Jerry Landis said. *Whir-pffft whir-pffft whir-pffft.* "An era of miracle and wonder where those in need of new organs are no longer victims of a heartless supply-and-demand curve." The crowd in the back of the room cheered weakly. Jerry Landis massaged himself and felt stronger for it. He raised his warm hand to call for quiet, then gestured at the video monitors and the old corporate logo morphed into a slick new one. "Xenotech, Incorporated delivers life," Jerry Landis said, echoing the words incorporated in the new logo. "Now, are there any questions?"

A reporter from one of the networks jumped to this feet. "Arty, what was wrong with your heart that you were willing to take such a risk with a baboon organ?"

Whir-pffft whir-pffft whir-pffft. Jerry Landis suddenly looked like he might pitch forward off the stage. If Arty told the truth here, Xenotech would have all the credibility of a congressman—a biotechnology company cutting a healthy organ out of an armless, legless, one-eyed man just to see if its new product worked. Jerry Landis looked to Dr. Putnam, hoping he would jump in and stop Arty from taking them down. But before Putnam could say a word, Arty fielded the question.

"Well, I'd rather not answer that," Arty said. "It's a personal matter and it's beside the point." Jerry Landis's eyes popped open in thanks. The little man in the acrylic box had just saved his ass. "As you can see," Arty said, mentally gesturing at himself, "I've been heavily involved in biomedical research for quite some time. I reached the decision to have the operation after lengthy discussions with the researchers. That, plus the fact that the FDA gave its unqualified approval, made me feel completely comfortable about going ahead with the surgery."

Another reporter stood and called out: "Who at the FDA gave approval on this?"

Mr. Luckett stepped forward and took the microphone. "That would be me. My name is Alex Luckett, that's with two *T*s. I'm with the FDA's Center for Drug

Evaluation and Research, which is a division of the Center for Biologics Evaluation and Research, which is a branch of the Division of Bioresearch Monitoring." The reporter asked more questions about the FDA's approval of such a radical medical procedure and Mr. Luckett answered. And all the while he was giving his answers, he was relishing the notion that his ex-wife was going to see this on the news. *Now* she'd be sorry for walking out on him. She'd be kicking herself hard over *that* miscalculation. Mr. Alex Luckett would forever be remembered as a man with the power to make history. He was the man who helped Xenotech, Incorporated deliver life. He was the man with stock options. By this time tomorrow, he'd be on easy street. The former Mrs. Luckett had fucked up and walked out on the wrong guy and *now* she'd be sorry.

A woman from the *New York Times* spoke up. "Arty says he feels good, but what is his exact medical condition vis-à-vis the xenograft?"

Dr. Putnam stepped to the podium, feeling important. "As most of you know, rejection is the main problem in any type of organ graft even between concordant species. But it's even more problematic with discordant species, where the phylogenetic differences are greater. The thing to remember here is we haven't simply put a baboon organ into a human being—that's been done before. This was a specially bred, *transgenic* baboon heart, which, for lack of a better word, is fooling the natural antibodies in Arty's system. On top of that we're treating Arty with the immunosuppressant cocktail we created in conjunction with the transgenic animals and which is, if you'll pardon the pun, at the heart of this revolutionary procedure. Arty has excellent cardiac function and the endomyocardial biopsy shows no evidence of rejection," Dr. Putnam said.

Someone from *BioScience Magazine* stood and called out: "How many of these transgenic baboons do you have and where are they? What sort of supply are you offering the public?"

Dr. Putnam yielded the podium to Jerry Landis. "I'm afraid that information must remain guarded for now," he said. *Whir-pffft whir-pffft whir-pffft.* "But let me say that supply is not going to be a problem. We've seen to that. Our breeding facility has been phenomenally successful. Now, since we don't want anything bad to happen to these animals, I simply cannot tell you where they are—as I'm sure you know, there are a lot of nuts out there who might try to do something crazy with them."

Arty had become hypnotized by the bright lights and the noise of the press conference. The words being spoken were now just ambient sound. He was adrift in his thoughts, calculating the value of his stock and thinking about all the things he'd be able to do for the orphanage. He couldn't wait to see all those kids smiling when he showed up with a truckload of goodies. Arty was glad he was able to do something for them. He smiled at the thought. But he wondered how he would do all these things without Bonedigger. Underneath Arty's one-eyed happy face he was worried that he hadn't heard from his big friend. He hoped everything was okay and that Bones would come to get him when it was time to go. Otherwise, Arty would be all alone.

Before the paramedics could treat H. Wayne Grigsby they had to get the four disfigured capuchin monkeys to let go of him. Ever since the big talking dog had let all the animals out of their cages they'd been performing their own little experiments on the vivisection executive. Most of the experiments seemed to be designed to ascertain the pain threshold of *Homo sapiens* when bitten by new world monkeys.

The San Mateo police had called some of Grigsby's employees to come in and round up the animals. They went for the monkeys first, but the feisty primates wouldn't give up their research without a fight. The employees finally resorted to tranquilizer guns. And while they were pretty good shots, they still managed to sink several darts into a grateful Mr. Grigsby.

Lance Abbott arrived ten minutes after the call to the police went out. The moment he saw H. Wayne Grigsby he knew he wasn't getting any organs, but he stayed nonetheless. Something that the talking dog had left behind caught his eye like a fishhook.

It caught the eye of the detective from the San Mateo police department as well. He was looking at it on the chalkboard as the paramedics wheeled H. Wayne Grigsby out of the lab. Mr. Grigsby was in full shock, and it was doubtful that even a corneal implant would help his eyesight. On the upside, he was holding up pretty well against the sublethal dose of the nerve agent with which he'd been injected.

The detective was new in San Mateo. Though it seemed like years already, he had moved to California from Michigan just six months ago after spending a dozen years with the Michigan State Police, where he had been assigned to the governor's detail. After all those winters in Lansing, moving to California was like stepping into the sunshine from an ice storm. Michigan seemed like a bad dream to him now, but it was because of his time there that the writing on the chalkboard caught his attention. He pulled out his notepad and wrote something.

Lance Abbott sidled up to the detective and pointed at the "!Terra tuebor!" "I've seen that before," he said, thinking about the notes that came from under the head of the man killed in the BART tunnel, from on the head of Edith Hazelquist, and from Shart Lemsling's pocket. "Have any idea what it means?"

"Well, *Tuebor* is a motto on the Great Seal of Michigan," the detective said. "It means 'I will defend.' I always thought that was a lot better than the state's motto, *Si quaeris penninsulam amoenam.*"

"Yeah? What's that mean?" Lance asked.

" 'If you seek a pleasant peninsula, look about you.' " He shook his head and gave Lance a can-you-believe-that look.

"Sounds like a slogan for a cheesy Cheboygan real estate company," Lance said. "How about the *Terra*?"

The detective cleared his throat. "I'm guessing *Terra* is like *terra firma*, which means 'solid ground,' but in this context it probably means 'earth,' as in 'I will defend the earth.' " The detective turned, looking at Lance suspiciously. "The question is, whose motto is that?"

Lance thought about it a moment before feeling indicted. "Well, it's not mine." But it was a good question. It was the sort of question the answer to which might be a career maker.

14

Georgette had several reasons to be worried. For starters she'd been ill for two days. At seven months, she knew it wasn't morning sickness, and since she didn't have any of the symptoms of intestinal flu, she knew it was something else. But what? It was a sensation Georgette had never felt before and it was severe enough to make her worried for her unborn baby. She took some comfort in the fact that her monthly prenatal doctor's appointment was later that morning. However, she didn't feel good enough to drive herself and she wasn't sure she could get Paul to do it for her. So she was worried.

Paul was sick and worried too, but for a different reason. Ever since returning from the aborted honeymoon, he had been on-line with everyone he had ever protested with and many whom he knew only by reputation. He had made contact with environmental activists in every state in the United States along with those in another two dozen countries. Georgette had never seen Paul this way. He'd always been concerned with his causes and periodically he would become borderline fanatical, usually when trying to get voters to vote on a particular bond issue or candidate. But he had always pulled back before reaching the edge of obsession, noting that moderation

was the best strategy in the long run. But this time was
different. Paul had become completely obsessed with lo-
cating Xenotech's baboon-breeding facility.

He'd slept only six hours in the three days since Xenotech announced FDA approval for the transgenic baboon
heart transplant. When Paul did sleep, his sleep was fitful
and haunted by a nightmare featuring an ancient and
cackling Jerry Landis counting his money as he stood
among the bloody carcasses of hundreds of mutilated
baboons. The nightmare would shock Paul awake and
leave him even more consumed with the need to stop it
all from happening.

As he clicked from hyperlink to hyperlink, Paul wondered what he would do if he actually discovered the
location of the baboon farm. Would he set up a protest?
Seek an injunction of some sort? Call the media? Would
any of that be sufficient? Could he bring himself to actually do something or would his cowardice be exposed
once again as the baboons were led to slaughter?

Over the past seventy-two hours, Georgette had looked
in on Paul every now and then, hoping that he had either
worked through his anger or that he'd found what he
was looking for. She knew if Paul could locate the breeding facility and start organizing against it, he'd feel better
about everything. But every time she looked in and saw
him hunched over the keyboard with the blue-gray glow
of the screen on his tired face she could tell things were
simply getting worse.

About an hour before her appointment Georgette poked
her head into the room and saw Paul typing furiously as
he composed another urgent E-mail. "Sweetheart, I need
you to drive me to my doctor's appointment," she said.

"Hang on." Paul typed with two fingers and tended to
hit the keys harder than necessary.

Georgette went to Paul and rubbed his neck and
shoulders. "You're going to break that keyboard if you
keep typing that hard," Georgette said.

Paul finished his sentence with a flourish and three

(!!!) exclamation points. "What doctor's appointment?" he asked as he clicked Send.

"My monthly prenatal," she said. "I've been feeling pretty crappy the last two days." Georgette dug a knuckle into a fibrous knot in Paul's thick trapezius. "Whaddya say, can you give a pregnant girl a lift?"

"I'd like to but . . ." Paul gestured at the table. There were six legal pads with web site addresses, E-mail addresses, newsgroups, paths, mailing lists, patterns, FTPs, and scores of names and indecipherable notes scrawled all over them. He wanted to say something about the importance of his mission, the urgency of his cause, but he couldn't find the words. And as he glanced at the screen he saw Georgette's reflection and he suddenly found perspective. "But . . . nothing." Paul stood up. "I'm sorry, let's go. I guess I got carried away." Georgette heard resignation in his voice, or maybe he was just exhausted; either way she was glad to be going to the doctor's and glad to get Paul away from the computer, at least for a little while.

Outside it was cloudy and cool. The neighborhood was quiet and neither Paul nor Georgette noticed the banged-up Ford pickup truck idling at the curb across the street. But the large, tattooed man in the truck's cab definitely noticed them. He was extremely alert and happy. His state of hyperacute awareness was the result of a recent snort of methamphetamine. His happiness stemmed from the fact that he was no longer incarcerated. Until late last night, Bones had been cooling his jets in the Mountain View City Jail. However, thanks to a minor violation of his constitutional rights, Bones had been sprung. And now, jacked up on the speed, he was having a hard time not shooting at anything that moved. In fact, twenty minutes earlier, he had almost surrendered his element of surprise by opening fire on a squirrel that appeared suddenly on Paul and Georgette's front lawn. But by the time he figured out where the gun's safety was, the squirrel had disappeared.

Bonedigger had ended up in the Mountain View jail

after the accident with the dump truck. He had plowed into the back of the truck and been knocked out cold. The cops found the bulky biker leaning headfirst against the steering wheel with a deep half-crescent-shaped subdural hematoma on his forehead. On the floor of the truck they found his loaded .22 Colt Woodsman and his peanut butter jar full of methamphetamine. Based on this, the police arrested him and read him his rights despite the fact that he was still unconscious (which turns out to be insufficient vis-à-vis *Miranda* v. *Arizona*).

Freed on the constitutional rights issue, Bones went to the impound lot to get his truck. Since he didn't have the sort of money necessary to pay for the towing or the impound charges, Bones had to sneak onto the lot and hotwire the ancient Ford. It was a tight squeeze for Bones under the dashboard of the old pickup, but he managed. When he got the right wires connected, nothing happened. Absolutely nothing. Bones eyed the fuse panel unkindly and spoke ill of its heritage. "Bastard," he said. He hit it a few times with his giant elbow but still nothing happened. He needed a new fuse, so he rummaged through the glove box, which was crammed with old road maps, packs of Taco Bell hot sauce, some ancient crumbling cigarettes, and a box of ammo for the .22 Colt Woodsman that the cops had confiscated. "Shit," Bones muttered. No fuses.

But just then Bones remembered something, or at least a part of something. Something he heard on the radio a few months back. Was it Frick and Frack the car dudes? Nah, that seemed unlikely. Regardless, Bones suddenly had the solution to his problem, and a minute later the Ford roared to life without a single kick to the fuse panel and Bones drove the truck straight through the cyclone fence off the back of the impound lot.

Figuring a change of vehicles was in order, Bones headed for the Los Trancos Trailer Park to retrieve his Harley and to get a meth refill. Then he would set off to finish the job Dr. Gibbs had hired him to do. To say the least, Bones was disappointed when he got to the trailer park and found nothing but charbroiled mobile home and motorcycle. He got out of his truck and cursed as he poked through the rubble. "Shit!" and "Sonuvabitch!" were used repeatedly. Bones went to Arty's trailer and banged on the door. "Hey, little man, you in there?" When Arty didn't answer Bones got back in his truck and drove straight out to the Los Altos Hills, where a buddy of his had a meth lab. He found his friend and beat the shit out of him since he didn't have any money and because the friend made a disparaging remark about Bonedigger's credit rating. Bones then filled a Folger's coffee can with fresh crank and stole his friend's Charter Arms Bulldog .44 Special. It didn't deliver a high-velocity round, but it would bring a victim to his knees long enough for some easy head shots. He would have stolen his pal's car as well, but it was currently up on blocks in the front yard.

Armed and refueled with the meth, Bones got back in his truck and went looking for Paul. He just wanted to finish the job, get paid, and move on. So he hopped on I-280 and started the drive north. Bones decided that the direct approach was more of a sure thing than the sabotaged-car routine. And he felt nothing was more direct than a .44-caliber slug in the old brain pan. So Bones went to Paul's house, parked the truck, and waited. He hoped Paul would expose himself outside so he'd already be in his getaway vehicle when he did the deed. If Paul didn't show himself by nightfall, Bones would go in to get him. That was the plan. It was his best plan to date.

He'd been parked at the curb for about two hours when Paul and Georgette emerged for the trip to the doctor's office. Despite the chill in the air, Bones was toasty—he'd been running the heater steadily for the last thirty minutes without once having to kick at the fuse panel. It seemed his jury-rigged circuit breaker was working just fine.

Georgette was first out of the house and was standing on the passenger side of their tiny car waiting for Paul to arrive with the keys to unlock the doors. Bones was

so hyped up on the crank that he almost shot at Georgette when she came out the front door. His heart was
pounding not just because of the speed but also from
the fear and excitement that come when you're about to
take someone's life. Paul was about halfway to the car
when Bones squeezed off his first shot. *WHBOOM!* The
.44 sounded like a fucking cannon in the quiet
neighborhood.

One of the problems with firing a weapon while under
the influence of substantial quantities of psychomotor
stimulants is how jittery you are. Actually, firing the gun
is easy, it's more of a problem in terms of hitting what
you're shooting at. The first shot shattered a kitchen window in a house on the next block.

Stunned by the thunderous report of the .44 and the
fact that they could tell someone was shooting at them,
Paul and Georgette froze. Actually, Paul crouched
slightly, but other than that he didn't move. Georgette's
system began secreting enough adrenaline to hairlip a
moose, and combined with the fear factor, her heart rate
soared much like Bonedigger's. She looked and saw the
big man with the dark muttonchop sideburns sitting in
the truck pointing a gun at Paul and before she could
say anything *WHBOOM!* The second shot hit Paul's left
shoulder and fractured his collar bone. If he hadn't
crouched it would have hit close to the heart. The impact
of the slug spun Paul around and sent him crashing face-
first onto the lawn. He landed hard on his ribs, knocking
the air out of his lungs. "Oooooofff." He couldn't breathe.

"Jesus!" Georgette yelled. "Paul, are you okay?!" She
could see blood staining his shirt. Unable to breathe,
Paul couldn't respond. He flailed a little with one hand
trying to tell her to stay down, but Georgette started out
from behind the car anyway. She had to . . .

WHBOOM!

. . . duck. She hit the driveway when the third shot
ricocheted off the roof of the car not two feet from her.
"Fuck!" Georgette's mind was racing. She wondered how
badly Paul was hurt. She wondered who the hell the guy

in the truck was and why the hell he was trying to kill
them. She wondered how she could get to Paul to get
him out of the line of fire. She wondered . . .

POP!

Pop? She wondered what the hell that was. The first
three shots were *WHBOOM*s, not *POP*s. The next thing
she heard was a man screaming. "Sonuvabitch!Shit!Fuck!
Goddammit!" She knew by the language and the growl
in the voice that it wasn't Paul. So who the hell was it?
The man in the truck? A wounded passerby? The whole
thing was insane.

"Georgette?" Paul was still on the ground but he had
his wind back. "Are you all right?" He looked around as
best he could from his prone position, trying to see
where the shots had come from as well as where Georgette was now. He had lost all sense of direction.

"Paul!" Georgette was relieved to hear his voice. "Can
you move? Are you all right?"

"Yeah, my shoulder's bleeding, but I think I'm okay."
Since the shooting had apparently stopped, Georgette
rushed to Paul's side. She kissed him quickly before
checking his wound. Paul rolled onto his back and sat
up. "What's that noise?" he asked.

What had been a voice venting a rapid-fire stream of
expletives had become a low moan. It sounded like a
large, dumb animal in pain, like a cow giving birth or
something. Then there was a rusty, screeching, squeaking
sound. Georgette watched the door of the banged-up
pickup truck open. She knew the man getting out of the
truck was the shooter but still she had no idea why.
Fueled by adrenaline, Georgette yanked Paul to his feet
and then to safety behind their car. She didn't know what
else to do.

Bonedigger fell out of the cab of the truck and onto
the street with a thud. He was still moaning, and Georgette could see that his pants were soaked in blood and
he was clutching at his crotch. She tried to piece things
together but nothing made sense. First this huge, tattooed man had shot at them for no obvious reason. Then

it sounded as if someone else had shot the huge, tattooed man—again for reasons unknown. And now it appeared that whoever had shot the big tattooed man had done so in his groin and then disappeared.

Though Georgette would never know it, the facts were these: While searching for a replacement fuse, Bonedigger had come across the box of .22 shells in the glove box. He remembered hearing a story about how a couple of good old boys down in Arkansas were coming home from a night of drinking and frog-gigging when their headlights gave out on them. The good old boys checked their fuse panel and saw they needed a new fuse. Since they didn't have any spares, they looked for alternatives and eventually discovered that not only did a .22 short fit perfectly in the fuse panel, but it completed the connection as well. The part of the story Bonedigger had forgotten was that after a while the electricity running through the .22 heated it up and caused it to discharge. Bones had been shot in the right testicle. After the bullet exploded through his scrotum it severed Bonedigger's femoral artery, and now he was bleeding to death on the street, undeniable evidence of the process of natural selection.

All Georgette knew was that the guy who had shot her husband was lying in the street, too hurt to shoot again. She was suddenly furious. This son of a bitch had tried to kill them and Georgette intended to find out why. Preoccupied with his bleeding crotch, the tattooed man seemed harmless, so Georgette stormed out from behind the car and charged him. She approached Bonedigger's head as if it were a football and she were trying to kick a field goal from forty yards out. She caught Bonedigger square in the forehead with the toe of her shoe. It's hard to say whether it was more surprising that Bonedigger's head didn't detach from his neck or that he remained conscious, but both were true. Georgette then came down knee-first onto Bones's chest, breaking two ribs and cracking a third. She punched him square on the nose. Paul heard it break from ten yards away. "Who the fuck are you?" Georgette screamed at the tattooed man.

Bonedigger's tongue slid out of his mouth like a tired pink snake. There was blood on it, seeping from his sinuses. He mumbled something that sounded like "Bitch," which was the wrong thing to mumble at Georgette at this particular moment. She hit him hard enough to break his nose a second time but there was no cracking sound, just a mushy noise as the cartilage and blood were compressed under the punch. "Why the hell are you trying to kill us, you son of a bitch?" Bonedigger was losing color in his face. His eyes rolled up in his head. He was about to pass out when Georgette slapped him to recapture his attention. "Talk to me, you big dumb motherfucker! I want to know what's going on!" Bones tried to articulate some words, but the going was tough what with this large, violent, pregnant woman kneeling on his chest while punching his badly broken nose—not to mention the pain in his crotch and the blood loss.

Georgette looked into the cab of the truck to see if there were any clues but all she saw was an open Folger's coffee can, a smoking .44, and a pool of coagulating blood. She stood and got the .44. Returning to Bones, she put the barrel to his head. "Talk, cocksucker!" She looked as if she had done this sort of thing before.

Newly motivated, Bones began speaking, though not in what you would call complete English sentences. Looking cross-eyed at the Charter Arms Bulldog .44 Special, Bones quickly gave up Dr. Gibbs as the man who hired him. When pressed about exactly who the hell Dr. Gibbs was, Bones said something about a company called Ex-eno-tech in Menlo Park. "What the fuck is Ex-eno-tech?" Georgette demanded. When Bones shook his head to indicate he didn't know, Georgette raised the gun to pistol-whip his memory. And just as she started to bring her hand down, someone grabbed her wrist. It was Paul.

"He means Xenotech," Paul said. "Dr. Gibbs works for Landis. Ask him if he knows where the baboon farm is." Paul let go of Georgette's wrist. *WHAM!* She smacked Bones in the jaw with the gun. "Where's the goddamn baboon farm?"

"I meant without the pistol-whipping," Paul said.

"Oh, sorry." Georgette asked Bones again about the baboon farm and, weakly, he said, "Missippi." Then he lost consciousness.

Paul helped Georgette stand. She looked at her fist, bloody from her interrogation. Then she wrapped her arms around Paul and started to cry. The adrenaline was still coursing through her veins, and now that the danger had passed her emotions flooded out. She had almost lost the man she loved. She had almost been shot herself. And then, suddenly, Georgette let out a scream. "Oh, God!" She put her hands to her lower abdomen. "Oh, Jesus!" She was starting to bleed. Paul didn't have to ask. Georgette looked into his eyes. "It's the baby."

Since both Arty and Mr. Luckett were thriving with their transgenic baboon hearts, Jerry Landis believed he had found a loophole in his contract with death. Werner's syndrome might age and destroy his organs, but now Jerry Landis could replace them at will. He could, in theory, live forever. And that set him thinking.

Immortality. *Whir-pffft   whir-pffft   whir-pffft.* That must have been what God had in mind for him all along. Why else would He have sent Jerry Landis down this path? The mere fact that God had visited him in the form of the golden light should have been clue enough. Surely it wasn't just a random series of events that, by fluke, had resulted in this . . . this miracle, for there was nothing else you could call this without diminishing its significance. Difficult as it was to fathom, Jerry Landis was beginning to think he actually might have underestimated his role in the grand scheme of things. Perhaps he was more than a mere prophet. Dare he think it? Could he really be the son of . . . the Almighty? At this moment that seemed possible because according to the accounting exercise in which he and Dr. Gibbs were currently engaged, Jerry Landis would soon be as rich as God.

"What about advertising?" Dr. Gibbs asked.

Jerry Landis laughed out loud. "Advertising? You must be joking. We don't need to advertise. Advertising is for the kind of crap people don't need, the non-necessities of life. You can live without Lite Beer and a new car but hearts and livers, Dr. Gibbs, are *not* optional items."

Dr. Gibbs smiled. He knew his boss was right. Xenotech wouldn't be in a marketplace glutted with competing products from which they would need to distinguish themselves with some unique selling proposition—"Our hearts have 25 percent less fat!" Aside from the cereal manufacturer, Xenotech would be the only company on earth offering Life. You wouldn't need J. Walter Thompson to get the word out about that.

"Tell me the first harvest numbers again, Dr. Gibbs." Jerry Landis sat at his desk and looked at the plastic organs lined up across the desktop like wooden soldiers on parade.

"Well, sir," Dr. Gibbs began, "since the press conference, we've sold every major solid organ from the first five hundred baboons." Gibbs picked up a legal pad that was covered with numbers and he started reading from it. These were the numbers Jerry Landis wanted to hear:

500 livers	@	$125,00 per	=	$62,500,000
500 hearts	@	$100,000 per	=	$50,000,000
500 lungs	@	$75,000 per	=	$37,500,000
1,000 kidneys	@	$45,000 per	=	$45,000,000
500 pancreas	@	$35,000 per	=	$17,500,000

Dr. Gibbs paused and looked to Jerry Landis. "What's the plural? Is it five hundred pancreases or five hundred pancreas?"

"Perhaps it's pancrei," Jerry Landis said.

Dr. Gibbs nodded thoughtfully. "Perhaps it is," he agreed. The total for the five major solid organs was over $200 million. Add to that, say $10 million for bone marrow and another $30 million for bone, tendon, and intestine (possibly sold by the foot?) transplants and the total was in the $250,000,000 range *for parts only.* If Xenotech did, say, half of the surgeries, that was in the neighborhood of another $125,000,000. As if that weren't enough, there was income from Xenotech's exclusive immunosuppressant to consider. Say only half of the initial 3,000 patients survived long-term, that would still be 1,500 customers who would require the antirejection cocktail in order to stay alive. At $35,000 a year that was $52,500,000 annually per 1,500 patients. Based on these somewhat conservative numbers, Xenotech stood to gross $425,000,000 in the first year.

"And you know what?" Jerry Landis mused. "They'd say it's a bargain at twice the price." *Whir-pffft whir-pffft whir-pffft.*

There was something else that Jerry Landis loved about all this aside from the money and the possible immortality. It was something that touched the core of his being. Something Jerry Landis would have liked regardless of the healing aspects of the miracle he had performed. It was the fact that these organs would be outside the purview of UNOS, the United Network for Organ Sharing. Thus there was no waiting list on which recipients needed to languish, no set of arbitrarily manufactured priorities, none of that status one, status two business that put you in line after someone else simply because he was in worse condition than you. None of that. This was no meritocracy. This was the purest expression of money talks. It was Jerry Landis's native tongue. *Whir-pffft whir-pffft whir-pffft.*

When Paul lifted Georgette into his arms his shoulder wound opened wide, nearly exposing the broken collar bone. He was bleeding profusely. Georgette alternated between excruciating labor pains and semiconsciousness. She felt so bad she wanted to die. Paul got her into the car and took off for the hospital, leaving Bones hemorrhaging in the street.

Over the past seven months Paul had mapped out three different routes to the hospital. Route one was mostly freeway—it was the most direct and fastest during non–rush hour traffic. Route two relied on a combination of freeways and multilaned boulevards with the most favorably timed lights—it was less direct but would get them to the delivery room in time if route one was busy. Route three was an insane combination of shortcuts and illegal turns that required an average speed of about sixty miles per hour through suburban neighborhoods filled with children playing games in the streets. This was the route of last resort.

Since it was mid-morning, Paul was optimistic about route one. He nonetheless tuned in to the radio station with the most frequent traffic reports. "Hang on, sweetheart," he said. "I'm going to get you there."

Georgette twisted into a fetal position trying to minimize the pain in her belly. "It's too early," Georgette said. "The baby's too early." She sounded like a frightened child and she started to cry. "Something's wrong . . ." It didn't even sound like Georgette. In all their years together Paul had never seen her scared. Georgette had faced down angry, screaming policemen during ugly, heated protests. She'd been involved in covert and illegal activities—like when she helped a group of rabid environmentalists sabotage some bulldozers. Paul had seen others in these situations and he had seen fear in their faces. But Georgette was always cool and defiant.

And pain didn't normally affect her demeanor either. Paul had seen torn anterior cruciate ligaments reduce some of the toughest men he'd ever played football with to tears. But when Georgette ripped her ACL in a pickup game of hoops, she just grimaced and limped off to the hospital without saying a word. But right now she was screaming and crying and scaring the hell out of Paul. He knew this was serious. There's something about the way people scream when they're in pain that lets you know the truth. It's not so much something you hear as something you feel on your skin and in your gut. Georgette's scream was terrifying. She knew something awful was happening inside her and, worst of all, she didn't know what it was.

Paul was about to get on the 101 when the radio said traffic on the freeway had ground to a halt thanks to an accident involving a semi carrying ten thousand gallons of benzene. The poisonous, flammable liquid had spilled all over the road and was pouring into the estuaries that fed San Francisco Bay. A hazardous material team was expected to arrive sometime that afternoon. "Jesus Christ!" Paul muttered. He envisioned the gruesome deaths of countless fish and waterfowl. How many would this kill? The irresponsible bastards liable for this would probably get off by issuing a public apology and paying a ten-thousand-dollar fine which was covered by insurance. Except for the fact that it was a public relations nuisance, the death of an occasional ecosystem really didn't matter as far as those types of people were concerned. Paul started to plan a letter-writing campaign against the benzene manufacturer and the trucking company when Georgette let out a horrifying howl which refocused him on the task at hand.

With route one closed, Paul checked his mirrors and executed a brilliant U-turn, moving like a fist through the traffic, slicing neatly between a minivan and a pizza delivery car before jumping the poorly conceived concrete median designed to discourage such maneuvers. He could be on route two in less than a minute provided that at least one of the two boneheads blocking the two lanes in front of him got "the hell out of the fucking way!" as Paul put it. He flashed his lights and honked his horn, but the man in the BMW was so engrossed in his phone conversation that he didn't notice and the woman in the Explorer was busy dealing with her dog, who had snatched her Egg McMuffin. "Dammit! Move!" Paul screamed. But no one did.

Paul looked at the speedometer. They were going twenty-five in a forty and they were slowing. He'd have a stroke if traffic didn't start moving soon. "Hold on, sweetheart," Paul said as he gave Georgette a reassuring squeeze on the thigh. "I'm going to get you there, I promise." It was a no-passing zone but, since there was no oncoming traffic, Paul crossed the double yellow lines and went around the Explorer. He glanced over to see if the woman was, in any way, paying attention to the world outside her sport utility vehicle. She wasn't. When Paul looked up he saw exactly what he didn't want to see—six flashing arrows herding two lanes of traffic into one. And that lane wasn't moving. A little beyond the flashing arrows, there was a man wearing a hardhat and holding a Stop sign. "Fuck me running!" Paul said before he took a wild right turn onto a side street and floored it. He was opting for route three.

At first it seemed like a good idea—very little traffic, no toxic waste spills, no construction delays, just the occasional garbage truck lurching down the trash can–lined streets. They were making good time, all things considered, but Paul was no less tense as he worried simultaneously about all the garbage people threw out every day and Georgette, whose breathing had become horribly shallow. Paul turned left and had only eight more blocks of suburbia before they were dumped back onto a major traffic artery about two miles from the hospital. Paul had never made such good time during his trial runs through these neighborhoods so he took this as a sign that things were going to be all right. But that was before he saw another sign. Actually Slow Children at Play was more than just a sign—it was the truth. In fact, Paul nearly had to hit the brakes to avoid hitting any of them. He'd been honking his horn for two blocks before he came upon a group of kids playing in the street. He couldn't believe how slow they were to move out of the way of an oncoming vehicle carrying a sick pregnant woman. It was as if they felt a car had no business being on the street in the first place. But when Paul didn't slow on his approach, they scattered like little monkeys. "Stupid little shits, get out of the fucking street!" Paul was uncharacteristically tense. Where the hell were their parents? Why were these kids unsupervised? Why weren't they playing on a playground or in one of these tiny little yards, for Christsake?

"Paul?" Georgette sounded weaker than before. "Am I going to be all right?"

"You're going to be fine," Paul said. "We're almost there." They were just a few miles from the hospital and unless something inconceivable happened they'd be there in five minutes or less. Georgette was pale and was starting to shiver. Paul touched her arm and then her cheeks. She was cold. Was that shock? That couldn't be good. Paul filled with a sense of dread. What if Georgette didn't make it? And the baby . . . God, he couldn't think about it. And he couldn't *not* think about it. Georgette was his world. She was all that really mattered. Paul would personally help clear-cut every square inch of rain forest on this godforsaken planet if that would make Georgette all right. And what about their baby? Didn't their baby deserve a better chance than this? What kind of way was this to come into the world? Dead. Stillborn. Coffin fodder. Born at the wrong time. Jesus Christ! Was this really happening? Or was this just a new nightmare, replacing the one with Jerry Landis? That had to be it, a double feature nightmare due to sleep deprivation. Any second now Paul would wake up wet and screaming to find out everything was okay. Any second now . . . any second . . . any . . .

The sound of horns honking and tires squealing on pavement as brakes locked up told Paul two things: (1) this was all too real; and (2) he had run a Stop sign. Paul cut the wheel hard to the right and fishtailed the little car onto the boulevard that would take them directly to the emergency room. A minute later they were a mile closer to the hospital when suddenly traffic got thick and slowed. The light ahead was green but no one was moving. And before Paul could get off the boulevard he was hemmed in by cars on all sides. He was trapped. "Goddammit!" He slammed the steering wheel. Now what?

Ahead, Paul saw several people walking up the boulevard in his direction. They were handing out flyers to the people in the cars. They were with an organization called the Alliance for a Paving Moratorium. The flyer they handed Paul said, "Overpopulation isn't just people." It was a fact sheet supporting their position regarding problems caused by internal combustion engines. Paul glanced at it: "Driving delays are expected to waste 7.3 billion gallons of fuel per year over the next two decades, adding 73 million tons of carbon dioxide to the atmosphere."

"Jesus," Paul said. "Since the first Earth Day, 1970, we have lost more than forty million acres of farmland to development." There were dozens more disheartening statistics—all of which Paul knew were true. He wanted to help, he wanted to do something, but he was paralyzed. It was too much for Paul to take. His pregnant wife was in pain and possibly dying. He was trapped in traffic and being told things were only going to get worse. And he believed it. His eyes lost focus and, even though he was still staring at the flyer, he wasn't reading it. The soy ink was little more than a blur on the recycled paper. Not that it would have mattered, but had Paul read farther he would have discovered the reason he was trapped where he was.

It turned out that the Alliance for a Paving Moratorium volunteers had driven their own cars into the intersection ahead to cause the gridlock in which Paul and the other drivers currently found themselves. They did this so they could hand out their flyers, solicit donations, and dramatically make their point all at the same time. The local television stations had agreed to cover the demonstration only if the Alliance could guarantee "good pictures," as they called them.

Georgette was quiet now, her breathing shallow and her eyelids all but closed. Paul knew there was nothing he could do except offer her comfort. He was useless, trapped in his car, betraying his oath to care for her in sickness. The Alliance flyer slipped from Paul's hand and, as he looked all around, everything moved in slow motion. The hot, poisonous fumes from the exhaust pipe in front of him rose sleepily, almost peacefully, toward the ozone hole in the sky. The people walking through traffic in his rearview mirror were closer than they appeared as they moved dreamily from car to car. Things were strangely quiet and Paul had a vague sense that death was nearby.

In the car in front of Paul, a man was smoking a cigarette. His arm moved lazily in and out of the window as he smoked. His index finger tapped the cigarette and the ash drifted to the warm pavement below. The arm returned the cigarette to the man's mouth and a moment later a gray stream of thick smoke poured into the air. Then the arm came back out the window and came to rest on the side of the door, the hand dangling down. Paul stared as the smoke curled up and over the smoker's hand and forearm. And he knew exactly what would happen next.

The man didn't look to see if anyone was watching him. He expected no reproach for what he was about to do. Paul watched the fingers holding the cigarette as they slowly moved apart and, as casually as a tree drops a leaf, the man dropped the cigarette onto the street, where it lay burning into Paul's soul. And Paul could take it no more. Someone, he felt, had to say something.

There was a time, at least in Paul's mind, when people wouldn't have done such a thing. Their connection to—or their pride in—the community (or their respect for another's) wouldn't have allowed for such behavior. But that sort of self-restraint was long gone. Everyone's standards had been so lowered that people could no longer be bothered when someone simply tossed burning trash from a car. And the reason for this was simple. Because someone, somewhere along the line, had done something worse than toss a lighted cigarette on the street and the second violation overshadowed the first. And then someone did something else worse than that and so on and so on and so on. And before you could say "Give a Hoot,

Don't Pollute" one was hard-pressed to do anything that would draw so much as a disapproving glance. The bar had been lowered so, and so many people were jumping over it so frequently, that it was hard even to remember in what order they jumped. Did Union Carbide's leaking pesticide plant in Bhopal kill 3,500 people before or after the Brazilian government sent a million urban slum dwellers to farm the state of Rondonia, resulting in the destruction of the rain forest, only to discover that the soil wouldn't support agriculture? Did Christian Falangists massacre a group of Palestinians before or after North Korean terrorists killed nineteen people with a time bomb at the Mausoleum in Rangoon? Did Oliver Huberty kill twenty people at that McDonald's in San Ysidro before or after Wayne Williams killed the twenty-three children in Atlanta?

Compared to everything else that happened day after day, most people couldn't be bothered to say anything when some idiot tossed a cigarette onto the street. And Paul knew that was precisely the problem. Because by shrugging your shoulders at the first transgression, you make the next easier to overlook—and so on and so on.

And now Paul was trapped in traffic with his pregnant wife, who, as far as he knew, was dying. And if the child she was carrying somehow managed to live, Paul didn't want him to live in a world where people felt free to throw burning garbage on the street. So Paul exploded out of his car and stormed toward the man in the car in front of him. The man glanced casually in his mirror when he saw Paul coming. He must have thought Paul was going to see what was causing the delay. When Paul stopped at the man's door, bent down, and picked up the still-burning cigarette butt, the man grew curious and somewhat nervous. When he noticed the blood on Paul's shirt he feared there might be trouble. When Paul grabbed the man's jaw and dislocated it open, he became very worried. And when Paul put the burning cigarette out on the man's tongue and shouted, *"The world is not your fucking ashtray, asshole!"* he learned his lesson. He would never do that again.

Paul then leaned into the man's car, grabbed his anti-theft device, and charged ahead toward the gridlocked intersection. There, swinging the Club like Jose Canseco, he would do whatever was necessary to get traffic moving again. Paul wasn't in the mood to take no for an answer.

Georgette, alone in the car, arched her back and moaned as a sharp pain pierced her gut. She hurt terribly inside and the bleeding was getting worse. If she had seen Paul, she might have felt a little better about things. She certainly would have been proud that Paul had actually done something for a change—but she had no way of knowing for she was no longer conscious.

15

The pregnant mother sat on the ground with one child nursing at her depleted breast while her six others milled around, filthy and malnourished, their eyes too big for their sockets. Their father had long ago disappeared, so the mother did whatever she could to feed them, which didn't amount to much.

The forklift was at the fence lifting huge pallets of crated food and dropping them over into the compound. As always, the dominant and subdominant males came away with the majority of the best food. One of the larger males lumbered away from the feeding frenzy dragging a crate filled with fruits and alfalfa. He made his way down the path past the nursing baboon, who looked down and meekly held out a hand. The male baboon bared his teeth and kicked at one of the starving babies when it reached for an apple that fell from the crate. The mother pulled her child back toward her and the male continued down the path.

In the beginning, the employees of the Biomedical Research Center of the South who were in charge of food supply never saw the baboons when they delivered the fruits, vegetables, eggs, Gulf Coast crabs, and other edibles that the old world monkeys thrived on. At that

time the troops lived strictly in the center of the compound and ventured to the perimeter only when food
was dropped there. The food supply employees gradually
increased the amounts of food until, over the course of
a few years, they had nearly quadrupled the tonnage
they delivered.

As the population grew and the center of the compound became increasingly crowded, some of the baboons moved to the outskirts, where there was more
room to raise their offspring. It wasn't long before some
of the baboons began appearing at the clearings around
the perimeter when and where the food was brought in
and dumped over the tall, electrified fences. It didn't
take long for them to figure out that was the best place
to be since that's where the food was dropped. Soon the
troops on the perimeter began defending their positions
against interlopers from the inner compound. After that,
things turned downright Darwinian.

During the first seven years of the project, the baboon
population in Deckern County, Mississippi, had grown
according to the careful plans of the scientists who were
in charge of the breeding program. The females' gestation period shortened from six to four months. Multiple
births became common, with litters of four being the
norm. Finally, the physical stature of the individual baboons tripled so that full-grown males reached nearly
three hundred pounds, yielding organs of sufficient size
for human transplant needs.

Then, as often happens with careful scientific planning,
something went wrong. Actually, *wrong* wasn't the right
word; it was more that something unintended happened.
There is, in nature, a tendency for hybrid offspring to
be larger, faster growing, and healthier than the parents.
This phenomenon is known as hybrid vigor, and the experiment going on in the piney woods of south-central
Mississippi was no exception to this rule. Over the thirteen years that followed the first seven at the facility,
hybrid vigor had resulted in healthy litters of six being
born after a four-month gestation period. And the more

baboons there were, the more breeding there was—which breeding was beginning at younger and younger ages.

Even when the food supply began to dwindle in relation to the sheer number of baboons, the breeding continued unabated. There were pockets of the strongest, most violent baboons that managed to obtain all of the food they needed. And of course those with the best food supply got stronger and healthier and more able to defend against those with the least food. It turned out that roughly 10 percent of the baboons consumed nearly 70 percent of the resources.

During the last five years, hybrid vigor had led to full-grown males' reaching six feet in height and weighing almost five hundred pounds. Indicative of the highly dimorphic species, the females grew to only half the size of the males. Each baboon now required about eight times the amount of resources it would have required in normal circumstances. Interestingly, there was an inverse relationship between food supply and the efficiency of the baboons' eating habits. The more resources they had, the more they wasted. Apple cores and watermelon rinds, once lustily devoured, were now tossed aside into piles of garbage where the weaker baboons scavenged their meals.

Over the course of the twenty years that the Xenotech facility had been in operation in Deckern County, the primate population had gone from the original thirty-six baboons to nearly ten thousand. This was the result of the genetic manipulations, hybrid vigor, and the abundant food supplies. This was good news for Xenotech, as it provided them with an ample supply of the parts necessary for their research. But there was a downside as well.

Studies on the effects of overcrowding reveal a wealth of pathological responses to the condition. Ferguson's classic study of an overcrowded baboon colony in the Tokyo zoo, for example, noted many instances of unnatural viciousness, bloody fighting, and violence unrelated to

hierarchy. Females were sometimes dismembered, and
no infants survived to maturity. All of this behavior was
observed in an environment with *normal* food and water
supplies but with an *abnormally* high population density.
When basic resources became scarce in an overcrowded
animal population—as was the case in Xenotech's Deckern County facility—the amount of violence increased
dramatically.

In the aftermath of Merle's and his curious cousins'
ill-fated safari, the baboons had recovered all the weapons and, like Kubrick's ape with the heavy bone in his
hand, they had learned how to use them. The first baboon learned the hard way. He was the sub-adult male
who had chased Merle to the fence, where he had
dropped his shotgun while cutting the rope to lower the
ladder contraption. As Merle drove off through the
woods that day, several more male baboons arrived at
the scene. They got there just as the sub-adult male
picked up the shotgun and looked down the barrel. An
unexpected downside to having opposable thumbs on
what we think of as feet is the ease with which they
allow you to pull the trigger on a twelve-gauge shotgun
while looking down the barrel. When the gun discharged,
taking off the majority of the baboon's head, the others
screeched and hooted and scampered up the trees, where
they sounded distress cries for the next twenty minutes.
Eventually they came down from the trees and approached their dead troop mate. They poked at him,
trying to bring him back to life, but soon figured out
he was gone for good and for a moment they appeared
to mourn.

Then another one of the baboons picked up the shotgun. Exhibiting behavior that was demonstrative of a fast
learning curve, the baboon was careful to point the gun
away from himself. From there it was just a matter of
trial and error before he shot and killed another baboon
and ascended in the hierarchy. That same day, another
group of the old world monkeys found Brutha's twelve-
gauge and Jimmy's 30-30 in the clearing and, clever crea-

tures that they are, they also figured out how the weapons worked. This went a long way toward explaining why the baboons had stolen the guns from the trucks when they raided Merle's fund-raising barbecue. They knew what they were and how they worked. They were useful tools, especially in light of the unchecked population growth and the dwindling resources within the Xenotech compound. And that's why there were so many other dead baboons throughout the ten thousand acres.

As for Billy Bob, he didn't know anything about hybrid vigor or average litter sizes or resource distribution. All he knew was that the boss had called and told him to round up five hundred baboons and, after thinking on it for a while, he had finally figured out how he would do it. It was simple really. He would halt the food supply being delivered to the perimeter drop sites. Absent any alternatives the baboons would be so hungry in a few days that they'd walk right into the cafeteria for a block of moldy lunch loaf. In the meanwhile, Billy Bob and a construction crew would build a massive corral which would funnel into the newly finished building. Billy Bob would set up a huge baboon buffet in the center of the corral and the hungry primates would rush in for the food. Once inside, Billy Bob would shut the gate and have all the baboons they needed. It was like baiting a field for a dove hunt, except for two differences: first, this would be legal; and second, in a dove hunt the people are the ones with the shotguns.

Arty was depressed. It had been weeks since he'd heard from Bonedigger and he was beginning to think his big friend had just moved on without telling him—and that hurt. Next to his friends at the orphanage, Bonedigger was the closest thing to family that Arty had, and family was something Arty held dear. Arty's depression lifted dramatically, however, when the stock market opened on the Monday after his postoperative press conference. By noon, Xenotech stock had rocketed from $2.80 a share to $59 per. Arty's 200,000 shares suddenly translated to a cool $11 million. Now all he had to do was live long enough for the restrictions on the stocks to expire so he could cash them in. The first thing Arty did when he heard the news was to get his nurse to call his broker. Arty wanted him to buy all the Xenotech shares he could afford with the money in his brokerage account, which was all the money Arty had put away from the sales of his various organs. As good as he was feeling with this baboon's heart ticking away inside his chest, he felt certain the stock would double in the next few weeks and Arty wanted to grab all he could at $59. In the meanwhile, he planned to live on his accidental death and dismemberment insurance money, which he kept in a separate checking account.

Arty had big plans for his new wealth. With the kind of dough he expected to have soon he was going to do remarkable things at the orphanage. Hell, he'd almost be able to buy parents for everyone. He'd buy computers and TVs and redecorate the whole place. Then he'd pay for some landscaping and buy swing sets and maybe some ponies. He'd make a lot of people happy, and that, in the end, is all Arty really wanted to do.

And now that he had all this money, Arty thought he might actually do a little something for himself. He got his nurse to set him up with a computer that he could operate by tapping at the keyboard with a stick held between his teeth. Then he went on-line, keyword: PROS-THETICS. Arty was going to do some virtual shopping, and the range of products he found on the net was won-drous to behold. He found the finest lightweight, high-strength carbon fiber prosthetic feet and high-tech shins and mechanical knees and upper-extremity prosthetic components. There were body-powered voluntary-closing prehensors and specialized lines of recreational sports adaptors. He found the company that created the original clear vinyl skin that could be pigmented to Arty's exact skin tone. They also made removable vinyl skin sleeves to meet all of Arty's custom cosmetic requirements. And talk about high tech! There was user-friendly software and microprocessor technology that helped control things his body couldn't. One company offered a prosthetic lower leg with an integral sensor combined with 180-mm geometry which would allow Arty to walk at a full range of walking speeds. The adjustment procedure used a cordless radio-linked programmer with an audio feedback system and visual prompting to allow for integral speed detection. Arty could program the device to give him exact swing adjustment for various gaits. He'd never have to worry about gait deviation! Arty was, understandably, elated.

Arty figured he'd order one of everything and become a sort of cyberman or android or whatever it was called when you were part man, part machine. He envisioned himself with high-strength carbon fiber arms and legs. He decided it would look much cooler without the vinyl skin sleeves—he'd go with the whole high-tech robotic look. Now that he was thinking about it, why not get some extralong legs and arms? Arty could be six feet tall; hell, he could be a seven-footer if he wanted. Imagine that, he thought, a seven-foot-tall half-robotic pirate man walking into a bar. Talk about a babe magnet! As Arty continued to surf the prosthetic web sites he began to feel like he was the luckiest man in the world. Technology could solve everything.

Georgette was bleeding worse than Paul by the time they got to the hospital. As he carried her up the sidewalk toward the emergency room she regained consciousness long enough to tell Paul that she loved him very much and that she was sorry she had done this to him.

"Don't worry," Paul said, "you're going to be fine." He said it because he wanted it to be true. But the truth was far less certain than that. Georgette was pale and clammy. Her body seemed to be retreating from its battle with whatever it was fighting. The emergency room's automatic doors were slow to open as Paul approached and he nearly went straight through the glass. "Open

up, goddammit!" Once inside he shouted, "I need some
help here!"

A triage nurse took one look at Georgette and switched
into crisis mode. She hit the call button, causing what
looked like an air force base scramble for fighter jets.
She screamed at no one in particular, "Get a gurney over
here, now!"

The physician on duty, Dr. Jack Stanley, ran over to
help. "What do we have?" He pressed his stethoscope
to Georgette's chest before looking to Paul for some
answers.

"She's only seven months pregnant, she's premature,
she's been bleeding," Paul didn't know what else to say.

"Breathing's okay but she needs circulatory support,"
the doctor said. Georgette suddenly vomited a sour yel-
low-and-red liquid. It was stomach acid mixed with
blood—even the doctor didn't know what that meant.
She tried to lift her head slightly, then she blacked out.

"Doctor, please! Do something!" Paul yelled.

Dr. Stanley helped Paul put Georgette on a gurney.
Her heart was racing and her future looked grim. Paul
had never been so scared in his life. Wheeling the gurney
down a hallway, the doctor continued his frantic examination, probing Georgette's distended abdomen. They
rolled her into an examination room. Dr. Stanley yelled
at a nurse, "Let's go, Karen! Get me a BP, hook up the
monitor, and put her on oxygen, stat!" Dr. Stanley was
short, strong, and intense. Georgette's pulse was very
thready. "I want a saline IV wide open, now!" the doctor
screamed. Paul was calmed momentarily by the quick,
authoritative manner in which Dr. Stanley issued instructions and the way his staff responded.

Paul wanted to comfort Georgette, wanted to hold her
hand, but when he moved toward her, he was shoved
unceremoniously out of the way. Despite Dr. Stanley's
demands that Paul wait outside, he tried to stay with
Georgette in the examination room. It took a couple of
very large and persuasive security guards to remove him
and convince him he would only be in the way if he

stayed with her. So Paul stayed outside looking in as Dr. Stanley and the nurses worked to keep Georgette alive long enough to give birth. A nurse rushed over with the saline IV. Another worked feverishly to attach the fetal monitor.

Dr. Stanley snapped his fingers impatiently. "Okay, get her typed and crossed with four units." He turned to one of the nurses. "Put her on a hundred percent oxygen, not a nasal cannula." He sounded angry and it was hard to tell if his anger was directed at the nurses who weren't moving fast enough for him or if he was just an angry man. He gloved up and felt inside Georgette. "She's dilated," he said. "Shit. Feels like a frank breech. Get L and D. See if there's an OB in the house and bring me the ultrasound!"

Paul watched through a small window as Dr. Stanley put the transducer around Georgette's abdomen. A nurse turned on the monitor and suddenly Paul could see an image of a tiny skeleton and a heart pounding on the screen. "My God," Paul said. It was his son. Dr. Stanley moved the transducer around Georgette's swollen belly. Paul heard him say "There's free blood in her gut, possible ruptured uterus. No way I can reposition the baby."

Uterine rupture occurs in roughly one out of every 1,500 births. Though rare, it can also happen during pregnancy, as was the case with Georgette. This is bad news for both the mother and the child as it causes the mother to lose blood while simultaneously decreasing the baby's oxygen supply. Immediate surgical intervention is required to deliver the child and repair the uterine tear or both lives will be lost.

Paul suddenly felt a tickle on his cheek and realized he was crying. He instinctively lifted his arm to wipe the tears away, causing a terrible pain in his shoulder where he'd been shot. It hurt like hell and the blood and the tears mixed and painted half of Paul's face a bloody pink. The enormous stress combined with significant blood loss suddenly hit Paul and made him feel faint. The last thing Paul heard before he crumpled to the floor was Dr. Stanley demanding to know "Where the hell is that goddamn OB? I need a fucking OB in here, now! This doesn't look good!"

There was no ribbon-cutting ceremony when the building was completed. After the crates from Hamburg were opened and their contents put on-line, the contractors ran tests and simulations until the bugs were worked out of the software. And then the people left. The building sat quiet and cool and clean on the inside, waiting. It was sterile, though not in the aesthetic sense—for the gleaming stainless steel and the golden drain grates, the white tiled walls and the smoky tinted glass all came together to create a ghastly art form with a negative space begging for deep, dark red. The main room still smelled of sawdust and caulk but that would change. In time the room would reek of disinfectant and death.

The harvest itself would be an orderly thing, proceeding from one end of the new building to the other in assembly line fashion. It would begin outside in the corral, where a chute at the east end of the enclosure would allow the giant baboons into the anteroom one at a time. Once in the building they would be shot with pancuronium, which would paralyze the animals without anesthetizing them. Paralysis was necessary so the automated harvesting devices wouldn't have to operate on a moving target and accidentally cut any of the valuable organs in two. There would be no anesthesia for two reasons: first, they saw no point in worrying about whether the baboons were conscious during the harvest—as one of the designers had said, "They'll be dead soon enough," and secondly, why spend good money on anesthesia and its attendant problems if you don't need to? The pancuronium-only approach was viewed as cost-effective and efficient. Sure, the baboons would be aware of what was happening, but they wouldn't be able to move whatsoever and that's all that really mattered here.

After being subdued, a series of synchronized hydraulic arms operating on a sophisticated artificial-intelligence program would gently hoist the three- to four-hundred-pound baboons onto large aluminum operating tables and strap them into harvesting position. Next, two more arms would descend from the ceiling and steady each animal's head so a large breathing tube could be inserted down the throat. One of the downsides of pancuronium (or curarine, for that matter) is that it paralyzes *everything*, thus rendering one unable to breathe on one's own. After pulmonary support was in place, the tables were coupled to a conveyor belt which would carry the baboons into the harvesting room and on down the line.

The automated sternal saws, of which there were two on the parallel lines, were attached to more hydraulic, computer-controlled robotic arms. The blades themselves were the same diameter as those found on a carpenter's circular saw; however, these blades were thinner and their teeth less dramatic in order to reduce bone splintering when they split the sternum. The custom-designed electrocautery device looked like a giant soldering iron—the blue switcher triggered an electric current to coagulate tissue, the yellow switcher was used for cutting.

The paralyzed baboon would enter the harvest room on the aluminum table and be set upon by six mechanical "positioning arms" which would assure the primate was lined up correctly on the table. A separate set of probing tactile array sensors would measure the primate's exact dimensions and send the information to the mainframe which controlled the sternal saws, the Bovie (as the electrocautery was called), and the robotic hands that would remove the detached organs from the body cavity and place them into a slushy saline-ice and free radical organ-preservation solution.

Unlike an automated beef slaughterhouse, there would be no shots to the head with a captive bolt to kill the baboons prior to the operation. When harvesting organs, the fresher the better is the rule. So instead of killing them and then harvesting the organs, the baboons would actually be killed *by* the harvesting, starting with the heart.

Application of cardioplegia was the first order of business once the chest was open. A potassium chloride solution (KCL) would arrest the heart, thereby reducing its energy consumption, which energy it would need when implanted in the recipient. If the heart wasn't stopped prior to being harvested, it would continue to beat until it exhausted its energy, after which point it was about as effective as used dynamite. The heart and lungs would come out first since they had the shortest ischemic time of all the transplantable solid organs. Next came the liver, followed by the kidneys, then the pancreas and intestines. Corneas, ligaments, and the other bloodless tissues would come out last.

Wanting not to be stuck with the problems associated with disposing of piles of baboon carcasses, the marketing people at Xenotech had come up with what they considered a clever idea and a secondary, if relatively minor, income stream. This required a couple of additions to the new building, but in the end the cost-effectiveness committee agreed that they were worth the trouble. Thus the next room in the building was the "rendering" room. Here the largely organless carcasses would be skinned, decapitated, and cut in half down the backbone by common power saws. Separately, the heads would be carefully split open and the brains removed intact and flash-frozen like North Atlantic cod. The heads would then be reassembled, freeze-dried, and, along with the brains, packaged for shipment to markets in Africa and Asia, where they were sold as expensive curios, as ingredients for aphrodisiacs, and as components for religious ceremonies.

The dressed carcasses would be sent to a large cooler for up to thirty-six hours. Once below 45 degrees Fahrenheit they would be cut into edible joints of meat before being addressed with various knives and saws, eventually yielding steaks, roasts, and tenderloins which would be shipped to markets in the West Indies and sold as water buffalo. This traditional butchery was followed by an unsavory process which resulted in what they called mechanically recovered meat. These remaining bits of flesh and soft tissues were separated from the bone by high-power water sprays. These not-so-choice morsels would be run through a grinder to produce a sort of gray meat-like mash which would be colored, frozen, and shipped as nonspecific meat product to markets in eastern Europe, where people were hungry enough to eat anything.

There would be a fleet of small jets (the Xenojets) used for shipping the organs around the world. The less time-sensitive products, the meat and voodoo merchandise, would go by UPS or Emory, or Burlington Express. Whatever remained from the baboons at this point would be subjected to cooking at extremely high temperatures and converted into other salable products like gelatin, collagen, tallow, and keratin. These valuable commodities would be used in the manufacture of candies, lipstick, glue, soap, deodorant, margarine, shampoo, and sausage casings. All in all, the Xenotech marketing department thought, a very efficient use of natural resources.

After Paul passed out, the orderlies put him on a gurney and took him back to one of the trauma slots. While they treated his wound, things took a turn for the worse in the delivery room. There was nothing the doctors could do about the baby's breech position, so they prepared for a cesarean. Then, as is common with premature breech births, the baby's umbilical cord slipped out through the cervix. With each contraction the prolapsed cord was strangled and the baby's blood supply was dangerously interrupted. This, combined with the ruptured uterus, made the doctors unsure if anyone would survive.

But finally there was good news. The child was delivered by cesarean. It was a boy. He weighed only four pounds and he was weak—but at least he was alive. But Georgette's uterine rupture was far worse than first imagined and the surgeons were unable to repair it. The only way they could control her bleeding was by performing a hysterectomy. So they did.

Now, several hours later, Paul was struggling to maintain his composure, but it was obvious from the way his lower lip trembled that he was on the verge of crying again. He had been blinking back the tears ever since they rolled Georgette into the recovery room. Paul was sitting at her bedside, holding her hand, thinking about how close he had come to losing her. For the life of him, Paul couldn't remember a sadder day.

Finally, Georgette stirred a bit and opened her eyes. She tried to speak but, thanks to the tube that had been shoved down her throat earlier, she ended up just making enough noise to get Paul's attention. He quickly wiped his eyes and leaned over. "I'm right here," Paul said. "Everything's going to be okay."

The tube in Georgette's throat was gone now, replaced by nasal intubation. She swallowed once and tried speaking again. "Paul?" Her voice was weak and groggy. "Where's the baby? Is he all right?"

Paul forced a little smile and moved close to his love. "Hi, honey," he said softly. "The doctor said you're going to be fine, but you lost a lot of blood, had me pretty scared." He gently brushed the hair from her forehead.

"Paul, where's the baby?" Georgette asked again.

Paul looked into her eyes and tried to be strong. "The doctors are doing what they can. He's not . . . he's . . . they're not sure." Paul squeezed Georgette's hand and he leaned down and kissed her cheek. "But we're gonna be okay. I promise." He didn't want her to suffer any more than she already had.

Bless his heart, Georgette knew Paul was trying to protect her from something ugly. His face was like a dam about to burst. A flood of emotion was trying to break through, and Paul was fighting it with all his might. But no matter how hard he smiled, Paul couldn't hide the sadness and the grief in his eyes. God, how did I get this sweet man? Georgette wondered. She reached up and touched his cheek. "Paul, it's okay. Tell me the truth." And the dam broke. First his smile became a frown and then the tears welled up in his eyes. "It's okay," Georgette repeated. "It's okay."

Paul didn't know what he could say without hurting her. And before he could find gentler words he blurted out the truth. "He's sick, sweetheart. He's little and he's real sick and I'm so scared." And then Paul began to sob. His head dropped so his chin was near his chest and he just wept. Georgette wanted to pull him close to her and wrap both her arms around him, to offer some comfort, but one of her arms was tied to a board and there was an IV running to a vein so all she could do was reach up with her free hand and wipe his tears and cup his face in her palm.

"I love you so much," Georgette said as she began to cry with him. Paul leaned down and tenderly slipped his arms around her and began rocking ever so slightly back and forth. As they held one another against the sorrow a shaft of sunlight reached through the blinds and slowly began working its way up the wall above the bed like a golden spider. Paul and Georgette held one another for some time. When a gentle knock came to the door they pulled apart.

The door opened and Dr. Stanley entered looking like someone burdened with news he knew he had no choice but to deliver. He glanced at the chart in his hand and then at Paul and Georgette. "How're you feeling?" he asked.

Paul looked to Georgette, who sniffled and managed a sad shrug of her shoulders.

"How is he?" Paul asked.

"I'm afraid the news is not good," Dr. Stanley said. "Your son has a problem with his heart—hypertrophic cardiomyopathy associated with Sengers' syndrome."

Neither Paul nor Georgette heard much after the part about "a problem with his heart." Dr. Stanley knew that most of his explanation was lost before reaching them, but he continued talking while the shock set in. There was nothing else to do so he explained that the syndrome consisted of a triad of congenital cataracts, mitochondrial myopathy, and hypertrophic cardiomyopathy and that most patients die of cardiac failure in childhood or early adulthood. But this was a far worse case than most and the odds of this infant's reaching even toddlerhood were a million to one against. As Dr. Stanley droned on Georgette saw the door open behind him. Paul turned when he saw Georgette's face brighten. It was a nurse carrying the child wrapped in a soft blanket. He was tiny and he wasn't making a sound, quiet as a sleeping army. His little eyes looked around as if searching for an explanation.

"Here's your son," the nurse said gently as she handed the tiny bundle to Georgette. Paul leaned in to see the sweet little wrinkled face. Georgette kissed the top of his head and held him close.

Dr. Stanley continued reading from the chart, something about serum biochemical evidence of a long-chain fatty acid disorder and urinalysis evidence of a beta-oxidation disorder related to the underlying mitochondrial dysfunction. Despite the fact that he had been in this situation many times before, Dr. Stanley was no better at it now than he was when he was an intern. The doctor's problem wasn't that he was unsympathetic; if anything he was overly sensitive to their distress. But he was no good at words of comfort. He was more at home with words like mitochondrial.

Georgette smoothed the fine dark hair on her son's head and then looked at Dr. Stanley. "What are you saying?"

This was the part Dr. Stanley hated the most. There was no hedging the prognosis, so he told them straight out, "If he doesn't get a new heart, he'll die very soon."

"That's it?" Paul asked. "No other options? No treatments? No . . ."

"No," Dr. Stanley said. "I'm afraid there's nothing." He knew not to let a grieving parent get going about options. That invariably led to colloquies on the unfairness of it all and the problem with doctors playing God and why did this happen to my baby, and Stanley didn't want to go there, so he cut Paul off. "And I'm afraid there are no human hearts available. There's a shortage of organs . . ." He trailed off without finishing the thought.

Georgette couldn't bring herself to ask any questions. She was too numb. She knew there was nothing to do but make her son's short life as comfortable as possible. She would love him for every second he was alive and be there when he cried and needed her—and when he died. That's all she could do. But Paul wanted to do more. He didn't know what, but he at least had to ask questions. "So we just have to let him die?" he said.

Dr. Stanley rubbed his face for a moment. "Now, I don't want to give you false hope, but there is one alternative," he said. "There's a company called Xenotech that just received FDA approval for transplants of transgenic baboon hearts." He went on to explain the science behind xenografting and how Xenotech was having remarkable success with the two transplants so far. "But you'll have to decide soon," he said. Dr. Stanley started backing out of the room. "I'll call them and see what they say about availability. I'll be back later."

After the doctor left, Georgette offered the bundle to Paul. "Would you like to hold your son?" she asked.

Paul took the child and cradled him in his arms. "He's too warm," Paul said. "He doesn't need this blanket." He gently unwrapped the blanket and handed it to Georgette. Then he held his tiny, dying son to his chest. He tried to remember the words to a lullaby, but none came to mind so he just began to hum quietly what sounded like "Silent Night."

There was darkness and silence in Georgette's heart where there should have been singing and light. She was too weak and exhausted to cry or rage against the inequity of it all, so she clutched the baby blanket while she watched her husband and her son and wrestled with her thoughts. There had been a brief moment when she thought she could justify the xenograft but it passed. Something was either right or wrong and that judgment couldn't hinge on whether it impacted her or, in this case, her child. She wondered if she was to blame. She wondered if there was something she could have done. She wondered why she hadn't gone ahead with the abortion and she wondered if that would have meant less suffering for him. She wondered how much pain she had caused him. She wondered a million ifs and found no answers. And then she wondered what her son would have wanted if all the choices had been his. But they hadn't been. None of it had been his choice.

And then Georgette closed her eyes and prayed with all her might that her sweet, innocent son might live. And her prayer was answered. And the answer was no.

When Georgette looked again at Paul, she could tell it was over. Paul had found the words to a lullaby and was singing softly as he cried:

Time for rest,
Go to sleep,
Little child, little child.
God will bless,
Love will keep,
Little child, little child.
Rub your eyes, you're fading fast,
A thousand sighs, asleep at last.
Little child . . . little child . . . little child . . .

16

Lance Abbott was having what was referred to in California as a good day—for lying on the bed in front of him, in the form of one Vic "Bonedigger" Nichols, was Lance's ticket back to Hollywood, comatose and nearly ripe for the picking.

Even before coming in to work this fine day things had been going good for Lance. First he had finished a new draft of the story outline he was working on. The story featured murder, mystery, plenty of gore, and most importantly, it had a great starring role for Lance Abbott as the handsome organ procurement specialist turned crime solver. Granted, he didn't have the solution to the mystery part just yet, but he felt he was one or two puzzle pieces away from solving it. When he did, he'd return to Los Angeles attached to his own project, take a few pitch meetings, close the deal, and make his triumphant return to show business.

What Lance had so far was a list of victims, five of which had been found with the Terra Tuebor notes, the others without. The victims who had been found without notes had all been killed while only one of the victims found *with* a note was dead, so those waters were still a little murky. But in a couple of instances where no note was found, Lance reasoned it was possible the note (A) had simply blown away, (B) was there but hadn't been found, or (C) had been found but the police hadn't made that information public. There was an apparent motive connection to all the victims that pointed to a possible psycho pro-environmentalist avenger. Among those was the late Mr. Hirschoren, who, prior to being split in two in the BART tunnel, was the in-house attorney for the industrial solvent manufacturer that had recently wiggled out of paying a large fine for illegal dumping of toxic materials. There was the tuna boat captain and the veal tycoon. And there was the lumber mill owner whose business specialized in turning ancient redwoods into rec room paneling. He'd been found cut not-so-neatly in half by his own band saw.

Lance had two theories about who was responsible for all this but not enough evidence to support either theory fully so he couldn't dismiss either one just yet. At this point, he didn't want to commit himself to any single hypothesis. It also seemed that lately the Terra Tuebor attacks had stopped and he wondered what, if anything, that meant. He needed a little more evidence before writing his final draft. Then, if he still didn't have the truth figured out, he would opt for Plan B.

Plan B involved framing Bonedigger as the eco-terrorist Terra Tuebor and making it appear that he also killed all the noteless victims. Lance had enough information in his Terra Tuebor file to pull this off without a hitch. The best part about this was that if Bones stayed in a coma he'd have a hard time defending himself against the charges. And if Bones went the way most coma patients went, the commission Lance would make after selling the body parts would pay for Lance's return to L.A. Thus was Vic "Bonedigger" Nichols to be Lance Abbott's ticket back to Hollywood. It was a win-win situation for Lance, lose-lose for Bones.

Satisfied that Plan B would still be there when he returned, Lance headed downstairs to see his friend in the pathology lab. He hoped to find one of the missing puzzle pieces there. Lance had given his friend the tissue he believed belonged to Jonah Levin and asked if he could identify it. His lab friend had called and left a message that, after some sophisticated and expensive DNA testing, he had finally done just that. "It's baboon myocardium," his friend said ten seconds after Lance walked in. "But it's weird. It seems like it's mixed with human proteins or DNA or I don't know what. Where the hell did you get that?"

And in that moment Lance discovered the truth—or at least enough of it to finish his story and pack for Los Angeles. It was the missing bit of information that made his second theory more than just plausible. It was now "compelling," "must see," and "one of the year's ten best!" A couple of important recent events that Lance had failed to recognize as such suddenly seemed obvious, and they turned on the proverbial lightbulb over his head. Lance knew exactly what he had to do next. So he pulled his friend's face close and kissed him on the mouth. "Thank you," Lance said as he raced out of the lab.

"Don't mention it," his friend said, referring more to the kiss than to the favor he had done.

Lance couldn't believe it. He knew exactly how the story would work and now . . . by God, now he was in a position to produce. And his first act as a producer would be to terminate Bones and put a slightly modified version of Plan B into effect. Drunk with power he didn't yet have, Lance bounded up three flights of stairs and burst into the hallway. He walked briskly down the hall to one of the supply rooms where various "nonscheduled" drugs and medications were stored. Using a key he had long ago stolen for emergencies such as this, Lance let himself into the room, grabbed what he needed, which included both Regitine and Heparin, and quickly left.

A few minutes later Lance was back in Bonedigger's room preparing to display some nasty bedside manners.

❉   ❉   ❉

It was a strange and mournful day when they scattered little Freddy's ashes in a grove of old growth redwoods near Big Basin. They had named him after Paul's dad, Frederick, who had gone on before. It was intended to be a memorial more than a traditional funeral—a chance to remember the good things. Unfortunately, there wasn't anything good to remember; there was only pain. And no matter how sincerely anyone tried saying things like how glorious Freddy's short life was, there was no sugar-coating the truth: Freddy never had a chance and there was nothing glorious about that. The best that could be said was that Freddy's was a childhood that was mercifully brief.

Georgette was distracted, lost in a haze of grief as she clutched Freddy's baby blanket. She was sad but not demonstrative. She wore black and cried softly every now and again. When she cried she held the blanket to her nose and she could still smell her little baby boy. Georgette was deep inside herself, and friends sometimes had to repeat her name a couple of times or even touch her to get her attention to tell her how sorry they were. She would look in their eyes, a bittersweet smile underlining her feelings, and say thank you. She cried the most and seemed most thankful when she saw one of her oldest friends, Rosie, whom she hadn't seen in a long time. Rosie had recently given birth to a son, and Georgette asked if she could hold him. Rosie handed the child to Georgette, who took him and held him to her chest, just as she had with little Freddy. That's when she cried the most.

Paul cried too. Especially when he saw Georgette— her eyes closed tightly against her own tears—cuddling Rosie's son. He cried and he thought about what might have been. Paul wished his father could have seen his son. That day there was something different in the look of Paul's eyes. Something none of his friends had ever seen before. They had seen him grieve when his grandmother died but this was something else. This wasn't Paul. Everyone agreed with that. Paul had come to doubt all the things he once held as true, and that made him angry. He thanked his friends when they expressed their sorrow but he said little else until someone he hardly knew approached him. It was a guy Paul had met at a protest of one sort or another. Paul didn't even remember the guy's name.

"I'm very sorry for your loss, Paul," the guy said. He seemed sincere.

"Yeah, thanks," Paul said, expecting the guy to move on. But the guy stood there, obviously wanting to say something else. "Thanks for coming," Paul said, hoping the guy would take the hint and leave. But instead, the guy pulled a piece of paper from his jacket pocket.

"Listen, Paul, you know those Energy Department subsidies to the oil companies? I was thinking this would be a real good opportunity to get some signatures on this petition." He unfolded the paper and held it out for Paul to read.

Paul never looked at the petition. He just stared at the guy for a moment. "Put it away."

"What? Why?" the clueless activist asked. "Bad timing?"

"I said put the fucking petition away," Paul repeated. "It won't do any good. They never do. You don't even know what you're fighting." The guy slipped the petition back into his pocket and tried to walk away, but Paul grabbed him. "There's too much suffering. Babies and baboons and the whole world is suffering and petitions aren't changing a *goddamn* thing!"

A few heads in the crowd turned to see why Paul was raising his voice.

"Look, I'm sorry," the guy said. "I understand—"

"You don't understand shit," Paul said. "If you want to change things, you better actually start doing something besides waving that little piece of paper at people. You better fucking do something. And you know what else? You better do it soon."

Rosie walked over and put her hand on Paul's back. "It's okay, Paul," she said. "He's leaving."

Paul tightened his grip on the guy and lifted him onto his toes. "It's not okay!" Paul was angry and no one could heal it. "There's nothing okay about it." Several of Paul's football buddies who were standing nearby eased over and got Paul to relax his grip and let the guy go. "It's not okay," Paul repeated calmly. "It's not." In a minute the whole thing had blown over, the guy had apologized and left, and Paul calmed down. But he still had that look in his eye.

Half an hour later with the sun going down and the cool from the ocean creeping into the great, ancient forest, people started to drift back to their cars for the drive home. And with that, the ritual was over. Freddy would be among the redwoods forever, or at least until Conifer Lumber bought another senator and clear-cut this part of the injured coast.

For the first hour of the drive home Paul was silent as he carefully negotiated the twists and turns of the road winding through the Santa Cruz Mountains. He steered with one hand and occasionally caressed the baby blanket with the other. Georgette let him be. It was nice not to have to talk. But somewhere around Saratoga, as they began their descent into the Santa Clara Valley, Paul spoke. "Sweetheart, do you remember what the guy said after you pistol-whipped him that day?"

She had expected him to say something like "It was nice of Rosie to come" or "Can you believe the guy with the petition?" But instead he wanted to know about the utterances of the tattooed man she had put into a coma. "What did he say about what?" Georgette asked.

"About the baboon farm," Paul said. "Where did he say it was? Missouri?" Paul seemed to be calculating something.

"No, I think he said Mississippi," Georgette said. Something about Paul's tone of voice gave Georgette the sense that he had something in mind other than organizing a protest. "Why?"

"I can't let it happen," Paul said with no particular

fanfare. "I'm going to do something." He sounded embarrassed that it had taken him so long.

Georgette wondered if he really meant it or if it was just the anger talking. "I've never been there but I think Mississippi's a pretty big state," Georgette said. "How do you propose we find this place?"

Paul drove in silence for a moment. "Assuming we can find it," he said, "are you with me?" He was dead serious. This wasn't the Paul who preferred working within the system. This was a man who had suddenly discovered he had the capacity for wrath.

Georgette leaned over and kissed him on the cheek. "Love, I'm with you regardless."

When they got home they went on-line to spread the word. "The baboon farm is somewhere in Mississippi. We need to know where and we need to know now. Search county by county for land purchases by Jerry Landis or Landaq or Xenotech, Incorporated. Baboon organ harvest is imminent." After posting the message on every major animal rights and pro-environmental bulletin board, Georgette and Paul packed for the long drive east. Within the hour they got word from someone with the Covington County, Mississippi, Animal Rights Coalition: "County Clerk records in Deckern County show large property owned by Xenotech. Download map file attached."

There was no direct route from the South Bay to Mississippi. They either had to take I-80 north to Salt Lake City before heading east or go south to Bakersfield and across to I-40. They opted for the southern route. They raced through the San Joaquin Valley under stars as white as the bottles and the bones of the night, slipping unnoticed into the Mojave Desert. Barstow, Kingman, Flagstaff. The sun came up as they sped past Winslow. They stopped to do some unusual shopping just outside Gallup, New Mexico. Afterwards, they continued east, stopping in Albuquerque just after noon with the Sandias hiding the Sangre de Cristo Mountains in the distance to the north. They had a quick lunch at a place called

Sadies and then hit the road, not stopping again until
Amarillo. There they turned southeast on the 287 toward
Dallas, where they picked up I-20, which would deliver
them to the Magnolia State just after dawn.

They had been on the road for about thirty hours when
they got there. They were punchy and they weren't in
the mood to put up with any nonsense from other drivers. They were on a big bridge about three hundred
feet above the Mississippi River approaching Vicksburg
at approximately seventy miles an hour when a Pontiac
Firebird with a flashing right turn signal suddenly
merged left in front of Paul and Georgette. "Stupid son
of a bitch," Paul muttered as he braked to avoid the
collision. He turned to Georgette, who was way ahead
of him. "Is that thing loaded?" he asked.

"Ready when you are," Georgette said.

Paul signed, merged right, and passed the Firebird,
whose right turn signal was still flashing. Paul pulled in
front of the Firebird and Georgette leaned out her window and opened fire. *BAM!BAM!BAM!BAM!BAM!BAM!
BAM!BAM!BAM!* "Holy shit," Georgette said. "They
weren't kidding. It really does shoot nine a second." The
idiot driving the Firebird hit the brakes and, finally obey-
ing his turn signal, pulled hard to the right, where he
piled into the bridge railing and rained broken headlight
pieces into the muddy river below.

"Nice shooting," Paul said.

Georgette winked as she blew imaginary smoke from
the barrel of the Automag cp/pf Paintball Gun she had
bought at the store outside of Gallup. It was, the salesman told her, the flagship gun for serious paintball players who wouldn't accept compromises. The crown point
barrel power feed unit fired up to nine paintballs a second. It was a sleek and exotic-looking weapon with a
long slender barrel balanced nicely by the vertical ammo
tube rising up opposite the fingered grip. And the unusual high-pressure tubing attached to the coupling device at the rear of the chamber added a nice aura of
menace. They also bought a half case of 1,250 red paint-

balls. For power they had a 114 ci Nitro Tank setup with hose. A hundred and thirty years earlier they could've taken Vicksburg with this thing. While in Gallup they had also purchased a bumper sticker, which was on the back of the car. It said "Forget World Peace—Visualize Using Your Turn Signal."

"Okay, the exit for Highway 61 is coming up," Paul said. "What do I do?"

Georgette put the gun down and picked up the map. "Skip it. Looks like 49 South's our best bet. We'll pick it up at Jackson and be in Deckern County in two hours."

Paul gave the accelerator a nudge. "One and a half," he said.

Billy Bob decided to wear electrified hog chaps even though he knew they would provide little to no protection unless one of the giant baboons decided to attack him at the shin. He borrowed them from a cousin who raised pigs. The chaps kept his hands free while working among his swine and kept him from being bit. Billy Bob strapped them around his own calves when it was time for the big roundup. He also had a Hot-Shot Hog Prod and a .38, just in case.

Fortunately for Billy Bob, the roundup went off without a hitch. He simply filled the corral with crates of fresh vegetables and live crawfish, opened the gate, and got out of the way. Since he had cut off the food deliveries to the usual perimeter spots two days earlier the response was overwhelming. As soon as Billy Bob was out of sight and the gate opened, the hungry baboons eased from the woods and into the corral. Ten minutes later he hit the switch and the automatic gate closed in on eight hundred and seventeen of the largest baboons gathered together since the Ice Age. This process naturally resulted in a lot of the large, dominant males' being captured—baboons whose parts were too large for use in humans. But Billy Bob had figured out a way to solve that problem. There was a chute at one end of the corral which led into the anteroom of the new building. Billy

Bob had simply made the chute too small for the dominant males to pass through.

After the corral was filled, Billy Bob turned on the power electrifying the fifteen-foot-high corral fence before heading back to the security office. He would wait there until the Xenojet arrived. Then he would drive out and pick up Jerry Landis and his associate, Dr. Gibbs.

As he waited, Billy Bob had time to think, and he kept thinking about the baboons. Ever since that day in the woods, the image of the dead baboon and her orphan had lingered in Billy Bob's mind, and it still bothered him. Who shot her? And why? At least he knew the baby would be all right, he'd seen to that. But what was going to happen to the eight hundred baboons he had just rounded up? He figured the answer to that question was inside that new building, and the fact that he hadn't been allowed to go in made Billy Bob even more suspicious. He had a bad feeling about things to come.

"Sweet Jesus, that hurts," Jerry Landis muttered as he injected himself with a large dose of human growth hormone and testosterone. *Whir-pffft whir-pffft whir-pffft.* Jerry was in the Xenojet bathroom trying to maintain his hormonal edge when they hit some turbulence, causing his hypodermic to go somewhat deeper than originally intended. On top of that, the liquids burned as he forced them into the muscle tissue of his thigh. The effects of these shots were wearing off faster and faster, and the testosterone patches had become virtually useless. But Jerry Landis had grown accustomed to the feeling of youthful well-being and virility that the hormone treatments produced and he was damned if he was going to be denied. The worst part—the part Jerry Landis was in denial about—was that the effects of Werner's syndrome had returned and seemed to be overtaking the effects of Dr. Vines's hormone regime. His skin was taking on that wretched papery quality again. His hair was falling out in clumps, his erection looked more like a divining rod than a lightning rod. It was pitiful really.

But when he took an injection he forgot all about the negatives. With a fresh load of HGH, testosterone, and DHEA coursing through his veins Jerry Landis felt young and strong and invincible. It was at times like this that he realized he had more reasons to live than most men, and live is exactly what Jerry Landis planned to do. Guided by divine forces, he had been shown the way to everlasting life. He had been given a third testicle. He had planted his seed, and now, thanks to the miracle of transgenic baboon organs, he would actually live to see his new children. In fact, thanks to the endless supply of organs he had created, he might just live forever. Jerry Landis had beaten the Grim Reaper at his own game, and best of all, he was about to become one of the wealthiest men on the planet.

He forced the last of the juice out of the hypodermic, then quickly pulled the needle out of his leg and rubbed at the developing bruise. He pulled his pants up and looked at himself in the mirror. Some pink worked its way into his yellowing cheeks. "Thy will be done," he said.

Dr. Gibbs was seated comfortably in the main cabin of the jet looking down at the piney woods below. He was eager to see the Xenotech facility and the troops of transgenic baboons that would make him so wealthy. After so many years of struggle and humiliation he was, finally, a very rich man, and the money he had earned would give him power, and the power would allow him to make more money. It was a wondrous cycle to be a part of and Dr. Gibbs suddenly realized he was looking forward to the harvest. He knew it would be a bloody thing, but the bloodshed was part of what would make him so wealthy and he was beginning to embrace it all lustily. Dr. Gibbs felt something powerful inside himself and he believed it was real. He felt he had attained the power of life and death. It lubricated his ego and he liked it.

Sharing the main cabin with Dr. Gibbs were half a dozen "security specialists" that Jerry Landis had hired to be at the harvest, just in case some animal rights activists showed up to cause trouble. There was far too much at stake to allow a bunch of misguided bunny lovers to jeopardize Jerry Landis's life and the future of Xenotech. The security guys weren't exactly ex–Special Forces or Black Ops types. They were machos who had answered an ad placed in *Mercenary Today Magazine*. Some had managed to get themselves kicked off police forces while others were former military MPs with dishonorable discharges, guys who were no less dangerous because of their unimpressive résumés. They were gathered in a huddle comparing lies about fights they had won when the captain turned on the seat belt sign and asked everyone to put their seat backs and their tray tables in their full upright and secure positions in preparation for landing.

Georgette and Paul stopped for gas in Hattiesburg, right across from the campus of the University of Southern Mississippi. Georgette was looking at the map they had downloaded from the computer and was trying to decide whether they should take Highway 49 down to Wiggins and then take county roads to the Xenotech facility or take Highway 98 to Beaumont and then head south. She noticed a couple of college-age girls sitting in a brand-new red Mustang GT at the full-serve pumps. Assuming they were locals and would know the best route, Georgette went over and asked for directions.

The driver's name was Sue. She and her friend, Laurie, were sorority sisters. "Why in the world would you want to go to Deckern County?" Sue asked as she checked her hair in the mirror and made an unnecessary adjustment. "There's nothing down there."

"I like the woods," Georgette said.

"You sure have a funny accent," Laurie said from behind a staggering amount of makeup. "Where're you from?"

"California," Georgette said. "Let me ask you, what

would you say if I told you some men were about to kill a bunch of helpless animals down in Deckern County?"

"Is it deer season already?" Sue asked. She explained how she and her fellow sorority sisters hated deer season because all their boyfriends ended up spending more time in the woods than taking them out on dates.

"I'm not talking about deer," Georgette said. "I'm talking about baboons trapped in cages. They're going to cut them open and harvest their organs and transplant them into people."

The sorority sisters were appalled. Sue said they believed in animal rights and were, for the most part, vegetarians. And Laurie allowed as how they wore fur only to really important social events, like cotillions and such. On top of all that, they didn't believe God intended for man to have monkey hearts in him. Sue told Georgette to take the 98 to Beaumont and then head south. The Xenotech property was probably about forty-five minutes from here, she said. Meanwhile, Sue and Laurie would go round up some frat boys they knew who would do whatever they asked them to. "I mean, if it's not deer or dove season."

Billy Bob drove the Suburban out to meet the Xenojet at the end of the runway. He opened the jet's door and let the stairs down onto the tarmac. He helped unload luggage as the passengers deplaned. The security force, dressed in all black, came off first, followed by Dr. Gibbs and Jerry Landis. Billy Bob went over to introduce himself to Dr. Gibbs. "How y'all doin'? I'm Billy Bob Needmore, head of security. You must be Mr. Landis." He held out his hand.

"No, I'm Dr. Gibbs, Xenotech's VP of Procurement," he said with a great deal of pride. Gibbs gestured to his boss, who was discussing something with the security force. "That is Mr. Landis."

"Well, it's good to finally meet you fellers after all this time," Billy Bob said. "I rounded up a bunch of them monkeys lack you asked and they's ready to go."

"Good," Dr. Gibbs said. "We want to get started right away."

Billy Bob lowered his voice. "I hope you don't mind my asking, but exactly what're you plannin' to do with 'em?"

"That is none of your concern," Jerry Landis said as he passed by. "And if you ask again you will be terminated." *Whir-pffft whir-pffft whir-pffft.* He climbed into the back seat of the Suburban. "Now let's go."

Five minutes later Billy Bob pulled the Suburban into a parking spot outside the new building. They were met there by the two remaining Xenotech research scientists, who would help supervise the harvest. After the FDA announcement all the other local Xenotech employees had been reassigned to the Menlo Park office, leaving the labs and the dorm building quiet and lifeless. As Jerry Landis spoke with the researchers and the security guys at the entrance to the building, Dr. Gibbs took Billy Bob aside. "Mr. Needmore, how many entrances are there to this facility?"

"Ain't but one," Billy Bob said, pointing to the north.

"And how many men are guarding it?" Dr. Gibbs asked ominously.

"Ain't nobody guarding it right now." Billy Bob suddenly looked worried. "Why? We expecting some kind of trouble?"

"The only thing we're expecting is for you to guard that gate, Mr. Needmore." Dr. Gibbs dismissed Billy Bob with a wave of his hand and turned to join Jerry Landis and the scientists as they headed into the building.

Billy Bob hadn't known these guys for ten minutes yet, but he already didn't like them. He didn't like the way they were so secretive and he definitely didn't like the way they patronized him. He figured if whatever they were doing in that building was okay, then they wouldn't have any problem telling him about it. And the fact that they not only were *not* telling him but were also sending him off to guard the gate against nothing while a bunch of out-of-town ninja-lookin' yahoos provided security outside the mystery building, well, he figured they were up to no damn good and the farther away from it he was, the better. So he got in the Suburban and drove off to the entrance gate in a huff. But first he'd stop by the security office and get his friend, Clyde.

The food in the corral was long gone and the baboons were growing restless, cramped as they were in the electrified enclosure. After a couple of the baboons had been thrown to the ground by the 200,000-volt fence the others backed away from it, pressing closer to the building and the chute which led into the anteroom.

Inside the control room of the harvest building was a series of color monitors showing live shots of the corral, the anteroom, the harvest room, and the rendering room. The video system gave Jerry Landis and the others a sense of omniscience since they could see what was happening in any room at any time. But, except for the corral, it didn't show them anything that was going on outside, and that meant they didn't see the troops of baboons gathering along the entire circumference of the clearing surrounding the buildings.

Inside, Jerry Landis asked a few questions and then, satisfied with the answers, he gave the word and one of the scientists pressed a button which opened the large door where the corral chute met the building. The baboon nearest the door, a juvenile, barked and backed away at first, but then, curious, he entered the room. The door shut quietly behind him and for a moment the baboon stood still in the middle of the room, sniffing, and looking around, unperturbed.

One of the researchers turned to Jerry Landis. "Sir, would you do the honors?" He pointed at a blue button on the control panel and smiled.

Whir-pffft whir-pffft whir-pffft. Jerry Landis smiled back and pushed the blue button. "Thy will be done," he said quietly. All eyes fixed on the monitors, and a moment later the giant baboon jerked violently backwards as he was hit by the hypodermic loaded with the pancuronium. The baboon stood his ground for only a few seconds before he lost all control of his muscles. He pitched forward onto his face and lay helpless on the ground, his eyes wide open and terrified, not knowing what had happened to him but fully aware that something had. A moment later the synchronized hydraulic arms appeared from the edges of the monitor and gently turned the baboon onto his back. Then, like pallbearers, the arms lifted him and placed him onto the first aluminum table. The baboon's limbs were secured and the pulmonary tube was forced down his throat, causing only insignificant esophageal bleeding. Next, two sets of electric clippers zoomed in and shaved his chest clean. The aluminum table then moved to the next stage on the assembly line, where the baboon's chest was given a vigorous, automated iodine scrub. The table then proceeded into the harvest room, where it was greeted by a high-pitched whining noise. The baboon, though paralyzed by the pancuronium, could hear just fine, and it was easy to see that he was frightened beyond comprehension.

The black robotic arm with the sternal saw rotated out from its position and hovered momentarily above the baboon's chest while the tactile array sensors took measurements and calculated the precise point at which to start the median sternotomy. The baboon wanted to scream, but he couldn't. He could do nothing but watch when, a moment later, the saw descended toward his breastbone and split it in half in a fine spray of flesh and bone and blood.

Paul stopped the car when Georgette saw the sign for the Biomedical Research Center of the South. The fifteen-foot-high double fence stretched as far as the eye could see in both directions. Ahead, a dirt road ran to a gate which was chained shut. Next to the dirt road, on the far side of the interior fence, there was a small guard shack, and it appeared someone was inside. Paul suggested they just plow through the gate but Georgette argued for a subtler approach.

"They're not just going to let us in," Paul said.

"Just honk," Georgette said. "Trust me. We'll get in."

After Paul leaned on the horn a couple of times Billy Bob came out of the guard shack and walked to the gate. Because of the double fence configuration Billy Bob was still about twenty feet from Paul and Georgette's car. "Can I help you folks?" he yelled.

Georgette got out of the car. "Yeah, we're with the FDA. We're here to do an inspection of your facility."

Billy Bob was a lot of things, but stupid was not among them. "Then how come you got watwall tires?" he asked while pointing at the objects in question.

Thrown by the question, Georgette looked at the tires, then back at Billy Bob. "What?"

"Watwalls," Billy Bob said. "I ain't never seen no government car what's got watwall tires. So you're either driving your own car or you're lying. Plus, you got California plates."

At this point Paul got out of the car. "This property's owned by a California corporation, that's why they sent us out here. It's the law."

While it wouldn't be fair to say Billy Bob was stupid, it *was* fair to say he had very limited knowledge about laws governing federal agencies, so he couldn't argue Paul's point. "You got any ID?" he yelled.

Paul looked to Georgette since it was her lie to begin with. "Yeah," she said. "Hang on a second." Georgette leaned into the car, reached under the baby blanket, and pulled out the paint gun and the 114 ci Nitro Tank. She pointed the exotic-looking weapon at Billy Bob. "How's this?" she asked.

Now Billy Bob had seen a lot of guns in his time, but he'd never seen anything like the weapon this woman was aiming at him. He didn't know if it was a flamethrower or a particle beam weapon and he didn't want to find out the hard way. "That's fine, ma'am," he said with his hands held high. "Now I'monna reach inta my pocket and get the key to the gate, so don't be shootin that thang, all right?"

"Go ahead," Georgette said. "You're not who we're after."

Paul looked at his wife, beaming with pride. "You're very good," he said. She winked. As Billy Bob keyed the padlock and unwrapped the chain holding the gate closed, a Range Rover and a Toyota 4-Runner came roaring up the road. They were loaded with college-age boys, all of whom had shotguns in their hands and fraternity logos on their sweatshirts. Following them was a bright red Mustang GT. Sue leaned her pretty head out the window and waved to Georgette. "Haaaaay!" she yelled, somehow turning it into a two-syllable word. "We're not too late, are we?"

"It's never too late," Paul said, smiling. He felt more alive than he had in weeks. He was actually doing something that would make a difference. A real, tangible, positive difference.

Georgette kept the paint gun trained on Billy Bob as she approached him on foot. Paul, the frat boys, and Sue and Laurie followed in their vehicles until they were all inside the fenced area. "You can put your hands down," Georgette said.

"Thanks," Billy Bob said. "Tell me the truth, ya'll ain't really with the FDA now, are ya?"

"Nope," Georgette said. "But we are here to do an inspection."

"It's about them big monkeys, ain't it?" Billy Bob volunteered excitedly. "Dang! I knew they was somethin' funny 'bout that."

Paul and Georgette now knew they were at the right place. Georgette put her hand on Paul's shoulder and whispered to him, "I love you." Paul wondered what had prompted her to say that. "And you know what else?" she whispered, "I would even if you weren't doing this."

By now, Sue, Laurie, and all the shotgun-toting frat boys had gathered around to find out a little more about what the hell they were doing there. Truth be told, most of the frat boys had come along hoping only to score points with the pretty sorority girls, but when they heard what Xenotech was doing behind these electrified fences, they pumped their shotguns in a show of support. "That just ain't nat'ral," was Billy Bob's response. He stood there shaking his head. After a moment he looked at Georgette. "I wanna hep."

Paul and Georgette exchanged a suspicious glance. "How come?" Paul asked. "You work for Xenotech, don't you?"

"I just quit," Billy Bob said.

"How do we know we can trust you?" Georgette asked.

Billy Bob paused a moment. "Lemme show you something," he said. "Over here." Billy Bob led Paul and Georgette and the others over to the guard shack and pointed inside. There, on the floor, in a box lined with towels, was the little orphaned baboon Billy Bob had found that day in the woods. He was sucking on a baby bottle.

"He's so cute!" Laurie squealed. "I just love the way his little ears stick out."

"Let me introduce you to Clyde," Billy Bob said.

"Clyde?" Georgette asked.

"Named him after that monkey in the Clint Eastwood movie," Billy Bob said proudly before turning to Georgette. "Whaddya say?"

"Now that's a face you can trust," Georgette said.

Jerry Landis and Dr. Gibbs were taking turns pushing the blue button. And each time they did, the door would open, a baboon would enter the anteroom, and the harvest would begin anew. Every time one of the baboons disappeared into the building, those left in the corral barked and howled. They could sense something awful happening, and the rancid smell of their rendered brethren was beginning to burn in their sensitive nostrils. These sounds and smells had drifted deep into the piney woods, causing a thousand or more of the giant baboons to gather at the edge of the clearing around the buildings, an army massed on a border.

The harvest room, once stainless and pristine, was now a bloodbath. Odd bits of tissue and fur and bone clogged the drain grates and the blood was spreading out to cover the entire floor. And Jerry Landis loved it. By, God, this was power. Starting tomorrow he would be selling life to thousands of people. Life! They would worship him and give him enormous sums of money. *Whir-pffft whir-pffft whir-pffft*. And finally, Jerry Landis would get a heart that didn't make him sound like a sump pump. The thought of all that power and money and his new lease on life combined with the recent shot of hormones had resulted in an enormous erection which Jerry Landis secretly pressed against the control panel as the next baboon entered the chamber.

Dr. Gibbs had stopped watching the slaughter altogether, not because he didn't have the stomach for it but because he was busy with a calculator. Dividing and multiplying, Dr. Gibbs was running numbers and projections about his future wealth. The numbers were serious and eager to please. He looked forward to the day that one of the medical schools which had refused him admission came sniffing around for a donation.

Technically, except for the clogged drain, things were running remarkably well, especially for an operation as delicate and sophisticated as this. In fact, right up until the gunfire started, everyone in the building thought this was going to be a perfect day. "What the hell was that?" Jerry Landis asked when he heard the first couple of shots.

"Sounds like . . . gunfire," one of the scientists replied with a hitch.

Dr. Gibbs stopped his calculations and looked at the video monitor of the corral. He saw all the baboons hooting and jumping up and down excitedly. Because of the angle it was hard to tell for sure but it looked to him like there were a couple of people near the corral gate, possibly trying to free the giant baboons.

Jerry Landis jerked to his feet. "Goddammit! Where the hell is Security?"

Dr. Gibbs pointed to the screen. "I think that's one of them there." A figure dressed in black retreated across the screen chased by someone with a shotgun.

Much to Dr. Gibbs's surprise, Jerry Landis pulled a gun from a heretofore unseen shoulder holster and moved for the door. He stopped and pointed the gun at the scientists. "Whatever you do, don't stop." He then waved the gun at Dr. Gibbs. "Let's go, Doc. We're not giving up without a fight."

"But I'm unarmed," Dr. Gibbs protested.

"Grab a stick when you get outside," Jerry Landis said,

"but get your ass out there and do something!" He cocked the gun and encouraged Dr. Gibbs to join him.

Being the insider, Billy Bob had designed the assault. And, with little Clyde clinging to his back, Billy Bob had led the frat boys in the attack on Landis's security team. As they engaged in battle, Paul and Georgette raced to the gate of the corral, trying to figure out what to do. "Jesus," Paul said as he stared into the corral. "Those are some damn big baboons. You better be ready to run if we manage to get this open." Paul reached for the latch.

"Don't touch it," Georgette said. "It's charged. We need to cut the power first. Look for a box with a two-hundred-and-forty volt feeder cable."

Paul looked at her quizzically. "How do you know so much about this stuff?" he asked.

"You don't want to know," she replied.

Inside the corral was utter bedlam. The air was filled with dust and the stink of rendering. The baboons were both scared and excited as gunfire erupted all around them and the door to the building kept opening and swallowing them up one at a time. The huge primates were making an unholy racket, screeching and barking and howling in fright. And although no one noticed, there was an equally frightening amount of noise coming from the woods surrounding the compound.

Jerry Landis charged out the side door of the building, his gun at the ready. Dr. Gibbs followed wielding a pair of scissors he had found in the control room. They looked around trying to assess the situation. Fifty yards across the clearing, over by the lab buildings, they could see the dressed-in-black security forces in a firefight with what looked like armed refugees from fraternity row. "Go help them," Landis told Dr. Gibbs. Gibbs hesitated only briefly before he charged into the fray without considering the wisdom of taking scissors to a gunfight.

Jerry Landis started making his way around the building looking for whoever was trying to free the baboons. His plan was to insure that whoever they were would rue the day they fucked with Jerry Landis. When he rounded the corner of the building he could see two people on the far side of the corral trying to open the breaker box that fed the electrified fence. He recognized Paul immediately. *Whir-pffft whir-pffft whir-pffft.* "Son of bitch!" he yelled, though not loud enough to be heard over the din of the baboons. His first reaction was to open fire on Paul, but to do that he would have to shoot through the corral and risk hitting one of his valuable transgenic baboons. He chose instead to circle around the building and sneak up from behind.

"I can't get the damn thing open," Paul yelled as he tugged on the cover to the breaker box. "We need a crowbar or something." Georgette and Paul split up and began searching for some sort of tool. Looking between the large central air-conditioning units on the side of the building, Georgette found some shafts of rusted rebar, but they were too thick to wedge under the cover of the breaker box. Ten yards away Paul rooted through a large pile of postconstruction junk. It was mostly crumbles of Sheetrock, concrete, cinder blocks, and two-by-fours. Paul was pulling on the shaft of a broken caulk gun he'd found when *PIQUEEEEW!* a bullet ripped it from his hand. "Jumpin' Jesus!" Paul looked over toward the harvest building and saw Jerry Landis bracing for a second shot. He dove behind the pile of rubble and began building a concrete wall to huddle against.

Georgette screamed when she heard the shot and saw Paul collapse behind the rubble. She couldn't tell if he had been hit and she couldn't get to him without exposing herself to the shooter. She peeked from behind the AC unit and saw Jerry Landis heading for Paul. "Shit," she muttered. Georgette knew Landis couldn't shoot Paul without going around the rubble pile. And to do that, he'd have to get past her. Georgette picked up a four-foot-long piece of rebar and waited. If Landis kept on the same track, Georgette would be able to reinforce his brain with the iron rod in about ten seconds.

Meanwhile, Paul was making fast work of building a short wall of cinder blocks and concrete behind which to hide. He didn't want to be the second generation of Symons to die at the hands of Jerry Landis. The wall was coming together nicely until the ground began to rumble.

Georgette felt it. And so did Jerry Landis, who stopped and looked around curiously. The baboons in the corral were screeching louder and louder as the trembling grew more intense. Landis didn't know what to make of it all; still he thought hiding was more prudent than not, so he slipped into the shadows of a recessed doorway and cringed. *Whir-pffft whir-pffft whir-pffft.*

At first, Paul thought it was a small earthquake, but then he remembered he was in Mississippi and he didn't think they had quakes there so it had to be something else. Georgette thought maybe one of the frat boys had found a tractor or something and was driving it toward the corral to crash open the gate. When she peeked out from her hiding place to look, she was surprised to see it wasn't a tractor at all. It was a stampede of baboons charging from the woods. There must have been two thousand of them and they were coming from all directions: one million pounds of baboon bearing down on the harvest building without the slightest clue of what they would do when they arrived.

The moment Sue and Laurie saw the baboons, they ran screaming for their Mustang GT and escaped only because Sue's father had had the foresight to buy the eight-cylinder engine. The frat boys and the black-clad security forces dropped their weapons and ran like hell for the dorm building. Billy Bob and Clyde headed for the security building. And racing toward the corral, showing surprising speed for a man of his age and physical condition, was Dr. Gibbs—running with scissors. *WHBOOM!* A shotgun blast from somewhere peppered Dr. Gibbs in the back, but he kept running.

Paul's shabby concrete-and-cinder-block wall had collapsed as the tremors grew worse. Curiosity got the better of him and he popped his head up over the pile of rubble to see what the hell was going on. What he saw made his jaw go slack. "Good God," he said. Difficult as it was for him to believe, there it was: a stampede of industrial-sized chacma baboons, some of which were . . . *armed?* He saw at least six of them carrying shotguns or rifles. He wondered how in hell that had happened.

To a biped, it's no big deal. But carrying a loaded shotgun while running is dicey business for quadrupeds. The impact of slamming the weapon against the ground occasionally caused them to discharge. *WHBOOM!* And depending on which way the barrel was pointing the baboons were just as likely to kill one another as they were to hit anything else.

"Stay down!" Georgette yelled.

Just before taking Georgette's advice, Paul saw Dr. Gibbs being chased by several sub-adult males. He thought Dr. Gibbs's mistake was in running toward the corral, since that's where most of the baboons seemed to be headed. Although, to be honest, his only other option was to run straight at the huge beasts, which really didn't make any sense. In any event, it wasn't long before Dr. Gibbs was trapped between two dozen genetically altered baboons and a 200,000-volt fence. Dr. Gibbs didn't know what to make of it when the dominant male of the group displayed his milky white eyelids. He'd never seen such a thing and he hoped it was a good sign.

It wasn't. The male then bared his huge teeth and let out a satanic screech. *WHBOOM!* Another shotgun blast sent Paul ducking back behind the pile of rubble, so he didn't see what happened next.

Dr. Gibbs considered throwing himself onto the electrified fence but he couldn't muster the courage. At the same time he knew he didn't stand a chance in a fight with one of these things, so he did what many smaller animals do when attacked by larger ones. He curled up in a tight little ball on the ground and prayed the big baboon would just leave him alone. But he wouldn't. The baboon picked Dr. Gibbs up and served him over the fence like a volleyball. When he landed in the corral the other baboons shoved Dr. Gibbs toward the chute as if he were a sacrificial lamb. And then, in a classic example of bad timing and tough luck, the door opened.

For one brief, shining moment Dr. Gibbs believed he was saved. He based that belief on the assumption that the scientists in the control room would see him on the video monitors and would turn the system off when they did. So when the door opened, Dr. Gibbs rushed into the anteroom and waved frantically at the cameras, his delirious smile betraying his relief. However, Dr. Gibbs had badly overestimated the scientists' loyalty in the face of an onslaught of shotgun-toting gorilla-sized baboons, and in a moment he felt the sting of the pancuronium hypodermic. Dr. Gibbs flopped immediately onto the floor and watched, helplessly, as the robotic arms gently rolled him over, picked him up, and placed him on one of the aluminum tables.

Next, the large pulmonary support tube designed for the huge baboon tracheas was forced violently down his throat. And as horribly painful as that was, it was the least of Dr. Gibbs's concerns. He knew exactly what was happening. He knew exactly what was *about* to happen. And he knew there wasn't a damn thing he could do about it. In fact, right now, as the shiny aluminum table advanced him inexorably toward a terminal event, the only thing Dr. Gibbs could do was think.

And think he did.

Dr. Gibbs took the opportunity to reflect, however briefly, on his life in the organ procurement business, of negotiating with the destitute for their kidneys "and maybe a little bowel as long as we're in there." He wondered about what moral lines he might have crossed in the course of things. He wondered if he deserved what he was about to get. And even as the baboon-sized sternal saw ripped through his flesh he was unsure of the answers.

As Dr. Gibbs completed his accelerated philosophy course, Jerry Landis was busy reevaluating his immediate goal. He had ducked into a doorway when the giant baboons began their assault and now, like Dr. Gibbs, Jerry Landis was thinking. While he had every intention of killing Paul, he thought he'd let the baboon attack run its course first. Landis figured that once things settled down and the baboons retreated to the woods, he'd be able to kill Paul and the other activists and then resume the harvest. Yes, they'd be behind schedule, but these things happen. After all, it wasn't a perfect world. They could run all these bodies through the harvesting process and there'd be no evidence of any homicide. Satisfied with this plan, Jerry Landis shot out the lock on the door and hurried back into the harvest building to wait things out.

The baboons had scattered all over the compound, but a large group was gathered at the corral gate, apparently trying to figure out how to free the ones trapped inside. An ambitious young male charged to the front of the group, barking theatrically, and grabbed the gate as though he would simply pull it off its hinges. His macho posturing outnumbered his understanding of electricity ten to one. When he grabbed the gate, the 200,000 volts grabbed back. A more surprised look never crossed the face of a primate. All the hair on this body stood on end, puffing him to twice his already considerable size. Fortunately, there was a little amperage behind the voltage, and after a few seconds of screeching, the young male was hurled to the ground embarrassed but alive. The others backed away from the gate to consider alternatives.

Having seen this, Paul knew the electricity was the key. He had to get the juice turned off before the baboons would be able to escape. Paul had waited all his life to do something and he'd be damned if he wasn't going to finish what he'd finally started. He knew he might get shot. He knew he might meet up with a baboon who didn't understand that he was trying to help, but Paul was going to try anyway. So he grabbed a thirty-pound piece of concrete with rebar poking out the ends and he ran to the breaker box. Several baboons noticed the hairless biped and gave chase. But when Paul raised the chunk of concrete and began smashing it repeatedly against the electrical panel, causing a fountain of sparks and nasty electrical sounds, the baboons turned and ran back to the protection of their troop.

The veins in Paul's thick arms bulged as he hefted the block of concrete again and again, denting, but not yet opening, the cover. As strong as Paul was, the enormous effort started to take its toll. His arms bone weary, Paul lowered the concrete for a moment and took several deep breaths before hefting the block one final time. Flashing back to his days as a weight-lifting college line-backer, Paul started screaming as he mustered one final attack, heaving the concrete block against the breaker box with enormous power. "Aaaauuuugggghhhhh!" Again and again he smashed the block against the panel's cover. The veins and muscles in his neck and his back and his arms burned as Paul made one last, explosive heave, finally exposing the breaker panel. Like a madman, Paul reached into the sparking box and grabbed the main switch lever and yanked it to Off.

"Paul!" Georgette yelled from between the air-conditioning units. "Are you nuts?"

"I'm fine," Paul yelled back. "Thanks for asking."

"Listen," she said, "I've got an idea."

"Shoot," Paul replied.

"What do you say we make a run for the car?"

Paul hesitated for a moment before yelling back, "Yeah, I think we've done enough good here for one day."

"Okay then," Georgette said. "On three. One . . . two . . ."

"Wait!" Paul screamed. "Do you have the keys?"

"I thought *you* had them." Georgette felt her pockets. "No, wait, I've got 'em! Sorry."

"Holy shit!" Paul yelled.

"What's the matter?"

Paul pointed at two especially large male baboons.

They were rocking a telephone pole back and forth in the ground. The two giant primates then grabbed the pole and let out a loud, sustained grunting sound as they uprooted the thing and let it crash to the ground, disrupting phone service temporarily. It was the single most impressive display of animal strength Paul or Georgette had ever seen. The pole must have weighed four thousand pounds, and it must have been dropped ten feet into the ground, yet two of them had pulled it out like a straw from a milk shake. Four more baboons rushed over and picked up the massive log and started running awkwardly toward the gate of the corral. They were going to use it as a battering ram to free the baboons trapped inside. Unfortunately, not all the baboons inside were clear on the plan, so when the corral gate collapsed like the Buffalo Bills at playoff time a few of them got crushed underneath the thing. Those with the foresight to get out of the way managed to escape into the woods, another example of Darwin's theory.

Paul and Georgette stayed where they were and watched in awe. It was beyond surreal. It was an African savannah on acid. Mutant old world monkeys twice the size of a man, conducting an organized raid to free captive members of their species. Armed baboons, for God's sake! Pulling telephone poles out of the ground. It was enough to make Paul and Georgette forget about Jerry Landis and Xenotech and organ harvests. They weren't even thinking about the danger they were in. All they could do was watch.

The freed baboons bolted into the woods like escaped convicts. Most of the invading baboons followed them, disappearing at the tree line. But several hundred of the massive primates continued investigating the grounds. Some had gone into the dorm building after the frat boys and the security team while others had climbed on top of the harvest building and were sniffing around the rendering room's chimney.

The ghostly figure watching all this from a window in the harvest building was Jerry Landis. It was over and he knew it. When the press got a hold of this—and there was no doubt that would happen—Xenotech was doomed. And with that, any chance Jerry Landis had of finding a cure to Werner's syndrome was doomed with it. *Whir-pffft.*

Jerry Landis took a long, deep breath and accepted the fact that his struggle for everlasting life was coming to a close. And as the madness played itself out on the other side of the window, he found himself focused on the truth. *Whir-pffft.* Nothing could change what was happening out there. At the moment Jerry Landis truly needed one, there was no revelation telling him how to stop the inevitable. He could perform no miracle to turn back the hands of time. There was simply nothing he could do to prevent his life's work from falling apart right in front of his eyes. *Whir-pffft.* His only chance of eternal life had just escaped into a pine forest in south-central Mississippi. *Whir-pffft.* His shot at being God, lost. *Whir-pffft.* And though there was nothing Jerry Landis could do to stop what was happening outside, there *was* something he could do about the person who had caused this to happen.

He could still kill Paul Symon. *Whir-pffft.*

With two thousand baboons barking as they retreated into the woods, Georgette had to yell to get Paul's attention. "Paul! Let's go for the car!"

"I'm right behind you!" he yelled back. "Go!"

The car was parked on the north side of the harvest building. Georgette and Paul were on the south side. Since the baboons had shown keen interest in the bipeds they had noticed, Georgette kept close to the building so as not to expose herself on more than one side as she made her way back to the parking lot. As dangerous as Georgette could be on a basketball court, she knew she wouldn't impress any of these overgrown monkeys by throwing elbows.

Paul was way behind Georgette. She was already rounding the corner of the east side of the building.

Against his better judgment, Paul suddenly stopped. He cupped his hands around his face and tried looking into one of the building's windows in hopes of seeing Jerry Landis in defeat, but he couldn't see a thing. The dark tinting on the glass hid the fact that Paul's face was mere inches from the man who killed his father. Jerry Landis remained still and stared back at Paul for a moment before he remembered the gun in his hand. He raised the gun impassively and put the barrel to the glass at Paul's forehead. He closed his eyes and pulled the trigger and the glass shattered, but Paul had moved away, heading for the parking lot.

Georgette was at the car. She jumped in and cranked it up, then leaned over to open the passenger door for Paul. Suddenly there was a huge thudding crash overhead. The roof of the car began caving in as a subdominant male pounded on top of the car in an attempt to get Georgette out.

Thirty yards away, Paul was rounding the corner to the north side of the building when he caught a glimpse of something coming out of a recessed doorway. It happened too fast to dodge. Paul felt his nose break and his knees hit the ground hard. Then he heard a familiar voice. "You pain-in-the-ass son of a bitch!" Jerry Landis said. "I won't miss you again." *Whir-pffft whir-pffft whir-pffft.* He kicked Paul in the stomach, doubling him over.

Georgette was still trapped by the baboon. She turned around and looked out the rear window to see where Paul was, hoping he'd be able to save her. That's when she saw him on the ground, hands covering his face, blood seeping through his fingers. Jerry Landis was standing over him with a gun.

Paul could see little more than stars and a dirty pair of expensive shoes as he knelt helplessly in front of his foe. Jerry Landis leaned down and spoke to him. "If I've got to die, so do you," he said. "Now stand up!"

Paul struggled to his feet and blinked hard to clear his eyes. He hoped Georgette had made it safely to the car and that she wouldn't see him die this way.

"Well, Mr. Tree-hugger, any last requests?" Landis said with a laugh.

"Yeah," Paul replied. "Apologize."

"Apologize?" Paul might as well have told Landis to fly. "For what? Failing to love the spotted owl?"

"For my father," Paul said.

"Not guilty," Jerry Landis said with a smirk. It was the same smirk Paul had always imagined. "Your old man should have been more careful." *Whir-pffft whir-pffft whir-pffft.*

Suddenly Paul was unable to see Jerry Landis. All he could see was his father's face, laughing at the dinner table, winking to Paul after a private joke, smiling as he tossed the football in the back yard. And then suddenly, stricken. Terrified. Dead.

"Your old man should have been more careful," Landis said.

And Jerry Landis should have just pulled the trigger but he hesitated. And Paul didn't. He hammered his fist into Landis's face. The blow uprooted twelve of his teeth and knocked him backwards into the wall of the building, which is the only thing that kept him standing. The shock of being separated from so many teeth caused him to drop the gun. Paul picked it up and looked at Jerry Landis propped up against the brick wall like a man on the business end of a firing squad. He wasn't sure what to do next but murder crossed his mind. He pointed the gun at Landis's head. "At least you could have said you were sorry."

Jerry Landis spit some teeth at Paul. "Get over it," he said. "It's not a perfect world."

"Apologize before I kill you," Paul said.

"I don't think you'll do it."

"Apologize."

"You're too much of a coward to shoot me," Landis said. "You've always been a chickenshit and you know it. That's the only reason we got this far, isn't it?"

Paul cocked the hammer.

❊   ❊   ❊

Georgette screamed when the baboon started hitting the window. She knew she couldn't run for it. All she could do was back away from the door and hope he couldn't reach her when he broke through. It didn't take long before the safety glass surrendered to the pounding. The baboon hooted a couple of times before he stuck a hand in the window. When Georgette put the hot electric cigarette lighter in his hand he screeched and howled. A second later he stuck his massive head into the car and bared his teeth. Georgette opened fire. *BAM!BAM!BAM! BAM!BAM!BAM!BAM!BAM!BAM!* The force of the paintballs at that range nearly put the baboon's eyes out. He rolled off the top of the car and ran away screeching and crashing into trees and other baboons.

Paul looked down the barrel and felt the tension on the trigger. "It was your fault he died," Paul said. "He never even—" Paul stopped mid-sentence and gasped wildly. His eyes jerked wide open and he dropped the gun. He tried to speak but he couldn't. The pain in his chest was stunning. He couldn't breathe. His face blanched and he fell back to his knees.

"You must be kidding," Jerry Landis said, "a heart attack?" He laughed, spilling two more teeth onto the ground. "By God, it must run in your family." He walked over to Paul's side and picked up the gun. Then he put it against Paul's temple. "I think I'll shoot you right here, you piece of shit."

"Hey!" Georgette screamed. "That's my husband!"

"Then tell him good-bye," Landis said without looking at her.

"Stop it!" Georgette shouted. "Or I'll shoot."

"Don't miss," Landis said. *Whir-pffft whir-pffft whir-pffft.*

She didn't. *BAM!BAM!BAM!BAM!BAM!BAM!BAM! BAM!BAM!* Landis didn't know what hit him, but he knew it wasn't lead. He turned to look at Georgette and saw the paint gun. When he started to laugh she shot again. *BAM!BAM! BAM!BAM!BAM!BAM!BAM!BAM!BAM!* Several of the paint balls stung Landis's face and one actually went into his mouth. Jerry Landis sputtered and spit paint and blood. "Goddamn bitch!" he yelled. He was furious. "I'll kill you first!" *Whir-pffft whir-pffft whir-pffft.* He raised his gun to shoot her and *VUMP!* The ground behind him shook violently.

Georgette's eyes widened. "You better hurry," she said, staring at the huge baboon that had jumped down from the roof of the harvesting building.

Whir-pffft whir-pffft whir-pffft. The way his day was going, Jerry Landis knew what was behind him before he even turned around. He could smell it. *Whir-pffft whir-pffft whir-pffft.* He could feel the bursts of stinking hot, moist breath blowing on his paint-soaked neck. For a moment the abject fear of what lay ahead paralyzed him completely. His gun was aimed at Georgette but he couldn't pull the trigger. He couldn't move at all. Finally the unnatural amounts of adrenaline and testosterone in his system overwhelmed his fear and good judgment. He slowly lowered the gun. Paint dripped from the end of his hand and formed a puddle near where Paul lay.

Georgette thought she might die right where she stood, not from a gunshot or at the hands of a baboon but from worry and shame. Paul was struggling for air. He was taking desperate, short, gasping breaths and she worried that he wasn't going to live. And she was ashamed because she didn't move to help. She didn't do anything. Georgette couldn't tell if it was because she was unable to move or just unwilling to take the chance. Finally she managed to speak. "Hang on, Paul," she said. "Just hang on."

Standing in the hot Mississippi sun, Jerry Landis looked like some sort of primitive warrior, his face painted for battle. He took a full deep breath and very deliberately turned around, coming face-to-face with what had to be the largest dominant male baboon on the entire ten-thousand-acre compound. The baboon was stunning in his majesty, easily four times the size of Jerry

Landis, more than ten times as strong. He looked much more like a male hamadryas than a chacma with his regal, flowing mane framing his huge and beautiful and dangerous face. Large amber eyes, set deep under a prominent brow, looked straight into Jerry Landis's dark soul. His long muzzle leapt out from his skull with the massive canines unable to hide. *Whir-pffft whir-pffft whir-pffft*. The baboon lowered his head slightly and looked curiously at Jerry Landis. *Whir-pffft whir-pffft whir-pffft*. The baboon tilted his head to one side and listened.

Jerry Landis stood perfectly still. The future had arrived and, just as Jerry Landis had predicted, the space between its nostrils was narrow. Jerry Landis just had one last question. He looked at the baboon and shouted, *"What are you staring at, you stupid dog-faced monkey-looking motherfuckerrrrr!?!" Whir-pffft whir-pffft whir-* . . .

The baboon couldn't stand it any longer. He had to know what was making that noise. So he plunged his hand into Jerry Landis, grabbed the noisy left ventricular assist device, and pulled it out. He did it so fast that Jerry Landis saw his L-VAD in the baboon's hand before he crumpled into a useless, dead heap.

It appeared that Paul would have to live without that apology, assuming that he lived at all.

Out of her mind with fear, Georgette finally ran to Paul, who was clutching his chest and struggling for air. The baboon was too busy sniffing and tasting the bloody L-VAD to care that she ran within a few feet of him. Georgette had the baby blanket with her, and she wiped the blood from Paul's face. "Hang on, sweetheart," she said, her voice trembling. "I'm going to get you out of here. We'll find a doctor." But that started to look like an empty promise as more of the baboons came to join the first. Several of them set upon the lifeless remains of Jerry Landis, dismembering him and scattering his parts hither and yon. A hungry young male ate his liver in two bites. Others surrounded Paul and Georgette, slapping the ground, pant-barking, baring their teeth, and displaying the strange, frightening white eyelids.

Since most of the baboons had retreated into the woods, Billy Bob emerged cautiously from the security building. Clyde was perched on Billy Bob's shoulder, his tiny hands balled up and held out as if holding the reins to a horse. The report of a shotgun came from the dorm building, causing Billy Bob to wonder who was winning that battle. As Billy Bob scanned the clearing trying to find Georgette and Paul, he caught a glimpse of something near the tree line. He would never be sure, but he thought it was his long-lost cousin. "Merle!" he called out. A second later, Billy Bob heard an unusual bark come from the woods. He took it as a response and he started to run toward the barking. But when he got away from the walls of the security building and into the clearing he saw the baboons gathered menacingly around Georgette. He saw Paul's head in her lap. And he saw that she was unarmed. Billy Bob had a gun and he was just about to test it against the huge primates when he had a better idea. The only question was whether he could execute it before the baboons attacked.

Georgette gently stroked Paul's forehead and spoke softly. "It's okay, I'm right here." She was doing her best to be brave but it wasn't easy. "I love you," she said. Paul struggled to maintain as the pain continued crushing inside his chest. He managed a little smile and then mouthed "Love you too" before he closed his eyes. As the baboons pressed closer, Georgette knew she and Paul were about to die. Most probably in gruesome fashion. Georgette thought about all the things she had done in her life—things she had once been very proud of—and she wished she could have traded every one of them to save Paul, but she knew you couldn't make deals like that. Tears were streaming down her face, salting the diamond on her nose, when she looked up to the huge beasts surrounding her. "Please don't take him," she said calmly. "He's all I have left." Then she cradled Paul in her arms and rocked him gently.

Suddenly one of the baboons, a female, made an unusual hooting noise. The others stopped and looked at her as she stepped forward and sniffed the air. The baboon moved closer and leaned within inches of Georgette and again she sniffed. Georgette could have kissed the baboon on her muzzle, she was that close. The baboon breathed in as she brushed her nostrils against Paul's face and the baby blanket. Her acute olfactory senses took in all the details. She hooted once again. The female had picked up the scent of a newborn. Suddenly a couple of sub-adult males approached, barking. The female baboon quickly hooted to one of the dominant males, who, in turn, let out a series of terrifying barks and took a defensive position in front of Georgette and Paul.

The next thing Georgette heard was what sounded like an eighteen-wheeler blasting its horn. The baboons were startled and they stood to see what was going on, allowing Georgette a view between their thick, hairy legs. It was a knight in shining armor named Sir Billy Bob and his faithful companion, Clyde. Billy Bob was driving the big truck he used for carting his giant baboon trap around the compound. But this time the truck bed was loaded with crates of fresh fruits and vegetables. He drove the truck straight across the compound at forty miles an hour, heading for the woods. Georgette wondered what the hell he was going to do. When Billy Bob was about halfway between the buildings and the tree line, he reached across the cab and grabbed Clyde, pulling him close. He then cut the wheels hard to the left and flipped the truck onto its side, cab and all. The crates were launched from the flatbed trailer and exploded on impact, spreading food for a hundred yards.

Georgette broke into a huge smile. What a great idea, she thought. The baboons took off after the food, leaving Georgette and Paul alone. The moment they were gone, Georgette stood and began struggling to get Paul into the car. "Hold on, sweetheart," she said. "You're going to be all right." As she strained to pick him up, Georgette glanced over to see if Billy Bob would emerge from the truck. With each passing moment she imagined increasingly serious injuries—she wondered if he was even alive. When she finally got Paul into the back seat of the car she drove straight for the truck. Billy Bob had risked his life for her and she'd have to do the same.

A couple of the baboons were climbing around on the overturned truck chassis but all the others were gathering food. Georgette pulled up next to the overturned cab and jumped out of the car carrying the paint gun. She was on a mission and nothing would stop her, not even the two juvenile males who had just ripped the door off the cab of the truck and were reaching down into it. *BAM!BAM!BAM!BAM!BAM!BAM!BAM!BAM!BAM!* Georgette pasted them. The other baboons hardly looked up from their smorgasbord as the two painted males screeched off into the woods covered in red paint.

Georgette climbed quickly up onto the overturned truck and just as she looked down into the cab, a baboon jumped straight at her face. It happened so fast Georgette couldn't react. The baboon wrapped himself around her head and in a moment Georgette realized it was Clyde, who was scared and trembling. She managed to get Clyde onto her back. "Hey," Georgette yelled, "are you—"

"Hey yerself," Billy Bob yelled from somewhere inside the truck. "Them monkeys gone?"

"Yeah," Georgette said. She helped Billy Bob out of the truck. He was fine, not a scratch on him.

"What happened to Paul?" he asked. "He don't look so good."

"We've got to get him to a doctor," Georgette said.

"I'll drive." Billy Bob took Clyde and jumped in the driver's seat. Georgette got into the back and held Paul in her arms. He was pale and his breathing was shallow. And Billy Bob was right, he didn't look so good.

Lance Abbott was a little nervous as he waited to go in to his first meeting. He was on the lot of a major film studio about to pitch his story to a very important and successful producer. Lance Abbott's time had finally come. Thanks to the timely demise of Vic "Bonedigger" Nichols, Lance had returned to L.A. with a pocketful of cash and high hopes. He rented a furnished apartment in the Marina and, after just four phone calls, he had landed an agent. The next day Lance drove over to the Best Agency in Century City to meet with Marshall Best. TBA was a boutique literary and talent agency but was well regarded. Marshall Best set up a series of pitch meetings for Lance, saying, "Screw TV, Lance. This is a fucking feature."

So now Lance was sitting just outside the producer's office, looking at posters of the films the producer had made. Lance was going over the details, polishing and refining the elements of the story which had finally become clear to him while meeting with his friend in the pathology lab.

It was only after his friend had identified the mystery tissue as baboon myocardium that Lance remembered hearing that the FDA had given Xenotech approval to do baboon heart xenografts. That, in turn, reminded Lance that Xenotech had hired him privately to broker the perfectly healthy hearts of Mr. Luckett and a funny little guy named Arty, both of whom were alive and well at the Xenotech press conference. From there the story presented itself to Lance. Once Lance had it figured out, it was simply a matter of executing Plan B.

"This is a story about a biotechnology company willing to do whatever was necessary to perfect a transgenic baboon heart in order to corner the xenograft market," Lance said as he began his pitch.

"Terrific," the producer said. "Great words too, *transgenic* and *xenograft*. I love science thrillers." The producer's assistant nodded vigorously and took notes.

"Until recently," Lance said, "I was an organ transplant coordinator in the Bay Area. Because of my job I came across a lot of dead and nearly dead people. A few months ago I began looking into what I thought was a pattern of deaths caused by an eco-terrorist."

"An eco-terrorist?" the producer said excitedly. "I got goose bumps when you said that."

"It gets better," Lance said, his nervousness suddenly gone. "There's some weird stuff going on at a well-funded biotechnology company, which I'll call Xeno-corp."

"Terrific name, Xenocorp, very sciencey, I love it," the producer said.

"About a week ago, a biker by the name of Vic 'Bone-digger' Nichols died in South Bay Hospital," Lance said. "A gunshot had severed his femoral artery and he was in a coma. The shooter remains unknown. The only thing found at the scene was a .22 shell casing. Of course there's nothing strange about a biker getting shot," Lance said. "The weird part is that he didn't die from the gunshot wound or brain damage. He died from a large, unscheduled dose of medication."

"Jesus Christ, this is fantastic!" the producer said. "A fucking biotech mystery thriller!"

Everything Lance said was true. However, he failed to mention that he was the one who had dosed Bonedigger with the medications in order to have Bonedigger declared dead. Once he was declared dead, they could harvest his organs and Lance could collect his commission and move to L.A. The other benefit, as far as Lance was concerned, was that with his organs harvested, Bones was considerably less likely to object to the story Lance was now telling to the producer.

Lance also left out the part about how South Bay Hospital had been experimenting with the so-called non—heart beating protocol, which sought to improve the speed of organ donation. Bonedigger seemed a perfect candidate, if for no other reason than he had no known next of kin who might raise a stink about premature declarations of death.

As far as a lot of people in the medical profession are concerned, the brain death standard to which most medical centers still adhered failed to take into consideration that there were an awful lot of perfectly good organs going to waste. But, the director of health affairs at South Bay Hospital reasoned, if they could set a precedent with the new protocol, well, that would take an awful lot of pressure off the fund-raising committee to which he belonged. And that meant more golf time.

Knowing this, Lance had dosed Bonedigger with large doses of several commonly used drugs. One was Regitine (phentolamine mesylate USP), which, when given just as life support is withdrawn, helps keeps organs healthy. Regitine also blocks the body's natural release of adrenaline, which, especially in critically injured patients, is frequently the only thing keeping them alive. Lance also gave Bones some Heparin, an anticlotting drug that, in addition to maintaining organ viability, can lead to dangerous intracranial bleeding in head-injured patients. And for the coup de grace, Lance slipped some blood pressure medication into Bonedigger's IV. When he no longer got a carotid pulse, Lance called the attending physician to have Bones declared dead.

"He's dead enough," the doctor said. "You sure there's no next of kin?"

"Zippity-do-dah," Lance said.

"Well," the doctor said, "let the harvest begin."

After making arrangements for all of Bonedigger's usable parts (his liver was shot), Lance submitted an invoice for his commission and went home. There he pored over his Terra Tuebor file, which also included details of all the mutilation deaths. Lance drew up a list of potential items which he could plant as evidence to frame Bonedigger. He gathered a few things into an old canvas bag before returning to the hospital, where he presented the front desk with "all of Vic Nichols's personal effects," which, Lance said, the police might be interested in seeing.

"So," Lance said to the producer, "this Mr. Nichols is declared dead and they rush him out to harvest." Lance looked around the producer's office, then lowered his voice. "When everyone left the room I noticed a canvas bag on the floor that I guess the paramedics brought along from wherever it was they found Mr. Nichols. Inside the bag, along with some clothes, I found an ice pick, some Save the Whales bumper stickers, a page from the phone book with the address of a vivisection device manufacturer, and several more incriminating bits of evidence which, I'm told, the police are still looking into."

"He's the eco-terrorist?" the producer asked. "That's great! I love it. I never would have guessed it was him." The assistant nodded and took more notes.

"But *is* he the eco-terrorist?" Lance asked. "Or did somebody set him up to look like one?" Lance stood up and started to pace. "Here's what really happened." The producer leaned forward as Lance rattled it off. "Xeno-corp's area of R and D was xenografting," he said. "Everyone assumed they were doing transgenic swine research but *then* they announced FDA approval on a transgenic *baboon* heart transplant. Now, there's no way

Xenocorp got that far ahead of the xenograft curve without sneaking some human trials under the FDA's radar; all the experts I've consulted agree with that. But where do you find people willing to undergo such an experiment?" Lance let the question hang.

The producer loved it. "Goddamn, I don't have a clue. Really sick people, I guess."

"Sure," Lance said, "you'd be able to find lots of desperate, dying people willing to give it a shot, but those are the worst possible subjects for an experiment like this. What you want for a medical trial like this are healthy subjects. That way they're less likely to die of something else and waste the baboon heart. You also want them to live so you can try out your antirejection drugs. But the only way to get otherwise healthy people to agree to undergo a procedure like this is to force them."

"Oh, this is unfuckingbelievable," the producer said.

Lance had always wanted a Porsche and he felt he was getting very close to owning one. "Keep in mind that companies like Xenocorp typically invest five hundred million dollars over many years in order to bring a single product to market. And with potential billion-dollar payoffs, the incentive is there to cheapen and speed the process."

"You bet your ass there is," the producer said. He knew that was true based on the last film he made.

"So Xenocorp hired someone to kidnap specific individuals and deliver them to the Xenocorp facility for experimental xenograft surgery. Let's say that person was a biker by the name of Vic 'Bonedigger' Nichols."

"Why him?" the assistant asked in an attempt to justify his job.

"He's disposable," the producer said. "No next of kin, that sort of thing."

"Exactly," Lance said. "Now, this next part took me a while to figure out because it was such a great touch. First, someone at Xenocorp instructed Mr. Nichols to kidnap subjects who were in some way connected to ecologically unfriendly businesses. Second, Xenocorp 'created' an eco-terrorist who attacks ecologically unfriendly types and leaves a note behind. This muddies the waters so that if the police start putting things together, maybe they'll spend their time looking through the righteous eco-nut files instead of biker bars or the biotechnology industry."

"Who do you see playing Bonedigger?" the producer asked, suddenly casting the film.

"I don't know, Lyle Alzado?" Lance said. "No, wait, he's dead. Uh, how about John Matuszak?"

"It's not important. Minor role. Please, go on."

Lance continued. "So Xenocorp hires Bonedigger to kidnap and deliver these people for high-risk medical trials. But of course with trial comes error," Lance said. "And every time one of the experimental xenografts failed, they had to dispose of the evidence. So Bonedigger took them out and disposed of them in ways that destroyed evidence of the heart surgery and, just as important, immediately suggested another cause of death."

"Like being cut in half by a band saw," the producer said dreamily.

"Just like," Lance said.

"This is fantastic!"

Lance noticed a humidor on the producer's desk. "May I?" he asked.

"Please."

Lance selected a Dunhill Altamira and clipped its cap. He lit it and savored a beautiful, long draw before continuing.

"I love the guy split in half by the wind turbine," the assistant said belatedly.

Though Lance was unaware of it, he could have included in this group the first head of security at Xenotech's Deckern County facility whose badly mutilated body had been fished out of the old cotton gin. "So," Lance concluded, "when Xenocorp finally got the transgenic transplants to work, they no longer needed

Mr. Nichols's kidnaping and disposal services. In fact, at that point, Mr. Nichols presented nothing but downside for Xenocorp. So they hired someone to kill him. That person, whose identity is still unknown, caught up with Mr. Nichols, shot him with a .22, slammed his head against the asphalt, and left him to bleed to death in the street where the police found him. Unfortunately for Xenocorp, Mr. Nichols survived that attack. So the hired killer had to go into South Bay Hospital to finish the job. And that's who gave him the overdose of blood pressure medication which led to his harvest." Lance leaned across the producer's desk. "So, whaddya think?"

The producer mulled it for a moment. "First of all, the giant baboons *alone* make this an event picture. But this has such a great set of bad buys. I'm seeing Walken, maybe Hopper; hell, maybe Jack as the head of Xenocorp. Fantastic motivation for murder. All the weird, Frankenstein science . . ." The producer looked troubled. "But who's the hero?"

Lance took a step back and spread his arms wide like Jim Carrey in the *Liar Liar* poster. "You're looking at him." Lance handed a videocassette to the producer. "Have you seen my *Renegade* episode?"

"No, but I've heard great things," the producer lied. "Terrific is one of the words I've heard used."

"I'd play an organ procurement specialist who stumbles on the conspiracy, sets out to find proof, gets found out by the bad guys, and has to fight to stay alive long enough to prove his theory to the cops."

The producer stood and began to applaud. His assistant did likewise. They were both in awe but for different reasons. The assistant smelled a big fat sale to the studio and continued employment, as did the producer. But the producer also smelled some things he doubted were coincidences. He had a feeling that Lance hadn't told him the whole truth, which was all right. In fact, if the producer could confirm his suspicions that Lance had something to do with the demise of one or more of the victims, this could turn out quite favorably.

"Lance," the producer said, "you don't want to direct, do you?"

Lance considered it for a moment before the producer started to laugh. "Just kidding; of course not. You're going to be too busy producing and *starring*, don't you think?"

Paul lay still and quiet in the hospital bed. Georgette held his hand. Billy Bob stood next to her, a serious expression under his crinkled, concentrating brow. Clyde wiggled around on Billy Bob's shoulder, but he didn't make any noise. He could tell it was an important moment.

"It's called Prinzmetal's angina," the doctor said. "Muscle fibers circling the coronary arteries go into spasm." The doctor made a funny spastic motion with his hand to demonstrate. "When that happens, the lumen can narrow or close momentarily, resulting in silent ischemia, angina, and sometimes heart attack."

"So . . . it was a heart attack?"

"Nope, fortunately not," the doctor said. "Just angina. With Prinzmetal, spasm can occur even in the absence of excess function demand. In other words, the blood supply's cut off to a point less than the minimal requirements of the heart muscle even when it is at rest." Clyde mimicked the doctor's spastic hand motion as the doctor continued. "The spasms may occur without apparent cause but can also result from exposure to cold, uh, inhaling cigarette smoke, or strong emotional stress." The doctor touched Paul's leg. "You had any severe stress lately?"

"A little," Paul said. He smiled at Georgette, who squeezed his hand.

"Abnormal rhythm disorders are common during the periods of blood flow cutoff, which can cause you to pass out," the doctor said.

"Is it genetic?" Georgette asked. "Contagious? What?"

"Idiopathic," the doctor said. "Of unknown origin. At any rate, you'll be out of here tomorrow." Just before leaving, the doctor told Paul to avoid whatever kind of stress it was that had triggered this episode. Paul said he'd try.

Clyde suddenly jumped onto the bed and bounced up and down as if it were a trampoline. He then jumped into Georgette's arms and blew an affectionate raspberry on her cheek. "Thanks, Clyde," she said. "I love you too."

"Listen," Billy Bob said, "I talked to the judge this morning about petitionin' the court to let me run the place while everybody tries on all them lawsuits. He said he figured they'd be litigatin' for ten or twenty years and I thank by then it might be a goin' concern."

"As what?" Georgette asked.

"What they call uh animal way station," Billy Bob said. "Them girls from up at Southern, Laurie and Sue, they sure are nice girls; anyway, they got their daddy to put me in touch with some folks who know about this kinda thang and, well, we're gonna see if we can't turn it into a wildlife photo safari kinda place. I gots permission to get started soon as all them police is done investigating thangs." Billy Bob took Clyde from Georgette and looked at her nose. "I been meanin' to tell you how much I lack that there diamond you got stuck in there. Looks real cute." He secretly wondered how she picked her nose with the jewelry in there. He turned to leave. "Y'all take care now, and come on back to visit whenever."

The Deckern County sheriff and his deputies were working with the people from the enforcement divisions of the FDA, the Centers for Disease Control and Prevention, the National Institutes for Health, and the FBI. The CDC, NIH, and FBI people were keenly interested in the harvest room. They dusted for prints, took photos, and sealed things in evidence bags. The lone FDA official was in the packing and shipping room taking a general inventory. She had already counted up the various meat products in the freezer and now she was about to open the sealed boxes that were stacked on a table near the south wall. When she opened the first box she was shocked. She gasped and stepped away from the table.

After composing herself, she opened another box and then another. The first eight boxes each contained a dried baboon head. After a few more, she was used to it, so when she opened box number twelve she screamed.

The CDC, NIH, and FBI people rushed in to see what had happened. The FDA woman pointed at the box. They looked inside and saw it contained a head, but one much smaller than a baboon's. It was Dr. Gibbs. But unlike all the horrified expressions dried permanently on the dehydrated baboon faces, Dr. Gibbs had a look of surprising contentment, as if, in his final moments, he had come to terms with his life and his achievements.

It was Wednesday morning, about three A.M., when the car's headlights dimmed and the driver pulled to the curb. The people in the car sat in silence across the street from an institutional-looking building.

"Nobody's going to see us," Melanie said. "Let's just do it."

"Yeah, all right," Thelma agreed.

They got out of the car and opened the back doors. They each picked up a small bundle and then dashed across the street past the big sign on the lawn that said CUPERTINO CHILDREN'S HOME. They reached the front door of the main building, making sure to stay in the shadows, just in case. "This looks like a good spot," Melanie said. She laid her package by the door. Thelma put hers down next to Melanie's.

"Good luck," Thelma said. "You're gonna need it."

"Don't start gettin' all sentimental," Melanie warned. "It's not worth it."

"I know, but . . ."

Melanie grabbed Thelma by the arm. "Can you afford to take care of that baby?"

"No," Thelma said.

"And neither can I," Melanie said. "Now come on." Melanie and Thelma ran back to the car and drove away.

The problem was that after the baboon farm snafu, Xenotech had gone tits-up. Its founder and chief op-

erating officer had been found deceased (not to mention
heartless) in somewhat suspicious circumstances. The
FDA approval they had received was withdrawn, and Mr.
Luckett, the man whose name was on the approval documents, was suspended with pay while the whole matter
was under review.

After giving birth to their children, Melanie and
Thelma discovered that they would not be receiving their
back-end payments from Jerry Landis as per their con-
tracts. They also found that the two men whom they
might sue over the matter were both dead. So, instead
of eating the loss themselves, Melanie and Thelma decided it would be best for all concerned if they just
dropped the inventory off on the steps of the Cupertino
Children's Home.

A few hours later, with dawn casting a gentle light on
the two cooing bundles, it became clear that Dr. Vines
had been right. The two curly-headed babies hadn't received so much as a single gene from Jerry Landis.

Paul and Georgette had been home a couple of
months before they started to discuss their family options. Because of the hysterectomy they obviously
couldn't have their own children—at least not without
some weird biotechnological intervention and that was
out of the question. Besides, they felt the last thing the
world needed was another child just so they'd be able to
see if it came out looking like one of them. So they
decided to adopt. They talked to their friends, Will and
Ellen, who had gone to China to adopt a baby girl, but
the price was beyond their means. So they decided to
make an appointment at the local orphanage, though
their expectations weren't very high since they had heard
infant adoptions in the United States were hard to
come by.

The first thing they saw when they entered the Cupertino Children's Home was a poster-size photograph of
the organization's biggest benefactor and current head

honcho, smiling and hugging several children with his long, gleaming robotic arms.

Just before the shit hit the fan, Arty, acting on nothing but gut instinct, had dumped his Xenotech stock the moment the restrictions elapsed. He made a killing and immediately got a full set of top-of-the-line prosthetics. Standing six-foot-five on his carbon-fiber prosthetic legs with integral sensors that were linked by the cordless radio-linked programmer and the audio feedback system with visual prompting that allowed for integral speed detection, Arty was able to program exact swing adjustment for various gaits. He had decided not to get a glass eye since women responded so positively to the pirate patch. As long as Arty took his daily dose of antirejection drugs his baboon heart just kept right on ticking.

With his wealth Arty had commissioned several new buildings for the orphanage and the landscaping was almost done. When the board of directors at the children's home offered Arty the job of running the place he slapped his prosthetic hand on the arm of the chair in which he was sitting (tearing the fabric slightly) and said, "Now you're talking!"

The kids loved him and he loved them right back. It was a match made in Silicon Valley. Arty never knew what happened to Bonedigger, but he was so busy running the children's home he soon forgot to worry about it.

Paul and Georgette tried not to stare when they walked into Arty's office. He made lots of sleek hydraulic sounds as he moved. *Whirvvvv whirvvvv whirvvvv.* "Hi, come in," Arty said. Paul extended his hand to shake. Arty held his prosthetic digits up in the air as if being robbed. "Not a good idea," he said. One of Arty's arms suddenly shot forward with tremendous force, the result of some problematic wiring in his system. "I wouldn't get too close," Arty said with a chuckle. "They don't have all the kinks worked out of this stuff yet. I didn't hit you, did I?"

"No, you just missed," Paul said.

"Good, then have a seat." Arty extended an arm toward the chairs opposite his desk. *Whirvvvv.* "So, you're wanting to adopt?"

Without going into the story about the liberation of the baboon farm, Paul and Georgette told Arty about Georgette's pregnancy, her uterine rupture, the hysterectomy, and little Freddy's death. By the time they were done, Arty wished he had three or four eyes so he could cry even more. "Listen," he said between sniffles, "no one should have to go through that much suffering."

"Thanks," Paul said. "We appreciate that."

BOOM! Something suddenly exploded through the top of Arty's desk. "Whoa!" Arty nearly flipped backwards out of his chair but something caught him. It was his right carbon-fiber foot, sticking up through the desktop like a suddenly sprouted mushroom. "Dammit," Arty said. "Third desk this month." He struggled for a moment before Paul helped him dislodge the metallic metatarsus and they resumed their conversation.

They talked about the difficulty of finding infants and the problems of foster care and government regulations. And after a couple of hours of talking Arty felt he had a pretty good handle on the latest couple wanting to adopt. He leaned forward, putting his carbon-fiber elbows on his desk. *Whirvvvv.* "You folks seem like exactly the sort of people who *ought* to have kids. Seems like you're caring and smart and, well, perfect."

"But . . ." Georgette said, expecting the bad news. "There just aren't any infants and—"

"Not at all," Arty said. "As a matter of fact, you guys are in luck. We just had two little ones show up on our doorstep last night and it would save me a *boatload* of paperwork if you'd take them."

"Twins?" Paul asked.

"Boy and a girl," Arty said. "I assume they're twins; they look a lot alike. They both have lots of fine curly hair." Arty raised one of his artificial limbs and gestured at his own fine curly hair. *Whirvvvv. WHAM!* Another short circuit and Arty whacked himself hard in the head.

"Yowch!" he said. "I'm telling you, technology is *not* all it's cracked up to be. They said it was going to solve all my problems, but—*whoa!*" There was a shattering of windows as one of Arty's legs again kicked violently forward, tossing Arty backwards. His arms crashed through the plate glass behind him. "Everybody okay?" he asked when he righted himself. He looked at the twinkling shards of glass on the floor. "I think I'll get safety glass next time. Now, where were we?"

"We'd get both of them?" Georgette asked. She couldn't believe it. This was too good to be true.

"Yeah," Arty said. "I don't like to break up siblings if it's at all possible. Family's very important." Arty did a quick background check on the prospective parents and when they vetted clean, he handed the kids over. "Good luck," he said as he waved good-bye. *Whirvvvv whirvvvv whirvvvv. WHAM!*

After Lance Abbott and his producer struck a huge deal with the studio to make the movie, the producer took Lance out to the Ivy to celebrate. By the end of the night, Lance was toasted and bragging about his legendary organ procurement performances. "Hey!" Lance said, "*you* try getting a Christian Scientist to donate organs—see how far you get."

"You're the man," the producer said as he poured Lance some more wine. "You're money! But the studio just felt more comfortable going with a star in the lead with a budget this size. And you gotta admit, Clooney as the handsome organ procurement specialist turned crime solver is pretty appealing. I mean, George can open a picture, plus you've got the audience's subconscious ties to his *E.R.* role, which makes the whole thing seem more real in their minds."

Lance dismissed the casting with a drunk wave of his hand. "So what am I, transgenic liver?" he asked.

"What you are is a co-executive producer with gross points," the producer said. "You think George got gross points? Forget it. Acting's for schmucks; producing's where it's at, Lance. And let me tell you something else," the producer said as he put his arm around Lance. "I think you are major producing material."

"You think so?" Lance smiled at the compliment.

The producer winked at him before trying his gambit. He put his mouth to Lance's ear and whispered, "Lance, I know what you did, you little scamp."

Despite his inebriation Lance thought now might be a good time to panic. "What do you know?" he asked with just enough fear in his voice to tip the producer.

"Not to worry," the producer said. "What? You think you're the first? Please. Why do you think the job pays so well? Because it's easy? No, the decisions a producer has to make are anything but easy."

Lance felt comforted that the producer seemed, if anything, impressed by what he had done. The way he had said it, Lance felt the producer even sympathized with him. "Really? It happens a lot?"

"I wouldn't say a lot," the producer said, "but that's only because most people don't have the balls. But you!" He pointed an accusing finger at Lance. "You, my friend, will command respect. You are a player." He paused before giving Lance a little noogie. "You will be taking home some statuettes before your day is done."

Lance's ego opened the door and showed the producer in. He swaggered where he sat as the producer poured some more wine. "Okay, you're right," Lance said. "If you don't take matters into your own hands, nothing's going to happen for you. So I did what I had to do."

"And that," the producer said, "is the definition of a producer." With his arm still around Lance, the producer pulled him close and spoke softly. "Do you still have the .22 or did you toss it?"

Lance shook his head. "No, no, no. I don't have a fucking clue who shot the son of a bitch. I just finished the job with a little help from my pharmaceutical friends."

The producer started to laugh at Lance's clever turn of phrase. And the more he laughed, the more comfortable Lance became and the more he told the producer. "Another bottle of wine here," the producer said.

They talked late into the night.

Eighteen months later *Xenograft!* opened on 2,100 screens, grossing $21 million its first weekend on its way to a domestic gross of $145 million. Lance Abbott, a gross profit participant, was persuaded to turn over his millions to the producer, who pointed out that Lance would be in serious hot water if anyone ever found out the truth about Vic "Bonedigger" Nichols.

Soon thereafter, disillusioned with the entertainment industry, Lance Abbott returned to SCOPE and became a regional family approach supervisor with script approval.

The police closed all the Terra Tuebor cases as well as the mutilated corpse cases. Notes in the files indicated that Vic "Bonedigger" Nichols, the lone suspect in all the cases, had been, at the time of his death, in possession of overwhelming evidence that would have convicted him had he lived and been tried for the crimes.

The various police departments in the cities and communities around the Bay Area are still trying to get CrimePerfect tech support on the phone to get their software working right.

Georgette was in the kitchen making dinner and the kids were in their room screaming bloody murder for no particular reason. Paul, who loved hearing their voices even if they were screaming, was reading the paper when he came across a story that caught his eye.

NEW OWNER GOES TROPICAL WITH CONIFER

The article explained that a new investment group had purchased Conifer Lumber after the recent problems at Landaq. The head of the new group was Mr. Cory Richardson. Mr. Richardson said the group was excited about their new acquisition and that they were going to be expanding their operations into the tropical rain forests, where there were so many wonderful hardwoods that were so popular now. Mr. Richardson also unveiled some new technology that would allow them to cut and process the trees at twice the speed of current technology. He said it was the sort of advance companies like Conifer needed in order to stay competitive. The new technology would allow Conifer to increase productivity, which would show up in dividends. This was the sort of thing shareholders demanded of him. It was Mr. Richardson's fiduciary responsibility to do this and he took that responsibility very seriously.

Paul took it seriously too. All he could see was the sign outside the Hard Rock Cafe: NUMBER OF ACRES REMAINING. The number began diminishing at twice the speed it used to. Paul's face turned red and he suddenly crumpled the paper up into a ball. "Goddammit!"

Georgette turned around. "Paul, relax. Remember what the doctor said. No stress. You don't want another angina."

"What do you mean relax?" Paul said. "They've got new technology that allows them to cut the rain forests down twice as fast as they used to! How am I supposed to relax knowing that?"

Georgette nodded as she wiped her hands on her apron. "So you want to do something about it or do you just want to stew until you croak?"

"You have something specific in mind?" Paul asked.

"I might," she said. "Come with me." They went to the front hall. Georgette crawled into the bowels of the closet. A moment later she wrestled a large box out into the hall. Paul wondered what was in it. For all he knew it was a box of stuff he had stuck in there a long time ago and had forgotten about. Maybe it had some of his old Tico and the Triumphs records in it. But he couldn't imagine how that was going to help him relax, much less save the rain forests.

Georgette opened the box and pulled out a grotesque sort of dog mask–looking thing. It was sort of creepy and

Paul didn't know what to make of it. Paul looked in the box and saw some surgical scrubs, a stethoscope, and a small hairy thing that looked like—hell, he didn't know what it looked like, a scalp maybe, but that didn't make any sense. There were several other articles of clothing, a security company outfit, and a PG&E uniform. For a moment Paul thought it was a collection of old Halloween costumes but Georgette's bottle-nosed dolphin outfit wasn't in the box so he wasn't even sure about that.

"What's all this?" he asked.

"Try on the mask," she said.

Paul put it on. There was a pause as he adjusted the strap in the back.

"So. How does that feel?" Georgette asked.

"Feels great," Paul said from behind the mask. "What's it for?"

"It'll help you relax."

postscript

"Man has lost the capacity to foresee and to forestall. He will end by destroying the earth."

—Dr. Albert Schweitzer

acknowledgements

It is only because the following people graciously shared their expertise with me that I was able to write this book.

First and foremost I must thank my friend Dr. Bobby Robbins, Assistant Professor of Cardio-Thoracic Surgery at Stanford University, for answering a thousand questions, many of which were clearly absurd. In addition to being a practicing transplant surgeon and teacher, Dr. Robbins is involved in university studies related to pig-to-primate cardiac xenotransplantation as well as rodent investigations involving mechanisms of accommodation of xenotransplants. Without his patience, his patients, his knowledge, and his sense of humor this book wouldn't have a heart of any kind. Thanks also for the three A.M. heart-lung transplant and (Debbie too) for the *Pest Control* party.

Additional thanks go to:

Dr. Jeff Miller for his ER acumen and Dr. Kendall Hansen for helping with the anesthesia.

Dr. James D. Hardy, Professor Emeritus and formerly Chairman of the Department of Surgery at the University of Mississippi Medical Center. Dr. Hardy was one of the first modern surgeons to experiment with xenografting. Thank you for helping with the history of events.

Dr. Gretchen C. Daily, Bing Interdisciplinary Research Scientist at Stanford University's Department of Biological Sciences. Dr. Daily was invaluable in answering questions about population growth, resource use, ecological sustainability, and the earth's carrying capacity.

Professor James C. Baird, Professor of Chemistry and Physics and Chair of the Faculty at Brown University. Thanks for your enthusiasm and for solving my problem in the Cel-Tech lab.

Dr. Victor Tabbush of UCLA's John E. Anderson Graduate School of Management for his economic expertise; Alan B. Solursh of Bear Stearns; and Michael P. Fitzhugh of Kochis, Fitz, Tracy & Gorman for helping with various questions of economics and the stock market.

Dr. Robert M. Sapolsky, professor of biology and neuroscience at Stanford University, for helping a little with the baboons.

Kendall Fitzhugh for helping focus the Malthus document and for pointing out Clyde.

Matt Hansen for reading early drafts and offering encouragement and suggestions.

Jennifer Hershey, Andrea Sinert, and Tom Dupree for their editing skills.

Jimmy Vines for representing.

And finally to the brilliant and talented Leonard Gershe and D. Victor Hawkins who figured out how the story started, what was missing in the middle, and how it was supposed to end. I am forever indebted.

Other than that, I wrote most of the book.

—Bill Fitzhugh
Los Angeles, California, 1998